SKYGODS

Sarah Latchaw

OMNIFIC PUBLISHING
LOS ANGELES

Skygods, Copyright © Sarah Latchaw, 2014
All Rights Reserved. Except as permitted under the U.S. Copyright Act of 1976,
no part of this publication may be reproduced, distributed, or transmitted
in any form or by any means, or stored in a database or retrieval system,
without prior written permission of the publisher.

Omnific Publishing
1901 Avenue of the Stars, 2nd floor
Los Angeles, CA 90067
www.omnificpublishing.com

First Omnific eBook edition, August 2014
First Omnific trade paperback edition, August 2014

The characters and events in this book are fictitious.
Any similarity to real persons, living or dead,
is coincidental and not intended by the author.

Library of Congress Cataloguing-in-Publication Data

Latchaw, Sarah.
  Skygods / Sarah Latchaw – 1st ed.
  ISBN: 978-1-623420-86-4
  1. Contemporary Romance — Fiction. 2. Skydiving — Fiction.
  3. Bipolar Disorder — Fiction. 4. Authors — Fiction. I. Title

10 9 8 7 6 5 4 3 2 1

Cover Design by Micha Stone and Amy Brokaw
Interior Book Design by Coreen Montagna

Printed in the United States of America

*For Nathan,
who keeps me grounded and makes me laugh —
usually at the same time.
I love you.*

SKYGODS

*A skydiver,
arrogant in his ability to navigate the heavens,
rejects his fragile state
and calls himself a god of the sky.*

Chapter 1
BLUE SKY, BLACK DEATH

A skydiver's mantra or greeting.
Enjoy the exhilaration of the open sky,
but never forget the mortal earth below.

Hydraulic Level Five {working title}
Draft 1.22
© Samuel Caulfield Cabral & Aspen Kaye Trilby
22. *An Inheritance and State*

Three million dollars. All of it in a trust fund left behind by his dead parents, which now that he is eighteen, is at his disposal. According to the lawyer, the fortune would've been nine million if the estate hadn't been obligated to pay his mother's debts after she jumped. Not that he wants a dime of it. Caulfield snarls at the memory of the piggish man with squinty eyes and a stupid-looking bowtie that choked his fat neck. He doesn't need a stranger to remind him his mother had preferred ski slopes, sports cars, and spending sprees in Boston's Back Bay to her son.

"Caulfield, hit the on-deck circle!" Coach bellows from the opposite end of the dugout. Caulfield scoops up a bat and sprints to the circle for warm-up swings. He has to get his head in the game, his last ever with Bear Creek High. He's wanted the state title for so long, and now it's three colossal runs away – so impossible just fifteen minutes ago, yet Bear Creek managed to load the bases in a ninth inning rally.

Bright stadium lights wash the field in white, heightening the exhilaration of the night game. He pushes his hat brim down to shield his eyes from the glare.

"Straighten out that swing. You're a little wild today." Caulfield nods to the hitting coach and focuses on the next pitch, clobbering the imaginary ball. "That's better."

The odd thing is, baseball has begun to lose its sheen of magic. The University of Colorado, along with several other colleges, offered him baseball scholarships. He turned them all down. The idea of playing ball another four years seems daunting. Really, all he wants to do is plow through the next two years until Aspen graduates from high school and he can once again see her every day.

She's up there in the stands like she always is – screaming his name when he's up to bat, waving as he takes to the outfield. To her, he's Caulfield: attentive boyfriend, hell of a ballplayer, and best friend since five. How would she feel about Caulfield: child of a disbarred lawyer and nutcase socialite? Or Caulfield: sack-of-shit millionaire who's too scared to touch his inheritance, even to buy his girlfriend a reliable ride? Caulfield tears through another swing.

"Number Nine, you're up!" Caulfield shoulders the barrel as the hitter before him strikes out. A thrill shoots through him every time he hears "Number Nine." Ted Williams – the Splendid Splinter himself – wore the number nine for two decades in Boston. Someday he'll see that retired number flying high above Fenway Park. Maybe he'll use his mother's money to do it and hope she burns with revulsion, wherever she is. The more he learns of her, the more he can't stomach thinking of her as "mother." He should just call her Rachel Caulfield. No, just Rachel.

Caulfield digs one foot into the batter's box, then the next. *Time to focus. Ninth inning, down two runs. Runner on third, runner on second, runner on first.* He has to hit it deep. The crowd behind him is a roaring machine, all squeals and shrieks. He hears Aspen's voice, and Maria's and Esteban's. Zoning them out, he studies the pitcher as he shakes his head once, twice, and windup. The ball's coming in high – too high. He holds his swing. *Crud, slider.*

"Strike!"

Coach hollers at him to watch for breaking balls, as if he doesn't already know. He plants his feet, pure fury pulsing through his veins, his heart pounding *Ra-chel...Ra-chel*. Fuck her. Fuck her for distracting him during the biggest game of his life, for keeping him from Fenway Park, and for despising her only child. He hates her money. He swings hard.

Too early.

"Strike!"

"Fuck!" Caulfield growls, earning him a warning glare from the umpire.

"Come on, Caulfield! Get your head out of your ass and in this game!"

"This isn't tee-ball, this is State!"

The crowd behind him jeers, and Caulfield knows they will hang, draw, and quarter him, then stick his head on the fence post if he screws this up. He narrows his vision to the pitcher, watching his windup, the angle of his arm, bracing himself. This one's coming in low. He holds his swing.

"Ball!"

He whooshes out. *There we go, Caulfield. Eye on the ball—first rule of baseball. Channel the rage. Carry it through in your swing. Windup...no break, coming in fast, just how you like them. Swing through...*

Crack!

Yes. Caulfield tosses the bat and sprints for first as the crowd's untamed screams propel him forward. He rounds first as the other team's outfielders stumble around the fence, the ball out of the park and lost to them. A manic grin claims his face as he slows to a jog, savoring the trip around the bases. One runner crosses home plate...then two...then three. Caulfield's grand slam pushes the score to six-to-four, bottom of the ninth. The game is over.

His teammates flood from the dugout and Bear Creek students and parents spill onto the field, but the only face Caulfield seeks is Aspen's. Strong arms lift him and he can see above the hundreds of heads. He spots her, wildly waving her arms and jumping with sheer joy. Gone is the inheritance. Gone is the piggish lawyer, his father, and Rachel. It's only her. Always her.

Caulfield stiffens.

I love her.

Not some high school crush or infatuation with her hair, her eyes, her body. He loves *her*. Enough to forget everyone else. Enough to give her everything he can. Enough to protect her, to marry her.

He slides down from his teammates' shoulders and whips Aspen into his arms, clinging to her.

"You were...Ack! Amazing!" she cries into his ear, heedless of the sweat dripping from his forehead, his neck, his arms. "So brilliant, so perfect!"

He laughs and set her down, plopping his soaked ball cap on her lovely blond head. Framing her face with his hands, he kisses her, hard.

"Let's do the fairy tale. All of it." His voice quakes with adrenaline and emotion. She can't miss his meaning. *Don't scare her, you idiot. She's not even sixteen.* But it's not fear in her wide eyes. Nothing but joy stares back, and it fills Caulfield's own heart with trepidation.

He smooths her cheek, eases his agony. "That's a long way out, though, getting married? Far, far in the future." She nestles beneath his arm. He stoops and pecks her cheek.

"Only you, Firecracker. Don't forget it."

Kaye—Well, here it is. One hundred plus pages of our story, told as truthfully as I can recall. I know it's one-sided. It's missing your thoughts, your memories. Thank you again for agreeing to share them with me.

You should know: I feel like that eighteen-year-old kid again, terrified you'll read this memoir and lose respect for me. I'm ashamed of how I resented my adoptive mother. How I both idolized and hated my birth mother. Or the secrets I kept from you, for years. The way I longed for a thirteen-year-old girl who was little more than a child. But this is life, and we make choices and we suffer (and grow) because of them.

Read our story. Give me your honesty. Question everything, not just the passages I've marked, because this is us and I want it to be right. ~Sam

Neelie Nixie was a whip-toting, stiletto-sporting dominatrix. Stupid Hollywood, had to sex up poor Neelie. But still, I was giddy to finally get a glimpse of her long-awaited image. Indigo Kingsley's soft, full lips curled in the publicity photo, as if she were about to say, "Why yes, I *am* the only woman in the world who can wear skin-tight leather and not chafe my ivory thighs." Her sleek platinum hair was now a wild mane and previously blue eyes were some smoky, unidentifiable color. Mist and shadow swirled behind her toned, action-hero body. In the background, a beat-up road sign proclaimed *BEAR CREEK: Population 4,182.*

I wondered if Samuel had seen Indigo's publicity shot yet. Heck, he probably attended the photo shoot during their romantic stint. Bald, red, and unbecoming jealousy flared as I studied, with the eyes of a competitor, limbs lithe and long, freckle-less complexion, ample cleavage. I sniffed. Airbrushed.

A clap of thunder rattled the TrilbyJones walls and the lights flickered. Thank goodness for backup generators. Double-checking my surge protector, I turned back to my work and ignored the sheets of rain pelting my office windows. More rain. More gray darkness. We'd had nothing but a constant barrage of the cold, wet stuff—a peculiarity for midsummer Boulder.

It had been ten days since Samuel and Caroline had driven the suitcase-laden rental out of the Cabrals' driveway to resume his book tour. Ten days since his sister and her new husband, Danita and Angel, boarded a plane bound for a Maui honeymoon. Ten days and I was still digging out from hundreds of emails that had collected in my time away from TrilbyJones, my boutique PR agency. We were patroned by the local tourist industry, from Wild West museums to spelunking clubs. Assembling marketing plans often required shadowing our clients, like the upcoming caving expedition detailed in the email I was supposed to be answering, rather than fretting over Indigo's come-hither pout. Minimizing the *Water Sirens* images, I fired off another response.

> Re: July Caving Trip
> To: Kevin@GreatWestCaves.com
> Kevin—Groovy Adventures caving expedition is still on. Can you please provide gear for four instead of three?

I tapped a fingernail against my coffee mug and dreamed of Samuel decked out in spelunking gear…heavy-duty overalls, hard-hat, carabiners. If understanding our client's business meant donning harnesses and ropes like bondage enthusiasts and delving into the depths of the earth, so be it.

I opened another email. As I attached artwork files, my mind floated to the cautious kiss Samuel and I had shared on the ball diamond. So warm, despite the chill of the night. So soft, despite the hard ground. My gut twisted. Ever since I broke my resolve, I'd worried that my actions could be misinterpreted as "friends with benefits." When I shared my concern with Samuel in our brief conversation last night, he laughed it off.

"If this is 'friends with benefits,' Trilby, I think I've been cheated out of the benefits."

"But I kissed you."

"And it was hot, and wonderful, and…well…left me with a big problem when I returned home. Trust me, I don't feel as though you're using me for sex."

"A *big* problem, huh, Cabral? Someone's bragging." I'm positive he could feel my warming cheeks across the sine waves. Who was this bold girl?

"By the way, I mailed the manuscript today. Keep your eyes open for a FedEx package…"

My email notification dinged and snapped me from my daydreams, just as I loosened Samuel's tuxedo tie and flicked open those little buttons, ready to trail a line of wedding cake frosting from neck to navel. I was a pitiable bundle of hormones. Sighing, I buried myself in my client accounts until it was home time.

Shutting down my computer, I grabbed my briefcase and dodged from my desk, the last one to leave. I'd decided not to return to my hometown of Lyons this past weekend. After our intimate little show during Danita and Angel's wedding dance, small town gossip was rampant. According to my disapproving mother, her farmers market customers had commented how exciting it was "to see those kids back together," and had asked how she felt about her "small-fry daughter going after that Cabral boy again."

Dodging Lyons gossip wasn't the only reason for burying myself in work. It kept my mind off of other things, like Samuel's grand kiss-off note from seven years ago. I'd finally mailed it to him, knowing he wouldn't see it until he returned to New York from his latest publicity gig.

It's not that I'd been reluctant to unearth it. I spent every night last week tearing through memento boxes and yearbooks. (I had a good chuckle over Angel's and Samuel's gelled comb-overs and silk shirts.) It wasn't with my keepsakes. I'd found the slightly yellowed envelope several days ago, stuffed in TrilbyJones's basement, along with other divorce papers I hadn't wanted to taint my new home. I don't know what I'd expected when I'd unfolded the note, perhaps some big, neon arrow pointing to a clue: a misshaped Y, an open O that told me Samuel hadn't been the author. Ever since he'd questioned his ability to write such a missive, I'd fished for someone else to blame for the ugly words. But when I held the thing between shaking fingers, smoothed the wrinkled paper marred by water marks, I saw Samuel's handwriting—wilder than normal, but still elegant, still precise:

Kaye,
Go home to Colorado. I don't want to see you again. The roots between us are dead, we are dead...

I swiped a stray tear and jammed the unwanted memory back in the envelope. I'd forgiven him. It was the past. I'd made a photocopy and mailed the original to Samuel, waiting with baited breath until he returned to New York and saw it...

Had he picked up the mail, yet? Maybe he was still on his flight or in a cab. My fingers itched for my phone. Locking TrilbyJones, I flew up the Victorian's dark stairwell to my second-floor apartment. Samuel had been in Toronto, meeting and greeting fans at some sort of convention. When we last spoke, I asked if he'd visited the CN Tower. His only response was a groan and a mumbled "I didn't even have time to shave."

The publicity tour was hard on Samuel, though he rarely complained. He enjoyed crowds almost as much as he enjoyed lumbar punctures. Caroline was cramming as many book appearances as possible into the months before the movie premiered, and with *Water Sirens* fervor creeping like ivy across America, his events were packed.

I'd read on a celebrity gossip website how an off-kilter fan all but accosted him at a book signing because Samuel Cabral had well and truly put *Water Sirens* to rest. Horrible visions of a sledgehammer-wielding, wild-eyed Annie Wilkes swung through my imagination.

I caved. Punching in his number, I jiggled my knees and waited. No answer. I left a generic message, something cringe-inducing like "hope you didn't need the barf bag on your flight," and settled in for another Wednesday night of televised ghost hunting and wine. I was already biting my thumbnail as night-vision cameras swept through Irish castles, so when there was a sudden rap at my door, I flew from my chair with a yelp. Without waiting for an invitation, Molly barreled into my apartment, followed by a scowling Jaime Guzman. Both shook rain from their jackets and slipped out of their muddy shoes.

"Hi, Kaye! We've come for a night of drunken debauchery and popcorn."

Jaime snorted. "She tackled me in The Garden Market and promised to buy a Labrador if I came along." Jaime housed a pack of Labrador puppies under the auspices of breeding and selling them, but I suspected she vastly preferred their company over that of the human populace.

"Oh please, you went willingly."

How...odd. Was misanthropic Jaime actually being social? If temperaments were placed on this earth with diametric opposites, then Molly Jones, my bubbly best friend and business partner, and Jaime Guzman, my scorned and scathing divorce attorney, were such. Yet they'd somehow clicked in their incompatibility, and I suspected it was a mutual appreciation of mischief. Ever since Molly orchestrated my prank night kidnapping several weeks ago, Jaime seemed to gain respect for her. If Molly ever knocked over a bank, Jaime might even invite her to coffee.

I reached sunburned arms around my friend. She stooped her towering ponderosa frame and returned my hug, her frizzy wet hair tickling my neck. "So, what have you been doing outside the office?" I asked. "I've heard nothing from you at all since the wedding!"

Her eyes sparked. "Shouldn't you be asking *who*—"

"Never mind, I set myself up for that one." I shuffled to the kitchen to make popcorn.

Molly mooned like a schmaltzy schoolgirl, sprawled on my sofa. "Oh, Kaye, Cassady is...argh! He's such a gentleman, and he's smart, and reads a lot and only has documentaries in his Netflix queue, and his pecs! Oh, and he says he's had it so bad for me, he was 'as useless as gooseshit on a pumphandle,'" Molly prattled on. "He would have acted sooner, but he wasn't sure how long he'd stay in Lyons..."

I poured three glasses of wine as Molly listed Cassady's virtues. Cassady was something of a hippie rover who'd found employment as an outdoor adventure guide in Lyons a few years back, and settled nicely into our circle of friends. He wouldn't tell us where he was from, but I suspected Minnesota. Molly'd been panting after him since he first spoke that glorious "ya, you betcha," and "nice weather, eh?" Jaime turned a little green and downed half her glass the instant I placed it in her fingers. I had a feeling she wouldn't be joining us for many more girls' nights. She smacked her lips appreciatively.

"Good stuff, Trilby. Local?"

I nodded, anxiously shifting as she leered.

"You know, if the talk in Lyons about you and Cabral hooking up again is true, you'll have to kiss your boozing days good-bye."

I twirled the stem of my wine glass between my fingers. "I've thought of that. *If* we decide to hook up again."

"Just think...no more of that mouth-watering, heady drink of the gods. Never again will you press it to your lips and let it slide down your throat, warming every beautiful pipe and gullet of your body. Mmmm."

"Wow," Molly whispered.

I shrugged, refusing to let Jaime get to me. "It's a small price to pay to help him stay on the wagon."

She sighed. "You're a lovesick, cherub-cheeked Kewpie doll, you know that?"

Eleven o'clock rolled around and still no call from Samuel. Now I was worried. What if there was trouble with his plane? What if someone mugged him? *Anything* could happen in New York. For all I knew, he was slouched against a grimy wall of the subway system —

And, providentially, my phone rang.

"Oh thank God!" I mumbled, diving for it. Molly and Jaime stared at me strangely as my fingers fumbled to answer. "Hello?"

"Kaye, it's Samuel."

"Hi!" I shoved down the anxiety. "You got back to New York all right?"

"Yes, several hours ago."

"Oh. Why didn't you call?" I frowned, glancing at the clock again. "And for that matter, why are you still awake at one fifteen in the morning?"

"Kaye." Uh oh, not good. "I got my note in the mail today—the one I wrote to you."

I couldn't miss that he'd said "*my* note" and "*I* wrote." I moved our conversation to my bedroom and closed the door. "And?"

"It's my handwriting." I also couldn't miss the tremble in his voice.

No. "Are you sure? I mean, it's such a short note, anyone could have written it."

"I'm sure."

"And just a couple weeks ago, you were positive you couldn't have written it."

"Kaye," he persisted, "I'm sure. It's my handwriting. A little more slanted and swoopy than normal, but without a doubt, it's mine."

"But what if—"

"Think about it. I obviously wanted you gone, as efficiently as possible. In normal circumstances, I would have reasoned with you. But I was high off my butt with no inhibition and frankly, little care for whom I was hurting. It makes sense. Who else would know how much a stupid note would affect you? You made me promise a long time ago never to send you packing with a tree house sign, that I'd tell you to your face. I was a bastard for doing it, and it worked. You divorced me."

By the time he finished his explanation, his voice had grown low and hoarse.

"Samuel…" I didn't know how to finish. Yes, it had been a bastard thing to do? Tell him it didn't matter anymore because it was seven years ago?

"I was arrogant," he said quietly, "thinking I knew what was best for you. Even up to a few hours ago, I was so certain I could never again pull that stunt like I did with the keep-out sign on the tree house when we were kids—leaving you high and dry with no way down? I was ready to open your letter and find someone else's writing on that sheet of paper. You think I'd be used to this—discovering what I'm capable of. But it always shocks me."

I had an odd feeling that he wasn't really talking to me anymore. I cleared my throat, reminding him I was still here.

"What if we had a handwriting expert examine it? I mean, there *is* a possibility you didn't write it, correct?"

He sighed. "No, Kaye. Just let that idea go. I'm sorry I put it into your brain."

I shook my head, even though he couldn't see it. "No. I'm glad you told me what you were thinking. It makes the whole friendship thing a lot easier when we actually talk to each other," I teased.

"Yes, I suppose it does. I enjoy sharing my thoughts with you. But you know what I enjoy even more?"

"What?"

"When you tell me your thoughts."

"Well, right now I'm wishing I knew what your home looks like. This is embarrassing, but I have no clue where you live — the Upper East Side?"

"No, Inwood, near Fort Tryon Park. I'm a Westsider."

I blinked, surprised. So much for my visions of Samuel as a well-heeled, silk-stocking snob. "Maybe you can send me a picture so I can visualize you there."

I could hear his smile. "I'll do that. It's beautiful, lots of trails and wooded areas overlooking the Hudson River and the bluffs. At the base of my bluff is north Broadway, and it's a different world — grittier, vibrant. I think you'd like it. Kaye?"

"Yes?"

He cleared his throat. "For what it's worth, the content of that note is a complete and utter lie. It was a lie then and it's a lie now. Do you believe me?"

"Yeah," I exhaled. "I believe you." I glanced at the time, knowing I needed to let him go. "Good night, Samuel."

"Good night, Kaye. I miss you."

When I returned to the living room, Molly and Jaime lifted significant eyebrows at me.

"Are you going het on me, lover?" Jaime quipped.

I rolled my eyes. Ever since I'd pretended to be her lesbian life partner in a desperate bid to get answers from Samuel, she'd been merciless.

"I suppose this year's Pride rally is out," she continued. "I want my Bryn Mawr sweatshirt back. Oh, and I'll need to turn in my dossier of Samuel's evils."

I slapped a hand to my forehead. "Frickin' monkey junk, I completely forgot about that thing. Yes, burn it, shred it, whatever you need to do. I'll get rid of mine, too."

"Are you ever going to tell Cabral about our little research project?"

I thought of my lie list and the whole mess of crap we'd cleared up. But so much still lingered, like the embarrassing lengths I'd been willing to go for revenge. Heck, we hadn't even gotten around to talking about Samuel's public intox arrest several years ago. Would he be ticked over Jaime's and my plotting? Oh yeah. Would he forgive me? Yes, he would. Maybe if I explained I was concerned about Caroline's manipulations.

Caroline Ortega, Samuel's publicist extraordinaire. She was an enigma. She obviously hated me. But how much of her was genuine and how much was show? Samuel was certain he'd written the note, but I wasn't so sure.

"Molly, did I tell you that Caroline was the woman who helped me in New York City all those years ago?"

"No!" Her eyes widened.

Molly scooted over and I sat next to her on the sofa. Taking a deep breath, I launched into the tale of how Caroline had been the one to scrape me off the floor of the debauched brownstone where Samuel resided and offer the haven of her frilly bedroom. She'd called me Samuel's "addiction," and the idea hardened in my brain like one of his trilobite fossils.

I stared at my hands, debating. "Molly, do you remember me telling you about the note Samuel left in my backpack, in New York?"

She nodded, digging between the cushions for the remote and muted the television.

"For seven years, I just assumed Samuel had written it. But now...I don't know."

Her expression was rife with confusion. "Kaye, honey, why would someone else write the note?"

"Maybe because they thought I was a burden. Maybe Samuel's dad—"

"No way," Molly interrupted. "Alonso Cabral would never do something like that, especially to you and Samuel. But what if..." Molly bit her lip, unsure if she should voice her suspicions. "What if Caroline wrote it? You said she was there, right?"

"See, that's what I was beginning to wonder, but I didn't know if it was just bias talking. Why would she do that, though?"

Molly took another sip of wine. "Well, picture this. Caroline is miserable with Togsy, the magical loser fiancé. She sees Samuel is brilliant, handsome, and she'll do anything to snag him. The only problem? He's married, albeit, the marriage is shaky. So then you arrive and find him…you know. The perfect opportunity. He's high as a kite; you're passed out in her bedroom." She grabbed a handful of popcorn and dumped it in her bowl. "She doesn't think, she acts. She digs through the house and finds a sample of Samuel's handwriting—maybe a Post-it on the fridge, notes from a class. Very carefully, she forms a note, mimicking his letters."

I got excited along with Molly. "Oh!" I snapped my fingers. "And Caroline's a calligrapher. A very good one."

A groan interrupted our eager theorizing. "Now I remember why I don't have any girlfriends—they screw up your head," Jaime snarked. "The problem with your theory, *niñas*, is Cabral doesn't write in calligraphy. Caroline's an artist, not a master forger. Look, I get why you don't want to think your boy toy wrote this thing. But now you're making up a fairy tale with Caroline as the villain so you can vindicate the guy you love, plain and simple. Don't be embarrassed, that's the way women work."

"But you're the one who told me Caroline was a manipulator. It makes perfect sense. She wanted Samuel, so she twisted the situation—"

"No, she didn't want him, not then. Remember, Caroline was engaged to Togsy at the time."

"That doesn't mean she didn't want Samuel," Molly cut in.

Jaime scowled at Molly. "I found an old engagement announcement in the *Raleigh News & Observer* featuring one Caroline Ortega and Lyle Togsender. They were childhood sweethearts, like you and Cabral. *She* proposed to *him*. She didn't want Samuel. She wanted Togsy."

"But Togsy was a drug addict," I fired back.

"So was Samuel."

Ouch. That shut me up.

Molly put a calming hand over mine. "Maybe she didn't write the note, Kaye. Jaime's right—as much as Caroline's horrendous, we shouldn't accuse her unless we have all the facts."

"But Samuel's first instinct was that he didn't write it."

"Of *course* he thought he didn't write it," said Jaime. "Put yourself in his place. You said he can't remember what happened that night, and that's got to be scary as hell. Seven years later, he suddenly finds out that hurray!—he didn't screw that brunette woman you found him with. Now he's going to question everything. You skip in and tell him he wrote you a note—something he hasn't heard about until now. So he wants to believe that maybe he *didn't* write it, that someone was messing with him like the brunette did. But look at the facts. Just because someone's high doesn't mean they can't write a note. Samuel wrote a book while he was doing cocaine."

I bit my lip and forced that stubborn Trilby pride to bow out.

Jaime studied me with shrewd eyes, then took a deep, courtroom breath. "Look, I understand why you want to put this on someone else, but it's one stupid note. Let it go. Have I ever told you why the Latin neighborhood shuns me?"

"I heard you made your ex-husband's life a living hell."

"Yeah, prick. Juan deserved it. *Most* of it. Mothballs in his gas tank, gay porn subscriptions sent to his house—those were genius. But it wasn't enough." Jaime threw back her wine and swilled it in her mouth. She set the glass on my coffee table.

"I hated that woman for falling in love with him when he was mine. For a home wrecker, she was always kind of sweet. Juan, on the other hand, was a horny, egotistical jackass. The only brain he had was in his other head, so there was no way Juan didn't get into this woman's pants. I was convinced they were humping like bunnies and I was very vocal about it, despite what Juan's buddies told me. But I went too far." She dragged a hand over her eyes, her head falling back against the couch. "I called Juan's father pretending to be his weeping, 'pregnant' mistress. You don't know Juan's dad—he's a tool. The aftermath was awful. Juan's father went off on the woman, her parents, on Juan, pretty vicious."

"Let me guess—they really weren't sleeping together," I said.

Jaime shook her head, eyes down.

"Wow, Jaime," Molly murmured.

"Yeah, it was horrible. I left them alone after that, but it was too late. Once the families figured out what I'd pulled, the damage was done. It's amazing I still have a law practice. I guess there will always be a need for divorce lawyers, right?"

"Man. I am never stealing from your cookie jar," I said.

"My point is, divorce is never black and white, and the other woman isn't always evil. Hell, she probably fought her attraction for a long time. Now I can see, plain as day, they love each other, as wrong as it was." She leaned forward, hard black eyes meeting mine. "Stupid pranks are one thing. But if you love the asshole, don't start accusing his friends and family to make yourself feel better, unless you're absolutely sure they're guilty."

"The letter *does* reflect what Samuel said to me in New York," I conceded. "'Go home, and don't you ever come back here again.'"

Jaime nodded. "Sometimes the simplest answer is the correct answer. Occam's razor, bitch."

But the truth was, I'd rather blame Caroline than Samuel. If it turned out she had written the note, Samuel would have no choice but to eliminate her from his life. And despite her help in getting him clean and making him a success, that jealous, wicked part of me still wanted her gone.

"Out of all the questions you could ask me, you want to know my history with Caroline?"

My ire fermented over Samuel's attitude during our weekly Q-and-A, until the tip of my tongue was bitter. Why on earth was he surprised I wanted to know more about his relationship with the woman who, up until a month ago, he'd chosen to give his heart to? I told him as much, and he sighed.

"Kaye, she didn't have my heart. You *know* this."

I strummed an angry, disjointed chord, refusing to back down.

It was Sunday evening after a weekend of climbing in the mountains. Hector, Luca Guzman, and I had killed our muscles and blistered our hands scaling the National Park in hardcore training for the Longs Peak winter climb. Now I was tucked into my cozy apartment, the fragrance of baking chocolate chip cookies wafting from my oven. I'd dug out my heating pad and rested it on my sore shoulder muscles. My guitar was in my lap and Samuel was on speakerphone. A darn good evening, until he questioned my question.

He relented. "Kaye, I'm sorry I'm so bent out of shape. It's no excuse, but it's been a rough couple of weeks." Jagged exhaustion edged his voice. Worry began to replace anger and I wondered if that exhaustion ever went away. "If I tell you my entire history with Caroline, will you quit fretting about her?"

I harrumphed, neither a yes nor a no.

Samuel continued. "I first met Caroline when I was a sophomore at CU. Togsy and I were in the same major classes and became what you would call casual friends."

"You mean drug buddies?"

"Yeah, eventually," he admitted. "Caroline would fly out to Colorado a couple times a semester to visit…"

Samuel explained that Caroline was also a writer, but her real desire had been to be a senior editor with Berkshire House Publishing where she'd been interning. Togsy had shared one of Samuel's workshop pieces with her and she'd seen his potential. For months, she'd pestered him for his work-in-progress book, but he'd refused, insisting he didn't want anyone to read it until it was completed. But Samuel did send her his short stories, none of which had been picked up by publishers. It wasn't until he moved to New York, broken by drugs and disappointments, that he had folded and allowed her to read *Water Sirens*.

"She agreed the story was rough," he said, "but saw the marketability of the book—especially if I intended to make it a series. We spent hours poring over the manuscript when I wasn't high and she wasn't cleaning up Togsy's messes. It was a hard time for all of us. She wanted her fiancé sober and I wanted to get so high I wouldn't remember your name."

Then I visited and subsequently slapped him with divorce papers, setting the wheels in motion for Samuel's long battles in rehab. Though Samuel didn't say it, I got the impression Caroline expressed her disapproval of my actions quite frequently.

Once Alonso and Sofia talked their son into therapy and detox, it only highlighted Togsy's failures. Lyle grew to resent Samuel. Then Samuel's book deal came through and it was the last straw for Lyle Togsender. Just after Christmas, he broke his engagement to Caroline and moved out of the brownstone.

"Caroline was devastated. I think, more than anything, that's why she fought so hard to help me. My mother told you about my trouble in Raleigh and the court-ordered rehab?"

"Yes." Samuel politely refrained from mentioning that I had his arrest record. My oven timer buzzed and I set my guitar aside to pull out the tray. He talked while I laid warm cookies on a cooling rack.

"I spent six months in a rehab center while Caroline worked tirelessly to edit my book for publication. She was adamant, and it was good to have her in my corner, though I didn't really appreciate it at the time. In a way, she was vicariously helping Togsy through me. He wouldn't accept her love and support, so I was the next best thing. My achievements are inextricably tied to hers. It's caused problems in the past. The men she's dated usually end up upset over the time she spends promoting the *Water Sirens* series. And the women I've dated think she's a controlling shrew—not that those relationships went anywhere, anyway."

So it wasn't only me—Samuel's other love interests had also thought he was monopolized by Caroline. I knew she'd ruthlessly protected Samuel for years. Which would be wonderful, except she didn't see me as a friend; she saw me as a threat.

It dawned on me that, save for vague references, neither of us had broached the taboo subject of past partners. Though curiosity and, admittedly, jealously, simmered in my gut, I couldn't ask about them just now, not after what he'd told me.

I heard soft strumming on the line and I smiled. Samuel had his guitar, too. He continued. "It wasn't until after Thanksgiving two years ago, when I told Caro you'd rejected my attempts at reconciliation, that she even broached the idea of being more than friends. I said no. I knew if we ever went down that path, it would ruin our friendship. But she pushed and pushed. And before you ask, I never slept with her," he quickly added. "We never even rounded second base, for that matter."

"I wasn't going to ask," I replied, glad for that little bit of information. I grabbed one of the warm cookies and headed back to my heating pad.

"I wanted more than a dark apartment waiting for me at night. I wanted someone to spoil, and hold, and give myself to. I knew it was wrong to say yes to Caro when I still had strong feelings for you. But loneliness is a powerful motivator, Kaye. I'm thankful you've never had to experience it."

But I had felt loneliness, too. Going to sleep alone, longing for the warmth of another body next to mine. Freezing leftovers because no one was there to share my meals. *Complete* loneliness, though…no, I'd never felt that. In the aftermath of our divorce, Samuel never once tried to turn our friends against me, the way so many exes do. Companionship was only a half hour's drive away.

I wanted to fall asleep with him again. I wanted to hold him and rub his back, assure him he'd never be lonely. I wanted to tell him to quit this insane self-imposed isolation and come home to Colorado, but I knew pity would only embarrass him. So I strummed a few chords, the opening to an Elvis song—"Lonesome Tonight." He laughed. He always laughed at my disparate love for Elvis Presley.

"You remember this one?" I heard the harmonies of his guitar almost immediately.

"Just see if you can keep up, Trilby."

"Hey now, I was the first to learn Elvis and don't you forget it."

After an hour of playing, I heard Samuel yawn and noticed it was after midnight in New York. We reluctantly called it a night.

"So you'll be home mid-July," I confirmed. "Are you renting a car in Denver or should I pick you up?"

"No, I'll rent a car. Are you sure you don't mind my tagging along on your caving trip?"

My heart twisted. "I wouldn't have invited you, otherwise. Samuel, I want you along, believe me. You have no idea."

I wanted him here, now.

It was roughly two weeks after Samuel departed Lyons that I received a package from him.

I was ready to flee the office following a long, blah Monday. Samuel had an all-day event—a press junket for the new *Water Sirens* trailer (I didn't even know they had press junkets for movie trailers)—so we postponed his Q-and-A. He'd already given me fair warning that we'd be discussing Hector Valdez. I cringed. Throughout our history, my friendship with Hector had been a relentless argument between us.

My mail alert bleeped and a message from Samuel with the subject header "My New Tattoo" caught my eye. Oh no. Wincing, I flew through the email:

> I thought I'd get some ink, too. A tribute to our friendship vows, if you will. Tell me what you think.

I opened the attachment, praying that Samuel didn't do anything ridiculously cheesy and permanent. Then the image popped open, and I laughed aloud. It was a picture of him, his T-shirt bunched up around his neck to expose his tan, trim back. Between his shoulder blades was an intricate tattoo, red and puffy—four grinning geriatrics positioned on a mountainside like Rushmore. Beneath the monument in bold letters was the phrase: *Thank you for being a friend.*

Ha. I fired off a response:

> I see someone's been playing with photo-editing software. Don't you have a publicity tour that's keeping you insanely busy? P.S.—Want to see the *Three's Company* tat on my tush? It's next to the infamous heart freckle.

Smug, I turned back to my work, only to be interrupted two minutes later by Samuel's reply:

> If you send me a picture, would that be considered an improper use of company email?

I typed:

> Not when you're the boss. But I'm afraid sending you a picture of my pert tush would fall under the "friends with benefits" category.

There was a knock on my office door and I minimized my email, embarrassed to be caught e-flirting. My underling smiled and dropped the mail on my desk, including a FedEx priority package. Almost immediately, a new email arrived:

> Kaye, you've ruined me and I need to return to this junket. Behave. Yours, Samuel

I blathered over the "Yours" sign-off, then tore into the priority package. Anticipation hopped in my gut when out slid a rough-bound, incomplete manuscript. Dozens of colorful Post-it flags stuck out of the sides:

Hydraulic Level Five {working title}
A Novel
© Samuel Caulfield Cabral & Aspen Kaye Trilby

I flipped through the pages, seeing Samuel's scribbles everywhere—questions, comments, highlighted passages. Curious, I tucked into the first chapter. Warm nostalgia flowed over me as "Aspen" tackled "Caulfield" in the creek. I'd forgotten how runty he'd been as a child, before he shot up like a beanstalk.

A picture fell out of the envelope, a recent shot of Samuel leaning against a moss-covered stone wall. His hands were tucked in his pants pockets and he squinted against the sun. A river and rolling bluffs stretched behind him. Wind whipped his hair around his face, and my fingers ached to tug at that fabulous mop of messy hair. I looked at the label on the back: *Fort Tryon Park. June 23.*

I missed him.

Settling into my chair, I lost myself in Caulfield and Aspen and a long night of seeing our story, for the first time, through Samuel's eyes.

Chapter 2
BOUNCE CRASH

A diver who lands without the aid of a parachute "bounces." Generally not advised.

It would have been painless to dip my toes in that frigid river and test the cold, the power of the current curling around my ankles. Or even to stay in that metaphorical boat, experiencing the wild ride that was Samuel's manuscript, from the false security of a piece of plastic between me and the water. But if we were going to find each other again, I had to dive in and risk getting hurt. I had no trouble taking risks in every other facet of my life. So why was it so difficult with Samuel?

In Samuel's description of Caulfiend and Aspen, I could see how he'd thought I'd guarded my heart from him long before he ever gave me real cause. He'd told me a month ago at Button Rock Reservoir that getting into my head was like breaking into Fort Knox. I'd only reaffirmed that when I barricaded his questions regarding Hector until he let out a frustrated growl and informed me that the only way this reconciliation would *ever* work was if we were honest with each other.

"What do you want me to say, Samuel? That I'm in love with Hector? Because I'm not. He is, and always has been, my friend."

"At least acknowledge that whenever you are upset with me, you use him to make yourself feel better."

"That's ridiculous," I fired back. "I would never, ever use a friend like that."

"When we were dating and we got into a fight, who was the first person you always went to?"

"Hector," I begrudgingly replied.

"And when I was away at college, who took you out on dates?"

"They weren't dates. Just two friends having fun!"

"Kaye," he said in a patronizing tone that made me want to smack him, "Hector Valdez has harbored a crush on you for years, and I think you know it. You may not have considered your time together as 'dating,' but when people back home started warning me that my girlfriend was seeing someone else, it was a problem."

"I don't care what the Lyons gossips say and neither should you."

"But can you see how it would've stung? I'm not above feeling jealous."

Yes, I could see that. I tried to calm my voice. "For the last time, I chose *you*. And I'm *still* choosing you. In the seven years we were apart, I never once had a romantic relationship with him. Don't you think if I had any desire to snack on Hector, it would have happened already?"

"I know."

"And do you realize Hector kept me from tanking when you left me? Kind of like Caroline did for you."

He paused, and I pictured him running a hand through his hair, or squinting, or another one of his exasperated quirks. "I know. I just…I want to be the one you come to first. I don't want Hector involved in our relationship. That's all I ask. Can you do that for me?"

It clicked. He wasn't asking me to give up my friendships. He just wanted reassurance that I'd turn to him before I turned to Hector—an establishment of boundaries. It was still difficult to think of the godlike Samuel Caulfield Cabral suffering from such fallible human qualities as jealousy. Perhaps, by pushing the line with Hector, I was pinching Samuel to ensure he was flesh and blood.

"I can do that, Samuel."

He sighed. "Good. Thank you."

At Friday lunch, when Hector asked me to a movie, my argument with Samuel was fresh in my mind. Sooner or later, we'd have to clear the air about our romantic entanglements during our seven-year separation before someone was hurt. The specters of those nameless, faceless women ate at my peace, but I wondered if it wouldn't be better to let them remain nameless.

Everyone else in our small circle of friends was busy—Hector's brother Santiago Valdez was taking a new bluegrass chick to dinner. Cassady was returning from a hiking expedition, so Molly had him penciled in. And the new Mr. and Mrs. Angel Valdez were still "penciled in" long after their return from Maui. So I called someone I'd never considered socializing with other than to plot the downfall of Caroline Ortega. To my shock, Jaime said yes (on the condition she didn't have to sit next to the "caveman"). I was happy she'd joined us, but I had ulterior motives—to ask her about something that Samuel's memoir had brought to light.

I sat in the middle of a dark theater, Hector on one side, loaded with popcorn, soda, and chocolate, and Jaime on the other side, arms crossed over her chest. Previews rolled—some romantic comedy that caused Jaime to snort derisively every five seconds.

"Jaime," I whispered above the preview, "when you went through all of our financial information during the divorce, did you ever run across a three-million dollar trust fund?"

She turned, her mouth hanging open. Snapping it shut, she threw her arms up and abruptly tore into me. "Did you even *read* the paperwork I gave you? Did you even *listen* to me as I walked you through it? I distinctly told you that Samuel was the beneficiary of a trust fund established by his parents, naming Alonso Cabral as the controlling third party until Samuel turned eighteen. Whatever estate money he inherited went into that fund. It was considered separate property and therefore, untouchable in the settlement. Not that you would've let me go after it, anyway. I can't *believe* you operate your own business…"

I'd known Samuel had a trust fund, but had believed it to be an insignificant amount. Rather, he'd been a millionaire at the age of eighteen. I tuned out Jaime's huffing rambles and arm jabs as something in my memory was jogged. Samuel had told me weeks ago that using his mother's money for his own self-destruction seemed "fitting." This trust fund must have been the account Samuel once used for drug money.

Another preview rolled, yanking us to attention. A sweeping view of the Rocky Mountains filled the screen as haunting music wailed from the speakers. A shot of a sinister old Main Street rippled into view and blurred into a city sign… *Welcome to Bear Creek, Colorado*.

The theater audience erupted into shouts and cheers as they realized which movie trailer rolled.

Hector laughed and poked me in the ribs. Jaime laughed too, but more at my discomfort. I sank into my chair, praying they would lay off the Neelie Nixie jokes. Then the woman herself appeared as a camera panned around and captured her rappelling down a mountainside, her blond braid swinging.

"In the West, legend tells of an ordinary girl..."

I groaned while Hector shook my shoulders, forcing my eyes to the screen. I peeked through my fingers in time to see Neelie take a spill as she leaped across a creek.

"...who went to extraordinary lengths for the ones she loved."

The picture slowed as a dreamy Nicodemus reached down and grabbed Neelie's hand, pulling her from the creek. Ha! If only Samuel's readers knew that "Nicodemus" had biked off in a hissy-fit after getting tackled by a girl.

The audience ooohed and aaahed as a quick montage flashed across the screen, detailing the rise of the nixie clan and their archenemy, the Others. The music and drums spiraled out of control and then the screen went black and silent as the words *Water Sirens* flared bright and bold, followed by *November 26*.

I frowned. Wasn't the release date initially scheduled for early November? This meant that *Water Sirens* would hit theaters Thanksgiving Day, which foretold good, good things for Samuel's franchise. I tried to be happy for him, but it also meant that Samuel would be gone for Thanksgiving, and it stung.

Later that night, I dug through my divorce papers, looking for the information Jaime insisted was already in my possession. I had to admit, I'd never read through the financial stuff because I'd assumed there was nothing to discuss. Actually, I barely glanced at anything, too wrapped up in my pain to care about the details...guarding my heart. Sure enough, there was the spreadsheet Jaime had referred to—a breakdown of Samuel's inheritance after his parents' estate had been settled. Three million dollars.

What else had escaped my foggy brain during divorce proceedings?

"After all that rain, we need to embrace those blue skies, *mamacita*," a brown, bare-chested Hector cajoled. "Put that thing away and jump out of a plane with me again." The "thing" Hector referred to was the hard copy of Samuel's manuscript, which I'd carried like a security blanket since receiving it in the mail.

I held up a finger as I finished my notation, knowing I wouldn't be able to work much longer before we reached the dropzone. From the plane window, Boulder sprawled west and below. Saturday forecasts originally predicted an afternoon of strong winds and dust, but a late morning shower tamed the skies. The minute the weather shifted for the better, Hector called and told me to grab my gear so he could test the Birdman jumpsuit he'd acquired on a few diving runs. He also talked his older brother, Air Force Lieutenant Angel Valdez, into taking us up.

Hector yanked his arms through the sleeves of his new Birdman suit. He flapped his wings, an odd cross between Elvis and a bat.

"Kaye, are you in or not?"

"I dunno. If it starts to rain, it'll leave welts."

Honestly, I was ready to call it quits. Clouds had regathered, and only idiots and masochists skydived in rain. When your terminal velocity is about one hundred fifty miles faster than the speed of rainfall, those little suckers hurt like hell. But Hector was relentless, an unapologetic adrenaline junkie who ceaselessly strove to one-up his previous adventures. His technique was flawless and fluid in skiing, skydiving, and everything in between, and I often felt as though I was watching a bird slice through air instead of a man.

"Last call, Kaye."

"Let me think a minute." I waved him off and settled against the rumbling belly of Angel's plane, attacking the manuscript with a red pen.

- You've got this scene with cherry ChapStick girl all wrong, Cabral. I wasn't angry because Jennifer was stealing my friend from me. I was ticked off because I had a gigantic little girl, starry-eyed crush on you, and I didn't want you dating ANYONE.
- Barnacle-brained wombat... I'd forgotten about that one! It was one of my favorites, along with bitsy blubber butt. Maybe you can work that one in, too?
- Okay, the Weeping lady. Come on, Sam, I wasn't made of glass... but yeah, I admit I was happy to pretend she was real, even if we both knew the truth. Our avoidant coping mechanisms (there's some psychobabble) didn't do either of us any good...

If it was possible to fall in love with a book, I'd send flowers and sparkly things to Samuel's beautiful body of writing. Then again, I'd never feared a book quite so much—reading about the decay festering beneath the surface of my first and only love, the overwhelming sadness, the lost childhood. I hadn't realized how deep that cavity ran. But again, Samuel truly was a master of concealment.

Samuel's writing was innocent and raw, and it seared my heart. His *Water Sirens* series displayed his talent, yet he never quite let his readers veer too close to his personal pain, instead wrapping his prose in a protective gauze of fine words. But in this memoir, he laid himself bare. Reading the stories of our childhood was like watching him take a scalpel to his chest and peel it back, declaring, "Here is my weakness…it is yours to explore."

Above the roar of the engines, a stereo blared a mix of pure, happy summer music. Angel bobbed his head and flipped switches on his navigational panel. One raindrop, then two, then a dozen pattered against the plane's thick windows. Aw, frickin' hamsters. I'd come out of this dive looking like an acne-plagued teenager. I flipped the page.

When I read how Samuel'd slept with that silly fake bat on his pillow—a remnant of one of my more effective pranks—because it somehow brought him comfort, I had to break for fresh air before I became a blubbering mess. And his birth mother…no wonder Samuel nearly yakked up an intestine when, at the recent wedding, his great aunt compared him to that woman. It was amazing I didn't break every plate in my kitchen when I read Samuel's snippets of her. Even in this memoir, Samuel only hinted at the darkness that was his existence in Boston, but the tendrils that tethered him there were far-reaching.

I should have known how disturbing his early childhood had been when, so many years ago, he confided that his mother once left him alone at the ski lodge while she hit the Zermatt slopes. And this was *Camelot* to him, simply because Rachel Caulfield Cabral had bothered to take him along. Still a naïve child, I simply shrugged off the story and filed it away as another oddity in Samuel's mysterious former life. But now, Rachel's ghost lingered in every tragic snapshot of Samuel's existence, waiting to drag her only son down with her.

Static blared over Angel's radio, and he replied with some flight jargon that meant nothing to me, except for a warning about thunderstorms an hour out. He shouted back to us.

"Weather's turning, you two. I think you could still do the dive, but it'll sting. You sure?"

"No worse than a paintball hit," Hector retorted.

"Hundreds of paintball hits. *Eres tan estupido como un perro.*"

"*Callate el osico gordota,*" Hector sniped back. Ah, *hombres.*

It would have been easy to furiously dwell on the things Samuel had shuttered from me—the inheritance, his abusive mother, the guilt, the undeserving loyalty he gave her. Yes, I was hurt that he'd never trusted me with these deeply personal things. But I couldn't be angry with a child for wanting to avoid pain. Years later, I saw how he'd been robbed of his childhood and no matter how much I, Alonso and Sofia, or Danita and Angel tried to restore his innocence with love, there simply had been no going back for him. He was doomed to be a sad, six-year-old adult.

Yet our love had done him *some* good. He had a gentle, quiet heart that, as long as I'd known him, had never truly hardened. And in giving me this memoir, Samuel was now entrusting me with his darkest secrets. I loved him all the more for it. There was no way I'd sit through this green light—asking those tough questions about his life in Boston was long overdue. And I knew just where to start: Alonso Cabral, Antonio's older brother.

"Kaye, if you're going to jump again, it's now or never," Angel announced.

"My fingers are still numb," I whined.

Hector snorted. "Oh please. You had more than enough downtime while you were playing with those papers. Don't give me that 'I'm cold' excuse."

I lifted an eyebrow at his irrepressible grin. Darn it, he knew I couldn't back down from a challenge. "One more, Valdez. Then I'm calling it a day 'cause you'll be kissing my feet, utterly jealous of my awesomeness."

He winked at me. "Bring it, Kaye. Hope your lips like my big, stinky feet."

With a sigh, I tucked the draft in my bag. I needed to escape from Samuel's words, anyway. Grabbing my pack and helmet, I zipped up, secured my frizzed-out hair, and double-checked my harnesses for one more run.

Hector pumped his fist and hollered. "'Atta girl, Kaye! Thought you were losing your *cajones.*"

"Ha! Never. I'll just dive faceup."

Diving in rain wasn't necessarily dangerous. It just hurt like a mother, from what I understood. But I was never going to learn new things if I didn't push the edge, so what the heck. Nervous adrenaline rippling up and down my body, I braced my feet and flew into a world of lashing wind and rain.

Oh, fiery furnaces of hell.

A thousand BB pellets struck a line along my body and I writhed against the rain. I knew I should relax into the dive and put the pain in the back of my mind, but woman-versus-nature my ass—*it hurt!* The wind rushing around my limbs was a lot stronger than even a half hour ago. The minute I tucked into a ball, the biting rain pummeled my spine and stole my breath. I somersaulted once, twice. Cloud cover concealed the ground below and, for a second, I didn't know which way was up.

I sought out Hector through gray froths and saw even he had turned his back to the stinging raindrops, the thrill of his Birdman suit forgotten. This was, absolutely, the least enjoyable dive I'd ever experienced. Soaring toward me, he gave me a thumbs up for canopy deployment. I signaled back. A cascade of blue and white fluttered behind him and he jerked, already growing distant far above me. I flipped around into a box man position and my tingling fingers sought the pull-out cord. Fighting numbness, they released the canopy.

I braced myself for the hard yank. It never came. And then fear hit me because crap, *I was still falling.* My head screamed at me to stop! *Stop free falling!* A split second more and my panicked hands fluttered across my chest to deploy the canopy again, but then I saw it had already opened above me, horseshoed on my foot and collapsed into an uncontrollable spin, dragging me across the bitter sky. Far above me, like a tiny parachuting plastic soldier, Hector wildly waved his arms. This time, I feared the sky was too formidable an enemy. Cold gray churned all around and I stared up into that vortex…

Only a handful of seconds passed, but time had slowed in that last breath manner, and all I could see was Samuel…Samuel…Samuel. Samuel, afraid of heights. Samuel, tethered to me only weeks ago, his strong heartbeat pounding through his wrists and into my fingertips. Samuel's mother, plummeting to her death. Wasn't it horrendous that he'd lose another to unmerciful gravity? *Please God, not now,* I begged.

Damn it. *Think, Kaye! What do I do?* A bit of information cut through the blue of Samuel's eyes and I remembered: *Jettison the canopy.*

Right, I could do this.

Fighting for clarity, I cut away the main canopy and watched through slitted eyes as it fluttered up and away. Before I could deploy the reserve, the Automatic Activation Device beat me to it and the second canopy billowed out…and open. Open, thank God, saving my life.

Tears of relief flooded the corners of my eyes, streaked and dried against my wind-chapped cheeks. But I wasn't safe, yet. I didn't know how much time had passed between the main and reserve canopy deployments. Gravity sped me toward the ground much too quickly and I knew, just *knew* landing was going to hurt.

My heart hit my throat. I wasn't going to make this one after all—my landing speed was way too fast. *Crap, feet down! If you hit the ground face first, you'll have a nasty tangle with the pavement.* But I couldn't stop the momentum of my body and I pitched forward, feet over head, smashing hard into the forgiving pea gravel of the landing zone and tumbling over and over. Something smacked me brutally on the back of my skull, and stars and pain shot across the entire left side of my face. I flopped like a rag doll, wet fabric of my canopy smothering my nose and mouth and lungs until, long seconds or minutes later, a strong arm wrapped around my waist and yanked me out of the parachute's choke hold.

"Kaye!" I heard Hector cry, pure panic. "*Por Dios, mamacita,* I'm so, so sorry. Just don't move."

I whimpered and hacked, fighting to lift a hand to my throbbing head, but I didn't have the energy. A few other club members mumbled to Hector, somewhere behind my eyelids. *"Man, she totally biffed…brace her head, she might have a neck or skull fracture…that jump was seriously hazardous, you two…a coupla stupid skygods…"*

I felt my body settle into wet, slimy grass. Several shadows hulked over me, mercifully blocking the heavy gray sky from my light-sensitive eyes. I heard more rustling and then Angel's blessed voice: "Move over, she's my sister." Dang it. I groaned again, not from pain but from the chiding I'd get from him, then Danita, Alonso and Sofia, and probably even Samuel once word of my stupid stunt got back to them.

Another face hovered over me, this time a woman with soft eyes. "I'm a PA at Boulder General. Can you please tell me your name?" Hands cautiously unstrapped my helmet and another bolt of pain streaked through my head.

"Kaye Cabral," I rasped.

"Kaye *Cabral?*" Angel said with surprise.

I sighed, my body and head aching too much to go there. Hector gingerly smoothed wet hair from my face, and I smelled the sharp metallic fragrance of blood.

"Kaye *Trilby*," he corrected, his voice cracking.

"Did you black out at any point, Kaye?" she asked.

"I don't think so. I saw stars..."

I felt her fingers probing my neck, my head—I winced as she pressed the side of my skull. "Can you open your eyes?"

I complied, grimacing at the light. The young woman looked vaguely familiar. She had me follow her finger and checked for double vision while she ordered a couple of onlookers to fetch a makeshift gurney from the hangar.

"Well, Kaye, it looks like the ground thwacked you good. I'm pretty certain you don't have any neck fractures or severe head trauma—your helmet saved your life, you know—but I want to run you over to BGH to get checked out. What kind of car do you have here?"

I frowned. What kind of car did I have?

"A Jeep," Angel answered for me.

"Perfect. It will be faster to just drive you over than to call for an ambulance. Hector, help me secure her to the gurney and we'll carry her up to the Jeep."

I'm sure my blush was rampant as Hector and Angel lugged me through the small crowd to my Jeep Wrangler. Pain flared through my skull as they settled me into the back. I'd never been so thoroughly embarrassed in my life. I called for Hector to grab my gear and bag, anxious to have Samuel's manuscript next to me. It was childish, but like I'd said—security blanket. I didn't have a chance to ruminate over the memoir, though, because the PA kept me in conversation with her the entire trip to Boulder General Hospital, barraging me with questions in between monitoring my blood pressure, pressing a wet cloth to my forehead, and checking my eyes with an annoying little light from her medical bag. I tried to dull the pounding in my head by listening to the drone of the windshield wipers...quiet thuds of rain as it pelted the Jeep's soft top.

In my woozy state, I hadn't really noticed Angel calling Alonso. But when we pulled up to BGH's emergency entrance, my former father-in-law was already there behind the ER staff, opening the Jeep door and grasping my hand.

"I hear you've been doing dangerous things, *hijita*," he said, his face all compassion and concern. It was difficult to be angry with him when he looked at me like that.

"Alonso, just don't. Please."

He nodded and stepped back as medical personnel checked the extent of my injury, my vitals, repeating everything the PA'd done as she rattled off a list of symptoms...dizziness, headache, some confusion.

"I want a CT scan stat," she ordered. "She may have a mild to moderate TBI and I don't want to chance it. She'll also need a stitch or two on that laceration."

"Tricia, I owe you one," Hector said.

Tricia...that was the PA's name. She'd graduated from Lyons High with Samuel. I'd always liked her; she was one of the few older girls who hadn't been catty.

Somewhere between the confining cylinder that scanned my head and being wheeled to an exam room, the pounding in my head dulled, oh sweet relief. I caught a glimpse of myself in a mirror. To say I looked like I'd been slugged by the pavement was an understatement. A large bruise had surfaced around a nasty-looking gash on my left temple and cheek. Tiny pink welts covered my cheeks and neck. My stringy hair was crusted with dried blood just above the wound, and I couldn't help thinking it would look even worse by the time Samuel arrived in three days. I scowled. *Nothing you can do about that now, Kaye.* I'd have to tell him about the accident and face his "I told you so."

When we'd had our discussion about my relationship with Hector last week, one of his most fervent complaints was the "brainless risks" I took with this particular friend. "I told you why I do it, a long time ago," I'd fired back. He'd sighed, forcing himself to calm down. "Trust me, from an addict's experience—the 'why' is never a good enough reason for risking your life. I don't want to get a call some day from my sister, telling me you broke your neck..."

I moaned, realizing I'd just proved his point. I might be just as screwed up as he was.

Alonso and I bided our time in the hospital room, the quiet buzz of a twenty-four-hour news station a stopgap for the blessedly absent conversation. The pain medication Tricia gave me made a mess of my lucidity, but my eyes flitted over Alonso's person. He wore a starched dress shirt and tie, and I realized with chagrin he must have come from something important for his magazine. But my goodness, the man was handsome, even at fifty-five.

Some time later, Tricia tapped on the door. "Good news," she said, "your CT scan is clean. No internal bleeding, no swelling—you are very, *very* fortunate. You have a slight concussion, however. I'll stitch up that gash and send you home for observation. Is there someone who can watch you?"

"Mom has farmers markets. D-Dad and Audrey are in Denver for some hippie convention," I mumbled, my tongue thick and dry. "They w-won't be home for two days, and then they'll be wrapped up in new tie-dyes, believe me."

Alonso's mouth twitched. "I'll call Sofia and have her pick you up. Is that all right?"

"Hector Valdez is w-waiting in the lobby. He can help me out."

Tricia cast me a dubious expression. "Hmm. I think I'll admit you overnight and have a nurse check you every few hours." *Dang it, should have gone with Sofia.*

I spent a fitful night under observation in an elevated hospital bed, thin pillows stuffed around my shoulder blades to ease the aches and pains tumbling through my body and jostling for recognition. When Alonso returned for me the next morning, I was dressed and sitting on the edge of the mercilessly afflictive bed, ready to admit that I should have accepted the Cabrals' offer.

Golden sunlight bounced off the rocks and pavement, splitting my already pounding head. As we drove the winding road from Boulder to Lyons, I chanced a glance at Alonso. His lips were silently pressed together, eyes holding to the windshield. I couldn't pass up this opportunity for damage control.

"You won't say anything to Samuel, will you?"

"May I ask why you don't want to tell him?"

"You aren't exactly one to lecture me about keeping secrets, Señor Cabral," I retorted. A sharp ache watered my eyes and subsided. Alonso gave me a quick, ponderous look.

"Please try to rest, Kaye," he murmured.

I sank into the seat and allowed the curve of the road to lull me. When my eyes drifted to Alonso's again, I was startled to find them filled with pain. He sighed and rapped his fingers against the steering wheel, torn.

"You've been speaking with Samuel a lot lately, sorting through some of the confusion around your breakup, correct?"

"Yes, we're trying to."

"How is it going?"

"Long, tedious, enlightening, frustrating, wonderful…should I keep listing adjectives?"

Alonso smiled. "I get it. You know, I never really understood why you chose to divorce my son. Don't misunderstand me — what you found in New York was shocking. But I was surprised you didn't wait a little longer."

I cringed. *Good thing you didn't wave the note under his nose and call him a traitor, Kaye.* "You and Sofia were probably furious when Samuel received the divorce papers."

"We were upset, but we tried to put ourselves in your shoes."

I twisted my fingers nervously. "Have you ever considered that if you or Sofia had only *told* me Samuel was trying to get clean to save our marriage, I would have held off? Heck, I might've been able to help, especially when he had his setback."

"I've gone over it many, many times. In retrospect, yes, I could have handled things differently, and I apologize. But, Kaye, as much as I care for you, my first priority was to my son. It was *his* decision not to involve you. To do so would have opened up a whole new can of worms which, honestly, he wasn't ready to deal with. And as his father, I had to respect his wishes. Maybe if Sofia and I had dealt with circumstances differently, when he was younger…"

"The damage from his mother?"

Alonso blinked, taken aback. "You know about her?"

"Samuel has been sharing bits and pieces. I could hardly be kept in the dark forever," I replied, bitterly. "But, Alonso, I was still his *wife*—the papers weren't signed. You had no right to keep me away like you did. You had to know his judgment at the time wasn't exactly sound." I hissed as my head throbbed, and pressed a palm to my temple, forcing the ache back.

Guilt-ridden eyes darted over my pale, scraped face. He tugged his tie loose with a sigh. "With Samuel, I've made the mistake of being an overprotective parent. I have a multitude of regrets, Kaye, even things that happened long before you or Samuel were born. In my need to atone, I'm afraid I steamrolled you."

"Are you talking about your brother?"

"Yes."

"Can you tell me about him?"

"No. Not without speaking to Samuel first."

"But he was your brother," I argued.

"And he was Samuel's father," he said gently.

"Bull. I want answers, Alonso, not excuses." I again pressed the heel of my palm to my forehead as pain shot through my skull.

Alonso rested a calming hand on my shoulder. "Kaye, enough for today—you've had a head injury and you need to rest. I will tell you what I can, only let me speak with my son first. He'd like to be a part of that conversation, I'm certain—he's in a much better place than he was seven years ago."

I sighed, knowing he was right...to a point.

Tricia had advised me to take a few days off from work to rest. "Resting" consisted of raiding my mother's recipe books to find some new dish to spring on Samuel. In the end, I decided to stick with my tried and true summer fare and loaded up on fresh salmon, tomatoes, brown rice, and all sorts of colorful produce and pastries. My entire body was the purple ache of one deep bruise, but I found if I sat for any length of time, stiffness settled into my joints and it was best to keep moving. Light housework proved to be the cure, along with a liberal dose of Advil. My apartment was dust-free and sparkling, I'd aired out a few bed linens, and I'd even emptied my wine rack and stuck the bottles in the cabinet above my refrigerator, ever mindful of Jaime's snarks about Samuel's booze-free lifestyle.

At first, Samuel insisted on booking a hotel room in Boulder for his upcoming visit, the two nights we wouldn't be camping on the grotto trip. I told him that was ridiculous because I had a very comfortable sleeper sofa and wouldn't he rather spend the night with me? (Whoopsie). He groaned that I was making it extremely difficult to be a gentleman. I laughed, assuring him he'd leave Boulder Saturday evening, virtue intact.

"It's a little too late for that. You stole my virtue a long time ago, Aspen Kaye Trilby," he teased. "Just don't go to any trouble for me, please."

It took me two full days to finally tell him about the skydiving accident. There were no I-told-you-so's, no recriminations of Hector. But he was upset. Very upset.

"If you won't think of yourself, at least consider the people who love you," he pleaded, his voice edged with panic. "Your parents, Molly, Dani, me. If anything happened to you, we'd be devastated."

Despite the pain in his voice, his assurance that he'd be devastated if I died was morbidly comforting. "Would you be, Samuel?" I asked, wanting to hear it again. There was a pause, and I immediately regretted asking him to reaffirm something so horrible.

"I'd be wholly destroyed, Kaye," he whispered, his voice low.

Fear rippled up my spine, triggering a memory of Caroline's warning: *You'll destroy him and you won't even comprehend you're doing it.*

"I'm s-sorry," I stuttered.

"For what? Upsetting me or skydiving in storm conditions?"

I didn't know the answer to that, so I simply mumbled, "both."

That conversation with Samuel grounded me, for a few hours, before I was again caught up in the excitement of his imminent visit.

Just hours before Samuel was scheduled to arrive, I sat across from Cassady at an impromptu lunch as we discussed the whirlwind that was Molly Jones.

"So why haven't you asked Molly to be exclusive yet?" Ever the commitment phobe, Cassady ducked his sandy head at my direct question, stabbing his fork prongs into an innocent piece of wilted lettuce.

"Believe me, I want to, but the timing isn't right. With her stepsister not improving and Molly hanging on by a thread, I need to hold off until things get better." Molly's stepsister, Holly, had recently delivered a lovely baby girl, but now suffered from debilitating post-partum depression. Her husband was reluctant to accept help, and Molly was doing all she could to hold her family together.

"I call foul, Cassady," I answered honestly. "Don't you dare mess around with her heart."

"I really care about Molly." He shrugged, and I decided not to push further.

Lately, the abrupt shift my forlorn love life had taken made me overly optimistic. As the crater in my chest steadily filled with all things Samuel, I was convinced that all the world's problems could be solved with Q-and-As, friendship vows, childhood memoirs, and sweet, sweet humor. The past few days, especially, I'd been floating like Ginger Rogers across the Front Range, counting the hours until my Fred Astaire arrived and swept me off to cloud nine. Then again, it could have been my concussion-addled brain. But hearing of Molly's struggles with her sister hooked me, and once more, I was reeled down to earth. I set my fork aside and searched Cassady's face.

"Is Holly really that bad? I had no idea."

"The depression has gotten worse in the past couple of weeks. They thought counseling and medication was helping—she ate more, slept better, and she started focusing on the baby again. But then she had an episode this weekend, which set her back." He cleared his throat and reached for his ice water. "She locked herself in the bathroom, screaming and crying that she wasn't good for the baby and to get her out of the house. Molly was pleading with her to unlock the door. Derek finally got out his toolkit and took off the hinges. It was bad."

"So now what?"

"Well, her doctor is adjusting her medication and increasing outpatient therapy. If things don't improve, the only other course is inpatient therapy."

"Poor Holly. That's really sad." Usually inpatient therapy for postpartum depression meant the person was either suicidal or a danger to their family, from what Molly explained. Doctors didn't like to split new mothers and their babies if they could help it.

"Cassady, if you and Molly don't feel up to the caving trip this week, I can find a couple of replacements. Santiago and Hector could shuffle their work schedule around."

He shook his head. "No, it will be good for Molly to get away for a bit."

When I returned to the office I picked up the pile of mail on my desk and sifted through it, then hit my phone and email messages.

After hearing of Holly's mental health struggles, the turmoil with Samuel suddenly seemed not so bad—at least we were on the downhill slope after scaling our pile of problems. Yet, with the eeriness of a fleeting bout of déjà vu, panic palpitated in my chest as I recalled pounding on the door of Samuel's bedroom in New York, just as Derek had pounded on their locked bathroom and cried for

Holly. Cried, pleaded, nauseous with the fear and knowledge that we were powerless to save our spouses from the Stygian thing that had captured their minds. I shook off the dreadful memory and delved into my work.

I found Molly in her office later that afternoon, weeping over her file cabinet as if it contained Saint Helena's holy relics. I had a hunch her visit with Holly had not gone well.

"There's no *way* Holly and Derek can afford these medical bills," Molly choked out. "And they'll only let me help them so much."

"What about my alimony money?" I reminded her. I'd just received another huge check in the mail last week, this time with a sardonic: *Mickey, In Memorium* in the memo line.

She shook her head. "Derek won't take it. He's too stubborn and prideful. I swear he's in denial."

"We can try funneling it through a not-for-profit, one that Holly's center works with. Could they recommend somebody?"

Molly sniffed and blew her nose, dabbing at the mascara running down her cheeks. "I can ask tomorrow afternoon when we take Holly for therapy."

I soothingly scratched my nails across Molly's back as her sobbing subsided. "Hey. We'll do whatever it takes to get your sister better, okay? You and me — right?"

Molly nodded and wrapped her arms around my neck. "Thank you, Kaye. I don't know what I'd do without you."

I was completely furious with Derek for refusing a financial gift that could help his wife get better. Yes, it's hard to take charity; anyone with an ounce of pride understands that. But would he do it for Holly? His kids? Or perhaps he was frightened to the point where he'd deny the seriousness of Holly's illness. If I were in his shoes, I'd have a difficult time accepting it, too. I'd want my old life back, before the tears, the suicide threats, the extreme behavior like having your spouse lock herself in the bathroom to keep from hurting your children. I hoped with all my might that Holly's doctors, and therapy, and medication could work a miracle.

When I left work that evening, I darted out the door, intent on a run to the grocery store for a last minute cake mix before Samuel arrived. I stopped dead in my tracks. A roadster rental was parked along the side street, its engine still clicking and cooling. I squealed, ditching the grocery store plans, and tore around Trilby-Jones's backyard, wobbly heels, pencil skirt and all.

Samuel sat at the top of my staircase, looking utterly delectable in a travel-rumpled dress shirt open at the collar, blinding white against the brown of his neck. He hadn't bothered with a hat and sunglasses, not caring whether someone photographed him lurking outside my door. His feet were propped on a small carry-on bag and his head rested against the rail, eyes closed. How could he possibly nap at a wonderful, glorious time like this? I squealed again and eyes as clear as ice flew open, then filled with delight as I dropped my satchel and scrambled up the staircase, into his waiting arms. Tight arms wrapped around me and I felt my feet lift from the stairs as he stood and pulled me to him.

"You're here! And you're early!" I laughed into his neck. "How long have you been waiting?"

He chuckled. "Just ten minutes. I very nearly stormed your office but I didn't want to cause a scene. How's my woman?" He lowered me to the ground and inspected the four stitches along my hairline, his smile turning to a frown.

"I'm fabulous, thrilled, and ecstatic now that you're here. How are you?" I tried to tug him toward the door, but he held me firm. His lips lowered to my forehead, and he gently kissed the stitches there, then the bruises surrounding them. Lastly, his mouth ducked to mine and he softly, tentatively kissed me.

"I'm relieved to find you in one piece." Serious eyes met mine. "I mean it, Kaye. Please don't ever do something that reckless again. The thrill isn't worth your life."

It was all I could do not to open my mouth and demand he kiss me soundly, deeply. But I'd set the rules and now I had to live with them, darn it. I sighed, simply enjoying the feel of his warm body.

"Welcome home," I murmured against his neck, thinking those words would become a lovely tradition. Every time he came back to me, I'd say them.

He smiled and brushed my lips again. "It's good to be home."

Chapter 3
FLOAT OR SINK

Rising or falling in relation to another vertical diver, when both divers are in free fall.

Happiness; why is it that we frail beings turn happiness into something so unattainable? Happiness can be as simple as discovering the asparagus you hated as a child is quite tasty once you reach adulthood. It can be a shared, secret smile with a complete stranger in a grocery store line when they place chocolate, strawberries, and candles on the conveyor belt. Being grateful simply for a rain-soaked breeze cooling your face, soft grass under your feet, intricate veins weaving through a leaf. Or reveling in a strong, secure arm around your shoulders and just *knowing*, even though he hasn't voiced it, that you are completely and utterly loved.

This was the form my happiness chose as Molly, Cassady, Samuel, and I journeyed west into the mountains to Cloud Lake and the glorious chimneys and squirmways awaiting our exploration. I had Samuel almost all to myself for two more days, before we'd return and spend Saturday with his parents in Lyons.

We left Boulder before the sun was up, and thankfully, after a restless two nights' sleep, I didn't have to drive. Cassady steered our company SUV with Molly in the front. In the back, Samuel had situated himself in the middle and pulled me flush against his side, his seatbelt discarded for the moment. I knew for safety's sake he should put it back on, and he said he would when we neared city limits. But for now I relished my happiness and could only pray there wasn't a box trap propped above my unsuspecting head.

"What's running through that mind of yours?" Samuel whispered, toying with the curl tucked behind my ear.

I smiled. "I'm thinking about how happy I am right now."

"Do I make you happy, Kaye?"

"Yes," I whispered honestly. Because right now, nothing could overwhelm the contentment I felt. "How about you?"

He brushed his lips across my temple. "So very happy."

"I meant, what's running through your mind?"

"I was remembering the summer you literally broke the bank to buy us soft-serve ice cream cones from the corner station. I think I had just turned eleven, so you must have been eight."

I laughed. "I remember that! I counted out one hundred pennies and put them in a sandwich baggie. The cashier was so pissed."

"She stood there, sliding pennies into her hand one at a time and grumbling about how we should ride our bikes over to the bank teller and exchange the pennies for a dollar."

"But I had exact change, of course," I said proudly.

"No, you were off by two. I had to toss in a nickel."

"You did not! I had exactly one hundred pennies."

"Ninety-eight pennies," he corrected.

I lightly jabbed him with my elbow and he squirmed. "We sound like a couple of kids, bickering over pennies. Molly and Cassady will think we're dorks."

"I thought you were dorks back in college," Molly quipped, pushing her sunglasses up her nose. "Nothing new here."

"Says the girl who hosted Risk parties in our dorm room to meet guys," I said dryly. Samuel buried his face in my hair to stifle a laugh as Molly flipped me the bird.

I gazed at his face. Despite his obvious contentment, tired lines crisscrossed the corner of his eyes, around his mouth.

It had been like this Tuesday night and all of Wednesday—this mercurial shifting from serious to playful to serious. I loved seeing Samuel laugh and smile. I hated seeing him even more tired and strained than the days leading up to Danita's wedding. I hoped, no matter what secrets Samuel and I shared with each other—namely, the other people who'd warmed our beds—we could take them in stride without our feet sticking in the bog.

I'd slept restlessly the past two nights. Every single time Samuel turned, or moaned, or even flinched on the sleeper sofa, I heard him. Naughty, rash Kaye hoped that the quiet thud of footsteps would sound and the empty space on my mattress would sink with the weight of the handsome man who wanted me, who thought I was lovely. But I knew Samuel. He would rather be strapped down and forced to watch a *Dawson's Creek* marathon than presume to violate the sanctity of my bed without an invitation.

Jolts of longing had tingled through me Tuesday night as he'd grinned over his plate of salmon, brown rice, and sautéed veggies, exclaiming that I always was much better in the kitchen than him. He beamed with pride as I unveiled my complete first edit of our draft memoir and placed it in his lap like a Christmas present. My stomach flipped. And my heart—oh traitorous heart!—pulsed out of my chest when he tugged me to his side so we could read through my comments together. He *had* to hear how loudly it pounded, because it was deafening to my ears.

"Is this okay?" Samuel had asked, smoothing hair from my face as he flipped open the much-abused, much-loved hard copy of our story.

"Mmhmm." *More than okay.* "Are you sure you aren't tired?" I asked, dubiously examining his drooping eyes, his subtly shaking hands.

"I'm tired," he admitted, "but I'm not going to waste our time catching up on sleep. I'm more concerned about *you* and *this*." He lightly tapped the stitches on my forehead. I once more cursed my stupidity.

Samuel read through my first page of comments and his forehead immediately furrowed. "What do you mean 'why is Molly mentioned here?' She used to play in the creek with us, correct?"

I shook my head, smiling. "See, this is why you need me. Molly moved to Lyons *after* the creek games, so she shouldn't show up until chapter four or five."

"Well, who was your little friend that tagged along?"

"Are you thinking of Jennifer—cherry ChapStick girl? She played occasionally for Danita's sake, until she said it was a stupid game and she'd rather be inside with her Barbie Dream House. Then Angel made Jennifer cry because he said Barbie was a 'hoochie mama.' It was the first time I'd ever heard that expression. Angel got in big trouble when I asked Sofia what it meant."

Samuel scratched the back of his neck, completely puzzled. At last his face softened. "Huh. I'd forgotten about that. I'll have to rewrite it."

For a solid two hours, I'd listened to the smooth timbre of his melodic voice as he read his manuscript to me, occasionally pausing to make note of ideas or ask questions. Finally, my body betrayed me and I slipped under, conscious only of his warmth, the strength hidden beneath layers of flannel and cotton and skin, and a subtle whoosh of air as he lifted me in his arms and carried me to my bed. And even though he'd left my side, I was hyper-aware of him just strides away, on my sofa…in my apartment…in Colorado…all for me.

And I knew, because he'd do the same, it was time to humble myself and give him the dossier.

I'd sprinted from my office at precisely 11:29 a.m. Wednesday, anxious to see Samuel and anxious to excavate the dossier from my underwear drawer.

He was settled in my big leather armchair, his glasses perched on his nose, dark hair sticking up like a ruffled tomcat. He diligently worked on his laptop and seemed so comfortable in my home, it was as if he'd come with the living room set. His eyes flew up as I whirled through the door, taking in my restless appearance.

He smiled. "Miss me?"

I nodded and hurled myself at his lap, allowing him just enough time to move his computer to my coffee table before I pounced. I flicked a charcoal tendril from his forehead and pecked him there. I wasn't buttering him up before I gave him my dastardly file of revenge and blackmail material, oh no.

"Give me a minute to change and I'll whip together lunch."

"Already taken care of."

"Oh?" I uneasily sniffed the air for burned food. He gave me a shake.

"I picked up chicken salad from the deli across the street and chopped veggies and fruit. Don't worry your pretty little head about choking down burned or lumpy stuff."

"I wasn't," I lied through my teeth. As I shed my work attire for jeans and a top that cried whore-nun complex, Samuel called to me from the kitchen.

"Hey, Kaye, where are the napkins?"

"In the cabinet above the refrigerator." I flipped my head and tousled the wavy layers of hair. Then, like a crashing organ chord in a horror movie, I remembered what I'd hidden in that particular cabinet. "Crap," I muttered, sliding across the wooden floor in my sock feet.

Samuel leaned against the counter, his long legs crossed, arms folded. A single eyebrow lifted at my panicked face. A little smile played on his lips.

"Care to explain, Trilby, why you have seven bottles of wine stashed above your refrigerator, yet your wine rack is empty?"

My eyes flicked between my perturbed…whatever he was and the contraband in my cabinet. I decided to play it cool. "I wanted to be respectful of your lifestyle, Samuel."

He nodded, waiting for me to say more.

"It's not that I think you're weak or you'll cave, or anything," I added quickly. "I just didn't want to be insensitive, that's all. And Caroline never drinks around you, so…"

Samuel reached for my hand, giving it a squeeze. "I know you're being helpful, Kaye. I just want to make sure you understand you don't have to go to those sorts of lengths. If we have dinner and you want to enjoy an occasional glass of wine, don't hesitate because you believe I'll be offended, or tempted, or uncomfortable. You don't have to drastically change your life for me."

"But that's just it, Samuel. I *want* to change my life for you. I want to be supportive and consider your feelings and needs, and all that. If it upsets you that I put up the wine bottles, then I'll move them back to my wine rack. Or I'll just get rid of them altogether—whatever you need. You always want to take care of me. Just give me a chance to return the favor, please."

Some powerful emotion crossed Samuel's blue eyes, setting them alight. He tugged me to him and folded me into his chest, his chin resting on top of my head. "Why don't we take care of each other—make it a mutual thing?"

I chuckled against his worn Clash T-shirt, surprised it wasn't a cleaning rag by now. "What a novel idea."

As we dug into the chicken salad, I recognized my window to broach the dossier. "Samuel, do you remember number three of our friendship vows?"

He peered at me, instantly alerted to my discomfort. "Sure. Fight for your reputation, guard your back."

"Well, I have a confession to make." I took a deep breath. "I have something here in the apartment that violates number three, and it could ruin your reputation if it ever got out."

He lowered his sandwich, sharp eyes questioning. "Are you talking about my arrest record?"

"Not just that. Lots of records—school, arrest, newspaper clippings, any public record, really. I'm so very sorry, Samuel."

"May I see them?"

I slipped from the table and fetched the file. I watched silently as he flipped through paper after paper, hissing one minute, stoic the next. At last, he closed the file and laid it on the table between us.

"This is everything?"

I blinked. "Is there more?"

He shook his head, closed his hurt eyes and ran a hand through his hair. "How?" he choked out. "Why?"

"The 'how' was Jaime Guzman. Why? It's complicated." I explained how I'd approached Jaime for help in getting Caroline out of the way with a healthy dose of revenge on the side. I told him I never intended to make the dossier public and kept it buried in my underwear drawer. Ashamed, I wordlessly watched as he left the apartment. I stared at the door for a full hour, gnawing on a thumbnail, frightened I wouldn't see him again. Then he returned, noticeably looser.

"What do you plan to do with this file, Kaye?" he asked.

"Shred it, pitch it. Right now, if you'd like. I would have done it sooner, but I wanted to tell you the truth—give you a chance to chew me out."

He shook his head. "I won't do that."

"Why not? I deserve it."

"Because everything in that file is the truth, things you should have been privy to from the very beginning. It's my fault those records even exist."

I exhaled and squeezed his shoulder as I cleared away our lunch plates, sandwiches long dried out. "Samuel, sometimes I wish you'd just get angry at me instead of blaming yourself all the time."

"I didn't say I wasn't angry," he replied, his voice tight. "But it seems like a colossal waste of time to 'chew you out' when I'm only here through Saturday. You apologized. We'll destroy the file, no harm done. It's behind us."

I clutched the file in my arms as I led Samuel down the stairs and into my TrilbyJones office where the magical problem shredder resided. I truly hoped he was right, that it *was* behind us and we could leave for our grotto trip with clear air…

Cassady flipped the turn signal and exited the road at a pancake house south of Cloud Lake, not far from the caves, just as the morning sun burned the last of the fog from the sky. Despite the early hour, the parking lot was bustling, and Samuel instantly tensed. Without a word, he slipped on a broken-in Red Sox cap and pulled it low over his forehead, shading his face. But when we were seated across from Molly and Cassady in a corner booth of the packed greasy spoon, he looked torn between good manners and flashing his recognizable face. Manners won out, as always, and he tossed the hat on the bench next to him and smoothed his hair in a futile attempt to tame it.

Sure enough, minutes later a nervous woman, then a second, then a third crowded the table, camera phones whipped out. I tried to duck out of the pictures, praying no photos of me with a messy ponytail and shiny face surfaced on the Internet. Meanwhile, our poor waitress returned with a tray full of pancakes, syrup carafes, and sausage, and struggled to slide around Samuel's readers. Molly jumped up and squeezed past the women, guiding hot plates to the table.

Samuel turned on his best charming smile. "I'd be happy to take a picture with you *after* we eat—"

"Do you mind terribly if I steal your seat?" The second woman was polite, but strong-looking and could tie me in a death knot with her pinkie. Samuel mouthed a "sorry" to me. I nodded and slipped out of the booth so the woman could take her pictures. The third woman, a much smaller and non-threatening person, smiled apologetically. Suddenly, recognition swept across her face.

"Oh, you're Neelie Nixie! Can you sign my magazine?"

"Ah…sure." She fished through her monster purse, triumphantly pulling out today's issue of *A-Okay* and a pen.

"Here, you can use my back."

As I propped the magazine against her floral shoulder and scrawled my name on the cover, I froze. There, in all its pixilated glory, was my face—pinched brow, mouth hanging open. Not the best candid shot. Next to the box was a gorgeous photo of Indigo Kingsley decked out as Neelie Nixie. And hovering above both of us was a puzzled Samuel, with the following caption:

```
Cabral Confused: Kingsley jilted for real-
life Neelie?
```

Molly, peering over my shoulder at the article, loosed a low whistle. I inwardly groaned and returned the magazine. My apartment phone would be ringing off the hook again. The woman thanked me.

"You're a lot prettier in person. Still, Sam's an idiot for blowing it with someone like Indigo. That's what all the sites are saying—he has a reputation for messing around with fans, if you know what I mean. Lucky girls." She winked and I felt bile surge in my throat. Samuel grabbed my elbow and pulled me back into the booth, placing a protective hand in the dip of my waist.

"Okay then! Thanks for stopping over," Molly said too brightly, and attempted to usher them from our table. Cassady grunted through a mouthful of whole grain pancakes, already halfway through his breakfast.

"Nice meeting you, ladies," Samuel added kindly but dismissively and finally, they took the hint and left us to our cooling pancakes. He buried his face in my hair and breathed.

"I'm so very sorry, Kaye. I should have warned you about the article and the sites. All lies, I promise you."

I snapped around to stare at him, incredulous. "You knew? I thought you never paid attention to the stories."

His lips curled. "Number three: fight for your reputation. And that includes the trash the tabloids print. I've asked Caroline to give me a heads up if something runs that's out of her control. She warned that the gossip rags are getting restless because she hasn't fed them anything juicy lately."

"But, Samuel, what if they..." I couldn't complete the thought with Cassady and Molly sitting there, watching us with curious eyes, but he understood I was alluding to his drug years.

Samuel also glanced at Cassady and Molly, debating whether he could speak freely in front of them, and decided he could. "I've called in a favor to Indigo and pretty much begged her to go public with a new romance," he said quietly, just for our ears. "She's not thrilled to be pegged as the victim of a love triangle, so she's considering it."

Molly leaned in conspiratorially. "Who's the new guy? Someone famous?"

Again Samuel paused, considering how much he should say. "A coworker from the *Water Sirens* movie."

"Is that why the two of you broke up? Because she was seeing someone on the movie set?" Molly pried. Cassady rolled his eyes. I just shrugged, because I secretly wanted to hear Samuel's answer, too.

"Um…" He shifted uncomfortably. "Actually, that was just the final nail in the coffin. Indigo hadn't been happy for a while with our intimacy. Or lack thereof," he mumbled, red creeping up his neck.

If Danita had been privy to this conversation, she would have mercilessly said something along the lines of "No way! *The* Indigo Kingsley dumped you because you wouldn't put out? That's so girly of you, Samuel!" But Danita wasn't there, and in her place were four rather polite people who just cleared their throats and played with their coffee cups after Samuel's admission.

Conversation shifted, but the truth about Samuel's dysfunctional sex life with Indigo niggled in my mind. More than niggled — it brewed, stewed, and bubbled with curiosity and, more darkly, jealousy. Who were these women Samuel had chosen above the masses to pursue? What did he find attractive in them?

Justifications for prying into Samuel's missing years neatly aligned themselves. I knew he had not lived as a monk. Given his past drug use and erraticism, the practical thing would be to find out with whom he'd been, right? And with all the flirting, the innuendos, and the small yet intimate brushes and touches flying between Samuel and me, one of us would be hurt if we put off that discussion much longer. Today I would exorcise these long-legged, unfreckled ghosts and, with any luck, my jealousy.

Groovy Adventures Kevin was a stocky California transplant with blond "hang-ten" hair and the surfer-dude speak to match. He'd already pitched tents on a bed of pine needles by the time we found him amid skyscraper ponderosas of the primitive Cloud Lake campground. He tossed each of us a hardhat with a mounted headlamp, spare batteries, an extra flashlight, leather gloves, coveralls, knee pads, and a small first aid kit for our thin backpacks. I turned the hardhat in my hands, grateful Tricia had suggested I start a regimen of Advil and pack extra gauze for my stitches.

Samuel looked dubious.

"Are they sending us into the mines?" he whispered facetiously. "Do we get pick axes, too?"

I snorted. "Trust me, after several hours scooting around on your hands and knees in near freezing temperatures, you'll be kissing Kevin for the extra equipment."

Kevin broke us in with an easy foot tour through the largest, more traversed lower part of the cave. A path led to the cave entrance, flanked on both sides by a prehistoric world of rock layers, and I could see Samuel's mind churning in his love for science and discovery.

The cave itself was a system of colorful, sparkling walls and dripping stalactites and stalagmites found in limestone grottos, tapering off into pitch black caverns. An odd fungus also coated the caves. At first I thought it was shimmering silver, but Samuel pointed out that the shining effect was caused by condensation collecting on the tips and, under our lights, it shimmered.

After we finished the main tube, Kevin suggested we pair up and hunt down some of the other, more hidden caves in the area. We decided to meet back at camp by six o'clock.

"Here's the thing about serious grotto clubs," Groovy Kevin explained. "We don't like to share cave locations with anyone else, because it means stupid people come in and totally contaminate that delicate ecosystem, get it? It's kind of like *Fight Club*—the first rule is no one mentions cave locations. The second rule is…ha, gotcha. No touching those cute little stalagmites. Respect the cave, dudes. Respect the cave."

Samuel's fingers brushed along the inside of my arm, coming to rest around my gloved hand. "Come on," he whispered in my ear, his breath tickling my skin. "I think I spotted a cave entrance not far off the trail and I'd like to check it out."

I gripped his hand and let him lead me away from the group. My palm was clammy as I anxiously pondered ways to introduce the ol' "previous partners" conversation. Away from the group, I likely wouldn't have a more ideal time to broach the matter. We pushed through brush until we halted in front of a four-foot skylight in the wall of a moss-covered cliff. Samuel crouched down and shined his light into the hole.

"It's only about six feet and there's a slope—a natural slide," he announced. "Let me go first and I'll help you once I'm in."

I internally rolled my eyes but indulged him in his need for chivalry. "I feel like Alice in Wonderland, peering down the rabbit hole," I commented as I watched him disappear through the opening.

"Please tell me you're not imagining a white, fluffy tail on my ass," he quipped, his voice echoing through the cavern. I laughed, my nerves easing.

"I am now, bunny ears and all. It's very sexy."

I felt a tug on my ankle as Samuel pulled me through, flipping my world upside-down. I shrieked and fell into the darkness as cold air washed over my face. I was relieved when two arms caught me and eased me to the ground. But my relief soon gave way to shock as Samuel, rather than releasing me to the dank, black air, tugged me closer. One hand gripped my hip and pulled me hard against him. The other drifted up my side, slipping beneath my coveralls and settled in the small of my back. My heart hit my throat and I gasped. My head fell against his shoulder and my unbuckled hardhat tumbled to the ground, erratic light bouncing against rocks until it settled, casting us both in shadow. He dropped his own hat next to mine and his hand frantically sought me again, his fingers digging into my hipbone as if they could burrow through my layers of clothing and touch my flesh.

"Kaye…" he breathed, a strange mix of husk and whimsy. "Tell me what you want."

I released a shuddery breath against his neck, remembering this very question from that night we'd spent at the ball diamond. I knew the answer he was searching for.

"I want you," I whispered fiercely, clutching his back. I kissed his jaw once, twice, my tongue briefly darting out to taste the salt of his skin the way I'd desired to all afternoon. He growled and pressed me against the uneven wall. His hand slid from my back and braced himself against the grime above my head. Kevin's warning about cave walls flitted through my head, but it was gone just as fast because…well. His mouth feathered over the sensitive skin of my throat.

"You can have me, Firecracker. Just say the words and you can have me."

Flipping golden. I would have sold my soul to hear him utter those alluring words seven years ago. Even now, I ached for him to take me against this cave wall and literally screw the delicate ecosystem. Our fast and heavy breaths echoing over us like surround sound. I wanted to groan out like a ravenous romance heroine, "Forget the stupid window-waiting, you can have me too, you amazing creature." But as crazy as it was, that contaminated ecosystem smearing my back with basalt only served as an odd little parallel to another delicate balance I was desperately fighting to preserve. And nurture. And fortify so it could survive long, long years.

I shed my gloves and wove my fingers through his matted, wild hair, gently yanking his face from my neck. His eyes were shadowed, but I imagined they were glassy with lust, probably similar to mine. I slowly, silently stroked his scalp. Finally, I felt the frenzied tension begin to seep from his body and he released my leg, letting it drop weakly to the ground. Likewise, his head sank to my collarbone, resigned.

"Not yet," he sighed.

I traced his hairline and softly kissed it. "Not yet. Not until I know this man again. And I need to know you, so badly. There's something there, Samuel. Something vital you're not letting me in on."

Samuel allowed himself another minute of calm before kissing my collarbone and pushing away from the wall. I discreetly reclaimed our hardhats from the ground while he did some adjusting, then tossed one to him. He caught it, flipped on the light, and gave me a guilty, toothsome grin. Ugh, he was going to be the death of me.

"Kevin's going to be really pissed you smudged his cave wall," I teased.

"Somehow, I think the wall was ruined a long time ago. I'm not terribly concerned about it right now."

I laughed and playfully swatted his backside. "Get moving, White Rabbit. Let's go explore Wonderland."

"You know, Carroll's rabbit hole was allegorical for the back stairs into the main hall of Christ Church. Actually, most of the story is based around people and places at Oxford."

"Freaking rabbits, Samuel! Quit ruining my fairy tales."

He chuckled and gripped my hand as we ducked into the cave. And let me tell you, Freud had nothing on this. Unlike the main part of the cave, these tunnels were much narrower. We often had to lie flat on our stomachs and army crawl through mud and grime and bat guano. I kept my head low so it wouldn't brush against the small, phallic stalagmites calcifying on the top of the tunnel, but I only ended up banging my chin on a rock jutting up from the ground.

Samuel's lithe, toned shoulders pulled his body weight through the cave like he'd been born to belly crawl. My thoughts turned to our steamy moment at the cave skylight and my face flushed, not just from exertion. Though boyhood was long gone, I still knew every inch of him, every curve of muscle and joint. Yet there were moments, like now, when I felt as though a stranger crawled beside me, the very depths of him unreachable, undiscovered. Those women with whom he'd shared a piece of himself—no matter how small—grated at my narcissistic need to possess as much of him as possible. So much so, I couldn't travel another inch without knowing what they'd been to Samuel.

Decades later, we broke from the tunnel, spilling into the base of a sweeping cavern scattered with massive boulders Kevin called "cave balls."

"Could this place get any more suggestive?" Samuel muttered. I feebly chuckled, glad I wasn't the only one with a dirty mind.

He picked his way around an underground stream and tested each rock before easing his weight up and over. I braced a hand on my knee and grabbed his elbow, silently asking for a breather. We settled against a large, smooth boulder and situated our hardhats above us so we wouldn't blind each other. The cold light caused the fungus around us to glow, casting a strange illumination and shadow over the cavern. Samuel pulled out a water-filled canteen and offered me a swig before taking a long drink. I watched his Adam's apple bob in his neck as he swallowed, and another wave of lust swept over me. Did I just fantasize about sucking on his throat? I was toast.

My mind zoned in on Samuel's PG description of his relationship with Indigo. Raw need still quivered through my body, and I forced it down in a bid for a cool head. But how, exactly, does a woman ask her ex-husband about his post-marriage sex life?

So Samuel, had any good boinking lately?

I hear you've been enjoying a bit of the old in 'n out.

Bumpin' uglies is such a hideous term, don't you think? Speaking of which...

Only ambiguity dribbled from my mouth. "Speaking of Freudian caves, have you dated much in the past seven years?"

He choked on his water. I patted his back and murmured apologies for the randomness. He gave me a wary eye, but gained a modicum of control.

"Yes. And you've dated, too," he replied matter-of-factly, as if he were answering an annual exam question.

"I have. They were…well, total busts. But the women at breakfast today, what they said about hooking up with fans—"

"I *knew* this was going to come up again." He thumped the back of his head against the rock. "A lie, Kaye. Not once have I ever slept with a fan, I swear. It's wrong and I'd be taking advantage of them."

"Right, I get that. But I want to know…how many?"

"How many women have I dated?"

"Yeah. Or I guess, more specifically, how many…*how many*. Who were they?" Oh for the love of Tom, why couldn't I be an adult and say adult things?

What could only be described as sheer horror blanched Samuel's angular face, and he squirmed uncomfortably, desirous to be any place but next to me, having this conversation. "Kaye, there is absolutely nothing good that can come from knowing that. Are you sure—?"

Was I? What if he told me about these women and I happened to meet one someday? Or worse, what if I constantly wondered if a woman had been intimate with the man I loved? Given my enervating jealous streak, that was entirely possible. Perhaps it would be better to know for sure. "Yes," I answered. "We'll have to deal with this eventually, so now is as good a time as any." I squinted despite the darkness. *Please be fewer than twenty, please be fewer than twenty…*

"Three."

My gaze leaped to his, certain I'd see sarcasm. Samuel, however, was all seriousness.

"Just three? But all of the women from Page Six and TMZ…"

He groaned. "I told you not to believe a word you read there. It's pure trash. How could you possibly think I'd ever be so cavalier about sex? You know me."

I pondered his question, wanting to give him an honest answer. "After I found out about the drugs and your behavior in New York, I guess I questioned everything about you. If one fundamental part of you could change so drastically, why couldn't other parts?"

He admitted I had a point. "I'm still me, Kaye. Yes, I was becoming a different person — one I was terrified to let you have any part in. But fundamentally I'm the same, and I know that now." He placed a hand on my knee, urging me to see his sincerity.

"Listen to me carefully," he continued. "I have never made love to anyone other than you. Those three women — they were a means to an end and I was horribly selfish to use them, but that's the honest truth. Let's leave it at that."

I cringed, because in this case, I understood exactly what he was talking about. A means to an end. In my rash rebellion and anger against Samuel, I'd also used a few men — nice men who deserved better than a one-night-stand and ignored phone calls. It hadn't been *me*, and I'd felt wretched afterward.

"What happened? H-How — " I whispered, immediately embarrassed for asking.

Samuel was equally embarrassed. He ruffled his matted hair as he watched me with a wary eye. Then he heaved a breath. "This is going to bug you until you find out, isn't it?"

I nodded.

He slapped his thighs in resignation and grudgingly elaborated. "The first was barely a week after we divorced," he said. "I believed if I was going to self-destruct, I might as well do it thoroughly. I singled her out at a Greenwich bar because she had curly blond hair and big hazel eyes. I was angry and greedy and high, and when she asked for my number I blew her off like the asshole I was. Are you sure you want to hear more?"

"Yes," I whispered, because I needed to know.

"The second was the indie singer I dated five years ago. She was my first real try at a relationship after you. But she could tell I wanted her to be someone else. It was grossly unfair to her and I ended the relationship after a month. I loathed myself for what I'd done. After that, I added sex to my list of taboo indulgences until I found a woman I could give myself to completely."

That sounded more like the Samuel I remembered. I pressed on. "And the third? Was she someone you could give yourself to completely?"

There was a long silence; the only sound was our puffs of breath against the ice of the cave.

"Do you remember the disorderly conduct charge from three years ago?" he asked. "The one in the file Jaime gave you?"

"Yes—public intox."

"That was the third woman. Something shook the shabby foundation I'd constructed and I went out, loaded up on straight vodka, and brought a woman to a motel. I told her, 'turn your face, I can't look at your eyes.' The same thing my mother said to me." His voice cracked sorrowfully and I wondered if he was close to tears. "After she left, I found a bar and got into a brawl with a guy twice my size. Thus, the disorderly conduct charge."

I stifled a sob in my throat, but he heard it anyway. "What happened three years ago that made you—"

"It's not important, now."

"Samuel, it *is*."

"*Kaye*."

But I stubbornly insisted, and he relented.

"I was back in Boulder for my book tour, hoping to at least catch a glimpse of you. I had this grand idea of asking you out for coffee—maybe meet on friendly, platonic terms because I was an adult and should be able to have a cup of coffee with my ex. But when I arrived, Molly informed me you were out for the week, enjoying a magnificent Valentine's vacation at a ski resort with Hector Valdez. I think she was thrilled to see me squirm—a bit of payback."

I flinched. No wonder Samuel was so paranoid about Hector. "Yeah, that was more of a Singles' Awareness Day vacation," I explained, trying to soothe Samuel's ruffled spirit. "Separate rooms on the off-chance one of us got lucky. Hector did, I didn't. Typical."

"I'd be lying if I said I was sorry to hear it." I heard a hint of smugness in his voice and I nudged him with my shoulder. He went on. "Just like that, I reverted to a self-pitying, jealous ex and stormed back to New York. If you could replace me, why couldn't I replace you? Months later, Danita told me you weren't with Hector. I don't need to tell you how foolish I felt."

"I can only imagine," I muttered, remembering my harried inspection of Caroline's lotions and lingerie in her guest room, only weeks ago.

"After the incident with the woman and a night in jail, it fully hit me whose son I really was. Sometimes it's still difficult to accept, though."

There she was again—Rachel, that wicked specter. I hated her more than I'd ever hated the cliff-hucking floozy with her black lingerie luggage. "You are nothing like your birth mother, Samuel. Not one bit."

Samuel looked as if he might argue, but let it go. "Let's walk again." He grabbed our hardhats, and I strapped mine under my chin. Silence fell as we took turns pulling each other over boulder piles, scaling slick surfaces, navigating twists. After several minutes, he spoke again.

"So, Ms. Trilby, how many have you lured to your bed? And Jaime Guzman doesn't count."

Now, if those horrid cameras that snap action photos of wild-eyed roller coaster riders and display them for all of creation to mock had been installed in this very cave, the terror on my face would have been a side-splitter. Because, at some point in my heedless dash to get the deets on Samuel's bedmates, I'd forgotten three cardinal rules:

1. It's not fair to ask of others what you aren't willing to do yourself.

2. Do to others as you would have them do to you.

3. Sauce for the goose is sauce for the gander.

Crap. I'd have to pony up the deets, too. "There's a large boulder field ahead, Samuel. Watch your footing."

"You're dodging my question. I answered, now it's your turn."

I huffed, dreading this. "Fine. Four."

"Four?" I heard him hiss as he halted mid-climb.

"Wait a minute, here." Hurt and defensiveness surged through me as I wrenched myself over the next rock and onto a fairly flat surface. "You have no right to judge me, Samuel. It's not like I was slutting around for seven years because I've slept with one more person than you. I know men think sex is easier for women to go without, and maybe it is, but we have needs, too."

"I didn't mean—"

"And just like you, I hated myself after each time, because I couldn't get you out of my head. Heck, the first time I slept with someone who wasn't you, I cried and cried and freaked the guy out because he thought he'd hurt me. Do you know how embarrassing that was?"

An odd gasp echoed through the cavern, and Samuel's light beam tumbled across the wall as he stumbled to the ground.

"Are you all right?" I asked, my hand flailing around in the darkness for his. Samuel's fingers wrapped around mine, reassuring me he was still there.

"I'm sorry." His voice was pure misery.

"I'm sorry, too." I let him tug me down to his side in the muck and cold, black rock. We sat quietly, listening to bats fluttering somewhere in the cave, their squeaks bouncing off the walls and ceiling.

"Better now?"

I nodded.

"So, who were these men?"

"Just…just dates," I stuttered, my face a pink carnation in the blessed darkness. "The first was a friend of a friend."

"Whose friend?"

"Molly's. The second was one of our old classmates from Lyons High, and I won't tell you who because you'll go nuts on him."

"Was it Santiago?"

"Ew, no!"

"Clark? Martinez? Murphy?"

"Be content to know he doesn't live in the state anymore." I stood and wiped dirt from my rear. Samuel's flashlight beam flicked across the boulders in front of me as he also stood.

"That narrows it down. Did I play baseball with him?"

"*It was Teddy Veddy*," I admitted in a rush. Flashes of Ted's grunge hair and flannels invaded my mind and I shuddered. By the set of Samuel's mouth, I knew he was also being bombarded by Pearl Jam-accompanied recollections of the sullen boy nicknamed "Teddy Veddy" in high school. "Do you want to hear about the other two?"

"I don't know if 'want' is the right word. Maybe 'masochistic need' is more accurate." He scaled another boulder, slipping over the shining fungus, then handed me up.

"I met the third at a bar about four years ago, when Molly was on her blue-haired wild streak after a nasty breakup. Celebrity gossip had started keeping tabs on your love life and I was a bitter mess. So Molly and I threw caution to the wind and found a couple of guys for a one-night stand. Except for the skydiving stunt Saturday," *and introducing this conversation*, I silently added, "it was probably the stupidest, most rash thing I've ever done. I was really lucky he was a decent guy who used a condom and didn't steal my wallet or slip me a roofie."

Samuel scaled the boulders quickly, almost too quickly for me to keep up. I seethed and latched onto his arm. "Look, I know this is difficult, but don't you dare get self-righteous with me. I didn't cheat on you—we weren't together anymore."

"And the fourth?" he ground out between clenched teeth, his sad face unable to meet mine.

"Two years ago. A man from my skydiving class who wore the same cologne as you."

"Did I meet him when we skydived?"

"No. I never saw him again. I never saw any of them again." I wrapped my arms around my middle as the memory of that wretched night invaded my thoughts…The sweaty, broad body that certainly wasn't Samuel's, even though he'd vaguely smelled like him. The way I buried my face in the man's neck so I wouldn't have to see his face and ruin my illusion. It wasn't cheating. But why did it feel like it?

I ran a hand along the side of the damp, fungus-covered cave then promptly yanked it back, recalling that I shouldn't touch the walls. Freud would have a field day with that one.

"I never saw any of them again," I repeated, "because they weren't you. You've spoiled me for other men, Cabral. And I know, deep down, you're probably ecstatic about it."

His shoulders sagged, the fight leaving him. He flipped off his light so he could talk to me. I did the same, rendering us blind in thick blackness.

"Relieved, yes. Ecstatic, no. All I've ever wanted was for you to be happy, Kaye. And if that meant you found your happiness with someone else, so be it. But I don't think I'd be strong enough to watch it. In fact, I rather want to beat the piss out of them," he said through gritted teeth.

My heart pounded because his words could have been yanked straight from my brain. "When you were with Caroline, I told myself I could still be a part of your life. But now I know I could never watch you love someone else. I nearly went crazy."

I felt Samuel's ungloved hand slip down my arm, cautiously threading his fingers through mine. "I told you, Kaye—only you. It wasn't just a promise. It's reality."

I nodded, feeling in the maturity of my tired, twenty-seven-year-old self how far away we'd grown from the innocence of Caulfield and Aspen.

"I'm sorry I didn't wait for you," I said softly. "I just didn't know."

"I'm sorry, too. I guess this is yet another consequence of letting you go like I did—knowing that other men have seen your lovely body, and touched you, and had you."

I shivered, the chill air hitting my spine. "I'm not exactly thrilled about it either. I don't like to think about the shame I felt when I pretended they were you. And I don't like three other floozies sharing my memory of your body, or the faces you make when you're lost in the moment," I said plainly, because we deserved the plain truth.

He searched for the right words to give voice to the heavy emotion hanging between us. "Look how we've hurt ourselves, Kaye. We've both grasped at shards of life, hoping to reclaim some sort of wild elation only to find we cut ourselves a little bit more." He clutched my hand as we stood and listened to the quiet plops and trickles of water echoing through the cave.

"May I kiss you?" Samuel asked.

"No. I'm sulking."

"Thirty minutes ago, you were convinced I'd slept with the entire Eastern Seaboard," he gently reminded, his arms circling me.

"I'm not going to kiss you. I don't want to tie beautiful things like kissing you to the ugliness of this particular conversation." But I tugged his coverall strap and pulled him closer anyway, touched my lips to his, and rested my head on his shoulder.

He had the grace to refrain from pointing out I'd been the one to initiate this talk. "Come on, then." Flipping on his light, he maneuvered over the rocks and then helped me down. "Let's find some sky."

We made our way through the cave until the light beckoned us back to the world above. Gray day washed gray faces, revealing our scattered walls. But it also brought to light another ill-omened barrier rising between us, one that hadn't been visible until those other walls tumbled down.

I hoped, with all my might, we'd see the other barrier for what it was and knock it down before it strengthened and grew to insurmountable heights.

Chapter 4
GLIDE PATH

The predicted flight trajectory of a diver from plane to ground.

Hydraulic Level Five {working title}
Draft 2.25
© Samuel Caulfield Cabral & Aspen Kaye Trilby
25. Best Last Prom

Aspen is not a frilly girl.

She never has been, and swears up and down she never will be. Despite Maria's best efforts, she fights makeup brushes and flat irons like a feral cat.

"I can't believe Caulfield dragged me from the dorm just to have you claw and hiss at me for trying to make you beautiful."

Aspen tries to hide the sting of her words. Maria means well, but she's too blunt. "Caulfield asked you to make me over?" she says casually.

Maria pauses, flat iron hovering over Aspen's locks. "No," she admits. "I didn't mean for it to sound that way. He thinks you're beautiful just as you are. I'm the one who pushed. But it's *prom*, Aspen! You skipped out last year and threw a hissy fit over

Caulfield's senior prom, and there's no way I'm letting you out the door without the full treatment this time. So just sit back, let me fix your hair, and be grateful."

Aspen does, not without an exaggerated sigh that says "I will tolerate this but so help me I'll be in cargo pants before the weekend is over." If it were up to her, she'd hijack Caulfield for the weekend and they'd drive to the guitar shop in Boulder, mess with the equipment, then find a quiet spot for some horny teenager time in his car. She hates watching the back of him as he leaves for college after his weekend visits.

Gusts of wind skip over the rooftop and rattle the old windows of her mother's farm house. This spring is a cold one. Even so, she smells the cusp of summer, and with it comes freedom. She counts the days until she and Caulfield pack their cars and escape – together this time – to college.

It's hard, watching her classmates do the high school thing. Hold hands in hallways, kiss outside classrooms, hit the diner after evening practices. Caulfield comes home when he can, but she wants him around full time. Breaking up is out of the question – she'd rather suffer through her last years of high school in a long distance relationship than be without him entirely. High school is a bust. So what? She's ready for graduation, ready for college, and ready for carefree days when it doesn't feel like half her heart is missing.

"Ow! Flailing beefeaters, Maria!" Aspen's shriek floats down the stairs and into the living room, where Caulfield sits on the sofa, awkwardly bouncing his knees while her mother watches a gardening program. "Leave me some hair!"

"For crying out loud, you'd think someone who wants their own apartment would at least know how to use a brush!" Caulfield hears Maria fires back.

He glances at Aspen's mother, who pays no mind to the apartment revelation, but leans in when the televised gardener demonstrates a bulb transplant.

Caulfield is also ready for his girlfriend to join him in Boulder. Afternoons spent hovering over the photo album Aspen made for him...late nights in the computer lab, exchanging emails until the building closed...his dorm room long distance service suspended each month because he reaches his max limit...It's ironic that he'll finally have Internet and unlimited long distance in his apartment next semester. Aside from his parents, he has no one in particular he wants to email or call once Aspen is with him.

Aspen's mother clears her throat, piercing Caulfield with a look that absolutely tells him she can read his mind.

"Are you going to shack up with my baby girl?"

Two points of red spread across the young man's cheeks. "No, ma'am."

Her lips twitch once, then she turns back to the television. Caulfield flips the corsage box between his fingers.

That was another point of contention – the apartment. Aspen hints that she wants Caulfield to ask her to live with him. He'd side-stepped her hopeful looks and implications. She should spend at least a year in a dorm or she'll never have any close girlfriends in college. He knows from experience what the consequences of shutting out other students are – a slew of casual acquaintances and no real friends.

It's what she *claims* to need, anyway. A chance to be a kid after stressing over her parents' messes for so long. Parents who, after seventeen years, finally decide to be parents and insist she live in the dorm, no arguments, which only makes headstrong Aspen fight harder. The woman is a mess of dichotomies. One minute, bouncing on the heels of her feet in a mad rush to grow up. The next, lamenting the passing of childhood. Caulfield runs an aggravated hand through his somewhat tamed hair. Right now, he just needs to give Aspen the best last prom he can.

And Aspen. All she focuses on is keeping Caulfield from slipping through her fingers. But the moment she descends the stairs, gauzy plum fabric trailing behind her, neither Aspen nor Caulfield believe there is any danger of the other slipping away. Because they are Caulfield and Aspen. They are in love.

Caulfield meets her halfway up the stairs. She is gorgeous. Not a poofy, pastel prom queen sort of gorgeous, but elegant, unassuming, all Aspen. Taking her pale hand, he pulls her to eye level. "You are." He tenderly kisses the tip of her nose. "Lovely."

Aspen rolls her eyes and smooths his black lapel with her pretty fingers – fingers Maria tortured into submission with files and nail polish. "You're pretty sexy yourself." She winks, ignoring her mother's throat clearing. Leaning against her chest, she whispers into his ear. "Thank you for this. Not every college guy would escort his high school girlfriend to prom."

He pulls the delicate orchid from its box and slips it over her wrist. "He'd be a fool, then, to let such a chance pass him by."

................•●•................

All right, Kaye, let me have it. I reworked the dual thoughts with your suggestions. Despite your insistence, I'm maintaining that you were in a hurry to grow up because of your parents, not just to catch up with me. All you talked about (aside from your utter hatred of "MmmBop") was getting away from your mom and dad. ~Sam

Dr. Phil—Fine, I'll give you that. I wanted to get the heck out of Lyons because I was sick of my dad gushing about his girlfriend like he was a fifteen-year-old perv, while my mother was just down the street, pretending I didn't even exist during planting season. I will, however, forgive your shrink-like ways because you remembered my thanking you for prom. It was important to me, even though I acted like a brat. ~Kaye

You weren't a brat—you were seventeen. And having a moody, self-involved boyfriend didn't help. ~Sam

Thanks, cliff-hucker. Hey. Is chili okay for dinner? After getting half-drowned in our tent last night, something warm sounds good. ~Kaye

Kaye, I'm sitting next to you. You can just ask. ~Sam

You didn't answer my question. ~Kaye

Chili is...(kissing the tip of your nose)...Lovely. ~Sam

For someone who claims to hate The Creek with the fire of a thousand suns, that was a very "Dawson" thing you wrote there. Just say—

A quartet of groans echoed around our measly campfire circle as several more raindrops splattered our foreheads, half-eaten hot dogs, and s'mores, then plunked woodenly on Samuel's discarded Gibson guitar. We needed to keep an eye on this storm. We were surrounded by a massive alpine forest, and if the wind and rain were bad, falling tree limbs and wash-outs could be a problem.

Kevin, our caving guide, had retreated to his canvas sanctuary the instant his girlfriend, Kiki, arrived. She was a buxom, black-haired woman who breathed too heavily and vaguely resembled Elvira, minus the whole vampy cleavage thing. She had a fixation with *Water Sirens*, and when Kevin let it slip that one of his clients was Samuel Cabral, he couldn't keep her away. Luckily, her libido was stronger than her star-struck curiosity. Kevin whisked her off for a "spiritual reconnection." Or, as Molly crassly put it, the exploration of her foreboding cave.

The minute Samuel left the fire to take his guitar back to the car, Molly pounced.

"Okay, Kaye, you've obviously kept some big secrets and I've waited all day. Are you and Samuel officially back together?"

"I...I don't know. We're friends."

Even Cassady shot me a dubious look from across the campfire.

She twisted her ginger hair into a bun. "Right. Friends don't kiss necks and caress hands and *accidentally* brush each other's thighs. No offense, Kaye, but if you ever tried that on me, I'd freak."

Cassady's face was a study. "Uh, yeah. Hold off on that convo for a sec and give me a chance to clear out." Jumping up from his log, he gathered the gear at superhero speed and followed Samuel down the wooded trail to the car.

I grinned apologetically. "Well, perhaps Samuel and I are too affectionate to be friends. Honestly, I don't know what we are. With our history, I don't think there's a label for it."

She nodded. "That's fine. But you need to decide soon, because if you two are going public with 'whatever,' there will be questions." I knew she wasn't just talking about our friends and family. Samuel Cabral was well-known and once our relationship became more visible, our clients would ask if I planned to leave the business and move to New York, that sort of thing.

The dark gray sky opened, and Molly grabbed my hand. We darted around the fizzling fire and half-rotted tree stumps, toward one of three red dome tents staked in the clearing.

"It's way too early for bed. Let's chat in Cassady's and my tent," she said.

I lifted an eyebrow. "Oh really? Since when has Cassady replaced me as your tent mate?"

She zipped open the tent. "Since I've seen how *well* you and Samuel get along. There's no way I'm passing up a chance to have Cassady all to myself for an entire night. I moved your junk into the other tent."

I ditched my sneaks and followed her in, an uncomfortableness settling in my gut that had everything to do with whether I could keep my hands off of my ex-husband and whether the deepest recesses of my heart recognized him as my ex in the first place. Perhaps Samuel would take the decision out of my hands and hightail it to the nearest town for his own hotel room.

For a long time, I believed Samuel's values to be a product of Alonso and Sofia's influence, as well as years of Sunday School—something my parents never had any interest in (except during my dad's two-month stint as a born-again Christian). But now I questioned if those values hadn't taken root as a way for Samuel to distance himself from a mother who seemed positively immoral. The more I paid attention to Samuel's subtle winces and cryptic words whenever his life in Boston was brought up, the more I realized he was desperate to be the polar opposite of Rachel Cabral.

Molly tossed items out of her duffle bag until she came across a Ziploc baggie full of homemade "puppy chow"—a chocolate and peanut butter confection. I grabbed a handful and grinned at her in thanks.

"So whatever happened to Samuel's hot-shot Manhattan publicist?"

"Caroline," I answered through a mouthful of crunchy chocolate goodness. "As far as I know, she's in New York City."

"But she still works for Samuel. She's his agent-slash-publicist?"

"Kind of. She's his agent, and her firm collaborates with his publishing house for book publicity. But for movie publicity, I guess she outsources to some Hollywood PR machine."

"*And* she edits his books?"

I licked powdered sugar from my fingertips and brushed the rest onto my flannel pajama bottoms. "Yeah, before they go to the publishing house. From what Samuel says, editing was her first passion."

Molly's brow furrowed. "She's wearing too many hats, Kaye-bear. If she and Samuel have a serious falling out, she could really screw him over. She would, too—woman was a pain."

I sighed. Samuel and I'd already had this conversation. "I know, Molly. But he trusts her implicitly and there's nothing I can do about that. At least he's not dating her anymore."

"I guess if they had a falling out, she'd be royally screwed, too, losing her firm's biggest client."

Before long, Cassady and Samuel tracked us down in the tent and we had to share the puppy chow. We lit a battery-powered lantern and settled around its cold white light. Samuel dropped behind me onto a sleeping bag roll. I draped my arms over his knees and reclined against him. The rain had dampened his shirt and flannel sleep pants but he was rumpled and happy, and soon his cool chest warmed against my back. As we quietly talked with Molly and Cassady, his hand drifted across my collarbone. I knew he was only half paying attention to Cassady's animated description of the psychedelic Iron Butterfly poster he'd won on eBay.

"Cassady, you spend enough money on junk for your campervan to feed a small African country," Molly teased. "Ever think of doing something useful with your salary?"

Cassady scowled. "I tried, but your bone-headed brother-in-law wouldn't let me."

The tent fell silent as his stinging words brought reality crashing down. Molly's face crumpled, and Cassady immediately pulled her into his embrace.

"Uff-da, I'm sorry. That was really thoughtless."

Molly sniffed into his shoulder. "Did you just say 'uff-da'?" I *knew* he was from Minnesota. "It's okay. I'm just really frustrated." She looked at me and Samuel. "Holly won't take her antidepressants—that's why she's getting worse. And Derek still doesn't want to admit how serious this is."

"Why won't she take them?" I asked, a little too angrily. "Doesn't she want to get better?" Samuel squeezed my shoulder in a reminder to calm down.

"She says they make her nauseous and foggy all the time. And she's scared of gaining weight, especially after having a baby."

"And severe depression and suicide are preferable?"

Samuel pulled me closer. Despite his efforts to calm me, I couldn't comprehend the mentality of someone who would risk her life and her family's well-being, just because she hated the side effects of medication.

Molly wiped her eyes with the back of her hand. "I know."

"Kaye," Samuel said, "try to understand. Sometimes it's hard for people to admit they need the meds. And there's such a horrible stigma attached to mental illnesses, almost like it's shameful to be diagnosed as such. She's probably really scared, even thinking she's a failure because she has to depend on medication to be normal."

Yes, Samuel would see this in Holly. After all, his birth mother had been plagued by mental illness.

Molly's eyes went wide. "You're exactly right. I can totally see Holly thinking that. She's always wanted a big family, to be supermom to a dozen kids. I'm sure the idea of something being out of her control is really scary."

"So how do you convince her to stay on her meds?" Cassady asked.

Samuel scratched at the ground, in thought. "Her family, especially Derek, can go a long way in that. Her doctor too, or maybe someone who's been in her shoes. But Holly has to understand for herself what could happen if she doesn't take her meds, what losing her would do to the people who love her. She has to make the choice." I felt a small shiver run through his torso, though his eyes never wavered from the spot on the ground.

No, this wasn't just about his mother. I peered up at him again. His eyes were dark, unfathomable. "How do you know so much about this sort of thing?" I asked.

Familiar red streaks burned up his neck and in his cheeks. "Caro's agency has a client who published an eye-opening book about his wife's depression. Since then, I've taken an interest in the issue." He shrugged and hastily rubbed circles on my shoulder with his thumb.

Hmm. I studied his face, uneasy with his blatant lie. But Cassady and Molly seemed swayed by his answer.

Cassady nodded. "I don't think any of us really get what Holly and Derek are going through, not without it happening to us."

"I know," I said, letting Samuel's eyes go. "I can't imagine dealing with those sorts of struggles. Waking up each morning and wondering if it's a 'walking on eggshells' day. Holding my breath coming home from work, always terrified of what I'd find. I don't think I'd be strong enough."

Samuel went rigid behind me. His hand tightened on my shoulder, almost painfully.

"Don't be ridiculous," he said, his voice shaky. "Of course you're strong, Kaye."

Then it clicked. As soon as I felt his trembling hands and quickening breath on my neck — the same thing that happened at Danita's wedding when he made a mad dash for the bathroom — I got it. My comments hit too close to home and I realized, too late, *why* Samuel seemed to be slipping into some sort of controlled panic. He'd been on meds at some point, maybe still was. And why would he be on meds?

I remembered the weeks before he left for New York, the death knell of our marriage. The sleeping, the seemingly apathetic laziness for most anything except his music reviews and running off what I now knew were cocaine highs. His mother had almost certainly been mentally ill. Depression? The more I thought about those months before Samuel left me, the more I realized cocaine had masked the real problem. I'd seen it seven years ago in Boulder. Then in New York, in the possessed lines of his half-naked body and that dingy, filthy room. I began to see it now.

"Go home to Colorado, and don't you ever come back here again, Aspen Kaye. I fucking mean it. You think this is a joke?"

Smothering the terrible memories churning in the pit of me, I pulled his shaking hand between my two hands. Running my thumbs up and down his skin, I slowly traced his ligaments, veins, fingernails, dulling the edge of panic until and his shaking ceased. I admittedly knew next to nothing about depression, but his being on meds was certainly a good thing. Because it meant what happened seven years ago wouldn't happen again as long as he took his medicine, right? Gradually, his breath slowed and he began to relax. His soft lips kissed the skin beneath my ear in a silent thank you.

Cassady and Molly exchanged a look. They'd noticed Samuel's odd little panic attack, but said nothing.

"May I ask what, exactly, Derek is struggling with?" Samuel said after a while, his voice still shaky.

"He thinks Holly just needs a vacation away from the kids for a week or two, not therapy and meds," Cassady answered. "He doesn't want charity—"

"That's not it," Molly cut in. "I think he's scared, too. Like he somehow failed Holly, or he's not strong enough to cope with her scary thoughts and her tears. So he'd rather deny she needs help."

"And he's refusing financial assistance from you," Samuel concluded.

Molly nodded. "And Kaye."

"The alimony," I answered and he smiled, albeit unsteadily.

"Well, I'm glad you're finally spending it, guinea pigs aside."

"I very well wasn't going to spend that much money on myself."

"You should have. That's what I intended in our settlement."

"Samuel," I hissed, "I am *not* having this argument with you again."

He gave me a playful shake, then turned to Molly. "Have you spoken with any mental illness centers about financial assistance? Derek might be more willing to accept help from a foundation than from people he knows."

"Kaye and I have tossed around the idea. And I'm looking into government assistance."

"A local charity is your best bet, because Medicaid funding is wrapped in red tape. Then there are always the NAMI fund-raiser walks." He grabbed a piece of puppy chow from my stock pile and popped one in his mouth. "It's tragic, the number of people who go without treatment."

Molly hummed sadly. "That's what one of the nurses at the hospital said while I was waiting for Holly's appointment to finish. She called Holly one of the 'lucky ones' because she has family who care enough to help her. Did you know they only have a couple visitors on the floor every day? Out of all those inpatients."

"I can't believe that!" I was woefully unaware of what happened beyond my front door.

"And get this," Molly continued. "There was a patient there who talked to me between his fingers because he thought he was the ruler of Saturn, and that's how gods communicated. Do you know what that nurse told me?"

I shook my head.

"They were going to release him the next day. They couldn't make him stay past three days since he told them he could sleep on a buddy's couch, had fifty dollars in his checking account, and promised to fill his prescription and make a doctor appointment in a week."

"That's crazy," Cassady said.

"That's how they slip through the cracks," Samuel explained. I felt him sigh against my neck. "So many unnecessary deaths."

"We should just have our own fund-raiser and give the proceeds directly to local clinics for patient assistance," I muttered. "Then we could avoid the red tape."

"Why don't you?" Samuel asked.

I craned my neck to look at him. "Organize a fund-raiser?"

"Sure. You have the financial resources, plus the event planning knowledge."

"That's...that's a big undertaking," I stuttered. "I'd need a lot of assistance, and even then…"

"If you start small, something for friends and family, it would be feasible."

"Or, TrilbyJones could donate time and project work as long as we kept careful accounts." Molly's eyes filling with excitement. "If we started planning something a year out, it could be extremely successful. A website, TV and radio spots, entertainment."

"It would be a great opportunity for some of our clients to show local support," I added, the wheels cranking in my brain. I pointed at Cassady. "We could even do some cross-promotionals, maybe a benefit auction with ski passes, kayak excursions, that sort of thing."

Cassady grimaced. "Wait, wait, wait. What scale of event are we talking here? Bake sale or Planet Bluegrass-sized?"

Yes. That was it.

"Planet Bluegrass!" I could kiss Cassady. "Why not have an all-day music festival in Lyons?" Now in full brainstorming mode, I ached for my white board and markers. "There are *so many* local bands. We could screen groups over the winter and invite them to perform at a music festival, say, next June? They would waive a performance fee in exchange for the free publicity. We could have tents for food concessions, maybe volunteer groups through the high school or the Boy Scouts could help staff—"

"Child labor, Kaye?" Molly grinned.

"Merit badges, Molly. Oh! And we could get in touch with several regional music critics and see if they'd be willing to write reviews."

Samuel held up his hands, as if to keep our tangible enthusiasm from ricocheting off the tent walls. "I think all of these ideas are admirable. And don't get me wrong, a large-scale mental health benefit could certainly be successful — with time. If you'll allow me to be a bit of a downer, though, here's the truth of it: fundraising for mental health issues is a lot different than children's charities, disaster relief, other non-profits.

"People are uncomfortable discussing mental illness, let alone hanging a banner over their business. And getting the crowds out would be tough. Half don't want to be lumped with a 'bunch of crazies,' and the other half are too afraid to out themselves or someone they love." Red slowly stained his neck. "When it's local, it's too close to home. No one wants to know their neighbor might be the one taking mental trips around Saturn."

Uncomfortable silence settled into the tent as the excitement that boiled minutes ago fizzled out. Cassady cleared his throat as if to speak, but didn't know quite what to say. Samuel sighed.

"Look. All I'm saying is, realistically, it will be tough to find support."

At that moment he looked so lost, so sad. I reclaimed his shaking hands and squeezed. "You'd support us, wouldn't you? Maybe you could write a feature piece or two that national magazines might be interested in running."

Samuel met me steady gaze. "I could do that."

Cassady and Molly's mouths dropped open at Samuel's offer. The tent became so silent, I could hear individual raindrops plopping in puddles outside.

Molly cleared her throat. "You do realize the equivalent is having J.K. Rowling write our web content?"

Samuel shrugged, a bit embarrassed. "It could bring attention to your cause, maybe even draw some large donors you wouldn't reach locally."

Molly blinked, surprised. "You'd be willing to attach your name to this? A big-name New York author helping tiny health clinics in the backcountry?"

"It's not like he's a complete stranger, Molly," I retorted.

"New York is where I live," he explained. "But Colorado is my home. I grew up here and I want to help."

I pulled his hand, now clammy between mine, up to my mouth and kissed his palm. "We'd love for you to help."

Molly, however, was still doubtful. "Don't get me wrong, Samuel. Your help would be…well…beyond helpful. But here's the thing. If mental health fund-raisers are really difficult like you said, you can't back out once we tout your involvement or it would sink us. Completely. It would be horrible for the event, for TrilbyJones, and any of our clients who offer their services. Like 'Joss Whedon bailing on Comic-Con' horrible. Because that's what *Water Sirens* is, Cabral: the Rocky Mountains' *Buffy*."

I hid a laugh behind my hand.

"If I say I'm in, I'm *in*." He chuckled. "I'll help in any way I can, short of setting up a kissing booth next to the face-painting station."

I snapped my fingers. "You know, that's not a bad idea. Forget the bands and the Boy Scouts. Let's just pimp Samuel out to his female fan base! I bet there are a lot of naughty nixies who would pay big bucks for a minute with *the* Samuel Caulfield Cabral in a closet." My lips curling into a smirk. "We could talk to Alan Murphy about publicity—"

I squealed as Samuel suddenly flung me over his shoulder and my feet brushed the top of the tent.

"Enough of that, Firecracker. I think it's your bedtime." He gripped me tightly around my waist and crouched through the zipper door. Grabbing both pairs of our shoes, he strutted out into the rain. I waved good night to my loving friends, who were laughing so hard, they didn't bother to wave back.

Holy Mother of Tom.

I shrieked. Samuel tossed me on my sleeping bag and dropped to his knees next to me. I ran a hand between his shoulder blades, up into his damp hair, and pulled him down, my hungry mouth reaching for his. He met me hit for hit, our legs tangling around each other.

He'd been so freaking clever, flooring us all with his offer to help our fund-raiser—even though he probably believed it wouldn't succeed. I loved him for caring about my friends, about a woman he'd never even met. Frankly, it riled me up. The way he stared at me, eyes of blue fire, lust-clouded and hot and…argh.

I knew, I *knew* we'd decided to wait just hours ago, that there was a lot of badness between us. But flaming stapler, how was a woman supposed to treat the man she was once married to? Should I pretend

I didn't already know every square inch of his body underneath the sleep clothes he'd worn for modesty's sake?

I pecked his neck, and he half laughed, half groaned into my shoulder, his elegant writer's fingers dancing along my hairline, the bandage over my stitches. My own hands dug into the fabric of his T-shirt and clutched at him, begging for the pressure of his body.

He obliged.

"You are an amazing, amazing woman. You have no idea how much I adore you." He kissed me again. "For wanting to help."

"Naïve as I may be," I murmured, sneaking two hands beneath his shirt and sliding them across his fevered skin.

"Not naïve. Well, maybe a bit." He smiled. "I'd call it wholehearted optimism."

My lips grazed his sandpaper chin. "But are you sure you'll have time, with the movies—"

His hands smoothed my flannel-clad legs and grasped my hips, silencing me. He mischievously nipped a bit of powdered sugar from my chin, grinning as I wiped it with embarrassment.

"I said I would and I meant it," he rasped. "This means so much to me, I can't tell you how much. I just wish…"

And then his hands, his mouth turned frantic. He dug his fingers into my damp hair, catching the tangles and making me wince.

"Wish what?" Why was I still talking? Fire shot through my body and my arm flailed, sending the lantern tumbling across the floor and flickering out. Crap. Total blackness. No more blue eyes.

His hips stilled and he groaned again, his lips pressing against my forehead, my ears, my neck. Hovering over me, he wrapped hands around either side of my head as if he was trying to force some strange current from his fingertips to my brain. "Why can't you see how strong you are? I wish I could make you see." He kissed me again, hard, and I tried to kiss him back, but his mouth was too urgent and too consuming and too quick, and left my lips for my skin. He caught my neck again, sucking and biting hard enough to mark me.

"Why can't you see how fucking amazing you are?"

His sudden anguished, angry tone brought me to a jarring halt. *What the heck?* Samuel never swore like that. I couldn't see his eyes and, with the darkness, I had the unsettling feeling I was locked with a complete stranger. A flash of greedy hands, cold, hardened eyes flared through my memory and became the hands and eyes of the man above me. The bare New York room. The brunette. Fluttery white cocaine lines.

I froze.

He returned to my neck, then back to my mouth and I felt his teeth bite my sensitive lips. I tasted copper on my tongue.

"Ow! That hurt." My fingers flew to my bottom lip. Decisive, I pushed against him with my hands and knees. His entire body halted as something in him yanked to awareness and he rolled off of me, scooting several feet across the tent. Harsh breath beat a somber rhythm into the silence. Somehow the silence was more uncomfortable because of it.

"Care to tell me why you nearly emasculated me with your kneecap?" Samuel ground out.

Fear still coursed through my body, chased by a strong dose of defensiveness. "Samuel, what's the matter with you? Keeping up with you is like following a ping-pong match." I propped myself up on my elbows, twisting to see his black form. The only sounds were the soft thuds of the strengthening rainstorm and heavy breathing as we fought for control.

But as panic receded, excruciating embarrassment rushed to fill its cavity. I realized for the second time today, I'd demanded something of Samuel that was both exposing and personal, and I hadn't been prepared to reciprocate.

I crawled over to him in the dark. Reluctant arms went around me, followed by even more reluctant lips as we struggled to restoke the fires that had burned so brightly a moment before. But that moment was long gone and, with a sigh, Samuel pulled away and retreated to the other side of the tent.

Several beats later and a world of distance between us, my pounding heart slowed enough for words. "Why do you know so much about taking antidepressants, Samuel? Do you—are you—"

I heard the rustle of a sleeping bag and I assumed he was settling in for the night. I slid into my sleeping bag and zipped it up to my chin. "Look, I'm sorry I panicked on you. I feel like a skittish virgin all over again and I'm incredibly mortified by it. Can you please talk to me?" I searched for a comfortable position on the cold tent floor before huffing and flopping onto my back. I folded my hands over my stomach and waited.

"Your birth parents," I tried again. "That's why you're so passionate about mental health issues, isn't it? Tell me more about them."

There was another long stretch of silence, and then I heard more rustling as he moved closer to me.

"Do you mind if I lay next to you? I swear I won't touch you," he said without a trace of cynicism, and my fear and shame melted.

Finally. I patted the ground until I found the top of Samuel's sleeping bag. "You're still too far away." I tugged him until he shifted to my side. Satisfied, I placed my palm on his waist. His trembling hand slip out of his bag and rested on top of mine.

"Is this our weekly Q-and-A?" he asked.

"Yes."

"Very well."

I rested my head on his bicep, so close I felt puffs of warm, sweet air as he spoke. "My mother came from an old Boston Brahmin family, the Caulfields. Very wealthy, very prominent. Glittering gowns and cars, homes in Beacon Hill and Newport, big Harvard donors—that kind of prominent. Mr. Caulfield was a partner at a law firm, just like his father before him, and his grandfather, all the way back to colonial days.

"So you can imagine how the family reacted when my mother, only sixteen, stripped down to nothing except for a pair of sheepskin boots at Boston Aquarium's coral reef exhibit. A lot of school children got an education that day, needless to say."

"Oh my."

"Yeah. She was nearly torn limb from limb by raging mothers before security shuffled her away. Rachel Caulfield had always been considered a free spirit. Willowy in appearance, fiery in temper. I've been told I resemble her quite a lot. Anyway, it was also the early seventies, and it wasn't the first time a woman was arrested for public nudity," he said wryly. "Her family didn't outright disown her. Rather, they washed their hands of her. Tossed her a pile of money every year to keep her out of their hair, under the condition she stay clear of the newspapers."

"But she was only sixteen! She was just a minor," I said, shocked at the coldness of her family.

He shrugged. "Now you know why I never bothered to contact any of them. I met my grandfather once, when I turned eighteen. Apparently Granddaddy Caulfield had contributed to my trust fund throughout the years and made a special trip to Lyons with a warning to not be as foolish as my mother. He was a bastard. He died a few years after that, and I never once mourned the loss."

"I'm sorry," I murmured. "I wish you'd told me about his visit."

"I wish I had, too," he said quietly.

"What happened after your mother was cast out?"

"She was a socialite. Kept up appearances and never interrupted the money flow. Oh, there were parties and men and drugs. But she managed to graduate from high school with honors and stay out of the papers, so the Caulfields looked the other way. Soon after she graduated, I guess she became bored with the monotony of her social circle so the family pulled a ton of strings and got her into Harvard." He gave a droll little laugh. "She studied Psychology."

"Didn't Alonso do his undergrad at Harvard?"

"Yes, and my father. They were extremely brilliant, close."

My fingers skimmed along his jaw until I found his mouth. To my surprise, it curled into a smile. He kissed my fingers.

"My father met my mother at a punk rock concert in an underground bar, of all places. While the rest of the country was crazy for KC and the Sunshine Band, they were Ramones fans."

Fitting, I mused, though I didn't voice it. Perhaps obsession with punk music was genetic, after all. That would explain his undying love for The Clash.

"Was Alonso a punk rocker, too?" I asked. I laughed a little—I couldn't help it. The image of straight-laced Señor Cabral as an androgynous sex fiend in a ripped Johnny Rotten T-shirt and safety-pinned pants was irrepressible.

Samuel laughed a bit, too, as if he could see straight into my head. "No, *Papá* has always been a José José fan."

"So they were punk rockers—and embraced the whole nihilist, anti-establishment identity. Isn't that odd, considering your mother was a socialite and your father was an immigrant lawyer who rooted for the Red Sox?"

He hummed. "I've reflected on it, what caused them to swing so extremely. A lot of it is due to their respective illnesses, I'm sure. But they were just two very lost people, Kaye. They let undercurrents toss them around and sweep them away instead of fighting for their own path. And when they found each other, they found another person who was willing to justify their behavior, no matter how they lived or what choices they made."

"Is that why your father was disbarred?" I asked.

He gave my hand a small squeeze. "I'm getting there. They eloped two months after they met, and my father gained citizenship. The Caulfields, surprisingly, welcomed the match. Mr. Caulfield immediately took him under his wing with promises of a place at the law firm once he finished law school and passed the bar. I think they believed marriage would calm my mother, and they could keep the pair under their thumbs. The Cabrals were shocked, of course, but they accepted the marriage. All except Dad—Alonso.

"My mother was extremely charismatic, understand—she charmed the Cabrals on holidays, but it was really only Alonso who spent any time around her. He didn't trust her smiles or frivolity, and it caused a rift. He hated that his brother turned his back on their heritage for 'gringo ways.' For a long time, Alonso blamed the change in his brother's behavior on my mother's influence, but since then, he's come to recognize it might have been early symptoms of clinical depression."

"What do you think?" I murmured.

"I think it was the latter, though my mother didn't help. His grades began to slip, and it was only through Mr. Caulfield's influence that he was able to graduate from law school at all."

"But he still passed the bar."

"Oh yes, exceptionally. Intelligence was never my father's problem. It was dropping the ball. Which is what led to his disbarment.

"For three years, Antonio and Rachel Cabral played the happy newlyweds, but I think depression, combined with the backlogging casework, my birth, and the responsibility of becoming a new father finally broke him. The state discovered he was using Caulfield family money—the stockpiles of 'good behavior' cash paid to Rachel—to bribe prosecution witnesses and bring about swifter resolutions to his cases. He was immediately fired, of course. The Caulfield Law Firm was thrown into the newspapers, a multitude of their court cases were reexamined, and disbarment proceedings began. But he was never actually disbarred."

A lump formed in my throat as I realized what he meant. "Because he killed himself first," I whispered.

"In a closed garage with a running Chrysler."

"Oh my God." I gingerly touched his face and discovered that it was wet. It disturbed me as much as his story, because the Samuel I remembered hardly ever cried. Not the day we married, not the day he left. Until recently, I couldn't think of a single instance. His quaking hand wrapped around mine and pulled it from his face, returning it to his waist.

"My mother was devastated. She may have been self-centered, but she loved my father very much. Toss in her sudden status as a single mom to a baby she'd only ever thought of as a toy, and you can see how her illness spiraled out of control. Alonso tried to visit, but she threw him out and forbade him, or any of the Cabrals, from seeing me. They were so overcome with grief themselves that they easily gave in to her requests. Alonso took a job in Colorado as his escape from the pain. The Caulfields threw more money at my mother to satisfy their grandparent duties," he said bitterly. "You know most of what follows from the book."

"Some." I knew about her late night clubbing and drinking binges while her son waited in the car. Her frequent vacations, when she left Samuel with a babysitter for days at a time. The ridiculously expensive shopping sprees and the bills that piled up—there was plenty of money in the bank, but she never bothered to make credit card payments, Samuel explained. She'd put her son in a ritzy prep school not because she wanted the best for him, but because a neighbor had a child who also attended, and offered to drive Samuel as well. I knew Rachel had slapped Samuel and spewed vitriol, which only made him try harder to please her.

"Just after New Year's, the wild lifestyle stopped. It was around this time that my prep school shrink had a talk with me about what I could and couldn't say. For a five-year-old, apparently I was very cavalier about things like drug use and raucous sex. The shrink gave my mother a stern warning. After that, she didn't go out anymore."

"So she must have at least tried to be a good mom," I said hopefully.

I felt him shake his head. "No, Kaye. She stopped because she was sliding into a deep depression. She couldn't have cared less whether a social worker came knocking and took me away. My mother shut herself in her room all day, all night. Occasionally she'd leave and I never knew where she went, though I have my suspicions."

"Where?"

"Fenway Park. She'd leave the house with my father's urn because she had this crazy idea that she was supposed to dump his ashes there. She fixated on getting into Fenway with the urn, mumbled about it all the time. She stopped eating, stopped buying food. That's when I started sneaking food home from kindergarten."

I frowned. "Why didn't your neighbors contact anybody?"

"I really can't say," he replied, too nonchalant for my peace of mind. "Maybe they just didn't want to get involved. Or maybe they did say something, but there were road blocks. I was too young to comprehend what was going on. You know what happened next."

"Your mother jumped." I brushed a lock of now dry hair from his furrowed forehead. "And you came home to Colorado. To me."

He exhaled.

The storm chose that moment to unleash its fury on our flimsy tent. Another gust of wind shook the tent walls and one corner, then two, snapped loose. The entire thing collapsed. Canvas tumbled over our heads with the wind, wrapping us, our belongings, and our sleeping gear in miserably cold wetness.

I yelled, my hands flying over my head, struggling to push the pile of slick material off of me. Samuel did the same, and I even heard him loose a startled laugh at our predicament. Together, we fumbled for the wall that was still partially standing and found the tent zipper. Samuel pulled me outside after him, shielding my body from the wind.

I tossed up my hands. It would take work to re-stake the tent in the dark.

"Roadside Motel?" Samuel asked. I saw his face a little better now, outside. The corner of his mouth turned up in that oh-so-familiar grin. But his eyes. His eyes were unreadable.

I shook my head. "No way, Cabral. If you were in the wilderness, there'd be no Roadside Motel three miles back. We're staying here."

He shrugged "whatever" and followed my lead. Before long, we'd managed to pound the stakes firmly into the ground and re-pitched the tent, though the inside of it was now as wet and wretched as the outside. I resigned myself to a soggy sleeping bag and pillow.

We stayed outside for a ridiculous amount of time, heedless of the pelting rain, the twigs and leaves flailing in the air, smacking and stinging our skin. His arms tightened around me and I hugged him hard, trying to squeeze all of the hurtful memories out of him like toothpaste from a tube. A plethora of questions raced through my head. Had he seen a therapist as a child? Why had the fact that he was a Boston Caulfield never become public? But none of them were so important they couldn't wait. Finally, his hold on me loosened and I sensed a change in his demeanor. He wanted to move on.

I tugged his hand. "Hey," I said, attempting a grin but failing miserably. "Let's save our pillows before they float away."

"It's going to be a cold, wet night in that tent. Are you sure I can't talk you into a room at that dumpy little motel outside the park entrance? I bet they even have a vibrating bed." He forced a chuckle.

"No quarters. You can tough it out for one night, city mouse."

"As long as you're sleeping in frigid rain puddles next to me." He squeezed my hand and crawled into the tent behind me, splashing through muddy water at the entrance.

And if I already hadn't known, those words sealed it—I'd never be able to let him go back to New York. Not after tonight.

Chapter 5
TRACK

At the tail end of a dive, a skydiver sometimes must track horizontally across the sky to distance themselves from other divers before they can deploy their canopy.

Soaked, shivering, and wretched after our camping trip, we ended up heading back to Boulder a day early. The minute we turned on our cell phones again, all sorts of message alerts dinged and we knew vacation was over. I fielded calls from gossip reporters about the "Kingsley-Cabral-Neelie" love triangle (I finally pulled the plug on my landline), while Samuel poured through numerous voice mails from Caroline. Tweedledee and Tweedledum, my pet photogs, had returned and set up shop in the TrilbyJones parking lot. I even took them blueberry muffins and cups of coffee, much to Samuel's annoyance.

Finally, the news we'd hoped for broke around seven thirty Friday evening—Indigo Kingsley confirmed she was in a long-term relationship with a man she'd met on the set of *Water Sirens*.

We lounged on the couch, Samuel's arm casually draped over my shoulders as we watched the tail-end of some indie movie he'd found on IFC (I didn't even know my cable package included IFC...huh). His cell phone blared, startling us both from the swampy Louisiana diner on television. I groaned. Caroline had already called six times today. But to my surprise, it wasn't Caroline.

"Indigo!" Samuel's face erupted into a grin.

The green-eyed monster hit my heart with a bull's-eye shot as I pictured Indigo's pouty lips whispering words on the other end of the line. But then I got over it just as quickly because: No. Freaking. Way. Indigo Kingsley called my apartment. Well, technically she called Samuel, but still, he was in *my* apartment. Molly would squeal. Samuel, however, saw the monster peek through and winked at me, planting a reassuring peck on my lips.

I barely heard the throaty lilt of Indigo's familiar Aussie accent while Samuel nodded along, his fingers nervously pinching the ends of his hair.

"Flip the channel to E!," he whispered.

Sure enough, stock footage of Samuel and Indigo at the Oscars rolled, followed by a series of clips from the *Water Sirens* movie.

"...*While rumors of the couple's split have persisted for weeks, her announcement makes it official—no more nixie love for Indigo. 'Ms. Kingsley and Mr. Cabral quietly parted company months ago,' comments Kingsley's long-time rep, Natalie O'Malley. 'She and Mr. Caldo are very happy, and very much in love.'*

"*And how is the playboy playwright handling the news of his former flame's fling with the set caterer? Just fine, apparently. His rep tells us he's taking a hard-earned breather in the midst of heavy book and movie promotions, spending time with friends in Colorado before he hits the West Coast...*"

Indigo and the set caterer? I stifled an incredulous laugh, turning it into an unladylike snerk. Celeb gossips had to be doing back-flips over this. Mr. Playboy Playwright smiled again.

"Indigo, thank you so much," he said. "I truly appreciate this...Yes, tell Nat thank you, too..." More throaty accent, then a muffled good-bye. Samuel snapped his phone shut and jumped onto the couch next to me. His arms snaked around my waist and I loosed an embarrassingly school-girlish giggle when he nuzzled my neck, the buzz of his breath tickling me.

"So, Indigo Kingsley jilted you for the caterer, huh? You failed to mention this bit of hilarity to me."

"Marco is an extremely talented caterer."

"Seriously, how does something like that even happen? It's so bizarrely *Cinderfella*."

Samuel flipped the channel back to his dull indie flick and settled in. "A little secret about Indigo: she loves burgers. Insanely loves them, which drove her trainer crazy. But she always complained about how it was impossible to get a good Aussie-style burger in the US — fried egg, pineapple, beetroot, the works — without special-ordering. So, after a long morning of filming, Marco overheard her telling another actor she would kill for an Aussie burger. After that, you can guess what lunchtime staple was added to the table."

"Romance blooms over burgers. That's sweet," I said, "though I'm sorry you were dumped for Marco, the catering sex god."

"It was devastating. I should have listened to *Mamá* when she tried to teach me how to cook."

I nudged him and he snagged my elbow, using it to gently twist me toward him. My breath caught in my throat as I saw his eyes, bright with elation. Soon I was lost in a celebratory kiss, grateful to Indigo (and Marco Caldo) for taking some of the heat off of Samuel.

The second piece of news to arrive that night was not as welcome. Just as I took a deep breath and dove in for another "hello" with Samuel's lips, his cell rang again. And again. And *again*. I groaned when he tore his mouth from mine. He flipped open his phone.

"Hi, Caro," he sighed, lips red and swollen.

I watched in staunch concern as his face fell, then crumpled, then grew angry. He leaped from the couch and paced the room. Long fingers wove through his hair, tugging so hard I thought he might worry a bald spot right on the crown of his head.

"That's not enough time. Simultaneous publicity tours are already swamping me. I can't turn around a script by Thanksgiving."

Crap, that didn't sound good. Samuel's face went fiery.

"Well tell them it's not possible! I can get one to the studio by early January."

When Samuel strode past me, I grabbed his arm and pulled his fingers from his hair, threading them with mine. He absently squeezed my hand.

"I don't give a *damn* about the contract. They *broke* the contract when they chose to bump up filming…"

Caroline screeched something on the other end, her voice sending cringe-inducing shudders through my spine. Samuel also winced, holding the phone away from his ear. Finally, he slumped down next to me. "Fine," he said stiffly. "We'll try for Thanksgiving. But my Labor Day trip is still on...*yes*, I'm serious. We'll talk about it when I return to New York—Caro?"

Samuel growled and stared at his phone for a long moment. Then he suddenly launched it across the room, sending it clattering against my wooden floor. I sat, stunned and frozen. Heady, dark emotions stirred in his face and all the extremes of his visit—the dossier, our sex life confessions, his parents, his career demands—brewed together, creating a potion that would overwhelm him.

"I can't do this anymore," he rasped. His head wearily fell against the back of the couch.

Pained, I dropped down in front of him, resting my arms on his knees. My hands smoothed over his legs. "What's going on?" I asked.

He sighed, relaxing under my fingers. "The movie studio plans to film the next five *Water Sirens* movies back-to-back, did I tell you this?" I shook my head. "They want the next script by Thanksgiving, a full two months earlier than they'd originally requested. I told Caroline that was impossible, but she's already agreed to it."

"And she hung up on you?"

"Yes. It's a new habit of hers that's going to end, and soon."

"That's very unprofessional."

"She's not usually like this. But she's had her feelings hurt...her pride, too."

Then you shouldn't have dated your publicist. I couldn't keep my disgust from my face, and he saw it. A part of me didn't care. I wanted him to wake up before it was too late. Molly's warning flitted through my mind—Caroline Ortega wore too many hats.

"What if you let another writer adapt your books?" I casually suggested. Ha, fat chance.

Samuel's eyes narrowed at me, as I'd expected they would. "Never," he retorted.

"We could cancel the Planet Bluegrass trip. That would give you some extra writing time."

His hands gripped mine. "Kaye, I'm not about to sacrifice our time together for my career." *No, Samuel, of course you won't.*

I chewed my bottom lip, peering up at him beneath my eyelashes. It was a trick Danita'd taught me long ago, and Samuel had never figured out the look was intentional. "And I suppose you'll be too busy to help with the fund-raiser or our book."

"I know what you're doing." His lips quirked.

Okay, so maybe that trick only worked on seventeen-year-old boys. Nevertheless, fire flickered in his eyes and, trickery or not, it still affected him.

I turned my palms to meet his. "Samuel, it's too much. You can't make everyone happy, so something's gotta give." *Or someone.* "If you don't want to cut out anything else, that leaves the book and movie tours. May I see your schedule?"

He retrieved his phone and opened his calendar. A dense, color-coded planner popped up, rendering me speechless. He'd said it was a busy time for him, but I had no idea. Every day, weekends included, was packed, hopping from city to city from this coming Monday and on. The only free time blocked on his calendar was a weekend in late August — Rocky Mountain Folks — and then it picked up again until Christmas. And if his concern over the rapid five-movie schedule was any indication, this insanity wouldn't end any time soon.

I closed my eyes in silent fury at Caroline for her obvious control ploy, and even at Samuel for allowing her to ride roughshod over him. When I opened them again, Samuel watched me intently, unsure if I was about to go Annie Oakley on his tail.

"This." I tapped the screen. "This is a big problem. I don't know what Caroline is thinking, but this will kill you in a week. You think you're exhausted now? There are *five more* movie promotions waiting around the bend."

"I know," he said soberly. "I've never done a simultaneous book and movie tour, and I'm hoping I won't have to again. That's the only reason I agreed to this, but once the events started piling up—"

"You don't plan to publish another book someday?"

"Of course I do."

"Then there will be more simultaneous book and movie tours. Don't set a precedent, Samuel. Put your foot down, now. Caroline and her agency don't own you."

His eyes searched mine. "You're an expert with this kind of thing. What do you suggest?"

I bit my lip and scoured his event schedule, trying to determine which appearances could be dropped. Unfortunately, only Caroline could answer that and I wasn't about to call her. "In my opinion, you should draw a hard line. No more than five appearances a week, with two days completely free, and only through Christmas. Everything else can be done via phone and social media. Let Caroline decide which are the most important commitments to keep—that's what she's paid to do." I looked him straight in the eyes, all business. "If she doesn't bend, go over her head."

Samuel nodded, agreeing with me. What the heck. I pushed a little further. "After Christmas, I suggest you decide what role you ultimately want Caroline to hold: editor, publicist, or agent. She'll probably come out fighting, so be prepared."

He stared at our hands in contemplation. Finally, he spoke. "You're right." I swear, somewhere, choirs sang, victory bells tolled, and cherubic children strewed brightly colored flower petals. "Caro's too invested in my career, to the point where it's not *my* career anymore. It's not fair to her." He bent forward and softly kissed the top of my head. "It's not fair to you."

"Samuel. It's not fair to you, either. Don't let these people use you."

He smiled and rested his forehead against mine. "It's going to be a long week. But I'll get this straightened out."

I actually cried when I watched him stuff his carry-on in the back seat of his rental car. I stood on the sidewalk in the early morning dew, clad only in my pajamas and robe. I hadn't even bothered with shoes, so I shifted my bare feet as the cold concrete numbed them. I told him I was tired of watching his back as he left, that for once, I wanted to be stuffing my own carry-on next to his on a plane to New York.

He wrapped an arm around my waist and pulled me flush against his chest, no longer asking permission to kiss me. And what a kiss it was…which only made me cry harder.

"Kaye," he murmured against my tear-streaked cheek, "you should know by now I'd never let you load your own suitcase." His voice teased, but his eyes brimmed with the same sadness as mine. He leaned down to kiss me again…a slow, sweet good-bye kiss. "Please don't cry. We'll figure this out."

I pushed away from his chest, stupidly denying I was crying. I swiped my traitor tears away with the back of my hand and steeled myself for my empty apartment. *But, Kaye, you've lived seven years with an empty apartment.*

"I'll be fine in a minute. Besides, you'll be here in less than a month for Rocky Mountain Folks. It'll go fast."

"Rocky Mountain Folks," he repeated, a solemn vow. He traced my jaw line one last time, his fingernail lightly scratching my skin. Then I felt an actual, physical rip in my chest as he tore himself away and climbed into the car.

It took all my strength to keep from desperately clinging to the bumper like Marty McFly sans skateboard as my "whatever" journeyed back to his stress-filled world in New York.

"Dang, Kaye, that kid is a monkey!" Hector's voice echoed through the lush canyon. "Look at him scale this thing—he's faster than any of us."

"I think he'll make a fantastic lead ascender on the Longs Peak trip," I chimed in, encouraging the young climber.

Luca beamed at us from halfway up the craggy cliff face, his tan body swathed in harnesses, pitons and ascenders. Then he turned to the rock wall and fitted another safety device.

Our entire team—Hector, Molly, Cassady, Luca, and me—was brushing up on belay techniques using the towering, sun-bleached cliffs of Big Thompson Canyon. The river gurgled beyond in a breathtaking stretch of green, dappled in wildflowers and tender moss, as we ascended with a belay partner guiding us from the ground. The Saturday afternoon was pleasantly sunny. It warmed my shoulders and freckled my cheeks, and I found myself drowsily floating back to my time with Samuel, a week ago.

When I was out of his blazing presence, I could almost convince myself I'd imagined the shaking hands and restlessness. Almost. Though I was now certain he'd once been depressed, what I'd witnessed from him ran more along the lines of anxiety. If he indeed struggled with some sort of mental health issue, as I suspected more with every passing day, then his work schedule would do him in. And Caroline *had* to know she was hurting him.

A hummingbird whizzed past my head and my eyes flew open, pulling me back to the canyon. The bird darted to Danita, sprawled across a beach blanket. Bikini-clad, she frowned over a bestseller. The bird buzzed her ear. She yelped and waved the thing away. Next to her, Molly's new puppy dropped the rawhide it was panting over and barked at the hummingbird.

That's right, a puppy. Jaime Guzman was dead serious when she told Molly the only way she'd go to Girls Night was if my friend bought a Black Labrador. Molly gazed forlornly at the gangly, drooling animal as she guided the belay rope.

"His name is *Juicy.*" She sighed. "He doesn't like me. He bites all the time."

Danita rolled her eyes. "*Ave María Purísima*, Molly, he's a puppy. Of course he bites you! Don't let it bruise your ego."

"I didn't know you could have pets in your apartment," I commented.

"He's staying at Cassady's. Cassady has a big back yard—I can't even give my puppy a proper home! No wonder he hates me." She cast another sad look at her pet. "Everyone likes me. Everyone except Juicy."

"Good, Luca," Hector instructed calmly as he tightened the rope. "Now put the ladders and carabiner in the jumar…test the weight… not too fast…"

Luca eased his foot into the resting point he'd created, making sure it held. It did. He grinned again as we cheered—the kid would be more than ready to climb Longs Peak with us this winter. It was obvious he'd trained extra hard to catch up, and his skill level had vastly improved. When temps dropped, we'd log some practice time on winter terrain. Ice and snow were nothing new for Hector, Cassady, and me, but this would be Molly and Luca's first cold-weather climb.

"Ready for descent, Cassady?" Molly called out. High above us, Cassady hovered at the top of the cliff, sun-streaked hair whipping around his face.

"A little more tension, sweetness," his voice echoed down. Molly tightened the rope, braking it while her boy toy leaned away from the cliff. Juicy, however, chose that moment to embroil Molly's belay rope in a death battle. He chomped down on the end and snarled, then scuttled off toward the river, rope firmly ensconced in his strong puppy jaw. Molly was yanked backward, and so was Cassady.

"Juicy! No! Drop the rope!" Molly screeched, her high voice reaching new decibels. She edged closer to the growling dog. Poor Cassady yelped, yanked even higher until he was close and personal with the cliff face. He shielded his boys, already precariously tucked between leather harnesses.

I jumped up to chase the dog. Juicy braced his wobbly legs and then dodged to the right just as I leaped. Molly screeched again as she was yanked the opposite direction, followed by Cassady's desperate cursing.

Juicy growled. I growled back. "No you don't, dog."

Somewhere behind me, Hector and Luca howled as Molly sank to the ground, determined to keep Cassady stable. Dani wavered between helping me tackle the dog or anchoring the rope for Molly. Finally, she flung her scantily-clad body over Molly and wrapped manicured fingers around the rope.

"*Me cago en tu pinch perro*, Molly, Cassady's package better be worth a bruised kneecap. Who buys a dog named Juicy?"

"It's the name he came with," Molly said, gasping and trying to stand without being knocked off balance. "I can't help it if Luca's sister has bad taste! The stupid dog won't even listen to me, anyway. I might as well call him Humpy."

"Juicy!" I whistled and snapped, my eyes fixed on the dog. He crouched again, only to dodge me when I snatched at his collar. "Freaking mutt!"

"Tito, sit!"

"Juicy" halted his rope massacre and sat. Then Luca descended, his angelic baby face bright with laughter. Hector lowered him to the ground and they both collapsed against the rock wall, loud guffaws rolling from their bodies.

Something stank of Jaime Guzman.

"Oh man," Hector gasped out, "that's the funniest thing I've seen all summer! Your sister is a crazy woman, Luca! *Juicy!*"

Molly righted herself and scowled at them both. "Let me guess," she said flatly. "His name's not Juicy."

The guys' roaring doubled as Luca shook his head. "Molly, meet Tito." Tito thumped his tail at his name.

I peered at the dog and whistled again. "Tito, come here!" And just like that, the puppy dropped the rope and trotted to me, pink tongue lolling over his gums.

"Oh perfect!" Molly cried. "Now my dog likes *you*, too." She whirled on Luca and jabbed a finger at his chest. "Tell your sister to sleep with one eye open, or she'll find herself in hair rollers and heels!"

But her irritation dissipated when she, too, tried out Juicy's real name. "Tito!" she called, one hundred percent beaming when her dog bounded toward her, dried grass hanging from his mouth.

As we took turns huffing over cracks and crannies, I tried to focus. It wouldn't do for me to slip and crack my tailbone. But my thoughts kept straying to Caroline.

I had a hard time discerning her motives. When I'd interacted with her during Angel and Danita's wedding festivities, she'd been a warrior for Samuel's well-being. But then she'd been jilted. Rejected by the very man on whom she'd pinned her loyalty, professional expertise, and her heart. Caroline was not a woman who would roll over and die, that was for sure. Was Samuel's jam-packed publicity tour her version of revenge? Or did she simply not care if he was healthy, as long as he was pimping their brand?

"Kaye," Hector shouted, "are you planning to sleep on that safety device tonight or are you going to descend?"

I snapped out of my ponderings and waved to Hector to tighten the belay rope. Once my feet were firmly on the ground, I unhitched my gear and flopped next to Danita on her blanket.

"Good book?"

She didn't say anything.

"Oh, so you're ignoring me now. Is this about lunch last week?"

She glowered at me over the top of her paperback, and I knew I was still in the naughty corner.

Samuel and I had lunched with his family the day before he left. The more I stewed, the angrier I became with Alonso and Sofia, and their skeletons in the closet. By the time we arrived at the Cabrals' picture-perfect home, my anger had extended to the entire Cabral *familia*. I spent the afternoon glaring until Samuel slyly warned me my face would stay that way. At one point, Sofia anxiously asked if I didn't like barbecued chicken and could she fix something else. I politely told her the food was delicious.

"So what's the problem, Kaye?" Danita snipped, her eyes not leaving her book. "Why were you shooting daggers at my family last weekend?"

"Why is your family dead set on keeping secrets from me?" I snipped back. "I think I had a right to know the truth. No wonder Samuel was so messed up."

Her black eyes darted to mine. "Samuel finally told you?"

"Better late than never, no thanks to the rest of my *familia*."

Her mood suddenly shifted. She flipped her book shut and exhaled. "*¡Gracias a Dios!* I warned him back in May that if he didn't come clean with you by the wedding, I would. My brother is lucky you're an understanding human being."

Danita and her ultimatums. "I don't see what the big deal is."

She gaped. "Are you serious?"

I waved my hands. "That came out wrong, let me rephrase. I don't see why all of you felt the need to hide the truth from me. I know I'm rash and sometimes say the wrong thing, but am I really so unreliable I couldn't be trusted with this?"

"It's not that, Kaye. You are more than capable—that's what I told Samuel and my parents. But he was so scared he'd ruin your dreams and your plans. He didn't want you to have to deal with him, which is absolutely ridiculous if you ask me, because you had every right to make that call yourself. But you know Samuel and his twisted logic." I tried to follow her rapid speech. She caught my confused look and fell silent.

"We're talking about his birth parents, right?" I frowned. "His life in Boston, the trauma it caused? I don't…why would he think he's responsible for what his parents did? I mean, they were sick."

Danita's lips pursed into a thin line, a ring of paleness forming around them. Then the rest of her face blanched. Her eyes flickered closed. When she opened them again, a sudden, angry fire burned there, so like her brother.

"The trauma, of course," she said evenly. "Just like you said. He didn't want it to affect you."

"I'm not following. Does this go back to his drug addictions? Or maybe…is he on meds for depression?" Once again, that odd feeling settled over me, the sense that something was being kept from me. Whatever it was, it waved its macabre hand right in front of my eyes, taunting me with a key dangling from its fingers. And yet I still couldn't unlock that maddening door.

She gracefully hopped up from the blanket. "Excuse me," she muttered, and gathered up her summer tote. I watched as she sashayed up the hill, flip-flops flapping, and then pulled her cell phone from her bag. I gnawed on my thumbnail. I knew who she was calling—Samuel. I'd stepped in something, and I wasn't quite sure what. But from her flailing arm and pointed air jabs, I could tell she was reaming him over it.

I was so caught up in watching Danita yell into her phone, I didn't notice Hector had finished his descent and plopped down next to me on the boulder. He reached over and pulled my half-eaten thumb from my teeth. Molly would kill me when she saw what I had done to yesterday's manicure.

"What did Mexi-Barbie's brother do to piss her off?"

I sighed. Even the big horned sheep could hear her hissing Samuel's name like a curse.

"It's a long story," I mumbled.

"You can tell me."

I gazed at my scuffed Scarpa boots, a bit sad. "No, Hector. I really can't."

Another stream of Dani's colorful Spanglish floated through the canyon.

"So, Kaye." He wrapped his rough brown hands around my knees. "You and Cabral again, huh?"

My eyes snapped to his face. It was pinched and rutted, and he was dying to say something. "Just spit it out, Hector."

"Sure. I think you're a moron for taking him back."

I scowled, sliding my knees from his grasp. "Well geez, that was tactful."

"One thing I've never been is tactful, *mamacita*. But just listen, okay? The guy doesn't bother with you for seven years, then all of a sudden, everything's rainbows and roses? I don't buy it. There's more to this, and I think you should seriously consider if taking him back is worth laying yourself on the line again."

"Look. I know Samuel has issues, okay? Heck, I have issues, too. But we're doing the best we can to work through them and make it last this time. I wish there were instruction manuals to come with this sort of thing but frankly, I think our relationship is beyond even Oprah's wisdom."

Hector snorted. "That's an understatement."

I punched his shoulder. "You don't have to agree with what I'm doing," I said, my voice calming. "Just...just keep being my friend."

"Always." His eyes were black with emotion, and it hit me how truly awful I'd been to him with my half-promises. I placed a hand lightly on his forearm, knowing what I had to do—for him *and* for Samuel.

"Hector, you shouldn't wait for me."

His eyes glittered, but not with amusement. "*¡Pobre de mí!* You almost get a gal killed with a parachute and she ditches you for life."

"I'm serious. It's always been Samuel. And…I think it might always be Samuel. You deserve better than second best, Hector Valdez. Don't waste any more time on me."

He grew quiet. I could tell he was chewing over my words, the lack of levity between us. His expression was a study in disillusionment. Disillusionment filtered through me, too. Why had I deceived myself into thinking second best was okay? I should have cut him loose a long time ago.

"Can you tell me a Hippie Tom joke?" I asked, in way of a peace offering.

Hector rubbed his thumbs together, a sad little smile warring with his gloom. "No, Kaye. Not today."

I collapsed into my comfy leather chair Sunday evening. It was only six o'clock, but my weekend in Lyons had exhausted me. I wasn't even hungry. I settled for a mug of hot chocolate, even though it was the middle of summer. I pulled my crocheted afghan around me, blew across the top of the mug, then sank into my chair…

Epic strains of arena rock startled me awake. Like usual, I couldn't place the noise and I fumbled for the TV remote, nearly knocking my lukewarm mug of cocoa from the end table. Then awareness hit me, and I realized my phone was ringing. Shoving the afghan from my legs, I reached for my purse.

Caroline, ugh! I'd answered her call earlier this week, only to have her bawl me out for "hooking" Samuel into our mental health clinic fund-raiser by using a well-placed guilt trip on him. I tried not to snark back…I really did. But when she hissed once again that I would ruin him, I'd had it.

"You're just ticked off because Samuel's laying down the law over your ludicrous publicity schedule. You can't control him, so you're pestering me, instead." Her indignant stammering told me I was right. "Nice try, Caro. But Samuel can make his own decisions."

"If you're making the calls on Samuel's publicity tours, maybe you should be his publicist," she'd snarked. "I'd like to see you try to swim in the big kids' pool."

"Good-bye, Caroline." I hung up on her. Utterly childish, I know, but she had it coming. So I wasn't keen to answer my phone now, given the last time I'd spoken with the woman.

But Caroline trumped me by leaving a voice mail. Seriously, who can ignore that little message icon on the display? I listened, bracing myself for the woman's wrath…

"*Kaye, this is Caroline. I know you're angry and not answering my calls, but hear me out—I've got an emergency on my hands. Please call me, ASAP.*"

I groaned and dialed her number, praying this wasn't a setup.

"Kaye," she rushed, skipping over greetings. "Have you heard from Samuel today?"

My stomach flipped. "No. Why?"

"He's gone AWOL on all his appearances, and even skipped a black tie reception last night."

"What? Have you tried calling him?" Duh, Kaye.

"He's not answering. I even stopped by his apartment around noon and he wasn't there. This is just perfect! We're supposed to fly to LA tomorrow morning."

Skipping out on commitments without telling anyone? This wasn't like him. I racked my brain, trying to think of where he could be. But fear gripped my mind and the only scenarios I came up with involved gruesome car accidents and hospitals.

"I don't know what to say, Caroline. I don't have a clue where he is."

"If you hear from him, please, *please* call me. I won't argue with you, I promise. I should have known better than to load his schedule, that something like this would happen. But understand, I push him, I've always pushed him to be better—that's what I do. That's what he *wants* me to do." This was turning uncharacteristically confessional, for Caroline.

The call ended. I was stunned for a full minute, my cell phone dangling loosely in my fingers. Then full-fledged panic clamped down on my heart and I sprang to action.

First, I tried Samuel's phone—no answer. In fact, it went straight to voice mail. I left a message begging him to call.

Next, I tried Alonso and Sofia. Not wanting to alarm them, I calmly asked if they'd heard from him at all this weekend. They hadn't.

"Is everything all right, dear?" Sofia asked, worried.

"He's just very busy, and I haven't spoken with him in a couple of days." There was no sense in upsetting them until I knew more. My mind calculated the last time I'd had contact with Samuel. He'd called Thursday night, and then a text message Friday. After that, nothing. Saturday…

Danita! She'd talked (well, fought) with Samuel for a long time Saturday afternoon. And that was supposedly right before he'd gone missing. My fingers fumbled over her number.

She answered. "Hey, Kaye, still glaring—?"

"Dani," I interrupted. "Have you talked to Samuel since yesterday?"

A pause. "No, why?"

"Caroline called. He's missing and neither one of us can get hold of him." I filled her in on what I knew. "You're the last one to have spoken with him, Danita."

Another pause. And then incoherent grumbling. "*Mierda.* Has Caroline checked his apartment?"

"Yeah. Dani…" A lump swelled in my throat. I picked up the now cold mug of cocoa and chugged half of it. "How did he seem when you talked to him? Was he okay?"

"Honestly, he was freaking out. Kind of frantic." She cursed again. "This is my fault. I should have left him alone, but I just couldn't, could I? Angel's right—I'm too pushy."

I waved my hand, even though she couldn't see it. "Focus, Dani. Why was he frantic? What did you say to him?"

Her voice cracked. "I can't tell you. It's not my place. Kaye, please understand—"

"Seriously?" I snapped at her, frustrated and frightened. "You surprise me, Danita Maria. You pretend to be blunt and honest, but you're just as bad as Alonso and Sofia and Samuel, aren't you?" My doorbell rang and I jumped, spilling my half-full mug of cocoa down the front of my hoodie. My quaking hands shuffled my cell phone and tried to catch cocoa as it dripped onto my wooden floor. "Dani! Please, just—"

I opened the door and froze.

There was the missing man himself, on my doorstep. He was haggard in a rumpled tuxedo jacket, his white shirt untucked, bowtie long gone. His eyes were bloodshot and baggy, as if he hadn't slept all week. He looked like crap...and I'd never been happier to see his beautiful face in my life.

I dropped my phone and threw myself at him, sobbing with relief into his neck. "What on earth, Samuel? I was this close to calling the police!"

His hand smoothed over my hair, and he clung to me as if *I'd* been the one missing, not caring that cold cocoa soaked into his shirt. "I'm so very sorry, Kaye. I told you that you don't need to worry about me."

I slapped his shoulder out of anger and the simple need to touch him. "It's hard not to worry when your agent and sister are freaking out because you're missing. Lord, Samuel, is it too difficult to give someone a call and let them know you're alive?"

He mumbled another apology. I vaguely heard Danita's shouting from my phone. I picked it up.

"Aspen Kaye Trilby! If you don't speak to me, I'm coming over right now!"

"It's okay, Dani," I said, my voice unsteady. "Samuel's here. I'll talk to you later, all right?" I ended the call to the sounds of her protests. My eyes swept over my erstwhile husband—he was this close to collapsing. Taking his hand, I pulled him into my living room and shoved him into my comfy chair, then plunked down next to him. Even when I tried to slide my hand away, he wouldn't let go, so I left it where it was.

"Where have you been?"

"Airports. La Guardia last night, then Dallas for most of this morning. I'm afraid I let my cell phone die."

"No luggage?" I asked.

He held up the corner of his chocolate-stained tuxedo shirt. "My trip was rather spur-of-the-moment. I was halfway to a Berkshire House reception for a big name author, and the mere thought of another champagne swilling party was revolting. So I headed for the airport, instead."

I glanced heavenward. "There are easier ways to get out of cocktail parties, Samuel. You certainly scared Caroline—she was actually nice to me for once."

"Again, I'm so sorry about that. I warned Caroline, but she didn't take it seriously."

I studied him hard. "This isn't your way of sticking it to your publicist by creating a PR nightmare, is it? Running away without giving her warning?"

"You aren't glad to see me. I'm sorry."

"Quit apologizing and just tell me *why you're here*."

He stared at his polished dress shoes. "All week, I've been thinking about what you said, how you hate watching my back every time I leave. I hate having a long distance relationship with you too, Kaye. I didn't like it in college and I don't like it now, especially since I've already lost so much time with you. So I came up with a plan." He took my hands and turned to me. "Please remember you can tell me no. This is just an idea, and you aren't obligated to me in any way."

"*Samuel*," I growled, impatient.

"Sorry." He brushed the pad of his thumb across my knuckles, then slid to the pulse point at my wrist. Mother of Tom, the man was an expert at disrupting my thought pattern. He winced, then breathed in.

"I want you to tour with me."

"What?" My eyes widened. "Tour, as in, your publicity tour?"

"Hear me out. One of our struggles has been how little we know of each other's lives after seven years. I've had all summer to see what your life is like now. But you still don't know much about mine, other than what I've told you or what you've seen in the media, unfortunately. So here's my proposal: I'd like you to travel with me until the movie premieres over the Thanksgiving holiday and get a taste of my life. Then, if you still want me, I'll leave New York City and buy a house in Boulder."

"You'll move to Boulder permanently," I repeated.

"Yes."

A thrill shot through me. He'd move *home*. "Is this what you and Danita were arguing about yesterday? I swear she's become as cryptic as you."

He tried to crack a smile. "In a roundabout way," he said cryptically (of course).

My fingers floated along the lapel of his tuxedo. I couldn't believe he'd move home. "What about TrilbyJones? I can't just pass my accounts off to Molly, and I certainly can't take any more vacation time."

He grinned rather smugly. "I've thought of this, too. Caroline's firm can outsource to TrilbyJones. Some things need to change, and

Caroline's overworked as it is. They'll hire you to keep the publicity tours manageable. Most of the events are already in place, so you'd just have to sit down with them to discuss which to cancel and which to keep. Then, you'll accompany me to events and do your PR thing—coordinate with the event sponsor, make sure everything runs smoothly."

I rolled my eyes at his description of my work—"PR thing."

"Caroline's agency is okay with your plan?" I listened to him as I scooted to the kitchen and grabbed a dish towel, dabbing at the cold cocoa dribbled down my shirt.

"I've already spoken with Caroline's boss and he's fine with it. Truthfully, I think he's too nervous to lose the account to say otherwise." Just as I thought, Samuel went over Caroline's head. She'd be hopping mad.

"I'll need a week off in November for the Longs Peak climb," I warned. "That won't be convenient for you." I handed him the dish towel. Instead of fussing over his tux shirt, he knelt and wiped my wooden floor clean.

"You're still planning to do that, even after your skydiving accident?" He frowned. "At least Molly and Cassady will be along to keep you from being reckless."

I ignored that. "And my TrilbyJones clients? I can't just ditch them."

"Telecommute. Everyone does it." Criminy, he had given this a lot of thought. "I can promise you, Kaye, landing this account will make it worth TrilbyJones' time to take us on, even with the short notice."

I began to fold. "When do you want me?"

He tossed the dish towel in my kitchen, then pulled me back to the chair with him. "As soon as possible."

The low, seductive way he spoke it sent both tingles and warnings racing up my back. A part of me thought mixing business and romance wasn't a good idea. After all, look what happened to Caroline and him. But then again, I wasn't Caroline, and I'd loved Samuel long before I could even spell "Public Relations Nightmare." Besides, this was only a temporary solution until his tours were over and he could finally, *finally* settle where he belonged—in the mountains.

So the tingles won a convincing argument over the warnings. Because, when it came down to it, I was hard-pressed to say no. City-hopping with Samuel? Spending every day with him? Getting a glimpse into the inner workings of his life? Yeah, couldn't turn that one down.

"Okay. I know I'll be in over my head, but what the heck. Just let me talk this over with Molly first before you confirm with your people, please. We might have to hire a temp before I can leave."

He blinked. "Really? That's it?"

"Don't sound so surprised. I'm not an over-thinker like you."

A toothy smile flooded his face. "I just thought I'd have to work a lot harder to convince you, pull out the fancy PowerPoint and graphs. Not that you should be worried," he said quickly. "We'll take very good care of you. Five-star hotels, sightseeing, and great exposure for TrilbyJones. You won't regret this," he added softly.

Honestly, I couldn't care less about the five-star hotels and sightseeing. I just wanted to visit his New York apartment and see Fort Tryon Park. I told him as much.

"Don't put on a show for me, Samuel." My fingers toyed with his lapel again. "I'm in this for us, so I want to see the real you, not Mr. Perfect Sexy Man who is never frazzled. As mean as it sounds, I kind of enjoy knowing stress rattles you like everyone else."

He pressed my fingers to his lips, ice blue eyes on mine. "I promise. Nothing but the real me, stress headaches and all."

"Good." I smiled, matching his gaze with a scorcher of my own. "Then you can be the one to call Caroline."

Chapter 6
ONE HUNDRED JUMP WONDER

*A relatively new diver
who arrogantly believes they know everything
there is to know about skydiving,
and ends up breaking a femur
when the ground greets them too quickly.*

You are sophisticated.
You are fast-thinking and clever, and can easily keep pace with Hollywood's publicity machines.

You can wear heels if you have to. No, you love to wear heels, and it shows. That's right. Those Prada pumps tucked away in your carry-on will not terrify you or your wobbly feet, no! You will own their leather hides. Own the shoes…own the shoes…

I white-knuckled the armrests of my business class seat. The dry, recycled air on the plane made a static mess of the hair I'd carefully groomed, and I was ready to sweep it into a ponytail. Around me, tired-looking passengers either caught some shut-eye or read magazines under yellow oases of lights. The strong-jawed man next to me typed away on a laptop. I tried not to disturb him with my fidgeting.

I'd caught the evening flight from Denver to Los Angeles, which gave me roughly three hours to freak out over the banana bread and airport coffee I'd carried onto the plane for a nightly fix. But neither my latte nor my mantras erased the palpable fear that I was too backwoods to be Samuel's publicist.

I'd barely talked to Samuel; I had been so busy putting my affairs in order before I blindly hurled myself into the maelstrom of his messy life. After Samuel's phantom-like appearance on my doorstep, he'd vanished just as mystically. I'd begged him to stay the night, if for no other reason than to prevent him from falling asleep at the wheel on the road to Lyons.

"Samuel, stay," I cajoled, wrapping two tempting arms around his middle. "You don't need to drive all the way to your parents' house tonight."

He groaned and leaned into me. "Firecracker, I can't. I have things there that…that I need." His voice faltered as my thumbs kneaded the tightness in his back. Every cord of muscle gave way and I thought I had him.

"Stay," I whispered against his neck. "I don't care what you sleep in. You can buy something to wear tomorrow. You can even borrow my toothbrush. Just *stay*." He knew what would happen, what I wanted to happen if he stayed the night. With a reluctant sigh, he untangled his arms.

"I'll call you when I get to Lyons." Kissing the top of my head, he slipped away into the night, leaving me frustrated in a silent apartment. Early the next morning, before I'd even poured my cereal, Samuel had traveled directly from the Cabral home to Denver International Airport, and flown to LA.

And now, a week later, I also slipped away into the night, cutting through black clouds and stars thousands of feet in the air, putting hundreds of miles between me and everything I'd ever known. Everything, save for Samuel.

Despite my age, I'd seen embarrassingly little of the world. Samuel was the one who had an insatiable wanderlust for faraway places. I'd never desired to stray beyond my mountains unless it was by his side. Lyons knew me. I defined myself in the comings and goings of its greasy diner and rusted-out gas station. I breathed with the ebb and flow of St. Vrain water sloshing against creek banks, a trickling current of life. I marked my years in tree rings. If I left, how would I know me? I began to understand why Samuel seemed so lost. I was already homesick for the Rockies and I'd barely left.

Fingers trembling, I peeled open the package of banana bread and dipped it in my coffee. Once again, I stared at those spiky designer shoes.

Own the shoes…own the shoes…

They mocked me, those pointy suede beasts nestled under the seat, next to my old ballet flats. The elegant curve of the peep-toe, the sharp stiletto heel…Danita said they were sexy. Molly said they could double as a lethal weapon if I needed to take out the competition. She even stole all of my ballet flats and sandals (save for the pair I'd snuck into my suitcase). For all I knew, they were now displayed on shoe racks at the local Goodwill.

"You've seen the way women dress in southern California," Molly asserted as she played tug of war with me and a tasteful dress I'd tried to cram into my suitcase. "Show off those beautiful shoulders of yours. And your legs. Honey, let them come out to play!"

I gave a sharp tug back, yanking Molly over my chair and woefully stretching my dress in the process. "Molly, that's television. Real publicists don't dress like hookers, even if it's LA."

In the end, I compromised and bought three new shorter, flashier dresses and two very expensive pairs of shoes, including those Prada monsters, which, at the moment, were giving me a bad case of buyer's remorse. Fortunately, my friends were more concerned with how I could prep for a publicity tour in five days than whether my skirt hit above or below the knees.

"Let's be realistic," Danita had said at Fisher's Deli Monday morning. "Los Angeles is a big pond compared to our little puddle — a shark-infested pond at that. An overpopulated, California shark pond that will go into a feeding frenzy at the first sniff of blood in the water and rip apart fresh meat."

My mouth fell open. "I know I don't have the experience for this—"

"But you've got great instincts," Molly interrupted, glaring at Danita. "You'll get the experience on tour."

"Kind of like being dropped in the middle of the Congo with no translator," Danita added. "You'll learn to speak Bantu really fast."

I didn't even blink. "Your Discovery Channel-esque metaphors strike fear in my heart, Dani, truly. However, Samuel has my back. I trust him. And there are a whole team of people who will be a phone call away if I have questions. Caroline will also be there for movie publicity. I'm sure she'll help."

Molly and Danita stared at me dubiously.

"Okay, so I'm counting on assistance from my stressed ex-husband and his bitter ex-girlfriend. On paper, not a good idea. Which means we need to come up with a game plan as of yesterday."

"Kaye?"

"Shoe thief?"

Molly grinned. "I bought you a US travel guide. Let's plan this mutha."

For five long days my TrilbyJones staff made calls, researched, and connected with other literary publicists. We tinkered away at Caroline's original PR plan, hammering out a rough "quality, not quantity" strategy to present to the NYC dream team. Our TrilbyJones intern lackeys finally had a chance to prove their mettle. Friday afternoon, when our new temp overnighted the last hard copy proposal to New York, Molly and I collapsed around our break room table in silent back-patting.

"I bet Gail's ready to go vigilante on Samuel and hunt him down with her pitchfork," Molly had teased.

I frowned. Ever since I'd made my intentions to go to Samuel in LA known, many of my acquaintances had cast themselves as foreboding soothsayers. My dad's girlfriend was angry at me for "chasing some man" to Hollywood, as if I'd met him on the Internet. Hector was angry because he thought I'd bail on the Longs Peak climb. And Danita was just angry, period. But Mom had been supportive, in her way.

"Actually, no. Mom seems fairly calm about the whole thing. She said 'you gotta do what you gotta do,' and left it at that."

"Strange."

But I knew what Mom meant.

Now, the new PR plan rested on my lap, the luminescence of my tablet dimmed so as not to disturb the passengers in the cabin. Most of them appeared to be business travelers who grasped at their valuable moment of imposed cell phone silence to rest. I turned to my small window. Dusk chased the last rays across a patchwork land far below, and then entire cities flickered to life, their trailing interstates like the haunting glow paths of the fireflies we used to catch in the forest line of the Cabrals' backyard.

My thoughts turned to my mother. She had always been a woman of few words. Mostly, she was simply uncomfortable without a garden spade in hand. When I was a teenager, there were times I intentionally tried to tick her off, just to evoke some sort of feeling from her. I remembered one particular occasion when I was fifteen, right after my father quit his third job that year. I'd gotten my belly button pierced despite my mother's "ears only" rule. As I'd made breakfast two weeks later, I'd stretched and flashed the bit of metal, and it was downhill from there.

"Dad doesn't care," I spat at her.

"Your father probably doesn't know."

I flinched. It was true…not because I'd hidden it from him, but because he spent so much time at Audrey Wexler's place, I hadn't even seen him long enough to show him. Mom saw the flinch, though, and her eyes softened.

"You can't let him move in with Audrey," I'd whispered, my voice hoarse.

"Nothin' I can do about that, baby."

I shook my head, begging her. "Yes you can. You can tell him you still—"

"No. It wouldn't make a bit of difference. I did what I had to do a long time ago, and it didn't change a thing. Still, I did it." She ruffled my hair, then put on her stern mama face. "Take that thing out." She flicked my belly button ring. "You're grounded for two weeks."

After that, my mother and I had an unspoken comradeship. Out loud, our official position was "Audrey's a nice woman." But really, we both desired to see Tom kick her to the curb. And that was why, when I told her about my plans to go to Samuel in Los Angeles, she told me "you gotta do what you gotta do" and I knew exactly what she meant…

"Excuse me, miss?" The man's voice broke through my wandering thoughts. I turned to the strong-jawed passenger next to me, in the aisle seat. "The flight attendant asked if you'd like a beverage."

"Oh!" How long had I been staring at my heels like a space cadet? "Nothing for me, thanks," I said, nodding to my cold Starbucks cup and bread.

The passenger eyeballed me like I was nuts. He may have believed there were tiny bombs nestled in the soles of my Pradas. If he did call an air marshal, I couldn't blame him — if I sat next to a high-strung woman muttering Stuart Smalley affirmations while glaring at teal pumps, I'd call security, too.

Glossy hair streaked with silver curled around the edge of his earlobes, short enough for the boardroom but long enough for the bedroom. Tan, pressed, and expensive, he looked like he'd stepped out of an advertisement in *Golf Digest*.

Before long, the captain's static voice crackled over the intercom, announcing our descent into Los Angeles. With a sigh, I struggled into my new heels and tightened the strap, girding my ankles for battle. The man lifted an eyebrow at the death traps.

"I'm a publicist," I stammered.

"Ah." Apparently that was all the explanation he needed. "What sort of publicity do you do?"

"Mainly tourism, arts, and culture, but I'm venturing into celebrity PR."

The man flashed a row of capped white teeth, reminding me of a grinning giraffe. "Well, young lady, you're heading to the right city. With all the agent jostling and back-biting that happens behind those pretty faces you see on television, LA could support a football franchise. The *Los Angeles Spin Doctors*, don't ya know?" The man barked at his own joke.

I gulped. "Banana bread?" I offered.

He shook his head, giving me the once over. "A bit of advice. If you really want to exude high-power take-no-prisoners ball-buster, wear your hair up. Coupled with those heels, you'll seem six feet tall."

I blinked at him, wondering how Molly had disguised herself as a middle-aged, male jet-setter. "I'll ruminate over that."

I. Was. Toast. Even Mr. PGA Tour knew more about making an entrance than I did. Flipping snowboarders, I was going to break my ankles. I'd de-board the plane, then promptly flail into my tanned airplane buddy and together we'd tumble onto the baggage claim conveyor belt, be rendered unconscious, and cycle through those black rubber flaps with unclaimed duffel bags until airport security handcuffed me and wheeled me away to some secret Homeland Security holding pen. Then they'd send me straight back to Lyons with a stern warning to never, *ever* again set my Prada-clad foot in Los Angeles.

And Caroline would sneer and say "I told you so."

The man watched me expectantly, and I realized I'd missed part of what he said. I fumbled back to our conversation. "So are you in the business, too?"

He whipped out his wallet and slid a crisp white card from its folds. "My wife and I are what you'd label 'behind-the-scenes' people. We used to be in the thick of celebrity networking, but we've scaled back to a select few. Still, call me if you or your clients need a consult."

I read the card:

Patrick O'Malley
ARTS & ENTERTAINMENT PUBLICITY
"Helping your talent shine through"

Cute. A publicist for a publicist: Welcome to Hollywood. I smiled and thanked him for his offer to make me over, then stuffed his card in my purse.

"If I may, who are your clients?"

"Oh. Um, Samuel Cabral," I answered tentatively. "Have you heard of him?"

The man's eyes widened and he whistled. "Who hasn't? Not only is he a brilliant writer, he has the 'it' factor—sexy and elusive. And in the entertainment business, people gobble up that stuff. Every producer, media hound, leading lady, and purse poodle wants an hour with that man. Very humble guy, though, on the few occasions I've met him. Refreshing—'humble' isn't even *in* this industry's instruction manual."

Pride snaked up my back and I straightened my shoulders. "Yes, he is a very good man. Definitely in-demand."

Patrick's mouth curled knowingly. "So you're more than his publicist. You're his manager."

"I…no. Sort of."

Patrick nodded thoughtfully, sizing up my frizzed-out hair and unpolished nails in a new light. "Word is the *Water Sirens* movies will blow the vampire boys out of the water. We're talking a mass-media franchise potentially worth billions of dollars. There are a lot of jobs and money tied up in Mr. Cabral's yays or nays. I wouldn't want to be in his shoes." *Or yours, for that matter*, he added wordlessly with a piercing gaze.

My stomach roiled. "Which is why he needs me."

Patrick leaned back in his chair. "Ah yes, there's that spin doctor ego. For a moment I thought you were a rare breed. So you're Buitre, then." My new acquaintance's demeanor chilled, and I suddenly felt the darkness of the plane circle our little pool of light. "Last I heard, Mr. Cabral was signed across the board, unless he has new representation…there's been buzz, lately."

"Technically, I'm not with the Buitre Agency." Inexplicably, I wanted to stumble back into this man's good graces. "I'm contracted to handle book publicity. I'm my own woman."

I'm my own woman? Who said that—Disney's next pop sensation? Patrick smiled at me indulgently, as if I were thirteen and had declared I'd bought my first training bra.

"I was under the impression that Buitre liked to do everything in-house, pretty nepotistic. But they're New York and I'm LA—what do I know?" Patrick winked, and his chill lessened. "It sounds like you've already got a solid foot in the door, Miss…"

"Trilby. Kaye Trilby."

Recognition flickered in his eyes. Once again, his gaze swept over my plane-rumpled appearance and decided lack of anything designer, save for the wretched shoes. Then, as if I'd slipped a whoopee cushion under him, he chuckled in delight and extended his hand. I took it.

"Kaye Trilby. I should have known, but it's always nice to be caught off guard. I've changed my mind." He waved his hand at the pumps dismissively. "Ditch the ice-pick heels and go with the sturdy flats. You'll do fine without them."

Breathing a sigh of relief, I yanked the Italian monstrosities from my feet and crammed them in my carry-on, then slipped into my ballet flats. But, just for good measure, I put up my hair. Patrick O'Malley nodded his approval.

"Perfect."

Long minutes passed. I pressed my forehead to the window, anxious. We sailed above nighttime Los Angeles now, millions of lights stretching over the earth. Directly below us were the glowing pylons of LAX reaching toward the plane like giant pastel birthday candles. The airport itself was a sphere of purple-lit arches, curvy and flashy—the embodiment of everything LA loved.

Ten minutes later, passengers scrambled to gather their bags, filing along the aisle like antsy movie-goers in a ticket line. I didn't expect to see Samuel right away. Caroline had warned me that LAX was always crawling with paparazzi, so celebs didn't do the "kiss and greet" thing like the "little" people. Instead, I was to find Justin, the publicist from Berkshire House, who'd then drive me to the hotel where Samuel was tucked away until his next event.

With a final wave to Patrick, I darted around passengers crawling along with rolling suitcases or hovering below departure/arrival screens. I didn't spare a glance for the gift shops, though it was my first time in Los Angeles. Instead, I whipped out my phone and punched in Samuel's number, aching for his voice.

"I'm here. I'm in LA," I said eagerly, the minute he answered. I heard his breathless laugh.

"I'm so glad. Did you have any trouble?"

"None, but I did get some unsolicited image coaching. Although, the advice wasn't half-bad." I silently thanked Patrick as I breezed by other women teetering in high heels.

He tsked. "Imagine that, on a flight to the celluloid capitol of the world. Where are you?"

"I'm almost through the gates, then off to find my suitcase." And the guitars I'd brought as a surprise, praying they weren't damaged in transit. I glanced around, searching for someone who could be a publicist. "What does Justin look like?" I asked.

"Utter hipster, that one. No, worse: he's a scenester dirtbag." I heard a commotion in the background, followed by a string of cussing and Samuel's laughter. He continued. "Skinny as hell, scruffy, Camel Light super-glued to his lower lip. He's wearing a keffiyeh the same color as your purple skirt, even though it's southern California. And it's the middle of August. And his mother's Jewish." More commotion, then a muffled "leave my mom out of this, man."

Realization tiptoed through my brain and my head shot up, scanning the throngs of people. My heartbeat raced toward Samuel with the velocity of a cannonball.

"Where are you?" I squealed.

"To your left, Kaye."

I skimmed the row of concierges holding signs and landed on a short man in skinny jeans and a plum scarf, Justin. Next to him was a man with wild brown hair—*my* man. Plain tee and jeans, bright eyes and a dimpled grin out-dressed anyone or anything times infinity. In his tawny hands was a sign of his own: Neelie Nixie.

Cheeky.

He stepped forward, catching me up in his arms as he dropped his sign and I dropped my bag at his feet. I buried my face in the crook of his neck and inhaled cardamom and cedar.

"Welcome to LA, Trilby," he murmured into my hair.

"Thanks for having me, Cabral."

He tilted my face up to his and kissed me hard, dragging my body in, his sensitive, full lips moving against my own, his smile touching mine.

"This is the way it should have been," he said.

"Hmmm?" My eyes fluttered open.

"Seven years ago, in New York. I should have been waiting for you at the airport. I should have held you, just like this. I should have taken you home with me and never let you go."

Tears burned my eyes. I shook my head. "Samuel, stop. Let's just be happy right now, okay? You can take me home…or to the hotel, I guess."

He brushed his mouth against my forehead and cheeks in silent agreement. Suddenly, I was aware of the crowds of people around us. Justin studied the LAX ceiling with his hands crammed in his pockets. Three young women eyed us curiously, one of them sporting a *Deep in the Heart of Nixie* T-shirt. And of course, there was the occasional bulb flash from several of the paps who trolled LAX for celebs. Samuel really was too pretty for his own good. I clutched the back of his shirt, the fabric still damp from the outside heat. Then, remembering my manners, I slid from his embrace and held out a hand to Justin.

"So glad to meet you. You're a publicist with Berkshire House?"

"New titles." Justin shook it with a surprisingly strong grip. "With the show Buitre runs, I'm more like Caro's walking, talking Rolodex. Normally I'm off tour at this point and we leave ongoing PR to the agency, but this a-hole author called in a favor," he said in a thick New York accent. He punched Samuel in the shoulder. Samuel shoved him back, then tucked me under his arm and kissed my cheek, just as another camera flashed.

Over our shoulders, a man shuffled camera lenses in a black bag. Catching my eyes on him, he tapped the brim of his ball cap in a hello. I nodded back, then lifted an inquisitive eyebrow at Samuel. "Funny, how you dodged paparazzi like bullets in Lyons," I said, "yet here, on their home turf, you're kissing me in public. What gives?"

Rebellious fire flickered in his eyes. "Fuck the paparazzi. I've decided I don't care about them, anymore. They can print whatever the fuck they like."

I jerked my head back in shock. Was he kidding? "Whoa, Cabral. Signing on with Def Jam, are we? Don't let Sofia hear that mouth of yours or she'll ground you to your bedroom."

"I'd rather you grounded me to my bedroom." He leaned over and breathed hot air into my ear. I shuddered. His hand slid over the plum fabric of my skirt and gently cupped my bottom. "I've missed you."

Yeah. Felt that. If I was any kind of publicist, it was time for me to get my very horny client out of sight, pronto. Moving his hand away, I tugged him from prying eyes and toward the baggage claim.

"What sorta luggage do you got, Ms. Trilby?" Justin asked.

"A black suitcase with a red strap. Oh, and two guitars. I know they're impractical to carry around on tour," I said, turning to Samuel, "but we're long overdue for some jam time. I thought you might like that."

A wicked smile spread over Samuel's face, as if I'd just announced the two guitar cases were brimming with garters and thongs. "I'd love it," he said huskily.

Justin mumbled something crude under his breath and trotted away for my things. Snapping out of his lust haze, Samuel followed him.

Right. Apparently everything was about sex tonight. Now I was very anxious to get my client out of the public eye and into the back of a car. Er, just a car. "My client"...oh geez, I sounded like a hooker. Red spread from the tips of my toes to the roots of my hair at the thought of pushing Samuel's shoulders down into the leather upholstery of a BMW or Benz or whatever fancy car was parked outside, skimming my fingernails over his torso, tugging at the waistband of—

The shrill buzz of my phone broke into my lurid fantasy. I yanked it out of my purse and glared at the screen:

Caroline Ortega.

Now she was derailing my imagination, too. I stamped my foot in unbecoming peevishness, startling an older gentleman who dropped his cane. I picked it up for him with a self-conscious apology.

"Hello?" I answered.

"I take it you arrived safely? Good. Now try not to do anything that will make Perez Hilton scribble drool and hearts on your pictures, please." Too late for that. "I have a conference call arranged for eight o'clock tomorrow night in my suite at the Roosevelt."

The *Hollywood* Roosevelt? My inner Molly squealed with glee. Any classic movie buff knew the Roosevelt had been the playground of the stars for eighty years. I pictured Samuel and me sauntering arm and arm through hallways a la Clark Gable and Carole Lombard. I wondered if Samuel had requested we stay there, or if Caroline had chosen it.

"The partners will be on the call, as well as Samuel's business manager, his lawyers, and the marketing director at Berkshire House. Samuel has a packed schedule tomorrow, so any prep for the call will need to be done tonight."

"But it'll be eleven in New York," I stammered.

Caroline huffed. "Here's the Cliff Notes, don't bother with the book: Samuel Caulfield Cabral is a big deal. They'd ditch their wives during the best sex of their lives if Samuel called for a bestsellers report."

I snorted in spite of myself.

"Half of them will just be stumbling in from martinis at Bruno Jamais, anyway," she continued. "Eight will give you enough time to brush your teeth and go potty—that's *it*." I didn't miss the subtle inflection of her voice. "That is, if Samuel's dinner with the *Water Sirens* producers doesn't go late. You and Justin are welcome to come along, of course."

Dinner with Hollywood producers? I almost dropped my phone. Caroline had successfully made me a nervous wreck in thirty seconds flat. I craned my neck toward the boys. "We'll be out as soon as my guitars show up."

"Guitars." There was a pause, and then a hiss. "Do whatever you want, as long as Samuel continues to garner good press. See you in five."

From what I could tell of the city blurring by, Hollywood Boulevard was a mix of tacky tourist museums, tattoo parlors, and liquor stores, streaked in neon lights like a Pollock painting. Palm trees lined streets of old movie theaters with glittering marquees and gift shops with tattered overhangs. Star impersonators peddling post cards mingled among tourists and artists and prostitutes. Chicken shacks perfumed the air with grease, making my stomach rumble. Not somewhere I'd wander alone at night, but from the breezy back of Justin's rented convertible, I soaked it up.

"Justin, put up the top!" Caroline yelled as she pushed whipping black hair from her face, her voice swallowed by the cacophony of car horns and street music.

"No way, Caro! This is a Bentley Continental GTC. You're supposed to feel the summer wind in your hair with this baby!"

"More like car fumes," Caro bit out and scowled back at Samuel and me, looking for help. Her onyx eyes darted down to his hand on my knee, then up. "Samuel, we need the top up. Kaye and I have a lot to discuss before I leave."

I started, thinking I must have misheard her. Leave? Leave where?

He merely shrugged at her, his fingers still stroking the underside of my knee.

"Samuel, the top!"

Samuel sighed, his fingers absently squeezing my knee. "Caro, you'll have all the time you need with Kaye tomorrow," he said loudly. "Give her a chance to relax and enjoy LA."

Caroline turned her glare to me and said something I couldn't quite hear. I gave her an apologetic tap of my half-deaf ear and turned back to the lights and air rushing by. I probably should have given in and asked Justin to put the top up. But honestly, what was five minutes?

Though the August air was heavy with *eau de exhaust*, the Hollywood Roosevelt Hotel smelled heavenly, like tea and almonds. Before I even took in the staggering arched lobby or chandeliers, the scent pumping through their vents assaulted my nostrils. I'm not sure how I expected the Roosevelt to smell—something tropical to match palm trees and swimming pools, like coconuts. Chintzy, I know. The Spanish-style hotel towering around me, though, was not tawdry. Warm-hued woods, coffee and cream upholstery. Several guests milled about, posh in high-end lounge wear that probably cost more than my new shoes. Which, incidentally, I was seconds away from yanking out of my bag and shoving onto my feet.

We walked into the softly-lit lobby, a bellhop rolling my luggage cart behind.

"Normally we stay at the Biltmore, Caro's favorite," Samuel whispered. He shifted his guitar to his other hand. "But I thought you might like to stay here, given your love for ghost hunting and all things old Hollywood." He placed a key card in my hand and wrapped my fingers around it. His eyes searched mine. "Your suite is next to mine. Charge anything you like to it—food, dry cleaning, spa time. Enjoy yourself while you're here."

"Samuel you don't have to pay—"

"Yes I do," he interrupted. "Please. Let me."

My eighth-floor suite was just as incredible as the lobby, but it wasn't delicious-smelling air vents that made my jaw drop. It was the view. I waved good night to Justin and Caroline, then made a beeline for the wall of windows overlooking the neon-lit boulevard and the fanciful rooftop of Grauman's Chinese Theatre, and clapped my hands over my mouth in mute delight. Samuel laughed as he directed the hotel porter to put my luggage in my bedroom.

"I thought you might enjoy that," he said, plopping onto a sofa covered in plush, faux-fur pillows. He picked up one and smirked. "I don't want to know how many synthetic animals had to die to make these things."

"Careful, Cabral. Now that I'm your publicist, the PETA ad is back on the table."

His eyes followed me as I hopped from room to room, inspecting the pocket of Hollywood history where I'd be dwelling for the next few days. The suite looked as though it had been doused in melted chocolate then pressed into a mold from an old Spanish mission—a mission with fireplaces and flat screen televisions built into suede walls. And the bathroom. With a running start, I could slide across the sleek granite in my sock feet and still not hit the opposite wall. I'd try out the spa shower tonight, oh yes.

I jumped when Samuel's cool hands snaked around my waist. His velvet voice echoed through the bathroom. "I believe your bedroom balcony overlooks the Tropicana, so you can do a bit of ghost watching when you're not carting me and my nixie brood around LA." He slipped the elastic band from my hair, letting it tumble over his palm. "Maybe Marilyn Monroe herself will make an appearance—at the Tropicana, not my book-signing."

I smiled. "Don't get a big head."

His fingers toyed with the bottom button of my blouse, then deftly flicked it open. "Hmmm. You'll have to keep me in check."

Just like Caroline does. I tried to squash the thought, but it refused to leave. I slithered from his roaming hands and made my way to the bedroom to unpack. Samuel stared after me, his brow furrowed. He sighed and followed me, then took the stack of folded shirts from my arms and decidedly set them down in my suitcase.

"What's wrong, Kaye?"

I picked up the shirts again and stuffed them in a drawer. "Caroline mentioned she's leaving next week. Where's she going?"

He exhaled slowly, then put on that gorgeous, lazy Cabral smile. "I don't want to talk about Caroline right now." Sitting on the edge of the bed, he grasped my hand and tugged me to him. He rested his forehead on my sternum, his warm breath trickling over my skin, making me tremble. A single finger crept up the back of my leg to tease me, but I was persistent.

"She's still handling your movie publicity, right?" I swatted his hand away from my skirt hem. "She's not bailing on the tour?"

Samuel ignored my hand and caught the back of my knees, pulling them until they were nestled on either side of his narrow hips. My skirt rode up and he gave me a cocky smirk, as if he'd bluffed his way through a poker game.

"Yes, she's still doing movie publicity. No, she's not bailing."

I gave in to him, combing my fingers through his tangled mess of hair. Samuel all but purred under my fingers.

"She's flying out for a few days to meet with a new author. Now that she's scaling back her work with me, she has time to take on an additional client." Persistent fingers dug into my waist. "Now, Ms. Trilby," he murmured against my neck, "kindly hold still while I find the zipper to this skirt of yours."

Oh flipping...whatever. I was going to lose myself in him. My arms snaked around his shoulders and I tried to relax.

His fingers skimmed the thin white cotton of my blouse, coming to rest over the buttons. One by one, he undid the little pearls. He dropped his mouth to my chest, his tongue grazing the edge of lace on my bra. Cripes, I was tense. Not the good kind of tense, like I should have been with Samuel's beautiful body inches from mine, seducing me, begging me to play. My gut told me it was wrong to go down this road, here and now. *You have to be responsible, Kaye.* The tiny voice of protest grew stronger as Samuel shifted me closer, until it was earsplitting.

Threading my fingers through his hair, I halted, wavering. Finally, I tugged his mouth away. Cool air hit my skin and I shivered.

"You really want to do this now?" I whispered, breathless.

Samuel paused, his fingertips floating above the collar of my blouse. "Don't you?"

"Well, this isn't exactly how…"

When I didn't finish, he wrapped his hands around my knees and spun us around, burying me into the soft feather down of the comforter.

I searched his contorted, carnal face for a hint, a bit of love to let me let go. I wanted him to gaze down at me as he had the first time we made love in my old bedroom, the music of Planet Bluegrass still ringing in our ears. I wanted the Samuel of our wedding day, so considerate, so loving. I tried to match his hunger with hunger, his love with love. But there wasn't *love* in his grinding hips, digging hands and greedy lips, no trace of the friend I'd loved my entire life. There was no tenderness, no give-and-take. Only hunger.

I scrambled against him. "Time out."

He groaned when I slid off the blanket and stumbled to the living room, rebuttoning my shirt. Leaping from the bed, he adjusted his pants and followed me, his irritation painting the room red.

"Samuel, I'm so sorry. I have a lot of work to do tonight."

He shook his head and fixed me with a bold stare. "Not good enough, Kaye."

"You have a talk show appearance first thing in the morning, followed by a book signing all the way down in Santa Ana. Then apparently you have dinner with your *Water Sirens* producers, which I didn't find out about until tonight, by the way. After that is the conference call—"

He shushed my mouth with his lips. His clammy arms clutched at my waist and I felt us stumbling backward, into the overstuffed couch cushions.

"I have to prep for the conference call tomorrow," I said in a rush of breath. "If I blow it off, there will be a lot of angry people."

His mouth paused over my neck. "People who work for me. Now shut up, Trilby, and enjoy this."

I felt his teeth graze along my neck, my collarbone, then down the middle of my chest. His long fingers teased the hem of my skirt, and we were back where we were five minutes ago. Lust shot straight up my body, in spite of myself. He slowly, deliberately traced the trim of my cotton underwear.

"Samuel."

Hard blue eyes watched my reaction, waiting for me, *daring* me to shoot him down. Well, he did dare me. I pushed on his shoulders until I could breathe deeply.

"You've waited three years to get laid," I said, a touch too sarcastically. "You think you can wait a little bit longer?"

A flash of hurt passed over his face. He braced himself above me, putting some space between us. "You don't need to throw it in my face, Kaye."

I saw my opportunity for escape and rolled out from under him. "And I don't want *our* first time in seven years to be a quickie on a hotel couch."

Samuel watched with petulant eyes as I moved across the room, straightening my skirt and smoothing down my blouse.

"You were pretty willing last week," he shot back.

"Yeah, and you ditched me for your parents."

"Look, I already apologized for that." Frantic hands tore through his hair and he jumped up from the couch and stalked toward me, his face twisting in bitterness. "But fuck, Kaye, how much longer are you going to string me along? There's only so long a man can jack off to a fucking memory, and seven years is pretty damned close to my limit." He paced the carpet, his muscles bunched with unfulfilled energy. "*You* need answers. *You* need friendship. *You* need time. Then *you* need my life story. What else do *you* need?"

"What are you accusing me of?"

He narrowed hot eyes on me. "You're being a fucking tease."

Pain tore through my chest at his words, partly because there was truth in them, no matter how crassly they'd been spoken. I closed my eyes, trying to keep in my throat the harsh words I wanted to scream. "Out."

"Kaye—"

"Out!" I pointed to the door. "How dare you degrade me? How dare you treat me like I'm some whore you picked up in a bar then screwed in an alley?"

"I didn't mean—"

"Yes you did. If you haven't gotten any from me in seven years, it's your own fault. Now please leave before I say something I'll regret." *Too late.*

Samuel wavered, his hands clenching and unclenching in his hair, and I could see a battle being fought behind his eyes. He closed them, blinked rapidly, and swept a final, longing stare over me.

"I'm sorry," he mumbled and then fled the room, and me.

Before the door slammed shut, tears stung my eyes. What was wrong with him? What was wrong with *me?* I'd been dying for this man's touch the moment it was taken from me, all those years ago. Now I had his touch. Why had I sent him away?

A wave of homesickness and self-pity washed over me. I'd only been in LA for a couple of hours, and already, I knew I didn't belong here. I didn't know what I'd expected, but it had been more along the lines of a relaxing evening spent on a fluffy hotel bed, Samuel writing his book, occasionally asking my opinion while I skimmed his tour schedules with a highlighter. Then he would smile down at me with longing, gentle eyes and set his writing aside, drawing me to him with his touch, his words of love.

But his touch.

His touch was a little too forward. A little too voracious. And his eyes. I couldn't explain it, but it was as if someone had plucked the eyes from a defiant, lust-filled teenager and fitted them in the face I still loved beyond reason.

Perhaps that's the way he is, now, Kaye. Gooseflesh dotted my bare arms and legs, so I tugged the thin blanket from the back of the couch and swathed my body in softness.

What if Samuel was simply more sexually aggressive than I recollected? My Samuel of seven years ago was a boy who'd barely been a man. Now there were seven people between us in the bed. Tack on seven years of changes in him, in me…

No, a sobering voice persisted in my head. *This is the Samuel of The Dream, hunched over the brunette in the brownstone as white powder fluttered across her skin.* Like an apparition, The Dream lurked in the shadows of the hotel room. It breathed down my neck, dogged in its need for recognition.

I ran a hand over the rumpled fabric of my expensive blouse, studied the haphazardly buttoned little pearls that Samuel had laboriously tried to unbutton. What did Samuel see when I pushed him away? I wasn't a starry-eyed teenager anymore. I was a woman who had a sex hang-up. A woman who froze him out when things escalated. I'd made my share of mistakes with other men, and now knew the pain of using and being used.

Striding to the bedroom, I stripped away my travel-worn clothes. Even my lace bra was uncomfortably tight, so I unhooked it and dropped it on the floor. The Dream prickled my skin, so tangible I thought I'd see it skulking behind me. I risked a glimpse in the mirror at my nakedness, from my mascara-smudged eyes to the vanity of my sculpted shoulders. There was only me. My skin was a gradient of whites and freckles and sunburn. Tan lines gave way to pale breasts and a torso that never saw the Colorado sun.

Those four men I'd slept with after Samuel—had they seen me, Kaye Trilby Cabral, beneath my cotton sundresses and eco sneaks? Or had I been just another body to them: blond, shorter than the nameless writhing forms in porn mags and videos, but readily available.

I plodded to the extravagant bathroom, feeling very small and exposed beneath its reach of granite. I twisted my hair into a frizzy mess on top of my head, then turned on the sink taps and splashed my face with hot water. I scrubbed my eyes, cheeks, neck, wiping away all traces of grime, and car exhaust, and foreplay.

Did any of those four men have women waiting for them, women who'd loved them once, who wanted them for more than their bodies? With shame, I realized I'd never considered those women before I so callously used and discarded their men. I supposed it was the same for Samuel and his three flings. I'd been jealous of those women for so long, but now that I knew how he'd used them, I felt only pity. In the end, there was never anything nameless and easy about casual sex.

I trailed a fingernail along the line of my calf, where a multitude of little bruises from rock climbing faded to green. As I slipped into my pants and sleep shirt, my mind ventured to the last time Samuel and I had sex, before he'd left for New York. The disconnectedness, the aggression of it had left me cold, sobbing in the bathroom. I'd escaped to Lyons for the weekend because I'd felt used by my own husband, a means to an end rather than loved and cherished—just as I felt now.

The Dream was relentless in its stalking. It dragged over my temples, down my arms in a frozen trail. I saw Samuel's blue eyes as cold as ice, his body single-minded and hungry for something I could never sate. I wrapped defensive arms around my middle, but it was too late. The last Other had left my dreams. It painfully jabbed me in the ribs to get my attention.

You have to get over yourself, Kaye.

So I thought…Seven years ago I never confronted him about what happened. Instead I hid, and then he left our marriage two days later.

History has never been your strong subject, because what are you doing all over again?

Hiding in my hotel room, expecting him to knock on the door and send me packing to Colorado.

What are you afraid of?

I pressed my fingertips to my forehead, as if they could pull answers from my mind.

You know this; it's simple. You don't want Samuel to leave you again.

But rejecting his advances isn't exactly an incentive for him to stick around.

You believe he's going.

Was I rejecting Samuel before he could reject me?

You see the changes. Already his mind is turning away from you.

Yes. In the most vulnerable part of my heart, I thought he'd leave me again.

But there's more to it. Something has a hold on his mind, doesn't it? You see it in his eyes. His words.

And in The Dream. Holy hell. I fell back on the bed as the truth socked me.

Even now, the last Other leered as Samuel and I slipped apart.

Ten minutes later, the door to Samuel's room slammed shut. I flew to my own door and whipped it open. He wasn't there. I peered into the hallway just in time to see him pace in front of the elevators in a ratty T-shirt, running shorts and sneakers.

Jogging at eleven? I moved into the hall to call to him.

"Samuel!"

He stared straight ahead and hurried into the elevator before I could catch him. I frowned. Yes, he'd heard me. I was positive.

He wasn't ready to talk—loud and clear. I would just wait for him to cool down. I sat on the hallway floor with my knees tucked under my chin, but eleven became midnight, and still, he hadn't returned. When one o'clock rolled around, I admitted that I might not see him until tomorrow morning, and returned to my hotel room, fraught with worry.

I wanted to burrow further into the blanket and hide my face in pillows. I wanted to drift away. Like bleached driftwood, I wanted to float to sea and not return. Because returning meant facing whatever monsters waited for me on that craggy shore.

But I sat up and pulled myself together.

With a trembling hand, I filled a glass with water and quenched the burning tightness in my throat. I grabbed a wad of tissues from the colossal bathroom and stumbled back to the living room, swiping tears and fears from my cheeks. My stomach growled. I realized I hadn't eaten anything today save for banana bread and coffee, but I wasn't about to show my messy cry-cry face to the hotel lobby. Resigned, I opened a five-dollar bag of mixed nuts from the snack drawer.

I took a shuddery breath and set my shoulders. Okay. So I had my fears and baggage. But there was still something going on with Samuel—it wasn't my imagination.

A sudden slam made me jump. I pressed a hand to my fluttering heart and listened. Another slam, from the hallway.

Samuel?

Sure enough, he was outside his hotel room, fists digging into the solid door as if he were trying to push them through a wall of butter. He was a sweaty mess, hair plastered to his forehead, shirt clinging to his back. He favored his left foot and I assumed, given the telltale intensity of his run, he'd blistered it. Frustrated, he banged the door again.

I cleared my throat.

He whirled around. Cold sky eyes skittered over my face, then landed firmly on my neckline. "I locked myself out of my room," he said flatly.

I tugged up the vee of my sleep shirt. "Do you want me to—"

"No. I'll go to the front desk."

I shuffled my feet, then decidedly took a step forward. He held up reddened hands, a silent request for me to stay where I was.

I tried again. "Samuel, about tonight. I think we should talk—"

He laughed, a dry, bitter sound. "Firecracker, the last thing I want to do tonight is *talk*. You'd better go back to your room."

"But, Sam—"

"Go the *fuck* back to your room, Aspen Kaye!" He squeezed his eyes shut and breathed deeply. "Please. We'll talk tomorrow."

I nodded and backed into my room, my eyes not leaving his contorted face until I'd closed the door. I pressed my cheek against the cool wood and sighed, the feelings of New York flooding my veins.

At least he'd returned, thank God.

After some minutes, I noticed my chirping phone, telling me I'd missed two calls.

They were both from Hector. I stared wistfully at his name. An overwhelming urge to call him hit me and, even though it was after midnight in Lyons, my fingertip still hovered over the send button. It drifted to my contact list and found another name: Danita.

I texted her, asking her to call me when she woke. Two minutes later, my phone rang.

"Hey, Danita."

A gruff male spoke, instead. "Sorry, just me."

"Hi, Angel. Where's Dani?"

The rustle of what I assumed was a potato chip bag answered my question. "Sorry, Kaye-bear. She and Molly are having a slumber party—can you believe it? Some Welcome Home thing for Molly's step-SILF. Either Dani has a secret thing for chicks or she didn't get enough girl love in high school. She accidentally left her phone behind."

"SILF?"

"Yeah, Sister-I'd-Like-to—"

"Gotcha. Don't ever say that around Danita. Or anyone, for that matter."

"So what's up, *manita*?"

I sniffled into the receiver, feeling like a complete idiot. "I'm just a little homesick, I guess."

"On your first night out there?"

"Yeah, no. I don't know. Everything is just…off. These people, this place. Even Samuel."

Angel's jock-boy tone sobered. "What do you mean, Samuel's 'off'? Describe 'off.'"

I paused, weighing what I could and couldn't say. "He's, well… ugh, this is embarrassing. I went frigid on him because he's being a big-mouthed horn-dog. Kind of like how you were in high school, no offense. Which is totally normal for some guys, but, Angel — this is *Samuel*. Since when has Sofia's well-mannered son ever said 'fuck the paparazzi' and grabbed someone's tail in front of a hundred witnesses?" I waited on tenterhooks for Angel to speak.

"Uh, yeah. Wow, Kaye," he hemmed and hawed. "Look, my advice is to forget blowing off steam with Dani and go to the man himself. He's probably just all jacked up from getting you back. *Hombre* seriously loves you, you know? Tell him his gropey hands and naughty words are freaking you out, and you want to know why he's acting that way. That's what works for Dani and me. Then, if he's still being a horn-dog, you come talk to me, little sister, and I'll kick the piss out of him. *¿Comprendes?*"

Warmth for the man who'd been a big brother to me circled me like a long-distance hug. The tension in my neck and shoulders eased, and I began to feel like myself again.

"I'll talk to him as soon as I can."

"Hey, Kaye? Do me a favor and keep this conversation on the DL with Danita, okay? She's already this close to flying down there, chopping off Samuel's manly parts and feeding them to the sharks at Sea World. Dani means well, but sometimes she needs to chillax."

"Chillax? Seriously, Angel?"

Before I switched off the bedside lamp, I tossed my old-school day planner on the nightstand. A folded piece of paper slipped from the back pages — the photocopy I'd hidden away and forgotten. It was that wretched good-bye note from Samuel.

My fingertip traced the letters, seeing the hard press of a pen, the mental stress in each slant. The word choice was a succinct arrow to the heart. Meant to injure, to distance.

Go home to Colorado. I don't want to see you again. The roots between us are dead, we are dead…

Jaime had been right with her whole Occam's razor spiel. Dang it, I hadn't wanted to believe that Samuel had written the note, so I'd grasped at frayed strings, desperate to wrap the blame for his final good-bye around someone else's shoulders. But instead of despair, I felt clarity. Peace, even, because now I saw the truth.

Go home to Colorado. I don't want to see you again. The roots between us are dead, we are dead...

I considered not only what Samuel had written in the note, but how he'd written, when he'd written. The *how* was with a heavy, stressed pen. The *when* was sometime after going ballistic and then running up and down the streets of the East Village.

Go home to Colorado. I don't want to see you again. The roots between us are dead, we are dead...

Samuel had a mental illness, and it wasn't depression. Tonight I'd briefly considered that he was doing coke again, and I still wasn't ruling it out. But according to the articles I'd read on cocaine use, highs only lasted roughly half an hour, usually shorter. Unless he was lying about being clean and snorted a line whenever I turned my back, drugs didn't explain his prolonged agitated state and strange eyes. But I'd seen this before, hadn't I? That night in New York...

"Go home to Colorado, and don't you ever come back here again, Aspen Kaye. I fucking mean it. You think this is a joke?"

It was there in his bitter words. In the note. In the backpack.

It was there, that keep-out sign on the tree house, passed from his mother...to him...to me.

I'd forgiven him. But I couldn't ignore him, not anymore, or I would lose him completely. And knowing what I now did about his mother's own good-bye letter, tucked away in his kindergarten backpack just before she'd tumbled to her death, there was no room for a blind eye. This was too vital. I turned out the light, Samuel's long-ago words resonating through my dreams.

"Go home to Colorado, and don't you ever come back here again, Aspen Kaye. I fucking mean it. You think this is a joke?"

And when daylight came, I would rise to face the last Other.

Chapter 7
FREEFLYING

*An expansion of skydiving,
freeflyers experiment with different dive positions
to increase speed and thrill factor.
Freeflyers will find themselves in mortal danger
if they do not transition back to a traditional
dive position before deploying their canopy.*

Hydraulic Level Five {working title}
Draft 1.28
© Samuel Caulfield Cabral & Aspen Kaye Trilby
28. *Skygods*

We try to watch for the slip.
  It sidles up – a warship creeching unaware over planks – and bombards our sides, all hands and fire back plastic-coated pills till we sink that mother in murky silt graveyards of fishbones and rusted remnants of those other warships sunk by pills. Sometimes we don't see the slip until it slips into us and we fall *down down down* to the sea floor where gravity squashes our sorry asses. There is no air. There is no lung. There is no word in the place where fishbones and warships lie. Sediment crusts for a thousand years over our limbs and encases us in a deep cave where only blind fish and gilled symbiotic creatures swim. So deep, so deep. Othertimes we

slip and fall *up up up* to wide skies. Weightless, tumbling, pushing those words so high, so high. Cold virgin air burns off our gills and didn't we soar? Didn't we twine feathered limbs together like skygods? My God, Firecracker, didn't we fly?

We found the ground when we heard sine waves crawl across Planet Bluegrass, twanged from the guitar strings of an ermine Festivarian court. They wrapped diamonds around your finger and chained you to me. You heard it again when you pressed your ear against my chest. Take me back to my room, you said, and make me yours. Lyons misted our faces as you stumbled behind me to our second-story haven, your hands on my waist.

When will you ask me, Caulfield? I've loved you my whole life.

When can I have you, Aspen?

When you ask me. I want to know it's for my whole life.

But you already know I belong to you.

I want to be your wife, you said. My fingers pushed the denim off your hips and crawled like those sine waves over your skin until they found the places that made you sing. I'll marry you in April, you cried. April is a good month, I whispered. It's your month, snowless and green, waxy leaves and roots and life. I'll make you my wife in April. Now tie me to the dirt, Firecracker, before I slip from this throne of yours.

I took you on an old bed.

I kissed your diamond ring and swore I belong. I belong. I belong. I belong to you. You braided your hair so I could unbraid it. I buried myself in the cape of your body and your blood stained the white sheets red as the rubies you scattered over my thighs. Then you placed me on your throne and made me a king.

And still, I slipped.

................•◆•................

Sleep came fitfully that night, followed by a barrage of dreams. Samuel's greedy hands pawed at the brunette in New York. Wild eyes. Harsh words. Bits of notepaper fluttered over my shoulders, through my fingers amid fine dustings of white powder. Nicodemus, walking ten steps ahead, his back forever in front of me, plowing through snowdrifts. Yet I followed with my keyhole eyes. And then

I was face-to-face with the last Other. I was so close, I only saw its leathery pores and crackled skin, smelled its putrid breath. But if I took a step back.

And another step.

And another.

A sob tore through my throat and I awoke. My entire body trembled, clammy with sweat as I clutched at my pillow, a frightened child in the throes of a nightmare. I *saw* the last Other. Not just the beast's teeth, or clawed fingers, or porous skin. I saw the thing in its entirety, and it made me gasp at how I'd been so detrimentally blind.

Oh my God. I knew what was happening to Samuel.

My hand fumbled for the lamp switch. Light poured into the hotel room and drove back the last shadows of my dream. The red glow of the alarm clock said it was five fifteen: two hours before we had to leave for Burbank to tape the *Helen Boudreaux Show*. Wrapping myself in a hotel robe, I grabbed my phone from its charging dock. My brain raced. Before I could forget, I typed my observations through blurred eyes:

> History of drug use. Memory loss. Tragic past. Rigid schedule.
> Trouble sleeping. Anxiety. Sadness. Loneliness. Perfectionist.
> Creative genius. Secrets. Fear of being like his mother.
> Mentally ill parents.

And now:

> Excessive sexual energy. Wild eyes. Uncharacteristically rash.

My fingers brushed over the stark words etched on the screen. I'd been too close to him. As I gingerly backed away from those demons, I realized they made up a single, snarling creature. The same being that nearly killed Nicodemus. The same creature that plagued the man I loved. The last Other.

At the end of my list I typed a single phrase:

> Bipolar disorder?

The green room behind the soundstage was fragrant with coffee and muffins early Saturday morning. *The Helen Boudreaux Show* was filming multiple episodes to air the following week while Helen recorded the voice for a mouse or bug or toy — I wasn't sure which — in an animated flick. Samuel and Helen were shooting the breeze about it while a studio audience roared with laughter. I watched him on the mounted TV, my fists clenched, just waiting for his next cringe-inducing comment. To my right, Justin chatted up a familiar, thirty-something character actor while he browsed on his phone. To my left, Caroline was also on the edge of her seat while Samuel switched from topic to topic so quickly that neither of us had time to process before the next "but I don't want to talk about blah blah blah" spiel began. If Samuel bashed the *Water Sirens* movie one more time, Caroline would fly onto the stage, rip the wireless microphone from his collar, and say something like, "What Mr. Cabral means by 'schizo scene jumps' is the movie is a piece of film-making art and you should all see it in November."

"He's all over the place," Caroline grumbled. "We should have canceled."

"You think?" I snipped. I'd suggested as much to her after Samuel gave us a grunted greeting in the Roosevelt's lobby then prattled away while a bewildered Justin nodded, trying to keep up with his frenetic stories. "What did you think would happen when you overloaded his schedule, Caroline? He warned you he was stressed out."

She froze, then gave me an odd look. A chill ran through me, and I wondered if this was exactly what she thought would happen.

To someone who wasn't looking, Samuel Cabral was playful, witty, even a touch arrogant. He seemed to be perfectly at home giving an interview in front of a studio audience. But I was looking. I saw the way he bounced his knee and tugged his hair, brimming with nervous energy. The way his eyes flicked from Helen, to the camera operators, to the audience, then back to Helen. The way he impatiently twisted the arms of his chair.

"So you had a reader who actually named their daughter Cinsere?" Helen asked.

"Yes. I even asked her to spell it, because I thought I hadn't heard her correctly. So she said proudly, '*C–I–N–S–E–R–E*.'" *Bounce bounce bounce. Hair tug.* "She asked me to sign the front cover 'To Cinsere. Sincerely, Samuel Cabral.' I ended up writing something like 'May this bring you hours of happy reading,' because I couldn't make myself torment the poor child any further. The mother was utterly clueless."

Caroline's posh head dropped into her hand. "Cardinal rule: never bash fans, especially on national talk shows."

"We can still cancel the book signing." I sighed.

"No. We'll need it now for damage control. Make sure you get a shot of Samuel kissing a baby and float it on the Internet. See if anyone bites."

"Speaking of the Internet," Justin cut in, "check it out." He held out his smartphone so we could see the screen. Just as I'd feared, it was one of the photog's pictures from the airport last night. Samuel's hand rested on my rear, and from the camera angle, it looked like he was leering down my blouse. Or maybe he actually was leering down my blouse. Above the picture was a blurb: *Siren Writer Lures Back Neelie*. Seriously, even Juicy the Labrador could write a better headline.

"The picture and story is also on *Hollywood Days*," Justin continued, "and they confirmed the rumors. You two hottie patotties kinda went guns-a-blazing at the ol' kiss-and-greet. Very *sincere*ly, of course."

Caroline's head sank even further into her hands, and for a moment I thought she was blubbering, but she was only muttering, "I hate this job," over and over. I actually felt bad for her until I realized that, after Labor Day weekend, Caroline would be with her new author and it'd be my mess.

Samuel's eccentric behavior continued through the afternoon. At the massive two-story bookstore in Santa Ana, the three of us hustled to prep for the signing. Caroline walked me through protocol, everything from the positioning of *The Last Other* cardboard cutouts to handling chatty fans. Samuel paced aisle after aisle of books, lost in his mind, oblivious to the stares and pointed fingers. I couldn't tell if he was calming down or psyching up for a grueling five hours of signing his name ad infinitum.

"What do we do now?" I asked when lunch was eaten and Samuel settled behind a narrow table, stacks of *The Last Other* encroaching on his elbows. Already, a line of a hundred readers had queued, wrapping up the stairs and around the second-story railing.

"We multitask. Keep one eye on the signing table and one eye on your tablet. Try not to hover—it makes fans nervous and you don't need anyone upchucking on Samuel. But don't be so busy you fail to intervene when some crazed reader with thirty books and a blond wig asks Samuel to sign her breasts. It's happened more than once. Word to the wise—the crazies will be up front. This isn't Colorado—this is LA."

I actually gulped. Samuel peered at me over his shoulder and hit me with a charming smile, which only made me more nervous.

"You'll be fine," he mouthed. Then he turned that panty-dropping smile on a busty young thing in a blond wig and rock-climbing gear who'd camped outside the Barnes & Noble doors since three a.m., just to be first in line.

"Hey, Samuel, I'm Neelie," she crooned.

Mother cliff-hucker, I was in a parallel universe.

Caroline was right. For the first hour, nixie after squealing nixie presented themselves in elaborate costumes. One person even dressed up like an Other, though he resembled Swamp Thing more than a demon. Still, it was pretty darned impressive. After the more enthusiastic crowd filed through, the line calmed down and we fell into a routine. Eventually, I was able to do some crash-course browsing about mental illness.

I thought Samuel was in a sort of elevated mood related to bipolar disorder, but I had to be sure. So I found a list of mental disorders and swapped my girlfriend eye for a clinical eye. One by one, I checked them against Samuel's symptoms. I narrowed my list to: clinical depression, anxiety disorder, post-traumatic stress disorder, and bipolar disorder.

Clinical depression: this would have been the obvious answer, if not for Samuel's recent agitation and impulsiveness. I clicked on a blog that caught my eye. Seven pages of comments popped up and I read through them, each convincing me that Samuel had, at some point, suffered from clinical depression—especially during college and our brief marriage.

> "I didn't think anything of it at first, it was so gradual. I noticed that smiling felt wooden. It was harder to enjoy little stuff, like taking walks or going to a movie with my boyfriend." ~psy22kris

> "After a while, the stress started. I worried all the time. I was uncomfortable in my own skin, like I'd mess up at any second. Everything—work, relationships—what was the point?" ~tacoLibre

> "My body was heavy. I was tired. It was an effort to get up and go to work. Then it was an effort to come home. Then it was even harder to go to the grocery store or even fix food for the kids. I was drowning, suffocating under it all. And the worst part was, no one seemed to really notice or care." ~impossible_crumpets

Samuel himself told me how his sadness would come and go. What if he hadn't wanted to label the sadness? Naming it meant acknowledging it, and no one wants to admit they have a mental illness.

I bookmarked the forum, then moved on to the next: anxiety disorder. Apparently sixty percent of people with anxiety disorders also suffer from depression, which kind of shocked me. Stress, nervous ticks, insomnia. And panic attacks—definitely what happened at the wedding. He even had them as a child, before he grew out of his fear of heights. Which led to my next search item:

Post-traumatic stress disorder: well, young Samuel had certainly witnessed a traumatic event—his mother's suicide. Even with therapy, the effects of something so shocking could endure for years and years. Flashbacks, nightmares, guilt, insomnia, depression. But PTSD also brought out a lot of anger, and Samuel was rarely angry.

Finally I typed "bipolar disorder." This one was tricky to pin down, because it manifested in so many different ways. I had a hard time understanding how a person could swing from the depths of depression to manic euphoria. Then there were mixed episodes—both depression and mania occurring at the same time. I'd always thought of this disorder as a spectrum with mania on one end and depression on the other. But one doctor described it like a two-pronged tuning fork—"neutral" is one end, "depression and mania" is the other.

> "I hated my job, the pressure of responsibility to so many people. Rather than disappoint them, I'd end up avoiding them or even running away. I was fired six times until I got on meds." ~five19

> "When I was manic, I was a rockstar—I could seduce anyone. One time I walked into the bank and told the teller if she emptied my parents' bank account, I'd buy her an iPhone. I really believed she'd do it." ~purple_power

> "I get so addicted to the highs 'cause it's like a drug without the drugs. I'll hole up in my room for days and nights on end, writing music and books and poetry. Most of it's nonsense, but there's some really good stuff that comes out of it. But then a low hits, and I end up destroying half the writing because I despise everything I create." ~sacrecoeur82

Everything about bipolar disorder seemed to fit Samuel's symptoms, except for manic episodes. From what I'd seen, he'd never had manic delusions where he was slinging around Saturn or spending insane amounts of money. Granted, he'd lost a good chunk of memory that night in New York, but was it drug-related or was it mania? Also, I hadn't seen Samuel for seven years. For all I knew, he could've dangled from the Empire State Building a la King Kong, and Caro's crack-shot PR team covered it up.

*Hypo*mania, though...It was a milder form of mania. I studied Samuel's intense face, his hand enthusiastically scribbling in book after book—he was bolder today. Then there was the "horn-dog Samuel" of last night, which made me remember the story he'd told about the woman and the bar fight—his public intox charge.

The last forum contributor recommended several books. My phone was on the last five percent of its battery, so an e-book was out. Grabbing a receipt from my purse, I jotted down the titles and authors. I was in a bookstore, after all. But if anyone caught me buying *My Loved One is Manic Depressive* after seeing the "romantic" photos of us together (and in this crowd, that was a given), Samuel would be outed, he'd be furious, and I'd go down in history as the worst publicist ever. If I had a puppet, though...My eyes sought out Caroline. She was in the break area behind the floor-to-ceiling *The Last Other* banner. Good. I waved to Justin.

He moseyed over, hands jammed in his pockets. "Whaddya say, Kaye? Cawfee break?"

I forced a smile on my face. "Can you possibly be more New York, Justin?"

He grinned and smacked his gum. "Don't knock The Big Apple, baby."

"I need a favor." This was going to be awkward. "I have a friend who's looking for several books. Of course Boulder doesn't carry them, so she asked me to check while I was in LA."

"Did she look online?"

"She's doesn't believe in electricity," I lied.

"Gotcha. Want me to dig them up while you're babysitting?"

"Yes, please."

He patted my cheek and snatched the paper from between my fingers. "You hippie tree-huggers, you're so danged cute. Back in half an hour." I watched as he skipped away on his mission, feeling a slight twinge for lying to him. Fifteen minutes later, he trotted back triumphantly, swinging a green plastic bag.

"That was fast."

"I got two of the three—they don't carry *The Bipolar Disorder Survival Guide: What You and Your Family Need to Know*," he practically shouted, "but they can order it for you. Oh, and I picked up *My Horizontal Life*, but that one's for me."

I didn't know it was possible to actually feel blood drain from my face. But I was sure the light-headed, panicked sensation was every single capillary emptying into my stomach as Justin, clueless, held out that green plastic bag. I guess I wasn't the worst publicist in history—Justin could take top honors. My eyes darted to Samuel. He was still grinning and sliding books back to his readers, thank heavens. But when my gaze landed behind him, I saw Caroline, her wide eyes locked on me. She'd heard. Blood drained ever deeper and my entire body began to shudder as awareness hit me: Caroline already knew. Of *course* she knew—she'd been his closest companion through all of this, hadn't she? I felt Justin grasp my arm as my head began to spin.

"Kaye, are you okay? You're freaky pale."

"Cover for me," I mumbled as I pushed my way past the signing table and throngs of people. Oh crap, I was going to puke. I flew down a book aisle toward the restroom. Given the crowds, I'd probably have to yank some poor person off a toilet. But before I could reach the swinging door, two strong arms wrapped around my shoulders and yanked me into a hard chest.

"Kaye, what's wrong?" Samuel hissed in my ear, panic twisting the low tones of his voice.

"I swear on Tom's bell-bottoms, if you don't let me go, you'll regret it," I choked out. Inevitable bile rose in my throat and I tried to swallow it back. I struggled against Samuel's arms, but he held firm.

"Just tell me."

I opened my mouth to tell him, which was a horrible, horrible mistake.

Well, I had warned him.

"It wasn't that bad," Samuel insisted as Justin maneuvered the Bentley along Hollywood Boulevard later that night after dinner at Mastro's Steakhouse with the *Water Sirens* producers. "At least it wasn't a fan this time."

"Samuel, I yacked all over you in the middle of a crowded bookstore."

"Yeah, it was pretty hawt," Justin chimed in. "I tried to get my ex-girlfriend to do that for me, but she was having none of it."

"Shut up, Justin," Caroline and I both growled. We glanced at each other, then turned back to our respective windows. "I guess I'm oh-for-two at your book signings," I lamented. I cringed as I recalled the near-nixie riot I'd incited at the Boulder bookstore when

I'd inadvertently informed the crowd that Samuel had killed off their beloved heroine. Not my best moment.

"Well, I apologize," Samuel said for the twentieth time. "I shouldn't have tackled you. But, Kaye, I really thought you were going to faint. I've never seen you turn so white. Are you sure you're okay?"

"I'm fine." I sighed. "At least no one got a photo of it. Although, there are plenty of shots with you signing books for drooling women in your undershirt."

"And there was that one chick who tried to feel his nipples. Thank goodness the security guard intervened." Justin laughed. He was the only one who did laugh. Samuel returned to fidgeting with his cuff links, Caroline texted, and I was still caught up in a shocked stupor that even dinner with Hollywood big dogs hadn't shaken loose.

Mastro's was just what I'd expected. Over rib eyes and lettuce wedges, two suits demanded more of Samuel's time, wanting him to team with the cast—Indigo Kingsley included—in ten additional public appearances. I firmly reminded them if there were to be any future *Water Sirens* movies made, they'd need scripts. So unless they wanted their stellar cast of actors to ad-lib multi-million dollar sequels, Samuel's first priority was writing. Caroline gaped at me (was that a grudging respect I saw flicker over her face?) Justin high-fived me under the table, and Samuel…Samuel was as charming as ever, bright smile and clever words dazzling the producers so much, they were one step from casting *him* in their next movie.

Now, fifteen minutes later, he wouldn't even speak.

My phone vibrated with a new appointment from Caroline for Samuel's calendar:

Dr. Mili Gupta Thur., 10 a.m.

I peered at her from behind my hair. She caught my eyes, then turned back to her phone and texted something else:

**He might argue a little, but it's necessary.
He's seen her before.**

Curious, I Googled "Dr. Mili Gupta, LA." Her office listing came up—a psychiatrist in Beverly Hills.

All of a sudden, Samuel's illness was very real.

I caught up with Caroline outside her hotel room just before our conference call. "Why are you still helping him?" I asked, not bothering with small talk. "You ran him into the ground knowing full well he'd snap, and now you're scheduling his psychiatric appointments? I don't get it."

Cool eyes narrowed to slits. She tugged me into her suite and closed the door, then swiveled, her finger in my face. "Don't you dare blame this on me. Despite whatever your jealous little brain has cooked up, Kaye, I do care about Sam. I've wasted seven years caring for him. When his own parents thought they could cure him with warm fuzzies and Ibarra, I was the one who bailed him out of jail, got him hospitalized, and convinced him to return to New York. I've sacrificed friends and lovers. I've read dozens of books just like the ones you had Justin buy. But none of it mattered in the end, because he didn't care, did he? Bastard." She crossed the room to the wet bar in the corner and took out several mini-bottles of liquor and two shot glasses. Topping off each, she handed one to me, then threw hers down the hatch.

"You know, I swore off alcohol because he can't drink it with the meds he takes—he's never actually been an alcoholic. Just cocaine." She gave a cynical snort and poured herself another shot. "But he would have become one if I hadn't intervened. I kept telling myself that one day he'd come around and see how good I am for him. Seven years. *Salud.*"

So he was on meds. Whisky sloshed between my fingers as I warily set the full shot glass on the coffee table. Caroline threw back another.

"He appreciates what you've done for him," I said quietly. "I appreciate it, too. I can't imagine…"

She pressed the heel of her hand against her forehead and loosed a resigned sigh. "How long have you known about his disorder?" she asked.

"Only since yesterday," I hedged. I began to worry as she poured a third round. "Come on, we need to get to the conference call. If you toss back any more of those, you'll be slurring into the receiver."

"I canceled it. There's no way Samuel's up for it mentally." She tucked silky hair behind her ears. "And only yesterday? That's a lie. I believe you've known a lot longer, but you were too much of a timid little backwoods doe to face the big bad problems of the real world." I bristled, ready to spit out a denial. "Just shut up and think about it, Kaye."

So I thought... How long had I known Samuel was ill? It was true I'd witnessed some of Samuel's symptoms before we married, like the sadness and the stress. But I ignored them—we both did. My arms wrapped around my middle, an oh-so-familiar defense mechanism. We ignored them because we *had* been scared little children. Scared of losing our fairy tales, scared to lose each other. Maybe I had known Samuel was ill for a lot longer than I was willing to admit.

"How long have you known?" I fired back.

Caroline paused, tracing the rim of her empty shot glass. At last, she pulled her wallet out of her purse and removed a laminated card. On it were several lines of poetry:

> *Meaning of vacancy: The heart wants what it wants.*
> *Open me carefully.*
> *The binds are longing to be filled with your pages.*

"You've most likely never seen this," she said. "Samuel wrote it. It's not his best, but it spoke to me—the hopefulness. Most of his stuff from that time frame is much harsher. You should ask to see it sometime."

"It's... powerful?"

"My NYU professor thought so, too. Samuel asked if he could attend my poetry workshop to get a feel for the writing program. It was the first time he wanted to leave the brownstone since he joined Togsy and me in New York; he'd been so utterly miserable." Her thin face softened. "Samuel wrote this during an in-class exercise in less than two minutes. That very night, over a bottle of cognac, the professor read through his other work. Samuel's brilliance left him speechless. Within a week, NYU fast-tracked his admission and begged him to start that very semester before another program swooped in and stole him away. I may have mentioned to the department chair that Berkshire House was interested in his draft novel. I was a junior editor there, at the time." She met my gaze with catlike eyes so there would be no mistaking her great influence, even at the beginning of their careers.

"I know."

Caroline gestured to the card. "I'd always known he was a startlingly good writer. Unfortunately, brilliant minds are often ill minds.

I keep this card as a reminder of why I dedicated my life to his writing, especially when he's like this."

I handed the poem back to her. "Is he like this a lot?"

"No. He's very diligent. He only has episodes when he's stressed or requires a medication adjustment, and I can count those incidents on one hand. They all involved *you*."

Anger clawed its way up my chest as I really listened to what Caroline said. My face burned. "But it's stress from your insane schedule that's made him like this! Why would you do that to him? That's heartless—"

"Heartless? For years, all that stood between him and a jail cell was my 'insane schedule.' Samuel wants his name on the top of the *New York Times*' bestseller list and I can give it to him. It's the *only* thing he's let me give him." Her voice cracked tellingly. "No, I'm not heartless."

Caroline looked down at her manicured nails, then pointedly at me. "If you had a chance to win back the man you love above anyone else, if it wasn't too late, would you do it?"

"If it was best for him, then yes," I said, my brow furrowing. "But what does that—"

"Good," she interrupted, and threw back another shot. "That poem. For the longest time, I thought Samuel was just waiting for the right woman to step in and fill his books with her pages. But the heart wants what it wants, right? He already had the woman. He just didn't have her pages." She pitched the empty bottle in the garbage and gestured toward the door. I guessed that was my cue to exit. But before I could leave, her arm shot out and blocked me.

"I despised you for a long time, Kaye," she said softly, "even though I knew there was another side to this story. I saw you as the cause of Samuel's sadness, even before you divorced him. Even before you showed up at my door in New York, looking so lost and pathetic, I hated you." She met my eyes, and there was that grudging respect again. "But I think, maybe, you could be exactly what he needs. And the odd thing is, I don't hate you for it."

She sighed and lifted her shot glass in a toast. "Anyway, that's that."

Several days passed and, slowly, acceptance that Samuel had a mental illness seeped into my bones. I walked the well-known halls of my childhood, unlocking doors and peeking into rooms I never knew existed until now. With each new room I explored, I understood so much more about Samuel's actions. A too-thick wall here, a blocked-up fireplace there...I had no idea what this meant for us, except that everything was about to change.

But as the shock of finding new rooms wore off, other emotions rose. Grief. Guilt. Fear. And so much anger. Anger at myself for my blindness. Anger toward the Cabrals for locking me outside when Samuel needed me. Anger toward Samuel, too. At times, I was so furious, I was this close to kicking in Samuel's door and railing in his face: quit hiding things from me! Why did you and your family let me believe a pile of lies? Why are you still letting it tear us apart? Then I would breathe and mutter: open me carefully.

I asked Caroline if I could copy Samuel's poem. She dug into her purse and handed me the laminated card.

"Keep it. It's yours, anyway."

Samuel spent those days alone in his hotel room or running. Always running. Caroline and I rescheduled his appearances, telling our colleagues he had a bout of food poisoning. In reality, he'd gone into a creative explosion—I was somewhat acquainted with them, as he'd had them in college. I was sure when he emerged he'd have written something heart-rending and beautiful—yet another tragedy of the beast. I checked on him every few hours to make sure he was shaving, sleeping, eating the room service food I ordered. He'd gaze up at me with shame-filled eyes. My chest tightened each time I passed him. I'd pause and give his shoulder a squeeze. Samuel would place his hand over mine and draw it to his lips. Then it was back to avoidant eyes and fidgeting, flying fingers.

When I wasn't with Samuel, I read mental health books. Caught up on my TrilbyJones projects. Planned the Lyons benefit concert. I paid a visit to Samuel's Aunt Lucia and Uncle Carlos (Sofia's family in Mission Viejo), apologizing profusely that he was too sick to see them.

"You can make it up with a drive along the coast in that gorgeous car," *Tía* Lucia said, her pleasant face so like Sofia's. Of course, Lucia passed along Samuel's "food poisoning" news to Sofia and made her worry. But honestly, I was so incensed with my surrogate *madre*, I didn't care.

I also toured LA with Justin. He was a breath of fresh air, with thumbs ups and goofy grins that would melt the PBR-soaked heart of any hipster.

"Did you know the Santa Monica Pier is celebrating its one-hundredth anniversary?" I read from my tour book as we sauntered along wooden planks crusted with sea salt, past caricature artists and whimsical amusement rides.

"Uh, yeah. If you'd get your head out of that book and actually look at the pier, you'd see banners all over the place that say '100 Years of Summer Fun.'"

"Right." I tossed the book in my beach bag and adjusted the straps of my sundress. The Pacific Ocean was warm and sunny. If I closed my eyes, the roar of surf sounded like strong winds cutting over my mountains. I felt a pang of homesickness, and this time it showed.

Justin tweaked my floppy straw hat, his eyes sparking. "You are a beautiful woman, Kaye. I mean it." I ducked my head, taking a great deal of interest in my snow cone.

"Justin…"

"If I were a straight man, I'd do my best to steal you from Cabral right now. You're too pretty to go to waste."

I smiled, not caring that my teeth and tongue were stained pink by cherry syrup. "Thank you for showing me LA."

"He'll come around," he said kindly.

On Thursday, Samuel went to his doctor's appointment with Caroline and flipping left me behind. While the man who supposedly loved me sat in a mental health specialist's office with another woman supporting him, I took out my fear and fury on a rock-climbing wall.

What if something bad has happened?

He's safe at the doctor's office.

He should have asked me to go instead of Caroline. (Tighten your grip on the belay rope…Hoist…)

If you'd asked to go along, he would have said yes. He loves you.

If he loves me, why won't he trust me? (Wedge your foot onto the notch…steady…)

He trusts you. He doesn't trust himself.

But he's never actually said "I love you" since he returned, has he? (Hoist…strain for the next notch, now hold…breathe…)

No, he hasn't. But neither have you.

How can I possibly risk telling him? (Careful...you don't need any more broken bones.) He's the one keeping secrets, not me.

He's a man, Kaye. He's scared to tell you because he doesn't want to seem weak. Remember, on your camping trip, you said you weren't strong enough to be with someone who is mentally ill. What was his reaction?

He was shaken, badly.

He doesn't want to burden you...not seven years ago, not now. It may not be right, but that's how he is.

True. (Wedge your foot again...) Yet he asked me to put my career on the line for him without telling me his secrets. Isn't that burdening me?

His judgment is clouded.

That's another thing—how long has his judgment been clouded? Since April? (Tighten your grip on the rope...Hoist...) What if he comes back from the doctor completely normal and he realizes he doesn't really want me back?

He loves you.

Which he, though?

With an angry cry, I sobbed against the wall, just once. I clung to the notch under my fingers to steady my teetering body. Then I took a deep, determined breath, and continued upward.

When I returned to the Roosevelt Hotel after my climb, sweaty and aching from exertion, I found a happy Samuel. He beamed at me, exuberant and carefree, and I didn't know whether the doctor had stuck him with pure sunshine or if this was yet another symptom.

"How was your 'studio meeting?'" I asked acidly.

Samuel's eyes narrowed thoughtfully and there was that unnerving look, as if he could see right through me. "Productive. I think we got to the bottom of some things."

"You and Caroline?"

"No, I went by myself. I took a cab."

"Oh." Flaming monkey. I'd spent the entire morning freaking out over Caroline for nothing. "I would have come with you, you know."

"You wanted to go?"

I nodded.

His entire face unclouded again and his mouth curled. "Then come with me now." He grabbed my hand and pulled me toward the elevators.

"Where are we going?"

"It's a surprise."

I pulled back and gestured to my Spandex shorts and ponytail. "Er, Samuel, I'm a sweaty mess."

"I don't care. Unless…" He halted and frowned. "Did you have plans with Justin instead?" His voice carried that same smidge of jealousy I heard when he spoke of Hector, and I knew to tread carefully.

I poked his shoulder. "Nope. I'm all yours."

He grinned. I let him lead me to the elevators, through the hotel, and out to the Bentley rental. But when he began to climb into the driver's seat, I acted quickly. If he drove in his current mood, we'd be dodging highway traffic at ninety miles an hour.

"Can I drive?" I begged. "I'm loving the Bentley, and I probably won't get the chance to drive it again."

Samuel grandly stepped back and held the door open for me. I slid in and prayed I wouldn't knock off someone's side mirror.

We cruised south on Interstate Five, back toward Santa Ana. The top was down, and the wind noise made conversation impossible. Still, Samuel babbled on and on about the dashboard features—I couldn't hear what he was saying, but he pointed to different buttons.

"Where are we going?" I shouted over the roar.

"Newport Beach!"

My mouth fell open, then snapped shut as wind rattled my cheeks. "That's all the way to Mission Viejo! Your aunt will kill you for not visiting!"

"What?"

"*Tía* Lucia!"

His eyes widened. "Shit! I should see her!"

"Maybe next time!" I smiled at him and kept my eyes locked on the road, hoping he wouldn't see pity there.

An hour later, as we exited the interstate, I asked him where I needed to go. His lips quirked and he turned to me, handsome and wind-ruffled, eyes shielded by sunglasses.

"I'm buying you a Bentley."

Sweet mother of Tom. I slammed the breaks before I ran a stoplight. "No! Oh no, no, no, no, no!"

"Come on, Kaye. Let me do this for you as an apology for being such a beast last week, and to say thank you for all the crap you've put up with. I don't want to lose you over this, I'm so goddamned petrified you'll leave me when I love you so much, so I was thinking, instead of flying back to Denver for Rocky Mountain Folks next week, we could get away with several extra days of vacation since everyone believes I have food poisoning, and road trip. Think of all the amazing views! Vegas, the Grand Canyon, the mountains, we could even stop along Route 66 at one of those old kitschy diners, and we could do Leadville again, that old West saloon? It's supposed to be haunted…"

I don't know how I held back the tears. My knuckles whitened against the steering wheel. *No, please don't tell me you love me. Not like this, not now.* His face was bright and innocent and happy, and it made me want to weep.

"Why are we going all the way to Newport Beach for a car?" I asked, swallowing down the lump in my throat. He went on about how he'd seen a television spot for a Bentley dealership that was having a back-to-school sale (only in Orange County, I swear). I was so caught up in my thoughts, when he placed his hand on mine briefly, it freaked me out.

"Hands off!" I screeched, grinding the steering wheel, and he flinched away, remorse spilling off of him in torrents.

Then I felt guilty, so…I let him buy me a car. Not a Bentley. At the dealership, I talked Samuel down from his luxurious aspirations to a used BMW convertible for twenty-five thousand. (The salesman, of course, was no help. I paid the guy three hundred dollars to shut his wheel-dealing trap and follow us to the Roosevelt in the BMW.) Whenever Samuel came down from this episode, I'd give him the car and he could either sell it or keep it in Boulder to use when he moved. *If he moved.*

I also had to convince him not to buy a Bentley for Caroline and Justin. "You can take them out to a nice restaurant when we get to New York, Samuel. They don't need cars as thank you presents."

Whatever Dr. Gupta gave Samuel helped. After he went on his car-buying frenzy (why, oh why, hadn't Justin gushed over a candy bar instead of a Bentley?), his moods finally began to level out. Just in time, too. I'd been two digits away from calling Alonso and Sofia, I'd been so panicked. It wouldn't have been a polite conversation.

Over the next couple of days, the wildness left his eyes and the nervous energy drained from his body. He ventured out for meals. Finished his restless writing. Ran in the morning instead of at night. I watched him closely until I was sure he was stable enough to have the conversation chomping at our ankles.

My timing was precise—five forty a.m. I'd only sat in the hotel hallway for six minutes, clad in running shorts, tank top, and sneakers, when Samuel's door opened and he appeared, also in shorts and sneakers.

"What are you doing on the floor, Firecracker?" He crouched next to me. His fingers, at last, were fidget-free.

"I want to join you. You'll have to bear with me; I'm not very fast."

He smiled—not a leer, not odd and over-bright. It was gentle, genuine. "I'd love it."

Our soles slapped the pavement as we jogged along a quiet, low-lit Hollywood Boulevard. It was too early for morning rush hour, too late for party crowds. The sky was hazy and pink as the sun peeked between buildings. The air was already sticky—it would be hot today.

Samuel slowed his pace considerably for me, so he wasn't even breathless. Even so, I lagged (running was not my sport). I watched Samuel's muscular calves, tight bottom, and beautiful back move beneath his sweaty T-shirt in rhythm to his strides. He knew I was ogling, but didn't seem to mind.

"How is your…next book chapter…coming along?" I huffed.

"Not so well. I think you know that." His eyes darted down to me, then forward again.

"Perhaps I can help."

Samuel said nothing for several minutes. We rounded a corner and he halted, leaning against a bus stop bench. "I deleted it."

"All of it?" I collapsed onto the bench, stunned.

"Most of it."

"But you've been writing for a week!"

He razed me with agonized blue eyes. "It was sixty pages of nonsense, Kaye—so bad, it was the first time I've ever deleted my

141

work. I loathed every single word. The only thing that's left is one flipping page." His fingers wove into his damp hair and tugged. He looked so sad, and the destruction of his words hit me harder than anything else in this messy ordeal.

Tears pooled in my eyes and I wiped them away before they spilled over. "Can I read the page?"

He didn't answer, only hung his head. So I whipped out the big guns. I motioned for him to sit next to me. He did, careful to leave a foot of space between us. Reaching into my zip pocket, I removed a folded sheet of paper and pressed it against his chest. Samuel opened it with trembling hands.

"Our friendship vows," he said, air whooshing from his lungs. "I thought this might be a resignation letter."

"I already told you, I'm in this. But I want to remind you of these vows, because it's easy to forget them." I insinuated myself under his sweaty arm. "First, I will make myself available when you are down, as well as happy. I will provide emotional and physical warmth."

"Kaye, you didn't have the whole story when we wrote those."

"I'm not finished. I will fight for you and your reputation. Which apparently is going to be a much bigger job than I originally thought, but it's manageable."

"Firecracker—"

"I will always want the best for you," I continued. "I will be honest and truthful, even when the truth is difficult. I'm going to be truthful now, Samuel."

He buried his face in my hair, then kissed the top of my head. "Go on," he said quietly.

"I know you've kept things from me—important things. I'm asking you for honesty. Because without it, this—" I motioned between us "—doesn't stand a chance."

His jaw shifted against my head as he weighed his options. Then, coming to a decision, he jerked me to my feet. "Let's grab coffee to-go and walk back to the hotel, all right? We can talk there. Too many people..." Minutes later, we strode along Hollywood Boulevard, coffee cups and croissants in hand.

"Do you know why I wanted to do the Q-and-As with you?" he asked.

"Because we needed time to sort through our emotions." I took a gulp of coffee, wincing as it burned my throat.

"Yes, but there's more. I was buying time."

"Why?" I studied his face as we walked, not paying attention to the sidewalk ahead. Samuel casually tugged me to his side before I plowed into a fire hydrant.

"I was afraid," he said simply. "I wanted to put off this conversation as long as possible, but it's past time, isn't it? Weeks ago, you asked me why I never came back."

"You told me it was a long story and you weren't ready to fill me in yet. Which was kind of a cop out."

"Well, it *is* a long story." He shrugged, then saw the irritated set of my jaw. "Are you very angry?"

"'Angry' is an understatement. But I still want you to tell me."

We made our way through the Roosevelt lobby bustling with suitcase-laden porters and people checking out, toward the elevators. On our way up, he wrapped an arm around my waist and tenderly kissed my shoulder, just once. I saw his face in the brassy reflection of the sliding doors—it was twisted with fear, as if he couldn't bear to release me once the doors opened. But they did open, he did release me, and I did ask my question (in a bumbling sort of way).

"Why did you stay away from me, Samuel?" I asked softly. "I'm ninety-nine percent certain I know why, especially after the past week. I can't believe I didn't see it. Even now, I'm not entirely sure I wasn't reading more into your...your behavior. Maybe I'm completely paranoid and Caroline was messing with my head. But, I think—"

"Kaye," he said fervently. "You *know* me, so well. Don't doubt yourself." He smoothed several sweaty strands from my forehead and pressed his lips there. I tilted my face to capture his lips, but he backed away, his hand still on my face. Finally, he swiped his key and ushered me into his room.

"Wait here, please," he murmured. I plopped onto a plush couch while he disappeared into his bedroom. When he emerged, he held three things: his laptop and two orange prescription bottles. On the laptop screen was an electronic document, and I recognized the working title for his draft novel.

"Is that the page you didn't delete?"

"Yes. It's the only page that had a hint of sanity, which says a lot about those other sixty pages." He chuckled, but it sounded forced. "I wrote it for you, after...after I treated you so badly your first night in LA." That night wasn't all his fault, but that was a discussion for another time. "It was a half-crazed attempt to explain how much I treasure you, even when I'm slipping into lows and highs. I know it's bizarre and convoluted—"

"It will be beautiful to read. Thank you." I rested an open palm on his knee. "And the prescriptions?"

He cautiously put them in my hand. I turned the bottles to read the labels. "Zoloft?"

"It's sertraline—a low-dose antidepressant," he explained, his voice quaking. "And the other is valproic acid."

"Depakote." My eyes fluttered closed, the weight of reality heavy in my hand. "A mood stabilizer?"

"Yes," he rasped. "For my bipolar disorder—Bipolar II, to be exact. Money isn't the only thing I inherited from my mother."

My eyes held his and I simply nodded. I wasn't sure what to say. I didn't know much about Bipolar II, and "I'm sorry" wasn't enough. Then I set the bottles down, took the laptop, and began to read the only page to survive destruction:

> **We try to watch for the slip. It sidles up – a warship creeching unaware over planks – and bombards our sides...**

Chapter 8
LOG BOOK

As explorers, skydivers will often journal about their experiences and achievements to document them for posterity.

"Don't you think it would be fun to be married by Elvis at a chapel?"

"We're not driving up to Vegas, Kaye."

"I'm not suggesting we do it. I just think it would be unique."

"It's not unique, it's cliché."

"Boo to you. Who doesn't love Elvis?"

"Pretty sure Jaime Guzman doesn't. She does, however, love retainer fees from quickie divorces which result from quickie marriages."

"Too rash, right?" I bit my lip and tried not to feel rejected—we'd just been shooting the breeze with the Vegas wedding talk. But I'd also been gauging the air to see where we stood after the storms of LA, and I think Samuel understood that.

"Hey. Don't stress about tomorrow, okay? Just focus on today." His eyes crinkled. "Besides, Las Vegas is probably the worst place you can take someone in the throes of a manic episode," he teased, breaking the tension. "If I didn't go broke at the high stakes table, I'd end up hitched to a red-clawed cougar named Oona."

I threw back my head and laughed.

We pulled off of old Route 66 for a picnic west of Flagstaff. The low rumbles of the desert wind bewitched my ears and I breathed deeply, and stretched.

We'd risen early this morning and hit the road in his new BMW convertible, journeying at a lazy pace despite the rush of summer travelers. Even though he was still tired from his episode, he'd done most of the driving while I played deejay with his iPod. After I put "The Crying Game" on loop he revoked my deejay license. I primly pointed out that he was the one with Boy George on his playlist. "Not for long," he muttered.

Even though Samuel hatched the road trip idea during a hypomanic episode, it turned out to be exactly what we needed. What better way to get everything out in the open than being belted in a bimmer together for three solid days? Over breakfast in San Bernadino, we realized that the only recent photos we had of us together were from our skydiving excursion and Danita's wedding. So we bought an old school camera and made up for lost time, taking pictures of ourselves, the sun-bleached terrain, rusted motel signs and wide blue sky.

Stepping out of the car, I put my hand to my forehead and scanned the horizon like a trail-weary Sacagawea. I loved spending time with Samuel, but really, I'd never seen anyone fret over a squeaky dashboard quite like him. I snapped several photos of highway, curving for miles until it vanished into an azure haze. Then I turned the camera on my fellow road warrior, catching him mid-stretch, a strip of skin and boxers exposed beneath his tee. Mmmm, Samuel. Sacagawea who?

"Are you ready for that talk?" he asked. Removing his sunglasses, he waved them in front of my glazed eyes.

"Um, sure." I blinked rapidly. We spread a blanket and plopped down, my eyes still skimming over his muscled torso. He dug the cooler out of the trunk and placed it on the blanket.

"Ah...when did you first find out you were bipolar?"

"You mean when did I find out I *have* bipolar disorder," he corrected. "I was diagnosed not long after our divorce. Before that, doctors believed it was clinical depression complicated by anxiety."

"*Am* bipolar, *have* bipolar—is it that much of a difference?"

"I'm not bipolar. I'm *Samuel*." He smirked. "Being something and having something are very different, yes. I don't say you *are* curly hair because you *have* curly hair. Which is wonderfully soft, by the way." He reached for one of my waves.

"Point taken." I smeared peanut butter over a slice of bread, then dabbed a bit on Samuel's nose.

Yesterday, after reading his few paragraphs about the ups and downs of his disorder, my first reaction was to crawl into his lap and hold him, then violently shake him for being so stupidly self-sacrificing. I cried for a solid hour, my cheek against his knees. He remained silent the entire time, allowing me my grief, sometimes stroking my hair. I choked and trembled and got snot on his shorts. And then the tears faded, leaving me spent. I rolled my shoulders in the shower, unwinding until I could go five minutes without tears. When I returned to his suite, wet hair dripping over my shoulders, he was asleep.

He slept for hours while Caroline, Justin, and I haggled with talk shows and journalists to make up for Samuel's missed commitments. In the end, we appeased them with exclusives at an upcoming *Water Sirens* event in New York. They'd sell their mothers for a chance to cover Samuel and Indigo's first public appearance together since their "split."

Like cave creatures, we squinted against the sun when we emerged from the Roosevelt to wish Caroline good luck with her new author. I watched with blazing eyes as Caroline pressed her cheek to Samuel's and whispered her good-byes. When she walked out the door, I counted each step until she rounded the corner and left our lives. Step…step…step…gone.

Last night, as Samuel softly kissed me good night, he peered down at me with a curious face.

"Why aren't you angrier?" he asked.

Was I angry? I didn't feel angry. I wrapped my arms around a throw pillow. "Being angry doesn't solve anything," I concluded.

"There's such a thing as fair anger, Kaye. You can have that toward me and I'd deserve it."

"If I don't feel anger toward you, I don't feel it. Can I ask you something, though?"

"Anything."

"Were you ever going to tell me the truth?"

He toyed with a pillow tassel, pensive. "Storytelling has always been the way I express my thoughts." Yes, I knew this. "In my mind, I had this grand plan laid out. I'd write a book from childhood to the aftermath of our divorce as a way to explain my illness to you. I titled it after something you could relate to—the highs and crashes you experience in that Colorado whitewater. Then, after you had read it, you'd know everything and we could both move on."

"How very logical."

"I'm a man, Kaye—I'm hard-wired to fix and protect. Of course it blew up in my face. Once you were back in my life, I should have told you right away instead of waiting to finish our book."

"It's not too late, Samuel. You have an entire road trip to tell me your secrets. Please, help me to trust you again…"

So now, on the road to Planet Bluegrass, he was sharing his story—the entire story.

Samuel split an apple with a paring knife and gave me half. "Bipolar II is heavy on the depression, light on the mania."

"Hypomania."

His eyebrows shot up. "You've done your research." He leaned against the car tire, crossing his long legs. "I've never had a full-blown manic episode, though the night you found me in New York and my arrest in Raleigh are arguably borderline. The cocaine intensified them. That, and I was on strong antidepressants when I left for Raleigh with Caroline. High doses of antidepressants also exacerbate manic episodes."

"But you're taking antidepressants now."

"Just a low dose. Not enough to cause problems."

I frowned. "When were you diagnosed with depression? Surely not while we lived in Boulder?"

"No. My father had his suspicions when he found me in New York, but I wasn't diagnosed until Christmas."

"Alonso and Sofia conveniently didn't mention that. Son-of-a—" I mumbled.

Samuel flinched. "I asked them not to. Actually, I forced them—I held a figurative gun to my head."

"You threatened to *kill* yourself if they told me you were depressed? That's kind of extreme."

"Not exactly," he sighed. "I'm not being very clear, am I?" He drummed his fingers, then snapped. "Did you know in the Middle Ages, people believed in fate? That they had no control over their futures?"

"Is that supposed to be a segue?"

"Shush, you. So if your life was fated to suck and you couldn't do anything about it, you might as well accept it. For the longest time, I believed the same thing—I was going to end up self-destructing exactly like my mother, and there wasn't a thing I could do. It started as a black thought here, a disappointment there. When I went to college, those feelings grew heavier. I didn't know what the heck was going on in my mind or where this blackness came from, but I was desperate to maintain some shred of control. Thus, the drug use."

"Self-medicating."

"Yes." He told me how once he left for New York, he holed up in his brownstone bedroom, did lines, and wrote. Finally, Togsy had enough of his "moping" and made it his mission to get him high and laid. He leaned forward. "That day was the first time I felt a shift in my head. After months of hopelessness, I began to feel euphoric. Powerful. Angry. I actually looked forward to Togsy's party. I'd already messed up my life, so why not thoroughly destroy my soul? Very emo—I was three bucks short for black hair dye at the emporium." He gave a humorless laugh. "As fate would have it, you decided to fly to New York and visit the very night I had my first brush with mania."

I watched his hands clench and noticed they were trembling—either residual symptoms of his episode, or just plain nerves.

"Is the mania why you can't remember what happened?"

"Yes. It's only happened twice, though, in New York and Raleigh. Those memories are comparable to peering through a frosted window—I can see shapes and colors, but nothing's clear. My doctors believe the coke had something to do with it." He stilled his hands, but then his knees started jiggling. "You may have noticed I'm also a randy bastard during hypomanic episodes."

"Just a little."

"I am so very sorry for that, Kaye. You deserve better."

"Let me decide who I deserve." Dang it, his hands were shaking again. I buttered another slice of bread and handed it to him, something to keep them busy.

"When my father found me, I was frantically running up and down the street, rambling about my mother and begging him to send you home before I hurt you. He thought I was having some sort of drug-induced anxiety attack." He winced. "I think he was afraid I would off myself, or even you."

"Would you have?"

Blue eyes flared. "You, never. Myself…I'm not sure. But given my birth parents' suicides, can you blame him for believing I might?" Samuel explained how Alonso relented and sent me home. I went back to Lyons, and Samuel went to detox. As the drugs left his system and he visited a therapist, he started to feel like himself again, even hopeful. During this time, Caroline scored his first book deal with Berkshire House.

"Once I was 'cured,' I had these grand plans of sweeping back to Boulder and asking you to forgive me."

It was my turn to wince. "I bet all of you were really ticked when you received the divorce papers."

I'd hit the mark, but he didn't validate it. "I was angrier at myself. Rationally, I knew why you did it. Toss my cruel little good-bye note into the equation, and what choice did you have? I was so sure I knew what was best for you, but now I see how condescending it was. I don't need to be a perfect man—just your man." Samuel looked at me so hopefully, so nervously. "You're too far away. May I hold you?"

"Not yet," I murmured, absently digging seeds from an apple slice. "So you were planning to return to me, but you had a setback."

"The blackness returned. It was so bad, there was no doubt I was clinically depressed."

"What was it like?"

"Just as I described in my story—like I was imprisoned on the very bottom of the ocean, trapped under thousands of years of sediment buildup." His voice went flat. "I couldn't eat, couldn't sleep, couldn't breathe. I was afraid to write because I'd fail. Each morning I woke, I was heavy with the knowledge that I had to get through another day. And love?" He snorted cynically. "The connection was bad—I couldn't hear love for all the static, and I couldn't speak it because the line was dead. That's why I agreed to the divorce."

Samuel's haggard face flashed through my memory. "I remember how horrible you looked in Jaime's office."

"Our marriage was over, Kaye. My only consolation was that I freed you to be happy again. Seeing how heartbroken you were simply reinforced my belief that you were better off without me."

"I wish I'd known."

I wondered if our divorce also split the other Cabral marriage down the middle: Sofia sided with me, and Alonso, with Samuel. But, more than ever, the fact they'd kept me out of the loop while Samuel suffered was biting. And even more painful was this: I rarely asked how Samuel was. If ever. Heated tears pricked the corners of my eyes. I needed to move again. Grabbing Samuel's hands, I tugged him to his feet. "Come on. Let's get to Flagstaff before sunset."

We didn't return to Samuel's story until we'd safely climbed the hills carrying us up to Flagstaff, through lush ponderosa forests. After dropping our bags at the quaint bed and breakfast Samuel had selected, we wandered into town.

It felt like home. The mountains here were arid, where spots of green mingled with red rock plateaus below our inn balcony. Flagstaff itself was an Old West timber town and, if we weren't leaving at the flipping crack of dawn to visit the Grand Canyon, I would have explored more. Instead, Samuel and I took a quick jaunt along the main stretch for dinner before making our way back to the inn.

Knowledge of the Cabrals' seven-year silence ate at my peace. I envisioned Alonso villainously twirling a handlebar mustache, Sofia sporting a stove-pipe hat, and Danita leering at me with rope and two miles of railroad track.

"Okay," I said, my fingers skimming a hedgerow. "From where I'm sitting, it looks like your family either hated my guts or thought I was so incompetent, I couldn't be there for my own husband."

Samuel pushed up the brim of his ball cap and kissed my forehead, and my hackles smoothed. "I should tell you that Danita has only known since May. She found my meds in my bathroom cabinet and confronted me right before her bridal shower, of all times." Ah, that would explain her dourness during hors d'oeuvres. "And Angel knew something was wrong, though he never understood the extent."

I felt relieved that Danita hadn't been hiding this from me for seven years. But wow, no wonder she'd been angry with her brother.

Samuel continued. "They were walking a tightrope, trying not to upset the tentative balance and send me tumbling, but still be there for you. It didn't help that I threatened to disappear into Mexico if they called you — that's what I meant by holding a gun to my head. In the end, my parents were scared and went into protective lockdown mode."

"But they had seven years to tell me, Samuel. They could have said something after you got back on your feet."

"What would be the point? Everyone believed you were doing well — happy, even, so why drag you into my drama?"

I wanted to argue, but we were at an impasse. "So you were going to run away to Mexico, but Caroline held your publishing contract over your head. You followed her to Raleigh instead, and were arrested there. What happened?"

He explained how he'd fallen back into cocaine and slipped into another episode. The night of his arrest, the cops found him at two a.m., sprawled under a row of pear trees, no coat, reeking of vodka and fiddling with the drug paraphernalia scattered over his stomach. He told them he was counting tree branches. They, of course, tossed him in a holding pen with ten puking frat boys until Caro bailed him out. "Not a shining moment," he professed. "Part of my sentence was hospitalization — did you know this?"

"Caroline told me." I struggled to hide my hurt, but he must have read it in my face anyway.

"Kaye, please don't think Caroline means more to me because she knew. This may sound cruel, but I didn't care if she left me because of it. I do care, though, about losing you again." He began to walk. "The judge agreed to treatment in New York rather than North Carolina. I don't need to tell you how I felt about discovering I had the same illness which most likely killed my mother."

"The whole fate thing."

He nodded. "I drifted, fluctuating between bewilderment and anger — bewilderment that I actually had bipolar disorder, and anger that I couldn't fix it. I used my writing to channel a lot of the anger. I also used it to escape into a fairy-tale life where you and I were together, where I hadn't cut off my friends and family."

"That's very sad," I murmured.

"It was a way to cope." He explained how he struggled to hide his illness and live a normal life. He established a routine. Finished his degree. Furthered his career. Stayed on his meds. Alonso and

Sofia returned to Lyons, and he left bustling lower Manhattan for the quieter Fort Tryon neighborhood.

"What made you decide to return at Thanksgiving, two years ago?" I asked.

"I missed you. And I'd been doing well, so I thought I was permanently healthy. In reality, I was slipping again. Several episodes swiftly followed—a lot of *The Last Other* was written during that time. It was a mess to edit, chock-full of what Caro calls 'self-loathing metaphorical prose garbage.' The same kind of stuff I deleted a few days ago."

"So that's why she thinks I cause your episodes. Between our divorce and Thanksgiving—"

Samuel halted and grabbed my elbow, staring down at me with cold-sober eyes. "Caro is absolutely wrong. *Stress* causes my episodes, not you. *Never* you, Kaye. If we're going to be together, you must understand this." He gave my elbow a gentle squeeze, then dropped his hand.

Ugh, manipulative woman. "So why now and not two years ago?" I asked. "What's different? Do you feel you're 'permanently healthy'?"

He shook his head. "No such thing. Most days I'm healthy, other days I'm not, and it will be this way for the rest of my life. The difference is this: you asked for answers. You want me in your life. I'm hard-pressed to refuse you." He smiled down at me.

I lovingly traced his jawline with my index finger, and stood on my toes to place a lingering kiss on his lips. Then I glanced at my watch—seven o'clock. The sun would set soon, and I wanted to watch it ignite the mountains from our inn balcony.

"Are you ready to go?" Samuel asked. The edge of his pinkie brushed mine; he was unsure whether he should hold my hand.

I tangled my fingers with his.

Later that evening, Samuel and I reclined together on the patio's chaise longue, he with his Moleskine notebook and me with the sunset. A yellow pool of porch light circled us, growing stronger as the day dimmed. He leaned against me, shirtless back pressing into my stomach despite the cool mountain breeze. His long, jean-clad legs were bent so he could write against them. My arm rested across his sternum, claiming him. Every now and then, I'd run my hand over the soft hair of his chest and feel him tense as he wrote. He'd turn his face and kiss the crook of my elbow, then go back to his script writing.

"Why is it that serious writers use Moleskine notebooks?" I asked. "Is it a status thing? Or do you all want to be Bruce Chatwin and journal about chasing mammoth mummies in Patagonia?"

"Every serious writer must use a Moleskine, Kaye. Don't you know that?" Samuel bantered. "Really, I just like them because the elastic band keeps loose notes from flying away when I'm outside. See?" He snapped the band.

"That's not very romantic."

"It's practical."

"May I read it?"

He thoughtfully scratched one of his longish sideburns (Samuel needed a haircut), then handed me the notebook. I scanned his streams of thoughts and to my relief, they were completely sane. Flipping through the notebook, I settled on a passage:

> *I should tell you, eager hijo,*
> *says Miss America,*
> *I slept and kicked you off the bed.*
> *I didn't mean to.*
> *Even then I saw you flail*
> *at seventeen, playing*
> *grown up with a green heart.*
> *Unlike me, you meant to.*

Samuel peered over my hands to see what I read, and chuckled in embarrassment. "A little bad poetry to soothe the flagellant's soul."

"Hmmm. No, there's wisdom in it. Sofia said something similar—that we shouldn't get caught up in the American Dream, two-point-five kids and a minivan, because what works for some doesn't work for others. Now I understand what she meant. You and me—we make each other happy, don't we? As long as we don't fall for the world's version of happiness."

Samuel's entire body stiffened, and I realized I'd struck a nerve. He sat up. "Kaye, there's something else you should know." He tugged his hair, and I knew whatever came out of his mouth would be bad. "I...well...can't have children. Before we continue down this path, I want you to really mull over what this means to you."

"Oh." Talk about a smack upside the head. I sputtered for several seconds before finding my tongue. "When—and *how*—did you find out?"

"I, um…" Splotches of red climbed his neck. "It was a personal decision, not long after I was diagnosed with bipolar disorder. With my family history and reckless behavior, I had a…you know."

"The family jewels snipped? So I guess that means I can go off the pill. Sweet."

Samuel's mouth fell open. "Kaye, be serious."

"Sorry." My fingers danced across his chest. "Those are reversible, right?"

"It's not an option. I'm sorry."

"Down the road, if things go well for us, would you ever consider other options, like adoption?"

"Truthfully, I think I would be a horrible father. Imagine what Mommy tells the kids when Daddy buys them Bentleys on a whim." He ducked his head. "Ah, that's presumptuous of me, isn't it?"

My heart did a back handspring. "It's honest. You know I don't want anyone but you. If it comes down to being with you or marrying a baby-daddy, I'll choose you."

A world of tension slipped from his shoulders and he relaxed into my body. "My father said you'd miss out on life if you gave up children for me."

"While I appreciate Alonso's concern, I'm not him."

"You should at least think about this, Kaye. You say this now, but a few years down the road, when your friends are pregnant and planning baby showers, you might feel differently."

"Then we can talk options two years down the road, together. Because right now, I still have to survive this publicity tour of yours until your movie release."

"That's my other concern." His face turned to the mountains and he sighed. "Having a public life versus a private life. People will ask you questions, take your picture, and tell malicious lies about you, at least until I stop publishing and step out of the public eye."

"They do that now." I kissed his protests. "Samuel, I want you. If it means dealing with tons of baggage, so be it. I'm not naïve—I know there will be rough times. But I've lived with the consequences of throwing in the towel, and losing you is too agonizing." I pressed my hand over his heart, as if I were stemming my own pain. "So, any more secrets I should know?"

"Yes. When I left for college the first time, I stole a pair of your panties."

"Is that it?"

I felt him smile against my arm. "After seeing those whitewater rafting photos in Paddler's, I have this fantasy where I peel that snug wet suit from your body and then ravage you in an inflatable duckie."

I choked on air. "Frickin' A, Cabral!"

"What?" He glanced up and winked at my wide-eyed lemur face.

As the last of Samuel's secrets fell away (even the perverted ones), I thought, perhaps, our window had returned. It wasn't startling, or nerve-racking...it was peaceful. I also surmised that I wouldn't freeze up should he take me to bed. There was a new level of trust between us that hadn't existed before. While we weren't gurus, we'd *never* been this honest with each other, and it was glorious.

Ten minutes later, Samuel's hand stilled against his notebook and his breath grew slow and even. Puffs of air caressed my elbow—he'd fallen asleep. The evening wind rustled and flipped pages of his notebook. I slid it from beneath his hand, slipped the elastic band around the cover, and let it drop to the floor. The wind teased his messy mop of hair, tickling my face. I smoothed it down and kissed the curve of his ear. Strong feelings of protectiveness surged in my chest, thrumming for me to say words I'd spoken since I was a child, yet hadn't spoken in years.

I breathed into his hair, "*Samuel Cabral es mi mejor amigo*," because I was too timorous to tell him I loved him, even when he slept.

His slow breathing hitched.

Wait. Was he awake? He shifted, careful not to crush me as he turned under my arm. Oh crap, he was awake. His eyes lifted to mine, followed by the rest of his body. And oh, every inch of him was both burning and covered in gooseflesh.

"*Mi vida.*" His mouth brushed mine, blue eyes blurring in my vision.

I smiled against his lips. "I thought you'd fallen asleep."

"Mmm, no, just enjoying this. You make a comfortable pillow. Now come here." He opened his mouth and pulled me into him. His hands slid over my arms and circled me. Long, sensual kisses claimed our minutes, but when desire began to consume us, we broke away.

"Rocky Mountain Folks?" he panted into my neck.

"Folks," I agreed, and reluctantly slipped from his embrace. That night, I slept solitary and ached for morning.

After eleven hours of blurred yellow lines, we rolled into Lyons late in the afternoon and stumbled into my mother's silent farmhouse. It was no Hollywood Roosevelt, but it was clean and comfortable with its paisley bedspreads and worn enamel bathroom.

Never failed, Mom's heirloom tomato competition in Pueblo was always the weekend of Rocky Mountain Folks, leaving two teenagers to do naughty things in an empty house. A nervous tremor ran through my body as I stared at my old bedroom. I could almost see my youthful Samuel, naked and sweat-slicked and shuddering after we'd made love for the first time in this room, when we'd sneaked away from the festival.

Another image flashed across my eyes…Samuel, hunched over the brunette, a line of cocaine fluttering across her skin. I squinted, banishing it. Thirty-year-old Samuel skimmed a warm hand over my neck, followed by even warmer lips.

"Should we go?" He placed a light sweater over my shoulders, and I knew his memories were with mine.

I shivered and took his hand. It was Rocky Mountain Folks time.

I don't know if it's possible to explain how fanatical Samuel and I were about Planet Bluegrass. We came of age under the shadow of Lyons' folk rock scene. We embraced its guitars like old friends. And as old friends, we paid homage beneath Steamboat Mountain, swaying to music, shimmying and shouting lyrics.

Our plan typically went like this:

-Grab a schedule

-Find chicken curry

-Spread blanket, eat curry, talk bands on schedule

-Get tipsy

-Sneak away and make out or have sex, depending on our relationship time line

-Wake up the next morning, grumble about hangovers

-Hit Planet Bluegrass again for Day Two of music, curry, and sex (or almost sex)

This year, we had a couple of revisions. Obviously we wouldn't be getting plowed, which also knocked off hangover grumbling. The sex forecast was promising. And we weren't just highlighting bands for our listening pleasure—we scouted them for the mental health fund-raiser I wanted to plan.

As it turned out, celebrity can be awesomely persuasive. All Samuel had to do was shake a hand and introduce himself as the author of the *Water Sirens* series, and he had the musicians' attention ("I *knew* you looked familiar, dude"). But keeping their attention, once he mentioned "mental health benefit"? Sadly, he'd called it ("Yeah... yeah...that's *amazing*. Give us a call in a few years and we'll chat. Love the book!"). Now, over chicken curry and the Tripping Marys (our boys had returned to the stage, well into their fifties and still rockin'), we compared notes.

"Are you positive you don't want to talk to Folsom and Frantz? Because that's just inspired."

"I'd love to, but Folsom and Frantz are recording next spring," Samuel pointed out, peering at me over the rim of his reading glasses. "Hobogen's local and more likely to play a benefit concert. They're also quite open about depression in their lyrics."

I sighed in defeat, then highlighted the Hobogens. "Okay, so our Sunday schedule is five p.m.—Dada Economics. Six forty-five—*Hobogens*. Eight ten—VeeVeeVee Quartet..."

For three hours I was in bluegrass heaven. I reclined on our blanket and stared at the night sky...the stage lights flashing red and blue against contoured clouds...the feel of Samuel's abs beneath my skull as he too stared at the sky and soaked up strings and accordions. I had my man, my music, and my memories. The tumultuous revelations of the past few days were now little more than a dream. I could almost forget how badly I wanted to rip Alonso and Sofia new ones.

Almost.

My phone rang, breaking the spell. I looked at the caller ID—Alonso and Sofia. I didn't want to talk to them, so I handed Samuel my cell.

"Your parents."

He gave me a long look, then took the phone and answered. While he happily chatted about how we'd had a safe trip, yes, Rocky Mountain Folks was great this year and no, he wasn't still sick, I stewed. And stewed. And *stewed*.

Samuel tapped my shoulder. "*Mamá* wants to say hello. I'm going to buy a couple bottles of water, okay?"

I nodded and took the phone.

"*Hola*, Kaye. Lucia told me all about Samuel's food poisoning."

"Mm-hm. Food poisoning."

"You're okay, though?"

"Yep. Stayed away from that cream cheese." I waited until Samuel was a good distance away before launching in. "Hey, Sofia. Can I ask you a question?"

"Sure, *mi corazón*."

I kept my voice quiet, too low for eavesdroppers. "Is there something difficult about saying, 'our son left you because he has bipolar disorder'? Because it didn't seem too hard to articulate just now."

Silence. Then Sofia gasped. "He told you? He finally told you? Alonso!" she called in the background, slipping into Spanish, "Samuel told Kaye…*Si*…No, use the receiver in the library."

There was scrambling, and I stared at my phone in utter disbelief. Did these people not understand how bowled-over offended I was? The rage I'd struggled to suppress fought its way to the surface. Alonso picked up the other phone.

"Kaye, he told you?"

I couldn't contain my anger. "No, he didn't *tell* me. *No one* told me! I figured it out on my own."

"Oh."

"Yeah, *oh*. How could you, Alonso? Sofia?"

My entire life, I'd tried to prove how far from frail I was. I felt manipulated. I felt the grieving process I went through seven years ago was cheapened. So what, did I have to grieve all over again because the first time was a lie? Most of all, I felt bone-headedly blind for allowing it to happen.

"*Hijita*," Alonso said calmly, "I do apologize."

"No. Both of you betrayed my trust, and 'I do apologize' doesn't cut it. Fucking hell, Alonso!" I hissed. "You're his father! What did you possibly think you'd accomplish by keeping me in the dark…"

A shadow fell across the blanket. My vehement words fell away as I stared up at Samuel. His mouth was pressed into a thin, white line. His hands were on his hips, eyes burning, and I felt shame at my outburst.

159

"I forgot my wallet," he said flatly.

"Oh." Ooh, he was pissed. No one talked to *Mamá y Papá* that way.

"May I have the phone?"

I handed it to him, and he wandered several feet from the blanket. I watched his agitated pacing, his hand as it gripped the bill of his ball cap, his eyes squeezed shut. After long minutes, I grew nervous, then defensive. He lowered the phone and his eyes locked on mine.

"I'm sorry for my language," I said when he returned, my anger still sizzling. "But your parents should have said something."

"Why? We aren't married anymore. They are under no obligation to tell you."

"Like hell they aren't!"

"And what if they had?" he snapped. "Let's say they told you I had a mental disorder before I was in a place to talk about it, thereby forcing my hand? They'd either A: cause you needless pain because I'd still pretend nothing was wrong, or B: attach you to a man who couldn't be honest with you."

"Like now?"

"I have told you nothing but the truth since our talk at Button Rock Reservoir!"

"But only because I forced you!"

"You didn't force me—it was my choice."

He tossed my phone on my bag and stared at me, searching my hard eyes. Then the anger seeped from his face and he dropped onto the blanket, resigned.

"Don't blame my parents, Kaye. Blame me. It will be a long time before things are right between us. Maybe this is all too fast. Maybe we shouldn't…tonight…"

Rejection ripped through me. My phone started to ring again—the Cabrals. I jammed it into my bag. "So what, we're *not* having sex now? This time you're freezing up on me?"

"I don't want to make a mistake with you, Kaye! We're both angry—"

"You *gave* me this anger, now you should man up and take it away," I spat, though I knew the instant it flew from my mouth that it was unfair. I braced my elbows on my knees and took a calming breath, then straightened. "That was low. But why can't we *just have sex?* Why is this so difficult?"

He tucked a tangle of blond hair behind my ear. "Because there is no 'just sex' for us—that's why it's difficult. We still have the same problems we had a decade ago. Sex and a wedding didn't fix them then, and it won't fix them now. Frankly, Kaye, I believe there's some unresolved trauma here, and sex is the *last* thing—"

I opened my mouth to argue, when my phone rang *again*. Argh, why wouldn't they leave me alone? I answered. "What?"

But it was Molly who stammered on the other end. "I...I'm sorry, I called at a bad time."

"Molly! No, geez." I instantly filled with remorse. "I thought you were my in-laws." She sputtered and I rolled my eyes, correcting myself. "The Cabrals." Samuel snorted behind me. I gave him a warning point. "What can I do for you?"

"I have really, really exciting news. Ready? Derek's going to let us help with the bills!"

"That's...that's great! How did this happen?" Another band took to the stage. I hopped to my feet and wandered away from the bandstand, away from Samuel. I mustered every ounce of enthusiasm.

Molly said that her sister, Holly, had made vast strides over the past few weeks, and her situation was slowly, but surely, improving. She was sticking to her meds and finally beginning to feel the results.

"Please tell Samuel thank you, from the bottom of my heart."

I froze. "Why? What did Samuel do?"

"I thought you knew," Molly said, confused. "Ever since our spelunking trip, he, Holly, even Derek have been talking on the phone—which is kinda surreal because they never spoke much in high school. I don't know what he said to her and Derek, but whatever it was, it's working. He's even hammered out some sort of financial assistance in exchange for their volunteering with the benefit concert. Oh, that reminds me. I know he's been busy lately, but could you ask him to call her after you guys are done with Rocky Mountain Folks? She was worried last week...Kaye?...Are you still there?"

"Yeah..." I whispered. Her words had knocked the hot air out of me, and I rocked on my heels. "Molly, I'll call you later. Thanks for calling."

I said my good-byes, then closed my phone and wandered through the nighttime, the crowds, the lights, the music, thinking.

After a hard fall, resetting the bones in your body is downright painful. Even more painful is the anticipation of pain: the cringing, the gnashing of teeth, the tensing, just waiting for sharp stabs to shoot through your body before they actually do. When you have to set your own broken bones, then the anticipation is ten times as painful.

In the first aid training Hector and I did before we began to climb mountains, I learned how to reset a fracture by myself and... let's just say I hoped I never had to in real life. First, remain calm (ha!). Second, check for skin tears around the break and clean away the blood and dirt. Next, create traction by wedging your hand or foot into a V-notch of a tree and then push *away* from the tree. After you have traction and can reset the bone, splint the break. There. You've just caused yourself tremendous pain in order to heal properly.

My bones had been broken not for seven years, but for twenty-seven. Mom left me for her gardens and squished heart. Dad left me for his new young thing. Samuel left me for his demons. And the Cabrals—they left me for Samuel's demons, too. I'd spent most of my memorable life stumbling around with fractured limbs, checking them over and over for skin tears or nicked nerves and cleaning them as best as possible. But I'd been so busy hunkering down against the next break, I never let those bones heal. Like a little girl, I was so wrapped up in my fears, I'd forgotten the fears of others...namely, Samuel's.

I knew what Samuel said to Holly, though Molly didn't. He'd told her about his bipolar disorder. What else would have convinced Holly to take her meds, if not the personal experiences of someone who walked in her shoes? Samuel feared his disorder would become public knowledge. Yet he'd risked his privacy, his career, his mental well-being to help my friend's beloved stepsister. What if she'd gone to the media for a quick buck? What if people saw the disease and not the man? He was brave enough to deal with those consequences, because it was worth the risk.

And I remembered, all over again, that loving Samuel was also worth the risk.

It was time to reset the breaks.

I stumbled through lawn chairs, beer bottles, and limbs until I saw our secluded little blanket. Samuel slumped there, elbows resting on his knees. His gaze was fixed on the musicians stomping the stage, but I could tell he wasn't listening. His face was shadowed by his ball cap and stage lights, and I thought it was probably a sad piece of work. When he heard me, he jerked.

I dropped to my knees beside him.

"Kaye? I'm sorry—"

I put my finger to his lips. "You were right about the sex. We have a lot to fix. But you should know…" Pushing his ball cap from his head, I burrowed my fingertips into his matted hair and put my mouth to his, hard. His head fell back, eyes closed. I brushed my hands over his hair and kissed him again, slow and aching.

"What was that for?" he asked when we broke away.

"Because you are a good man." My eyes bore into his. "And because I love you. I'm so sorry, Samuel."

There. That wasn't hard, was it? I smiled with the freeness of it.

"Kaye." He enfolded me in his arms, his head buried in my neck. "I love you." His voice cracked. "I never stopped."

Beautiful relief liberated my body and I sagged into him. Breath came swift and deep between us, and I thought I could meld onto his heated skin like dripping wax. We stilled, not daring to move as the band ground out ragged chords and crowds swelled and swarmed the stage, leaving us alone in our dark corner of grass. When the music fell away and the fans with it, we slowly released each other. I'd held Samuel so tightly, I had to retrain my muscles to move. I stooped to pick up our blanket, but he wrapped his arms around my waist and swung me in again.

"Thank you for helping Holly and Derek," I said unsteadily when he released me, minutes later. "Molly told me."

He cupped my face, gently kissing my cheeks, my eyes. "I did it for you."

"You did it because it was the right thing to do."

Samuel pressed his lips to my hair, a quiet thank you. "So I take it you aren't angry anymore?"

"I'm *weary* of being angry." I sighed. "Your silence wasn't the only thing that's kept me in the dark. I didn't try to find the truth because I was too busy being hurt. I've been hurt and angry for so long, they became my crutches." My voice began to rise. "But I'm sick to death of being on crutches, Samuel. I'm done believing I don't have a choice. There's always a choice. And…and I'm going to choose not to be angry with you."

He brushed away the wisps of hair that clung to my cheeks. "You are fearless, Kaye. Full of life. I've always seen it, even if you didn't."

A not-so-bright light bulb flickered. "Oh frick, is that what the nixies' curse is in *The Last Other*?"

He laughed. "Yes."

I slapped a palm to my head. "I wondered. I thought it would be something better, like the curse of lethal sex appeal."

"You have that, too." He raised my hand to his mouth. When he lightly nipped my knuckles, I vaguely pondered how *I* wasn't the one with lethal sex appeal. Halfheartedly, he released my hand. "But not tonight. Let me show you how much I love you by *not* sleeping with you."

"Hmm. Thanks, I guess?"

He chuckled. But then he grew serious, voice full of grit. "I want you to understand, there will be times when you're furious with me, just like today. Earlier, you asked me to take away your anger. I wish I could, Firecracker. I can wait, though, and be patient, and as honest as possible. Will you do the same for me?"

I nodded. "Just don't tell me if my butt gets big. That's *too* honest."

His head fell back and he laughed, exposing the brown scruff of his neck. A powerful ache ripped through my chest, all the way to my thighs. A single image—Samuel groaning and clenching our bedpost as my mouth playfully bit that scruffy chin—hit me with clarity. I wondered if that still drove him wild, and vowed I would find out, some day.

A distant "thank you and good night!" reverberated through the small mountain town, followed by a final swell of cheers as we made our way home. Here and there, a window peered at us with yellow eyes, and I wondered why anyone would still be home on such an exhilarating festival night.

My phone rang again. The Cabrals. They'd called twice in the last half hour, and each time I'd evaded them like hippies evade neckties. If there was an emergency, they could leave a voice mail. If Samuel noticed, he didn't mention it.

"Will you sit with me tonight?" His fingertips reverently grazed the tendons in my wrist.

"Absolutely. Front porch of the farmhouse."

Such a heady thing, the power a woman can wield. My heart slammed with the knowledge that, even after long years apart, I could bring this man—this brilliant, sought-after man—to his knees if I wanted to. *Oh yeah, Kaye, you still got it.*

"Come with me. Or not." He winked. Ooh, naughty. It seemed he could still weaken my knees, too.

Chapter 9
CLEARED

*When a diver has completed training,
they are cleared to advance
to the next level of certification.*

"I'm going to take you to Graceland."

"Whaa?"

Samuel shifted beneath me, stirring me from my sleep. My mother's living room was entirely dark, save for a strip of moonlight escaping between the curtains and stretching across the couch. The digital clock read three forty—five hours since we'd stumbled back from the Folks Festival, and at some point, I'd drifted to sleep mid-conversation. Had he slept at all?

"Graceland. I think we should visit Memphis after the publicity tour ends and pay our respects to Elvis. It's no Vegas chapel, but you've always wanted to go."

I yawned and propped my chin on his chest. The pale light cast half his face in shadow, and the eyelashes feathering across his cheeks seemed even longer. "Sounds like a plan. Have you been there before?"

"A few years ago, when I toured with my third book. It was the epitome of sixties opulence, rather garish, touristy. You'd love it."

"Hey!" That woke me up. His chest shook in silent laughter. The man got my excitement over kitschy tourist traps—probably because I'd ventured so little outside of Colorado and certainly never went on a family vacation as a child, unless it was courtesy of the Cabrals. When I was eleven, Alonso and Sofia had taken the three of us—Dani, me, and Samuel—on a week-long road trip to Niagara Falls and back. I bought every postcard on the stretch between Wall Drug and the Maid of the Mist boat tour, and stuck them in a cheap photo album while Samuel helped me write anecdotes on the backs. It was the only thing that kept us from killing each other during long hours in the back of the minivan. "Okay, I'd love it; you're right."

My cotton sundress was twisted uncomfortably around my legs and waist, so I hurriedly dragged it over my head and replaced it with Samuel's discarded T-shirt. I burrowed back into his arms and closed my eyes, trying to find sleep again.

"Kaye?"

"Hmmm."

"Are our expectations too high?" His tone was now all seriousness. "Are we just setting ourselves to fail?"

My eyes popped open. I belatedly realized I hadn't done us any favors by stripping away my sundress. "Is this about sex? Or not having sex?"

"That's part of it. I'm worried that we'll make the same mistakes we made seven years ago."

I smoothed a hand over the smattering of black hair on his chest. "You mean how we used sex to avoid our issues?" I smiled against his skin. "Well, no one here is having sex, so I think we're okay."

"But I would have slept with you in a heartbeat if you'd wanted me to."

Ah, introspection at four in the morning. I bit my lip thoughtfully, my hand still stroking his chest. "We used to hold some pretty high standards when it came to sex outside of marriage."

"We still do, it seems."

"Then what gives? Why would you have had sex with me 'in a heartbeat'?"

His arms tightened around me, tension gathering again. "I don't know how to explain this without freaking you out."

"Please try." There wasn't a lot he could say now that would freak me out.

"Signing those divorce papers didn't change the way I feel about you, Kaye. I know it sounds terribly hypocritical since I left our marriage, and I've been with other women—perhaps all of that only reinforces what I've learned the hard way. You used to say you didn't need a piece of paper to be married. Well, if that's true, it goes both ways. It's the intent *behind* the piece of paper—not the paper itself. You're *it* for me. I promised to love you for the rest of my life, and that may be the one marriage vow I haven't broken."

There went my back-flipping heart again. I pressed my lips to his chest and felt the pounding of his own anxious heart. "I feel the same way you do, Samuel. Which is lucky for you, because if I didn't, I'd be the ex-wife taking out a restraining order," I teased.

"No freaking out?"

"No. But you said you're still worried about making bad choices. What are you referring to?"

He sighed and rubbed my shoulder blades. "That's what I need to figure out. Like I said, sex and marriage didn't fix our issues before. I need to make a change, do something, but I'm not quite sure what."

"We'll figure it out. But, Samuel, I think we're already making those changes. Rome wasn't built in a day, blah blah blah."

"Can I ask you a question?"

"Sure."

"Thanksgiving, two years ago, you told me you never wanted our marriage. Why did you say it?"

I thought back to that day—the anger, the pain, and the fear he would suck me in again. "To keep a shred of my pride. Marriage terrified the crap out of you, Samuel, but you did it because it was what I wanted. And I hope you know I didn't just marry you for your family."

"I know you loved me."

He grew quiet, retreating into his head to mull—he was such a muller. He was having a tough time right now, his confidence in his choices shot to hell.

Finally, he spoke. "We should have waited. If one of us wasn't ready to be married, it meant our relationship wasn't ready for it. And in our case, with my mental hang-ups and your family hang-ups, neither of us was ready."

We drifted into silence. I left him to his thoughts while I wondered how our lives might have changed if we'd waited to marry. Would we still be together today, or would the same problems rip us apart? Soon, the late hour and the strokes of Samuel's hand along my spine lulled me to sleep.

Dum. dum dum Dum. dum dum Dum...

I tried to bury my head under my pillow, blocking out that horrible, shrill arena rock chords. But the pillow wouldn't lift. What the heck? Not my pillow, but Samuel's arm.

Dum. dum dum Dum. dum dum Dum... "Whatever it is, kill it," Samuel mumbled, shielding his eyes against the stream of light pouring between the curtains.

DUM. dum dum DUM. dum dum DUM... "Argh! Stupid freakin' monkeytail-humping son-of-a-biscuit phone." I stumbled half naked from the warmth of the couch and pounced on my phone as it happily chirped its morning song for the sixth time in a row.

"What are you doing?" Samuel asked.

"Changing my ringtone." I thumbed through the menu. "How about 'Janie's Got a Gun'?"

"Ah...you do know what that song's about, right?" came his muffled reply.

Now, I loved Planet Bluegrass, don't get me wrong. But the way Samuel stretched his arms over his thoroughly tangled mop of hair, the top half of his bronzed body twisting, the dusting of hair trailing down his abdomen and beneath his sleep pants...Well, he didn't have to crook his finger to convince me to forsake Folks. Slits of blue followed me around the room. He offered a lazy smile, all stubbly jaw as I scurried under the blanket.

My phone started to ring again and "Janie's Got a Gun" blared, just as Samuel found my earlobe.

"Seriously, you didn't mute it?"

"I forgot." Stupid happy trail. Stupid Cabrals. But it wasn't the Cabrals—it was Molly again. I answered and attacked. "Molly, why are you calling me so ungodly early?"

"Oh, silly Kaye, it's eleven thirty!" Ah. So it was. "Did you hear me? Wake up, we're outside!"

"Who's outside?" Samuel circled my belly button with his finger and I swatted him away. Man was making my brain cells wonky.

"Me, Cassady, Danita, Angel, and Betty the Campervan. Actually, we're just outside your door. Except for Betty."

"What?"

"Yeah, you wouldn't answer your phone but we heard your ringtone." Oh cripes, it was Mystery, Inc.

Sure enough there was a knock on the door, followed by Angel's booming voice. "Open up, *hombre!* We know you're in there, and we know you're naked!" Then Danita's, "Shut up, doofus, then why do you want him to open the door?"

"Just a minute!" I hung up on Molly and ran a frantic hand through my hair. Samuel hunted for his T-shirt and I scrambled for my pants, only to realize I'd stolen Samuel's T-shirt last night. Samuel was in the middle of swapping sleep pants for jeans, when a fresh-faced Molly burst through the door, followed by the rest of "the gang," clutching blankets and cameras. If I squinted, I could almost see them in orange ascots and knee highs.

"I was right!" Molly shrieked. "Pay up, be-yotches." Hmm, Velma'd gone ghetto. She pushed past me and went straight to our window, flinging open the curtains.

"What are you doing, Molly?" Samuel cried, whipping the afghan around his waist. She tossed her purse on a chair, stepped over Samuel's jeans, and made a beeline for my suitcase. The other three filed in. Cassady flipped on the television. Danita started my mother's coffee pot. Angel jumped on the couch and spooned a thrashing Samuel. Yep, no boundaries whatsoever.

"You bet on us?" I shouldn't have been shocked.

"It wasn't my idea," she retorted. "Angel said you'd be humping like bunnies by Christmas, and I told him it would be sooner than that. So we started a pool at Friday Lunch—"

"Flipping weiner dogs, Molly," I hissed. "Who placed bets?" Our four so-called friends all raised their hands.

"Christmas—guilty," Angel said.

"Right after the movie premiere," admitted Cassady.

Dani gave her brother a fierce, meaningful look. "I said never, because after I chopped off your *verga*, you'd never have sex again."

Molly bounced on her heels. "And I said Rocky Mountain Folks, which means I win. Oh, Santiago said 'his birthday,' idiot, and his new woman guessed 'in the ocean'—I don't think she understood the 'pool' concept. Jaime said you'd never stopped boinking and had some lucrative frequent flyers arrangement. And Hector didn't play."

"At least one of you has some decency," Samuel muttered, his face darkening. "Now can you all leave?"

"Nah, Valdez just said it wasn't gonna happen." Cassady was kind of clueless to Samuel's "Hector issues."

"Nobody wins, not that it's any of your business. What are you even doing here?" I asked.

"We wanted to catch up with you before you left for New York," said Molly. Angel jumped up and poured a cup of coffee. Molly ripped away Samuel's blanket and motioned for him to get up, not noticing his scramble to cover his black boxers with a pillow. He gave me a pleading look, but there really wasn't much I could do to rein her in.

"Honestly, Sam, we've all seen you in less. Oh, speaking of Hector, guess what went down yesterday at Friday Lunch?"

Dani groaned, facing the wall. "*¡Ay Dios!* Molly, let my brother put on some clothes! Yuck." In a show of belated politeness, Molly turned her back while Samuel awkwardly jerked on his jeans and avoided fist bumps from Angel.

"All put away? Good. Now, as I was saying, Friday Lunch. Hector's started seeing this chic from Lyons named Tricia. You probably remember her, Samuel—she was in your class."

"Wait, PA Tricia? The one who works at Boulder General?" I said, whipping my hair into a ponytail. The same Tricia who helped Hector drive me to the hospital after my skydiving accident? Apparently I missed a bit after being knocked senseless by the ground. I dug out my toothbrush and floss, listening to Molly's story as I brushed my teeth in the hallway bathroom. I wished Hector was here so I could high-five him for the smooth moves on my doctor. If I was honest, I was also a teensy bit jealous. But that was ridiculously selfish, and I pushed the thought out of my head. I glanced at Samuel in the mirror and caught him staring back at me with an odd look. He quickly focused on Molly.

"So yesterday," she continued, "Hector decided to bring Tricia to Friday Lunch. Who else should be there, but Jaime Guzman? She's joined us lately, saying she needs to get out of the office before she cuts someone. When she saw Tricia with Hector, she pitched a fit! None of us saw that coming, but it makes sense, you know? She called him a bleeping man-whore doctor-bleeper then stormed out of Paddler's, leaving Hector gaping like a wide-mouthed bass. It was great!" She plopped next to Cassady on the sofa and swung her legs into his lap.

I followed her back to the living room and folded our discarded blanket, straightened the throw pillows. "Wow, that's..." Holy crap, Jaime had a thing for Hector. It was so utterly obvious now that beneath her switchblades and snarky T-shirts, she had a soft spot for the guy. He was the only person from the Latin neighborhood who continued to speak to her. She always bashed him, and Jaime tended to bash people she liked. Then there was the night she went to the movies with me and Hector, and I didn't think she went because *I* was there…"

"There's more," Cassady picked up. "So last night, I was at the bar, talkin' to the sheriff, who just got back from the station after booking Hector and releasing him." I gasped. "It seems that Hector showed up at Jaime's place to apologize. Instead of forgiving him, she locked him in a dog kennel and had him arrested for trespassing. Hector was sitting in a cage with a handful of Lab puppies, playing tug-of-war with one of their chew toys."

"That's kind of creepy," I said. I noticed Samuel was beaming like a frat boy at an undie run.

"No, that's foreplay." Angel tried again for a fist bump…still nothing.

The four of them spilled Lyons gossip for a good hour while Samuel and I took turns showering and getting ready for Day Two of Rocky Mountain Folks. Jennifer Ballister was currently dating so-and-so's seventy-year-old father, and the entire family was hopping mad because the old man rewrote his will. Alan Murphy's parents promised to buy him a house if he quit dating virtual people in Second Life and found a real girlfriend.

"Oh, and Jorge Garcia got kicked in the balls by his two-year-old while pushing a grocery cart at The Garden Market," said Molly. All three men winced as we walked up St. Vrain, weaving through dozens of Festivarian tents. "Rumor has it he'd just had a vasectomy because he and Mel are done popping out kids. I get that Jorge doesn't want more children, but doesn't it seem kind of crazy to have surgery? It was probably Mel's idea."

Samuel's hand tightened around mine, and I noticed he'd locked his jaw. Dani saw it too and deftly steered the topic to safer areas. "I'm sure they have their reasons, Molly. Anyway, Jorge ended up rolling in the freezer aisle, his crotch covered in bags of frozen peas."

"Then there's the usual gossip about you two," Angel said, earning another smack from Danita.

Samuel grimaced. "What now?"

"It's probably the same old story about how I've been trying to get my hooks into you since junior high, how I love the attention," I said.

"People still say that?"

"Samuel, I followed you to LA and ended up in tabloids. Of course they still say that."

As we reentered the festival, I may have rubbed the gate post a la St. Peter's toe, thanking the Planet Bluegrass deities for Samuel's return. The sun was high and the baking earth was musty and sweet. We found a patch of shade not far from the stage and spread blankets, drinks, and burger baskets on the grass. While we waited for the next band, Samuel wrapped an arm around my waist and whispered into my ear.

"Does it bother you? The Lyons gossip?"

"Not gonna lie—I don't like it. But we grew up with it, Sam. Between my parents' turmoil, then our drama and your books, I got used to tuning it out. And it helps that I have Danita and Molly in my corner." I nodded to our friends—Molly instructed Cassady and Angel where to place the second blanket, and Danita strong-armed another couple out of our land claim.

"I'll miss all of you when we're in New York." I sighed.

Cassady pointed a french fry at me. "Likewise, little girl. Training for the Longs Peak climb isn't the same without you pestering Luca Guzman to 'quit hollering or we'll get squashed by falling rocks.'"

Samuel stiffened into protective mode. I patted his hand. "We'll be fine. Luca won't cause a cliff to collapse on us."

"Or snow." Cassady was all seriousness. "Make sure you get in your ice and snow training sometime before the climb, for sure. November weather on Longs is notorious. I can do it, or you can find someone in New York—"

Samuel's arms squeezed even tighter. "I thought you said this wasn't a risky climb."

"All climbs have some risk," I answered. "But we're prepared and know what we're doing, trust me. The North Face approach is the best route in winter. Between the five of us, we'll be fine."

But he was still doubtful, and even Cassady's assurances that he'd look out for Samuel's "sweetie pie" didn't calm him. "I don't like this, Kaye."

"It's my risk to take," I said, my voice quiet. He kissed my shoulder, but I knew he wasn't conceding this battle.

By early evening, everyone save Samuel and me were off exploring craft tents. The singer currently on the main stage wasn't promising for the benefit, and we were this close to ditching to stalk The Twiggies. Then Danita reappeared with a scowl for her brother.

"I need some girl time with Kaye." She swatted the brim of his ball cap.

"I suppose 'please' isn't in your vocabulary," Samuel shot back. Siblings.

"I need half an hour, *please*. Go find music-y stuff."

With a last grumble, he moseyed off to the Wildflower Pavilion. Danita placed a small package between us, wrapped in pretty pink paper and a bow.

"*Feliz Cumpleaños*. Don't think because you'll be in New York, you don't get a gift."

I smiled and tore into the paper. A jewelry box. Giddy, I opened the case. Out spilled a small silver bracelet with a single charm.

"It's a locket," Danita explained. I fingered the charm, trying to open it. She reached over and pressed a tiny latch, and the oval sprang open. On the inside was a very old picture of Danita, Angel, Samuel and me with our heads pressed together, bandanas around our necks, grinning like fiends despite missing some of our teeth. "Sam was also going to get you a bracelet for your birthday, but I told him I had dibs on jewelry. He was cranky about it." She shrugged. "He owes me."

"I remember this picture. It was taken on your old front steps, on my seventh birthday. It was during my cowgirl phase, so Sofia and my mother threw me a 'hoedown' party." I grew sad over the memory. I'd loved the Cabrals with my whole heart, so naïvely. Snapping the locket shut, I carefully placed it back into the box and hugged Danita.

She tapped the box, meeting my eyes. "No matter what happens, you'll always have these friendships. We're worth keeping."

"Thanks, Dani. It's really thoughtful."

Danita wrapped her arms around her knees, dark eyes drifting to the stage. "The Cabral family has issues, too, you know. Most people never see them, but we're just as screwed up as the next household. I remember evenings when we'd have family fights about grades, or being out past curfew, or my dad's long hours at the magazine. Then the next morning, it was as if it never happened—even if nothing had been resolved. Arguments were referred to as 'little tiffs' or 'spats.'"

Little tiff…that sounded like Sofia, glossing over harsh words. "Samuel told me one thing he appreciates about my family is that Dad over-shares, and though Mom doesn't say much, when she does, you know exactly what she means. I thought he was full of it, trying to make me feel better about my dysfunctional folks. But now, I get it."

"A lot of the secrecy has to do with what went down in Boston when Samuel was little."

"Did he tell you about your Aunt Rachel?"

"No, but I put the pieces together. I heard his nightmares when we were little. I saw him freak out over open windows. I know now my parents had him in therapy, but at the time, I thought *Papá* was taking him out for ice cream while I had to stay home with *Mamá*. I probably would've needed therapy myself to get over my sibling rivalry, if I hadn't taken so much to that poor kid." She shook her head, eyes in the distant past. "But yes, we like to play the perfect family and ignore the unsavory crap. Well, my parents and Samuel do. I'm the black sheep."

I gnawed my thumbnail. "Did Alonso and Sofia put you up to this?"

"Since when have my parents been able to control me?" she scoffed, tugging my nail from my mouth. "I spoke to them last night and they mentioned the phone call—nothing specific, just that you're upset. Believe me, I get where you're coming from. I was so pissed at my parents and Samuel when I found out they'd hidden the bipolar disorder from me." I realized Dani had been forced to push a lot of anger aside for the sake of her wedding—quite the position to be in. "I'm especially pissed they validated Samuel's shame by hiding his health issues."

"Samuel and I have worked through so much this summer. But Alonso and Sofia…I don't even want to deal with them, right now. One Cabral at a time is my limit."

Danita sighed. "I just don't know what to say. I don't know how to fix *mi familia*."

"You can't, and neither can Samuel. Danita…I appreciate your desire to help. But until your folks return from LaLa Land and realize the damage they've done, I can't forget this. I don't think our relationship will ever be the same."

"Just remember, Samuel loves them."

"I know, Dani."

"And if you want something long term with him, you'll have to deal with the folks eventually. Did Samuel talk to you about his vasectomy?"

Dani really just laid it out there, didn't she? "What if he hadn't?"

"Now you'd know. Are you sure you've thought this through?"

I pressed the heel of my hand to my forehead. "Danita, this really isn't any of your business. But we did talk a little about the possibility of adoption down the road."

"I can tell you right now, because of Samuel's drug arrests, that's going to be next to impossible, Kaye-bear," she said, blunt as ever. "Sorry. Although, with his kind of money…"

"Danita. We are *not* buying a black-market baby." I choked back disappointment, which surprised me. Baby options were starting to look slim, and suddenly I felt uncomfortable with it.

"I know it seems premature, but it's stuff to think about."

"That's what Samuel told me." Dani and her pragmatic brain.

As the sun sank beneath the mountains, the joints flared. Pretty soon, our blanket neighbors shared their spot of grass in more ways than one. I glanced at my watch, waiting for Samuel and the others to return so we could find a space that wouldn't get us higher than a Dead concert. Somewhere behind us, "Janie's Got a Gun" irritatingly mingled with bluegrass.

"For crying out loud, that's the second time that annoying phone's rung today." Danita shot daggers at the young couple in front of us. "What kind of sick person chooses 'Janie's Got a Gun' as their ringtone, then makes the rest of us listen to it?"

Crud! I'd forgotten to change it back. "Ahhh, that'd be me."

Shock drifted over Dani's face, and then she laughed. "*Ay*, Kaye, I can't tell you how many things are wrong with that. Wow, I love you."

My face flushed red as I answered my phone, and I just knew the Festivarians in our vicinity planned to bail before I could spout "daddy, you bastard, I'm through" and break a few fingers.

"Justin, hey."

"Hey, honey. Sounds like a wild time."

"Some West Coast band, we—"

"Listen, I don't have much time to chat. You and your wunderkind need to hop on the next plane to New York."

I upped the volume on my phone. "We'll be there Monday night, Justin, I already told you. Our flight—"

He interrupted me again, his voice edgy. "Something huge is about to go down, and there's gonna be carnage. Buitre is circling the wagons. You need to be here for a meeting ASAP. Jerome himself will be at the table, as well as Cabral's business manager. Even Ace Caulfield is coming up from Boston."

I sat up, catching Dani's eye. "Wait, what's going down? And who the heck is Ace Caulfield?"

"Archibald Caulfield, one of Sam's lawyers—contract negotiator and secret keeper crackerjack. He's worked closely with Caroline in the past, so we'll need him for damage control."

Caulfield, as in Caulfield Law Firm? "Justin so help me, if you don't tell me what's happening, I'll climb through this phone and shove your Buddy Holly glasses down your throat!" I clutched a handful of grass, mindlessly ripping it from the ground.

"Caroline Ortega's gone rogue, Kaye."

"What does that mean?" I pictured Caroline decked out in guerilla gear, belly crawling between cubicles.

"She's broken from Buitre to start her own agency. Seven clients and two agents jumped ship with her. Apparently there's an unauthorized biography about Cabral in the works that'll make one of her authors the next Kitty Kelley, and she's been negotiating with this poison pen prick since early June."

I shook my head. "No, absolutely not true. Look, Caroline may be lethally ambitious and she won't be crying 'out damn'd spot' any time soon, but you're forgetting two things. One, she cares about Samuel. Two, she cares about her reputation. A move like this would *kill* both of those."

"Sorry, but the move's already been made. The poison pen's name is Toccani…Targasi…"

"Togsender." *No. No, no, no.* My voice went flat. "Lyle Togsender."

"That's it. If we move fast enough, we might be able to squelch the book before it hits the public."

Togsy. Caroline visited Togsy right after our bachelorette party. AKA, new author? I smacked my forehead, feeling utterly stupid for letting my guard down. "I should have seen this coming. I knew she was a freaking Svengali, but she just sucked me right in, anyway."

"We all got suckered, honey."

Vindictive cow. Jaime and Molly warned me not to trust her. After everything that happened in LA, I'd truly believed she wanted the best for Samuel, in her own misguided way. But this…this would devastate him.

"Can't we get an injunction? When does it hit the shelves?" I slapped the ground and pain shot through my middle finger. "Mother cliff-hucker!" I cried, shaking out my hand, certain I'd sprained my knuckle. Several people turned to check out the commotion—oh heck, I actually *was* breaking fingers. I lowered my voice to a hiss. "She signed a nondisclosure agreement! She has to know we'll sue her for every dime and then some. It'll ruin her career."

"Or make her career, if she pulls it off. That's the kicker. *She* signed a nondisclosure agreement, but Lyle Togsender can write whatever the hell he wants, as long as there's a smidge of truth to what he writes. And from what I understand, he's got insider info on Cabral and Caroline's just helping him dot his i's and cross his t's. Word is she can back up all of Togsender's claims with documentation and affidavits."

I hopped to my feet and began to pace. "Are you absolutely sure Caroline would betray Samuel?"

"Oh, honey, she already has."

My brain raced. Caroline warned me she'd do anything to be with the man she loved, and I'd just assumed she meant Samuel. But Caroline had only ever loved Samuel's words, hadn't she?—his beautiful, brilliant words and the success they brought her. So when Samuel distanced himself, she—what had Samuel called it? I grimaced. Used her Midas touch.

That was *not* going to happen. "Do you have a copy of this book?"

"Not personally, but I've been told it's scathing. Caro waltzed into Buitre's New York office yesterday and dropped this outrageous monsta on Jerome's desk. Called it 'fair play'—crazy, huh? Jerome sent a hard copy over to us at Berkshire House this morning so we'd be ready for fallout." He noisily exhaled into the receiver. "We need Sam in New York *now* to figure out what's true and what's false. Then we can slug Togsender with a defamation suit and get that injunction before this goes public. Lemme tell you, she's got guts."

"We'll leave as soon as we can, Justin."

"See you soon, killa."

I stared at Dani, who'd undoubtedly heard enough of the conversation to comprehend what was about to go down. Her eyes were wide, her hands frozen to her mouth. "No. Poor Samuel."

Without thinking, I punched Jaime's number, nursing my tender finger while I waited for her gruff voice. Before she had a chance to chew my tush, I spat out Justin's bad news.

"You're screwed," Jaime answered when I caught a breath.

"That's all you've got to say? Can she and Togsy even do this?"

"Oh yeah. I'm no media lawyer, but I'm pretty sure that publicist is right. Caro can't write the book herself, but Togsender sure can. Given he knows Cabral from his brownstone days, and he probably uncovered the same gory story I did in our dossier, I'd say your boy toy's about to have his Lego castle topple in on him. The higher they rise, the farther they fall."

"Thanks for that bit of wisdom, Jaime."

"Save the sarcasm for the boardroom, Trilby. You better hang up and get your little lackeys in order."

I ended the call and blinked at my phone. My head spun. They were not going to destroy him, these people who'd carved chunks out of my Samuel since the day he was born. I was going to shut down Caroline. First things first—find Samuel and get to New York.

"That puffed-up piece of plastic never once cared about Samuel's happiness," Danita snarled. "And, honestly, Samuel didn't care much about hers, either. Now it's coming back to bite him." She took my injured hand in hers and poked at my swelling finger. I winced. "*¡Hijo de la bruja!* You've got to wrap this before it gets any worse."

"*La bruja*, all right. I've also got to break this to Samuel." I hadn't even realized she'd meant my finger.

Chapter 10
FUNNEL

When a skydiving formation becomes unstable, divers find themselves in a turbulent burble and the formation must break off.

Hydraulic Level Five {working title}
Draft 2.31
© Samuel Caulfield Cabral & Aspen Kaye Trilby
31. Fate & Faces

Caulfield,
Come on, send me the book. No bigwig editor is ever going to give a short story a second glance, or even a first. My man said the excerpts you shared in workshops are phenomenal, but I have yet to see one. If you don't have the balls to share your writing with the world, then your career is as good as over. One more shot, Caulfield. Send me something I can pass to my editor, or this favor has run its course.
CO, Junior Editor
BigName Publishing House

Witch. Caulfield clicks open the piece he sent his buddy's girlfriend, "The Bard's Two Faces," which expounds on how a seemingly insignificant chain of choices determines whether a story will end as a comedy of errors, or a tragedy. Caulfield believes in fate, but after this evening, his future hinges solely on a choice.

They were ambushed tonight. Like two sheep hustled into a shearing pen, their parents invited them over for coffee after the rehearsal dinner, then pounced in a last ditch effort to talk sense into their children...

"Flower, I just don't want to have to say 'I told you so' in two years' time," Aspen's father pleads.

A muscle twitches in the small fingers laced with his, and Caulfield feels the miniscule movement race up his marrow and straight into the organ furiously pumping blood into his angry-red brain.

That single muscle spasm conveys only a fraction of the hurt screaming to be loosed. Aspen knows what her father truly means. He doesn't want his baby girl to stagnate, rooted to a place she doesn't quite love, shouldered with a baby who frightens her and a lover so bland, her tongue forgets how to taste...but not quite. Aspen hears his unspoken words: *if you marry, you will wither.*

At the same moment Aspen's fingers twitch, her mother grimaces. Neither she nor her mother observe it. But the same pain that keeps her mother silent spurs Aspen to speak.

"You won't have to say 'I told you so,' Dad. I swear to you, all of you, I want to be his wife. I love him."

"You're both so young," says Caulfield's *Papá*. "Just wait a few more years, please."

"No," she says. "We're marrying tomorrow."

"Caulfield?" his mother asks.

His eyes fix on the tops of her flip-flops, studying her pink toes as they clench, wiggle, then clench again. Aspen holds her breath as he raises his eyes.

"I love Aspen."

Tension lifts from her shoulders and she exhales. She doesn't notice he fails to say "I want to marry Aspen" or "I want to be Aspen's husband." His parents see. Her mother sees and grimaces again. But Aspen is too occupied by her defiance, hard and flinty and daring their mutual enemy to question their love. Caulfield loves her defiance. He'd cross the Rubicon – or a satin-covered church aisle – just so she can have what she wants.

She wants marriage. He wants her. No less will appease either of them.

But that night...just before bed...she notices.

"Still up, kiddo?" Her mother cracks open her door, all bleary and watery. "It's a big day ahead of you. This time tomorrow, you'll be a married woman."

"If he shows," she mutters.

"Oh, Aspen, he'll show. That boy loves you."

"What if it's not enough? Let's face it – he doesn't want to marry me, Mom. But he's going to do it anyway, and I'm going to let him."

Her mother awkwardly hugs her shoulders, as if she were an out-of-state aunt rather than a mother. "Aspen, you and Caulfield are meant to be together. You will be, whether it's tomorrow or ten years from tomorrow..."

The next morning, he is there. Her pale ankles skip over the lawn, fresh and lovely in white lace, and he is overcome. He knows this is right when he sees her dainty frame and a bouquet of daisies and roses between her fingers.

"May I touch you?" Caulfield's voice quivers. He can't bear to dirty her dress.

"Yes."

His hands quake as he brushes her waist. Then he grips her to him, head bent and buried in the crook of her neck. "Thank you, Firecracker. I love you, so much." How could he ever have considered letting her go? If marriage proves he loves her, so be it.

Aspen's hands find their way into his cub's mane, one of the last corporeal strongholds of his youth. She murmured against his lips. "I love you, Caulfield. Always have."

That afternoon, as a small gathering of friends wander beneath April leaves, he remembers "The Bard's Two Faces." It is tucked away in his boyhood room, and he still thinks it's pretty good. C.O. was an idiot. How could anyone not understand that hovering above the chaos was Fate's calm hand? One small choice might have changed whether Aspen and Caulfield found each other: If his mother hadn't left him to his uncle. If Aspen's parents had left Bear Creek after their split. If he and Aspen never had a penchant for ghosts.

But Fate pre-ordained them. He believes that old biddy will bind them, no matter what comedies and tragedies life whips up.

C.O., Junior Editor, could kiss his ass.

·········•◉•·········

Kaye—What were you thinking after our parents staged their intervention? ~Sam

I was scared we were making a mistake, too, but I wanted so badly to prove them wrong. I regret so many things. But, Sam, *never once* have I regretted loving you, even in the dark times. There's a difference.
P.S.—It seems as though you've got some serious passive-aggressive tension building, Mr. Cabral. Want to meet me in the bathroom? ~Kaye

Passive aggressive? I'm a rational adult and Caro deserves to be heard. Besides, the airline bathrooms are too small for this man, Firecracker. ~Sam

Caro deserves to be strung from the Chrysler Building by her tatas. And ego much? I don't want to touch anything in that nasty bathroom, anyway. Truly. ~Kaye

"Don't you trust me, Kaye?" Samuel asked.

He shifted the unfolded copy of *The New York Times* he'd picked up at La Guardia, using it as a barrier between me and the driver's rearview mirror. Subtle. I doubt the man could have seen into the backseat, anyway. We were passing through the Queens Midtown

Tunnel, and the blurs of light outside the window barely lit the interior. I worked a gray silk stocking up my prickly leg, careful not to snag it on my new bracelet.

"It's not a question of trust," I answered. "But the facts speak for themselves."

"Facts. As in, secondhand information from Justin — a man who tends toward the dramatic."

"*Facts*, as in Togsy's tell-all book and Caroline's split from Buitre. She can't possibly come out innocent in this mess."

Since we'd caught a red-eye flight, I'd barely had time to fish a professional-looking outfit from my suitcase before a bleary-eyed Buitre intern whisked us away. We were being carried straight to Midtown, where the agency's headquarters were located. It wasn't until we careened through Queens that I noticed my horribly rumpled skirt, cleavage hanging out of a half-buttoned blouse, and unseemly legs. I grudgingly donned the stockings I'd stuffed in my purse. Samuel, on the other hand, was immaculate in charcoal trousers and a crisp oxford. I didn't know how he did it — only that it was typical.

He stiffly refolded the newspaper. "She wouldn't sell me out."

"Oh no? You told me yourself that she's ruthless when it comes to business."

"Ruthless, but loyal."

"And it was loyal of her to overload your schedule?" I had him there.

"In order to advance my career."

"She knew full well what could happen to your health."

"I could have said no a lot earlier, but I gave her a green light," he retorted. "Caro and I were caught up in the publicity game years ago, whether I like to admit it or not."

I narrowed my eyes. "But when you finally told her no, she threw a hissy fit and betrayed you with that book. Samuel, this isn't friendship!"

Samuel sighed and pressed tired fingers to his temples. With only a two-hour nap in an uncomfortable airline seat, we really were too sleep-deprived to do this right now. "There's more to this story, and I owe it to Caro to get her side."

"You owe her nothing."

"Have you stopped to consider that perhaps you're biased against her?"

Ooh, now I was getting angry. I bounced to the defense. "But Justin thinks she's a snake, too. So do Molly and Jaime, Danita—"

"So you trust their judgment above mine," he said in a cutting voice.

"I could say the same thing. Trust is a two-way street, buddy."

And we'd circled back to trust. If I was honest, though, I really didn't trust him above the others, and it wasn't just because he'd lied about his disorder. I believed he was a fool to still have faith in Caroline Ortega.

I stared at his hardened face, trying to decide if it was disappointment or denial which brought out this calm — almost eerie — intensity. It first surfaced yesterday evening, when I told him of my conversation with Justin, and how we had to high-tail it to New York City. To my horror, he suggested there had to be some misunderstanding, and why didn't we keep to our original plans and finish out Folks? That led to an argument, which I won. But as I watched him shove clothing into suitcases with slumped shoulders, I didn't feel as if I'd won. I didn't like winning if it meant Samuel lost.

The whole incident irked me because, not two days ago, I swore I wouldn't be ruled by my feelings. Yet here I was again, allowing fear, and hurt, and anger to dictate my actions.

Samuel touched my hand. "We're leaving the tunnel."

I peered past a series of stone overpasses and into the city. Thousands of skyscraper lights flickered out as the sky became an amalgam of corals and blues. While we'd cruised along the expressway, the distant city seemed an adventure. It was the same rush of adrenaline experienced when riding a ski lift to the top of a slope — the closer I got to the point-of-no-return, the more anxious I became.

The gray buildings on either side were so tall, I had to crane my neck to see where they ended. Soon, Samuel tentatively showed me the place he now called home, pointing out the Empire State Building, Bryant Park, and Rockefeller Plaza. I recognized city backdrops prevalent in the *Law & Order* marathons my mother griped about yet watched religiously. As I stepped out of the car, I nearly tripped over the curb in my effort to take in the cacophonous surroundings and put my heels in pungent water streaming from an alley. Common sense told me the quickest way to spot out-of-towners was to find the people who looked *up* instead of *down*, but I couldn't help myself. Modern monsters shared real estate with sturdy, century-old bricks. There was a clutter of brightly colored signs — some fluttered from awnings, others were light boards three stories high. Despite the hour, sirens and car horns echoed along grid streets, and early risers pushed past Samuel and me, their heads bent over to-go cups of coffee. I wasn't sure what they were doing up and about at six a.m. on a Sunday, but it was New York—the "city that never sleeps" and all that.

"Wow," I breathed, nervously fingering the cuffs of my sleeves. No wonder Samuel found inspiration here.

He smiled and took my fidgeting hand. "I don't want to go in there on opposite teams, Kaye. No more cricket infestations or IcyHot on the toilet seat?"

I squeezed his hand. We did have a tendency to beat each other up, whether the weapons were stupid pranks or vicious words. And if he didn't have my back, I wasn't confident enough to go into an elite boardroom packed with Newhouse alums, guns a blazin'.

Samuel led me through the building's rotating door and into a lobby. An older man in a jacket sat behind a reception desk, head propped on his fist as he stared at a security screen. I wondered if he always worked the weekend graveyard shift—if so, what dreary surroundings. The décor was going for industrial chic, exposed pipes mixed with paint-splashed art, but it came across as cold and sterile. Our feet slapped across polished cement, and the man's face snapped up.

"Mister Cabral, welcome back. You'll need to sign in your guest."

"Um, Buitre's expecting me. Kaye Trilby?" I gestured to the elevators.

"You still need to sign in, ma'am."

"Oh. Right."

"I need ID." I handed the man my driver's license. At TrilbyJones, our receptionist just buzzed my office and I swung around the corner to greet my clients.

Samuel gave my shoulder a reassuring squeeze. "Sorry, I should have warned you. Security's really tightened up since 9/11, understandably. Don't let the hoops rattle you—you'll have to do the same thing on the forty-first floor."

"I'm not rattled." Trembling fingers peeled the back from the badge and I stuck it on my shoulder with the nervousness of a rookie.

We stepped into the elevator. The back wall was entirely glass. I felt like Charlie Bucket as we rose higher and higher, watching older buildings give way to rooftop gardens and AC units, and I wondered if the elevator would just keep going until it burst through the ceiling and soared into the sky.

"Do you see that black, glossy building with the stripes?" Samuel said. I followed his finger. "That's the Bertelsmann Building, where my publishing house is located. If we have time, I can show you their offices, introduce you around."

"For my career or personal reasons?"

"I'm taking you home to meet the family," Samuel kidded, a touch awkward. He wasn't fibbing about his nonsocial tendencies.

It may have been a joke, but Samuel's "family" comment reminded me I didn't need to be intimidated by these people. They worked for Samuel. So did I. This wasn't a competition — this was a valiant effort to save our client's reputation and so help me, I would give this my all. Families helped each other, right?

Oh sweet baby Jesus.

In Boulder, people at least pretended to like you. Heck, even in LA you could garner business-savvy respect if you glossed your lips and showed a little thigh. But in New York, you knew within a minute if someone thought you were a moron.

A crowd of hostile eyes stared me down as we strode into the boardroom, save for Justin's pitying expression.

If Samuel noticed the "you've got to be kidding me" looks when he officially introduced his odd choice of a publicist, he wasn't fazed. The eight-foot-tall, glass-encased promo banners of Neelie and Nicodemus that circled the room told me everything I needed to know: *Water Sirens* was their coffer, and Samuel, the crown jewel. Squaring my shoulders, I hitched up the strap of my messenger bag and found my fierce face. So they didn't like me. Big deal. I could at least make them respect me.

Sliding into one of two empty seats, I pulled the conference phone toward me and punched in Molly's direct line.

"This is TrilbyJones, Molly speaking."

"Hello, this is Kaye. Thanks for joining us — I know it's insanely early for you." Around the table, mouths silently yawned, fingers wrapped coffee mugs, men smoothed hastily knotted ties. A woman with plum lips and a sassy neo-fro (I assumed she was Lexi Rogers, from Samuel's description) picked fuzzies from her blouse.

Introductions began, and I quickly observed they'd divided themselves into three groups: Samuel's team, the Berkshire House Team, and The Buitre Media team. I discreetly pulled out the cheat sheet I'd created with the help of a book critic for an avant-garde magazine in New York—an acquaintance of Molly's who used to live in Colorado. Okay. He was also the first man I'd slept with after Samuel and I split, and calling in a favor was really awkward. (Thank goodness Samuel had been in the shower when I actually uttered the words "I swear this isn't a booty call.") But my former fling had insider information about these people, which dug beneath the polished bios on company websites, so it was worth a little humiliation. My finger drifted down the list as each person introduced themselves, until only the key players were left.

"Lexi Rogers, Editorial Director with Berkshire House Publishing." She turned beautiful black eyes to Samuel. "We're still working on finding you an editor you can really bond with, Mr. Cabral." Oh gag.

Actually, Lexi seemed pleasant enough. She was the type of woman who kindly touched the forearms of business associates when she talked to them. Samuel admitted that after their first meeting, he wanted to encase his forearms in bubble wrap with a Post-it that read "personal space." I had a feeling she and Caroline Ortega used to sip mojitos together.

"Ace Caulfield, just got in from Boston. When I said to call me day or night, Sam, I really didn't mean it, ha. Let's keep this brief. My kid's got a flu bug and Mischa'll kill me if I'm not back tomorrow."

Archibald "Ace" Caulfield, Samuel's lawyer, employed by none other than Boston's own Caulfield Law Firm. Not so incidentally, Samuel confessed that Ace was his cousin. This surprised me—given the bitterness he harbored toward his absent blood relations, I'd been under the impression he had no contact with them. He was a toned-down version of Samuel's sharp lines with a high brow and cheek bones, and those blue, blue eyes. But Ace didn't carry Samuel's strong jaw, and without it, the other marks of beauty were a bit too effeminate.

Finally, the last and most prominent:

"A pleasure to finally meet you, Ms. Trilby. And Ms. Jones, also, though the circumstances are lamentable. Jerome Buitre, and I'm very happy to have you join our family."

Jerome Buitre, Wielder of the Buzzword. Shaved head and glasses, his appearance was deceivingly slight. He was a silver-tongued ferret-of-a-man and if you didn't know he owned one of the more prominent agencies in New York, you'd assume he was either a lawyer or politician. In the past decade, Buitre had turned its eyes to Hollywood in a diversification move that, after several celebrated authors found movie audiences (Samuel Cabral included), proved to be a coup. Buitre Literary Agency became Buitre PR & Media Group, and Jerome bought a beach house next to Harvey Weinstein's.

"Colleagues…our esteemed Mr. Cabral…I thank each of you for canceling your weekend plans and banding together to proactively fight this challenge to our client's wholesome brand and aura of trust…" *Was this guy for real?* "As you know, one of our own has chosen, in an unfortunate manner, to break from The Buitre Group. Not only has her departure left us in quite the lurch with a string of blockbuster movies on the horizon, but she has egregiously threatened to defame our most critically acclaimed author. This cannot happen." Heads bobbed in agreement. "As business partners, it is our responsibility to protect our client and find a solution that favors Mr. Cabral's interests. Ms. Rogers, if you will?"

Lexi strode across the room to a laptop and projector. She squeezed Samuel's forearm as she passed and he shot me a silent "I told you so" look.

Bold, blue letters scrawled across the screen:

BrownStoners: A Houseful of Famous Pens and Crack Pipes

I nearly spit coffee down my front. If nothing, Togsy got props for creativity.

"Ace and I have taken the liberty of reading this 'tell-all' written by Lyle Togsender, entitled *BrownStoners*, and have accrued a list of details that may be of concern to our client."

Her words triggered a warning signal in my gut and I spoke up. "Wait. Will Samuel—Mr. Cabral—and I have an opportunity to read this book?"

Lexi tilted her head, puzzled. "But we've already done it for you."

I caught Samuel's eye and he lifted his chin, giving me the go-ahead. "I'd like a copy of *BrownStoners*."

"Ms. Trilby," Jerome said with a patronizing stare, "our concern at the moment is determining the veracity of Lyle Togsender's claims. Mr. Cabral's lawyer would prefer to file an injunction as swiftly as possible—surely you can understand our time constraints."

Samuel backed me up. "But you'll provide a copy. Ace?"

"My client will need a copy of that book, as soon as possible, preferably hard copy—electronic distribution's dicey."

"Without a doubt." Jerome offered Samuel a photo-worthy smile, but his eyes were hard. It reminded me of...well. Caroline. Something was fishy, and I had a feeling we wouldn't be getting our mitts on this book any time soon. Jerome extended a hand. "Ms. Rogers, please continue."

"As I was saying..." As the editor pulled up a PowerPoint listing potential defamation suit material, Samuel began to squirm.

Drug addict.

Cheating husband.

Demanding artist.

One by one, Lexi rattled off cool, clinical descriptions of Samuel's supposed misdeeds contained in the passages of Togsy's book. Stoic intensity crumbled to despair as each one hit him like a guilty sentence. And, one by one, he was forced to admit to their truth. After the third slide, I'd had enough. I *knew* what was coming next, and I was sickened that Samuel's private mental health battles would be announced with the click of a space bar in a business presentation.

"Ms. Rogers, surely there's a better way to do this."

"Kaye, let it go," Samuel whispered, a hand clutching my knee under the table. I shook him off.

"No. I mean, does Samuel's accountant really need to be here? Or Justin? They could just be given a summary after the meeting." I felt my face flush to the roots.

The accountant chuckled uncomfortably. "Actually, I'm not sure why I need to be at half these planning meetings. Someone could give me a five-minute re-cap and I'd be good."

"When we have crises arise at TrilbyJones that's embarrassing for a client," I nervously pushed, "we try to make the situation as painless as possible for them. There's no sense in trotting out their embarrassment to a room full of people. Molly, get my back on this?"

"Kaye, I don't..." she stuttered over the phone.

Samuel gave my knee a gentle warning squeeze, and Jerome used my distraction to smoothly take back the reins.

"Ms. Trilby, you are new. You don't comprehend the beast that is our industry, so we will afford you some leeway. Let me explain.

If Mr. Cabral wishes to keep his private life private, it takes a team such as this to achieve said privacy. The very definition of 'celebrity' is one who is *well-known*. Privacy, my dear, is the price of fame. To assist our clients in navigating the complex media landscape, The Buitre Group has a full-service platform of offerings tailored to—"

"*Platform of offerings?*" I gave a disbelieving laugh. "What, are we sacrificing to Huitzilopochtli now? Sorry, I forgot my headdress."

That comment gained the hard glares of the entire room. It wasn't clear whether they were stunned by my mocking of their buzzwords, or my ability to say Huitzilopochtli.

Samuel rose. "If you'll excuse me, gentlemen, Ms. Rogers. I'd like to confer with Ms. Trilby outside."

I followed him like a spanked puppy. The hallway was quiet, save for the faint sounds of copy machines and clacking keyboards. I braced myself for hard words. Instead, as the door swung shut, Samuel cupped my face between his hands, his eyes soft.

"Show-off," he teased, and brushed his lips against mine. "Crazy, brilliant, show-off." A woman with a handful of files scooted down the hall and around us, shooting curious glances our way. Samuel waited until she rounded the corner. Then he became serious.

"I love you, Kaye. I appreciate that you want to save me from embarrassment, and I know this mess is uncomfortable for you, too. But, Firecracker, this is the consequence of my screw-ups. And if having my indiscretions flashed on PowerPoint slides is part of my sentence, so be it." He smoothed his thumbs over my cheekbones then dropped his hands. "Besides, if this book isn't reined in now, it will only get worse. Those slides will become headlines."

Stop the book. That was the reason we were all here, wasn't it? I reached up and pecked Samuel's cheek.

"I'll behave."

He pulled me into a hug for a long minute before releasing me. "We'd best go back."

"They'll be discussing your bipolar disorder next," I warned. His jaw tightened, and I knew he was bracing himself for the inevitable.

"I know."

We slid into our seats, hands clenched under the table as we waited for the bold revelation to be broadcast to the entire room: "BIPOLAR DISORDER."

But it wasn't brought to light via a presentation slide. Rather, Lexi glossed over his disorder. Maybe she had tact after all, I don't know. I found it odd that she could so boldly speak about his arrest for drug possession, being busted with another woman by his wife, or "seducing away another man's fiancée in a misguided attempt to prove a point," as Togsy had written. But when it came to something that was not his fault, it was taboo.

She closed the presentation and flipped on the light. "As for Mr. Cabral's *secret*—it's all guesswork on Togsender's part, and I think we can pass it off as such. In my literary opinion, and you can quote me on this, Jerome, *BrownStoners* is sensationalistic tripe, more fantasy than fiction, and not worth the paper it's printed on. Minimalize it."

"But that's not accurate," Samuel murmured.

"You can't know that until you read the book, Samuel," I said gently.

"We were destructive and it ruined lives. I know the truth. So do Lyle and Caroline." He turned to the room. "As for my 'secret,' it would be impossible to *minimalize*. I just..." Samuel lowered shamed eyes to the table. "I don't want my readers to know about it. Any of it."

Jerome nodded thoughtfully. "Certainly not. Ace, I assume you will accordingly adjust your media sources' incentives, should the details of this rubbish be leaked to them?"

"I think my firm can arrange it." Ah, so *that* was it—Caulfield Law Firm was paying off the gossip tabs. This man was the secret weapon Caroline deployed whenever they encroached too closely. Who better to keep Samuel's personal indiscretions personal than an old-money family with industry clout and one-hundred years-on-the-job training? The longer I sat in this meeting, the more I realized how many complicated layers of secrecy had accumulated to protect Samuel's image.

"Excellent," said Jerome. "Continue to comb through the passages and pick low-hanging fruit which would warrant an injunction and potential defamation lawsuit. If that proves difficult, then we'll extend a monetary offer to Mr. Togsender via Caulfield Law Firm. Quick and easy." AKA, hush money. "Now, Mr. Cabral. You said you want to keep your, ah, secret...a secret?"

Samuel shrugged, resigned.

Jerome's eyebrows shot up. "Well, we'll operate under the assumption that you *do*. We deal with these sorts of things all the time."

The poor accountant was the only man who looked decidedly confused, and I realized that Samuel's "secret" must have been discussed at length before we arrived. Figures.

Molly was also confused. "I'm not sure I'm following this discussion. Which secret are we talking about here?"

Samuel opened his mouth to speak, but Lexi cut her off. "There's a reason it's a secret, Ms. Jones."

Now. If there was one thing that made Samuel fume, it was being discounted. He had patience, but it seemed to have reached its limits. His eyes flashed. "No, Molly has a point. Why call it a secret, since it's so obvious you all are privy to it. Call it what it is—my *illness*."

Mouths dropped open around the table.

"That's harsh," Lexi whispered.

"I haven't heard it called that since the eighties," Ace said thoughtfully.

"It's the truth. I live with this disorder every day of my life, Ms. Rogers, Mr. Buitre. I call it a *disease*, because that's what it is. What buzzword would you prefer I use?"

"I'm sorry. I don't know," she stammered.

"'Lifestyle choice,' perhaps? That seems to be the phrase these days," Ace offered.

"A *choice?*" Samuel threw up his hands in frustration. To my left, Justin stifled a chuckle.

"Have you considered that Samuel could just come out with his disorder and stick it to Lyle Togsender?" I offered Samuel an encouraging smile. "Then he wouldn't have to hide it anymore."

Justin's laughter was now audible.

Jerome frowned. "Well, it certainly has been done before. But I should warn you, Mr. Cabral's female fan base would be sorely disappointed."

"Really, Mr. Buitre, I don't think women are that shallow. That's an awfully archaic idea."

"So is calling it a *disorder*, Ms. Trilby."

"If anything, they'd be supportive!"

"Trust me, my dear, hearts will break."

Justin slapped the table with his palm, repressed tears leaking from the corners of his eyes. "Not all hearts." He snorted. "Some might be pretty damned thrilled."

Jerome cleared his throat, effectively calling for silence. "Perhaps we should leave this particular decision in Mr. Cabral's capable hands. If you do decide to come out, though, please give us plenty of advance warning."

Molly loosed a bark of incredulity through the speakerphone, right about the time comprehension coated me in a bucket of red paint. Oh holy schnikes. They thought he was gay? That's what this was about?

"There's a certain unspoken protocol to follow," Jerome continued. "Statement to *People Magazine*—we can mix it in with the marriages, divorces, and Malawian adoptions, then hope for a feel-good feature. Spot on *The View*, award show acceptance speech when the nominations for *Water Sirens* begin to roll in, et cetera."

Wow. Caroline was good. *Really* good. Next to me, Samuel's drumming fingers stilled.

"I'm not gay," he said plainly.

Jerome flashed him a thumbs up. "Which is exactly how you should say it to the media hounds when they ask, in my opinion."

Samuel's eyes widened. "No. I'm really *not* gay. This is pure speculation."

Expressions around the table ranged from sympathetic to dubious, but not a one—except maybe Justin—believed him.

"I have a girlfriend," he stammered.

Your ex-wife, their eyes answered.

"I'm in love with her."

Which is why you hired her as your publicist. Uh-huh. Samuel looked to me helplessly. Hey, he didn't need to convince *me* of his sexual preference. But we very well couldn't tell a room full of PR execs that Samuel and I once dented a wall, could we?

"I've had relationships in the past," he grumbled.

*That didn't last the blink of an eye and remained relatively sexless, according to…*ah crap. Caroline's signed affidavits. No wonder these people didn't believe Samuel. And the public wouldn't, either, when the book was released. Jerome was right. Samuel's female fans could spout the typical platitudes—"good for him…so glad he can be himself…I always wondered"—but secretly, part of his appeal, other than his addictive books, was the idea they could screw him silly if given the opportunity. Jaime would be impressed. Heck, we probably *gave* Caroline the idea with our faux-lesbo diner antics. In another life, the floozy could have been my friend.

But, in the midst of this Shakespearean misunderstanding, truth struck: the book never once mentioned Samuel's bipolar disorder.

I didn't know what to make of Caroline Ortega. For some reason, she hadn't told Togsy. Or, if she had, he'd refrained from writing about it.

No bipolar disorder. Dodged a bullet. As for the rest, aside from the potshot at Samuel's sexual prowess with the female species, everything Lexi'd shared in her PowerPoint was the truth—nothing a little digging wouldn't turn up. The question was, how *accurate* was Togsy's truth? For that, I needed the book.

"Samuel's telling the truth: he's not gay. Now can we please move on so I can get a copy of this book?"

Jerome's smile twisted. "Bottom line. In Buitre's professional opinion, the publication of this book would be detrimental to Mr. Cabral's career. Ms. Ortega and Mr. Togsender must be stopped."

The rest of the meeting was a blur of contingency plans. But the one thing no one seemed willing to discuss was the possibility of simply opening up about Samuel's past and letting the public make of it what they will. Buitre was hell-bent on playing Merry Maids. I tried to catch Samuel's eye, but he clandestinely scribbled away in his Moleskine. I wasn't sure if he was taking notes or composing poetry.

Finally, we broke for lunch.

"Jerome," I said, "while I'm thinking about it, I'd like a hard copy of that book this afternoon."

A look passed between him and Lexi. "I'm afraid I have it under lock and key at the Bertelsmann Building," she answered. Jerome patted her back and left the room.

"Well, can someone bring it over?"

"It's Sunday."

I pursed my lips. What happened to the "expediency is everything" mantra? I searched the room for Samuel and Ace Caulfield, hoping for some backup. They were tucked away in the corner, immersed in a somber conversation. Samuel's hands vaguely trembled as Ace handed him some sort of brown-wrapped package no bigger than a shoe box. Curious, I watched them for a moment, then turned back to Lexi.

"The book?"

Lexi sighed. "It'll be two days before I can have a copy made. Even then, I can't allow it to leave my office."

"Then I'll just hole up in your office to read it." Son-of-a-monkey. Time to seek other paths.

To my frustration, Justin fell in line with Lexi. "Just forget about the book for an hour and come to lunch with us, Kaye." He grinned. "We'll hit a sushi place down the street, maybe find Cabral a boyfriend."

Samuel appeared at my side and wrapped an arm around my waist. He kissed my neck…then my shoulder…then my temple. Man was still hung up on the fact that the entire room believed he was gay. "Lunch?" he asked.

"I'm going to stay behind and take care of some stuff."

"Try to rest a bit in one of the conference rooms." He kissed me again for good measure. "I'll bring you a turkey and Swiss."

When the room was empty, I whipped out my phone and got to work. Forget the nap. I had roughly one hour to get my hands on a copy of that book. Instinct told me there was something in it they didn't want Samuel to read, and they planned to put us off indefinitely. I had a feeling they were desperate to show a confident face to their client while, behind the scenes, they juggled hoops. Caroline had the right idea in dealing with Buitre—strike before struck.

Caroline…

Eh. Might as well go straight to the source. I sucked it up and punched in her number.

"The number you have dialed is not in service. Please check the number and dial again, or dial 6-1-1 for customer assistance…"

A minute later, the email I'd fired off to her account bounced back, too. I tapped my fingernails on the table, baffled. Then, snap—she no longer worked for The Buitre Group, did she? So kind of her to leave a new contact number.

Time for Plan B.

I called Berkshire House and worked my way through their phone system until I got Lexi's voice mail:

"My office hours are Monday through Friday, seven thirty a.m. to six p.m. If this is an emergency, please contact me at 2-1-2—"

I quickly hung up. Dang it, I'd hoped for an out-of-office contact name—someone else I could finagle into getting me a copy of that manuscript. Did I even have a Plan C?

Yes I did.

As I dialed my former fling's number—the critic for the New York mag—guilt crept up my throat. I was glad Samuel was out to lunch, so I wouldn't have to explain. Mr. Avant Garde answered, his tone playful.

"Kaye, two calls in one weekend. Are you sure you aren't looking for a hookup? Maybe a little phone fun?" he teased.

I pursed my lips, stifling a chuckle. "I told you, I'm happily taken. But I do need another itsy-bitsy, teeny-weeny favor from you."

"Whaddya need?"

"A name and number. The assistant to Lexi Rogers, Editorial Director with Berkshire House. You know her?"

"Sure. I know her assistant, too. I met both of them while rubbing elbows at a book launch several weeks ago. Berkshire House knows how to throw a party for their authors." I wondered if it was the party Samuel bailed on when he fled to Colorado. "Her assistant's name is Robin something-or-other. Here's the number…"

I jotted it down, then half-promised Mr. Avant Garde a cup of coffee to get him off the phone. I punched in this Robin person's number, praying she'd answer.

"Robin speaking." *Craaaaaap.* The voice was confusingly androgynous, and I realized "Robin" could be either a squeaky man or a woman who'd kick my tail.

"Robin, hi. This is Kaye Trilby—Samuel Cabral's publicist." I heard a quiet gasp on the other end. Still no clue as to gender. "Listen, I'm in a bind. I need an advance read hard copy of a book sent to me ASAP, but I can't get a hold of Lexi. Lyle Togsender's *BrownStoners: A Houseful of Famous Pens and Crack Pipes.* It's absolutely imperative Mr. Cabral receives it this afternoon, you understand." I kept talking, not giving him/her a chance to object. "Now, I'll need you to write down this address. Are you ready?"

"Ms. Trilby, I'm not even in the office—"

"Are you in town?"

"Yes."

"Well, like I said, it's an emergency. You'll find it in Lexi's office."

He/she sighed. "Go ahead."

Yes. I rattled off Samuel's apartment address, reminding Robin once again I needed the book couriered there immediately.

"Okay. I'll give Lexi a quick call."

Wait. Call Lexi? No!

He/she mumbled a good-bye and hung up, leaving me slack-jawed and freaking out. For five minutes, I bit my nails and stared at my phone, terrified Lexi would call me back and ream me. When it finally did ring, I exhaled. Robin again.

"Ms. Trilby, I couldn't get a hold of Lexi, either. She typically won't take calls over lunch. And according to her schedule, she's in a meeting all afternoon. I can try back this evening—"

"No!" Dang it, desperate times called for desperate manipulation. Hoping Robin was a dude, I mustered my best pathetic, sniffly girl voice. "Robin, *please*. I really, reeeally need that book now, or I'm as good as sacked. Mr. Cabral is absolutely livid he didn't receive a copy of the book. I mean, *livid*. Eyes-bulging, hand-flailing, hair-pulling L–I–V–I–D. I even heard him mumble something about a rival publishing house."

"*No,*" Robin gasped.

"*Yes!*" I exclaimed. "I know Lexi would send a copy if she could. I really don't want Berkshire House's most acclaimed author upset with her, you know? No telling what he'd decide to do…"

"Say no more. I'll get Mr. Cabral a copy as of yesterday, Ms. Trilby."

I polished my nails on my shoulders. Oh yeah, I was good. "Thank you so much, Robin," I said sweetly. "I'll be sure to tell Mr. Cabral how helpful you've been."

I probably should have felt like a manipulative ho-bag for scaring the kid, but for now I'd won, so it kind of voided the ho-baggish feeling. But I could see how, if you moved in this playing field long enough like Caroline had, you could grow used to manipulating people and situations to get what you wanted. I'd have to tread carefully.

Before long, Samuel's crack-shot team filtered back from lunch, and we dived in again. He slid into the seat next to me and plopped a deli bag under my nose.

"Did you rest?" he asked, smiling down at me.

"Enough." I returned his smile, crossing my fingers that Robin wouldn't disappoint.

Chapter 11
FIRST

*New skydivers should be aware
that every time they utter the word "first,"
they must buy veteran skydivers a case of beer.
To avoid this particularly expensive pitfall,
it is in the first-timer's best interest
to forget it's the first time.*

A tide of people washed us underground like autumn leaves down a gutter, and into a passage that led from the neon chaos of Times Square to the Port Authority. The stale tunnel hadn't breathed fresh air in eons. Mucky-white tiles blurred as we hoofed it to catch the northbound A Train. Ball cap brim tugged down, Samuel secured my hand in his, releasing it only to drop a few bucks in a busker's guitar case.

He insisted we take the subway, determined to cure me of my aversion by tossing me headfirst into big, scary NYC. I begged for a cab, brain-weary after a long day of what The Buitre Group called "lateral thinking" (the rest of the sane world called it problem solving). I wanted to get to Samuel's apartment as quickly as possible to see if Robin followed through.

When I'd last been in the subway, I was a twenty-year-old kid blindly stumbling through a foreign city. I was still stumbling, but not alone. Samuel was beside me, guiding me to his park-side home in Inwood with all the tenderness and hope and fear of a new lover. He was anxious to please me. I didn't want to let him down, either.

Now I just had to master the stupid subway turnstile.

I swiped the flimsy card and pushed the bar again with my hip (there was no way I was touching that germ haven with my hands). It didn't budge, for the third time.

"Swipe it the opposite direction," Samuel said.

The monster machine beeped at me.

"Try it again, a little slower." Samuel was a picture of patience, but the man behind us was not.

"Come on, crazy woman, what's the holdup? It's not that hard!" Apparently harder than saying Huitzilopochtli.

Samuel swiveled to face the guy, body tensing. "There are four other turnstiles—" he gestured to them "—so lay off, man."

"Yeah, packed with people." The guy smacked a weathered hand over an equally weathered Yankees cap, challenging Samuel's Red Sox cap.

Ignoring him, Samuel shifted the brown package under his arm and asked for my MetroCard. All it took was one swipe, and so went my life.

We found a corner in the subway car, cozy against the press of people making their way home to West-Side neighborhoods. A woman reeking of alcohol hovered over me, a picnic basket at her feet. I subtly turned my nose into the soft cotton of Samuel's shirt, breathing in his scent. It didn't seem to bother him. He was used to the mix of stench and sweet, grunge and color—a dissonance that strangely made sense in the city.

Ever an observer, Samuel was enthralled by the stories around him. My eyes drifted, seeing what he saw. Advertisements on bludgeoned walls, rough-and-tumble people clinging to poles, swaying with the subway. To the left, a raven-haired woman peeled blinding-yellow polish from her nails and let it flutter to the floor. To the right, a man with temple locks flipped through the latest suspense novel. A little further into the car, a bum sprawled on a seat, slurring a Sinatra song between plaque-darkened teeth. So many stories.

He drew my attention when his warm breath hit my ear.

"There's a sort of unspoken subway etiquette you pick up if you spend enough time in the city," he said. "First, stay to the right of the stairs unless you're in a hurry."

"We did that."

"Let everyone off the train before you get on. Don't touch someone's hand with your sweaty palms when you're holding a pole. Give up your seat for pregnant women and the elderly. Also—never, *never* eyeball the homeless."

"Oh." Whoops.

"And, under *all* circumstances, avoid completely empty cars on an otherwise full train."

My eyes widened, thinking of stabbings and crime scenes. "Why?"

Samuel grinned. "Because there's shit in the car and everyone knows it."

I wrinkled my nose. Several people around us chuckled, probably because they'd been there before.

Gradually, the car emptied with each stop as we rattled north to Washington Heights, until there were only a handful of people remaining. Samuel thrummed his fingers against the package resting in his lap, nervously describing all of the places he wanted to show me. Central Park, the Met, the Morgan Library, Chinatown…

"And The Dakota, of course. If we go to Graceland to pay our respects, we have to lay it down for Lennon. Do you remember the class project I helped you with when you were twelve, about the assassination? Angel told you the shooting was a government conspiracy engineered through a complex code in newspaper headlines, and I had a terrible time convincing you otherwise. You were such a stubborn girl, still are. Of course, the way that Lennon treated his son Julian was quite shameful, so it's difficult to pay respects and not remember that aspect. Everyone has their personal failings, I suppose…"

He rambled on, and I began to get that "off" feeling again. His chatter wasn't like the over-enthusiastic manic-babbling of LA. Rather, it seemed as though he did it to focus his mind so it wouldn't stray—namely, to Caroline Ortega's betrayal. He'd had such faith in her, but even he couldn't deny she'd played some part in this mess.

And yet, I couldn't help but wonder if it was an eggshells day…

"Samuel, did you take your meds?"

His story about John Lennon's spectacles ground to a halt. His eyes went cold. "Kaye, did you wear clothes today?"

The rest of the ride was chilly and silent.

The train slowly pulled in to the 190th Street station. Samuel ground his teeth as we left the platform and stepped into an industrial elevator, brusquely nodding to the attendant.

But the odd discomfort melted away when the doors opened and we stepped into a world of green, green, green. The picture Samuel sent me weeks ago didn't do the place justice. Some brilliant city planner made wondrous use of the naturally hilly terrain, and what emerged was a fairy-tale blend of stone arches and shady foliage. As we climbed higher into the Fort Tryon Park, I caught a glimpse of the Hudson River far below, gray and hazy.

"Are you sure this is Manhattan?"

"Oh yes, we're on the edge of Washington Heights. Take a jaunt south down Broadway and you'll hit the Dominican neighborhood, follow the merengue. But these bluffs…I always feel as though I'm walking through a Thoreau poem when I'm here," Samuel murmured. "'Give me thy most privy place, where to run my airy race…' The park's still something of a secret. Or it seems that way, to me."

My lips quirked—Samuel and his poetry. For him, musing over the Romantics was akin to breathing, it came so naturally. If I tried, I'd sound like a haughty snoot.

"So, which bench do you sleep on?"

He laughed. "None of these. My apartment building is across that grassy stretch—see the archway?—then down a set of stairs. This is a roundabout way to get there, but I couldn't wait to show you the park."

We walked in silence. Suddenly, Samuel dragged light fingers along my spine and I jumped. His face was full of apology.

"I'm sorry I snapped at you about my meds. It was a fair question."

I waved him away. "It's okay. I'm not your parent."

"I'm trying to be more open about it."

"I know."

He rubbed the knuckle of my ring finger, squeezed it, and let it go, his face twisted in defeat. It made me sad. No, no defeat, Samuel. Look how far we'd traveled on this third road. Two months ago, I wouldn't have even known to ask about the meds.

I watched him shuffle the package between his arms. "Speaking of being open, are you going to tell me what's in that thing?" I nudged him with my elbow. "Did Ace bring you a bust of Ted Williams?"

"Um…no. It's an urn."

I cocked my head. An urn?

"It contains my mother's ashes."

I pivoted so quickly, my purse swung off my shoulder. "You've been carrying a cremation urn all afternoon? Your…y-your mother." My hands flew to my mouth as I eyed the package that contained the earthly remains of Rachel Caulfield Cabral. "I wish I'd known. Oh Samuel, I'm so sorry." I had no idea what to say, so only awkwardness spilled from my mouth. "We should have taken the taxi so you didn't have to carry them—her—onto the subway. What if you'd been robbed?"

He shrugged. "Then some thief would be sorely disappointed."

"Where did it—she—come from?"

"Ace's relatives came across them in the family home. He called and asked if I wanted the urn. I guess no one else did."

"That's really heartbreaking." Sorrow for Rachel Caulfield Cabral crept into my chest, in spite of myself. I eyed the morbid box as we descended the park stairs into the neighborhood below.

He was right—the bottom of the bluff was a different world of Art Deco and fire escapes.

"Is it legal to fly with remains?"

"I don't know. Ace took his family's private plane. Here's my place." He stopped in front of an eight-story façade with awnings. I noticed he refused to refer to the Caulfields as his own family. I knew he'd never cared about them, but his omission was so deliberate, it was almost passive aggressive.

As he collected his held mail from the doorman, I took in the lobby. Cracked tile floors, mint walls—nothing like the gentrified East Village brownstones. According to Samuel, Inwood suited him perfectly, unlike the "bohemian" neighborhoods south of 14th Street. I jokingly called him a snob. Yet another dichotomy of Samuel Caulfield Cabral, formerly of Lyons. He turned up his nose at pretension, but kept his own secrets and failings guarded beneath a veneer of flawlessness.

"So, what are you going to do with the urn?" I hedged.

He sighed. "No clue. I'd rather not talk about it anymore."

Yes, Samuel's head needed some serious *fēng shui*, but like he said, he was trying. Open him carefully…I fingered the laminated poem in my purse.

There was nothing more I could do for Samuel right now, and frankly, he didn't want me to. I wrapped my arms around his middle and murmured a last "I'm so sorry about your mother." Then I promptly collapsed into the first bed I was steered toward, where sleep came to collect.

Mmmm, soft bed. Beautiful, cozy bed. A very nice smelling bed.

Then why was I yanked from its bliss?

I burrowed into the right side, but my body slid to the left, where the mattress sagged. How funny that, after years of sleeping alone, we both preferred our respective sides of the bed. I savored the warmth of the familiar quilt, almost positive it was the comforter we'd had on our bed in Boulder.

Actually, this *was* our bed from Boulder.

And wasn't that the armchair we'd salvaged from a university Dumpster?

I didn't know when or why Samuel had acquired our ratty old stuff, but I vaguely recalled asking Sofia to get rid of it when she helped decorate my place above TrilbyJones. My heart hammered in my chest. If Samuel's pilfering of our rag-tag furniture wasn't such a testament to our obsession with the "glory days," it would have been sweet.

As I hovered just above dreams, I heard it again—Samuel's low voice. He was talking to somebody in Spanish, but the door muffled most of his conversation and my bad ear didn't help. I strained to hear and translate.

"...we're staying in the city for now, *sí*...I don't know how long... No, it's fine, *Papá*..."

It was Alonso on the phone. A sudden pang of fear twisted my gut. What if Alonso flew to New York again? Would he try to force me out? Send me home? My fingers fisted around the comforter. Well, I wasn't going without a fight.

Dragging the quilt with me, I rolled from the bed and pattered to the doorway, my feet cold against the oak floor. I peered into the softly lit living room and saw Samuel beyond the sofa, his lilting Spanish words echoing through the vaulted ceiling. A brown grocery bag sat on the counter, abandoned for the phone. He'd gone to the store while I slept. I pulled the blanket around me like a cape and watched him. One hand clutched his cell, the other gripped the fireplace mantle, where his mother's urn now rested.

"...I said it's fine, you and *Mamá* stay in Lyons. We can handle this on our own."

My fingers slowly unclenched. Samuel told them not to come. He wanted to face this *together*. Was it wrong to feel giddy?

"...Yes, she's okay. Sleeping right now, it was a long day...She is staying here, not a hotel. We've been married, *Papá*, it's not as if..."

A frustrated grunt, and then, "...I told you, no more episodes... *Yes*, I'm still on my meds...Well, if I sound irritated, it's because I am irritated."

I shifted, and the floor squeaked beneath my feet. Samuel's head shot up. His troubled face softened, and he beckoned me into the room. I crossed quickly and wrapped my arms around his waist.

He switched to English. "I'll talk to you later. Give my love to *Mamá*. Tell her not to worry." He set his phone on the mantle, then folded me into his arms.

"Did you have a good nap?"

"Yes. Almost like I was in my own bed," I hinted.

"I liked our old bed—sue me." Samuel laughed quietly. "It's actually the only bedroom in this place. But honestly, if I had a guest room, I still would have put you in my bed."

Because I belonged there, on the right side. "Your father thinks it's wrong that I'm staying here with you, doesn't he?"

"He's more concerned than anything. But I think he understands the unorthodox position we're in." It was odd, not feeling as though the eyes of Lyons were upon me. The seclusion of Samuel's New York haven was freeing. Here, we were only answerable to God. I nipped his chin and he smiled down at me.

"A Berkshire courier dropped something off for you," he said, holding up a package. "It's marked urgent."

"Oh!" I took it from his hands and ripped it open. Out slid a freshly printed copy of *BrownStoners: A Houseful of Famous Pens and Crack Pipes*. Thank you, Robin.

"I'm not even going to ask what you had to do in order to pry that from their hands."

"Nothing illegal. At least, I don't think so." *Only unethical.* I cringed. "But I should warn you, Lexi's PA now believes you're the devil incarnate. The next time you see Robin, he/she might douse you with holy water."

His eyebrows shot into his hairline. "He/she?"

"I wasn't sure," I admitted and handed him the book.

"Robin's a man." Ha, I knew it.

As he flipped through the pages, I scanned his apartment. Like Fort Tryon, this small space suited Samuel. Sofia's handiwork was everywhere—warm colors, iron accents, even a few scented candles that had never been lit. There was a digital piano I'd never seen before, and he'd placed our guitars next to it. Mixed in with newer pieces of furniture were our flea market finds from Boulder. The woven screen we'd used as a room divider now separated the living room from an office space. The mismatched end tables I'd sanded and painted blue were tucked against either side of Samuel's sofa. There was the stained glass floor lamp I'd mooned over at an art festival. Samuel had returned the next day and bought it for me, despite his measly copywriter's salary.

I now knew he'd never touched his inheritance, not even to buy me things. But I was glad he hadn't—we didn't have much money then, but our resourcefulness made for some beautiful memories.

I slipped from his arms and ran my fingers along the intricate lamp shade. Its soft glow flecked colors across an array of framed photos. I studied them and saw they, too, were from the studio apartment. Two children clinging to their fathers' necks…making fish-faces at the Denver Aquarium…Samuel with a baseball bat slung over his shoulder, me in an oversized jersey that hit my knees. Even the picture of Samuel's graduation I'd found in his Lyons bedroom now rested on one of the end tables—its original home. Next to it was a five-by-seven of—gulp—our wedding.

A lump formed in my throat. The only way I hadn't drowned was to hide my photo albums beneath the dust ruffle of a new bed, surrounded by new things…albeit, in a familiar city. Samuel had done the opposite. He'd surrounded himself with familiar things in a new city.

Samuel answered my unasked questions. "Mom put our old things in storage for me. When I finally got my own place, I had it shipped to Manhattan."

"It must have cost a fortune to ship. Much more than it's worth."

"It was worth it."

I felt his warmth behind me. His fingertips grazed my neck as he pushed my tangled hair over my shoulder. I dragged my palm up his forearm and circled his wrist, cuffing him to me. A thought flitted through my head—I hadn't seen the Rolex Caroline gave him for a long time, not since he left Lyons after Danita's wedding.

"It must have been awkward when you brought a date over," I whispered. "Can't really pass the gal in those photos off as your sister... especially the wedding picture."

"I've never brought a date here," he murmured.

"What about Caroline?" I blurted, then internally smacked myself when his hands froze.

"Caro's been here before, but not as a date." I felt his scowl turn into a smile against my neck. "She was seconds away from calling my psychiatrist. Quite an image, isn't it? The tortured writer, alone, save for the pictures of his past. The last remnants of love, a dusty shrine hung upon his wall for all posterity...or the next tenant, at least."

I turned and gave him a wry grin. "Good grief, are you a writer? I never knew." Trailing a finger down his chest, I hooked it under his belt. He flinched, but in a good way. "So, tortured writer. Think you could scrounge up some dinner in this dusty shrine, or do you only live on purple prose?"

His eyes widened at my mocking and he answered me with a bruising kiss that, I swear, made my lips go numb.

He always did know how to make me shut up.

Samuel got the first crack at *BrownStoners*.

A small television mounted above his dresser quietly aired reruns of some low-budget sci-fi show, but he was engrossed in the manuscript resting against his thighs.

Clutching my bath towel around me with one hand, I tried not to steal glances at his shapely torso as I dug through my suitcase, hunting for my camisole and sleep shorts. I found them at the bottom and dangled them from my fingers, frowning at the wrinkled mess.

He watched me with murky eyes.

Okay, so I was a bit of a tease. I couldn't help it—his silent attention made me feel sexy. I shimmied into my night things, my shyness long forgotten.

"Are you trying to kill me?"

I lifted an eyebrow and tied the drawstrings of my shorts. "If I'd wanted to kill you, I'd have dropped the towel."

Placing the book on his nightstand, he patted the bed. I climbed into his lap and gently kissed his lips. "It's after midnight, Samuel. I know we're still on West Coast time, but we really should try to sleep."

"I should have put you in a hotel," he groaned. "This is a lot harder than I thought it would be."

I bit my lip, stifling my laughter. But it broke through anyway, and peals echoed through his apartment until tears blurred my sight. Samuel tossed me off his lap.

"And now you've killed that too, cruel woman." He stretched his arms over his head then fumbled for the TV remote while I pulled the lamp chain.

It never was truly dark here, in the city. I settled against Samuel's chest and absently toyed with his chest hair. It was quiet, save for the rumbles of cars and an occasional heavy bass blaring from cracked speakers. A cool breeze wafted through the open window and blew across our faces. It wasn't a Midtown penthouse, but Samuel's apartment still had an unreal view of the George Washington suspension bridge spanning the Hudson. At night, its lights glowed against the water like Christmas strands. Ripples pulsed with Latin beats floating down from northern blocks, and they lulled me. I could get used to gazing at the city with Samuel sprawled beneath me as I fell asleep.

"Kaye?" Samuel dragged a lazy thumbnail up my spine.

"Hmmm?"

"Thanks for watching my back. I know I wasn't much help today."

"No problem," I mumbled into his chest.

"Just don't do anything to compromise yourself, especially not for my sake. Okay?"

I nodded. "How is the piece of tabloid trash?"

He paused for so long, I nearly drifted to sleep. "Actually, Lyle's book is good."

"What do you mean?"

"The writing is clever. Engaging. I've only read the first twenty pages, but I can already tell it's quality work."

"But it's a poison pen."

"I don't know if it is. And don't forget, Caroline has the ace in her back pocket — my bipolar disorder — and she didn't use it."

I frowned, his quiet logic not making sense in my addled brain. "If you're right, why would The Buitre Group and Berkshire House lie? What do they have to gain?"

"I have no clue. That's what I find troubling."

I sighed and tugged the covers tightly around our bodies. "We'll get to the bottom of it tomorrow."

Even though my heavy eyelids drew shut like magnets, alarms kicked in. If Samuel couldn't write off this book—and Caroline Ortega—as money-grubbing tripe, then maybe I shouldn't, either. At least not yet.

We spent the morning exploring the Cloisters, an annex of the Met which housed Medieval art. The Cloisters had been plucked from monasteries in Southern France and reassembled right in the middle of Fort Tryon Park, on a hill overlooking the Hudson.

While Samuel studied a gold-leafed gradual, I wandered into the next room. A handful of sarcophagi graced the walls, each topped with a depiction of its former occupant. Some were cracked, others missed noses and toes. I peered down at the figure of a robed lady, her stone face sanguine. Was she still inside her tomb? I thought not. After eight hundred years, she'd long since turned to dust.

As my finger ghosted over the woman's aquiline nose, my thoughts strayed to Rachel Caulfield and her urn, resting prominently above her son's fireplace. Maybe he felt guilty she'd been tucked away in a closet at the ancestral home in Boston—it would be a very "Samuel" sentiment. I watched him unawares…hands stuffed in his pockets, rocking on his heels as he explored with unabashed curiosity, and glimpsed the boy I once knew. I was certain he'd used this place for inspiration in *Water Sirens*, and my heart lurched because he'd shared it with me.

He caught me staring. Smiling, he crossed the room and took my hand.

"Are you finished in here?"

I nodded.

"Come on, I'll show you a bizarre plant in the garden called a Dragon Arum. It has this huge spadix that's overtly phallic—the docent told me it's supposedly an aphrodisiac." He winked. Such a nerd.

"Why would monks grow aphrodisiacs?"

"They probably made a killing selling it. That, or it had another use, like curing constipation."

"That's the most romantic thing I've ever heard."

Hours later, we left the Cloisters and settled beneath a shade tree. Samuel paged through Togsy's book while I flicked bread crumbs at fat sparrows hopping around our feet.

Aside from Togsy's acerbic portrayal of Samuel as a spoiled mandiva who caved in to drugs and drove away his wife (which was a big "aside") there was a lot to like about the memoir. It painted a witty portrait of destructive young writers living together before their careers skyrocketed or failed. Samuel called it an "Allen Ginsberg shakes hands with Evelyn Waugh" tale. I thought it sounded like a *Rent* rip-off, but hey.

Then there was the speculation around Samuel's sexuality. Every time he came across one of those passages, he'd clench his jaw.

"My sexual preferences shouldn't be a spectacle in the first place," he muttered. "Why would they ruin a perfectly good book with this tabloid garbage?"

"Because tabloid garbage sells?"

"No. Caroline's not a sell-out."

"But maybe Togsy *is* and Caroline doesn't want to rain on his parade."

While he highlighted, I scrolled through over a hundred email forwards from Justin. Caroline had been looped in on everything. Viral stats on the latest *Water Sirens* movie trailer release. TV commercials that would air in a month. The original *Water Sirens* book re-release with a new cover that screamed: *Now a major motion picture!* And my favorite, a fast food promo deal featuring plastic cups with Indigo Kingsley's curvaceous Neelie Nixie scaling the straw.

I'd hopped onto the world's tallest roller coaster just as it began its wild descent, and now scrambled to buckle my safety harness. I dropped my phone and groaned into the blanket. Immersed in *BrownStoners*, Samuel thought I was sympathizing with him.

"Here's another one," he snarled. "'Mr. Cabral sent Mrs. Cabral packing, though the method of disposal was needlessly complicated. The end of the marriage would have been less destructive had he chosen to embrace his true nature…instead of a feisty brunette co-ed.

Thus, the bohemian prodigy found he was both spineless and wifeless. Also, sexless…'"

"He forgot 'humorless,'" I teased.

"Flawless?" Samuel waggled his eyebrows.

"Tireless."

He swatted my bottom. "Clueless."

"Clothesless." I crooked my finger.

Samuel growled, tugging me onto his chest. "Pointless. Come here, mean thing."

For the rest of the afternoon, we enjoyed the last days of summer. I was now absolutely certain Caroline played Jaime and me like a pair of finger cymbals when we pulled the lesbian routine at the Lyons Diner. There was even an excerpt straight from Jaime's big mouth about rainbow wigs and gay pride parades.

Soon, the sun began to sink behind the tree line. Samuel dragged his reading glasses from his face and we called it a day.

"So I guess we're both in agreement the book isn't a poison pen," I said. "If anything, it's a satirical shooting spree through the New York artist community. Unfortunately, you happen to be its biggest casualty." I playfully shoved Samuel with my shoulder. "The question still is, why did Jerome and Lexi lie about the book?"

"Here's a thought," Samuel said as he swung our arms between us. "I hate to admit it, but *BrownStoners* has bestseller written all over it. And that's the last thing Buitre wants, because it will financially make Caro's new company. If she's successful, she becomes competition with insider knowledge."

I picked up his reasoning. "And Lexi claimed it was garbage, but maybe her true opinion is in line with yours. But the kicker is, there's no way Berkshire House can pick up *BrownStoners*."

"Not without publicly compromising my reputation." Samuel caught my elbow before I tripped over a curb. "However, that doesn't explain why they don't want me to read the book."

I snapped my fingers. "I know why. Because you're a good guy."

He jogged up his apartment building stairs and held the door open for me. "I'm not following."

"You try to do the right thing, Samuel. You have industry clout and they want to keep you in their corner. They want to manipulate your anger to quash Togsy's book—don't you see? They trot out their nasty PowerPoint slides, get you breathing fire, and boom! The book goes down and so does Caroline. Unfortunately, I was the one who got angry. *You* were the picture of composure." The elevator dinged. We waited for a couple in matching bowling uniforms to exit. When the doors closed, Samuel jocularly leaned into my side, then caught my waist to keep me from stumbling. He smelled like cut grass from the park.

"So you believe Buitre's afraid that if I read the book and saw it was legit, I'd relent because I'm a good guy, and Caroline gets her bestseller," he repeated, his voice tinted with humor. "Even though she supposedly sold me out."

"I think so." It seemed stupid when he spoke it. Or it may have been my brain short-circuiting when Samuel's hip subtly brushed against mine. He kissed my nose, my lips, then released me as the doors opened to the eighth floor.

"That makes me sound like a pushover. Frankly, there's a lot of objectionable crap in those pages and I'd rather it not see the light of day. I don't want to know who submitted the supposed affidavits confirming that nonsense."

"Well, I don't particularly like being called a 'waifish child-bride.' If I ever see Togsy, he'll get a kick to the groin." Samuel shut the door behind me and began flicking on lights. Dropping my messenger bag on the table, I kicked off my shoes and wiggled my toes. "But I know from experience that nothing hinders a PR campaign like a hesitant client, so they get marginalized. It's unethical and firms will never admit to it, but it happens. It's all about control."

"Or maybe they simply didn't see the urgency in providing us with a copy. Maybe we're being overly paranoid."

I shook my head. "I know stonewalling when I see it. We never would have gotten that book…at least, not in its current form."

Samuel plopped onto his sofa. He clasped his hands between his knees, head bent in quiet contemplation. At last, he raised resigned eyes.

"Kaye, I know how you feel about her, but I need to get Caroline's side of the story. We're missing something here."

"You're right." I dropped down next to him and rested my head on his shoulder, ready to eat yesterday's angry words. "There's a problem, though. Short of sitting outside her Upper East Side place while poodles piss on our shoes, we have no way to contact her. None of her old numbers and email addresses work."

A slow grin spread across Samuel's face. "Yes we do. My cousin can track her down."

"Can we trust Ace?"

"He's never given me a reason not to."

∞

That evening, the call I'd dreaded finally came. Lexi Rogers. Before I even answered, I felt her ire bouncing from cell tower to cell tower.

"This is Kaye."

"Ms. Trilby, my personal assistant just informed me you coerced him into sending you a copy of *BrownStoners*."

"Hello, Ms. Rogers," I said dryly.

"Did you, or did you not trick my PA?"

"I simply requested a copy of what you'd already promised my client. He had some reading time today, so I thought—"

"I specifically told you the draft was *not* to leave my office."

"Well, now it's under lock-and-key in Samuel's apartment."

"This is risky."

"Lexi—can I call you that? You truly have nothing to worry about. After reading it, I highly doubt he'll want it making the rounds. It's not exactly the trashy unauthorized bio your team portrayed, but it's hardly kind to Samuel."

There was a long stretch of silence, then what could have been a sigh of relief. "Jerome is going to be furious when he finds out we gave you the book."

"Why should he be?" More silence. It was my turn to sigh. "I'll be straight with you. I don't know what sort of office politics all of you are playing behind Mr. Cabral's back. But here's a bit of advice—the less you involve my client in them, the better. If Jerome will be furious about the book, fine. Just don't tell him."

"Perhaps," she replied, uncertain.

"Look, we'll discuss it later this week."

"Please remind Mr. Cabral that by the next meeting, he needs to decide whether he's coming out. Our publicists have to know how to respond."

I groaned. "He's not gay, so it won't be an issue. Thank you for calling." I hung up before her anger recovered and she dragged me into a second round.

I heard Samuel laugh from the kitchen as he fixed dinner.

"That sounded like an interesting call."

I scowled and picked a mushroom from the stir fry he tossed in a wok. "She had it coming." I tried to steal another mushroom, but he batted my hand away. He returned my glare with a mock scowl of his own.

"So fierce."

"Just hungry. And sick of this bull."

"It's only going to get worse, Kaye. If you want out—"

"No! I'm fine. I'm just not used to dealing with corporate bureaucracy, that's all. My TrilbyJones staff is all I can handle."

He looked at me steadily, doing that thing where he searched me out for a bluff. At last, he was satisfied I wasn't hiding my true feelings.

Samuel was right. It was about to get worse. And much, much more complicated.

Tuesday morning brought word from Ace Caulfield, who'd returned to his vomiting children and exhausted wife in Boston. Caroline Ortega was still in New York. She agreed to meet with Samuel and me, as long as it was on her turf—which meant trekking to the Upper East Side.

"I'm adamant about listening in on this meeting," Ace said, when Samuel put him on speakerphone. "I'm no literary critic, but I know what is and isn't libelous. You won't hear a peep from me unless you start promising her things or sharing info that could be used against you."

Samuel and I exchanged a look. His mental health would most likely come up in conversation. Was he willing to discuss aspects of it in front of Ace?

He nodded. "That's fine."

So, just before two o'clock, the two of us swept up pristine sidewalks not far from the Metropolitan Museum of Art. Townhouses ran the length of the street, a hodgepodge of styles from bulky Federals to airy Italian villas. Beyond the row of homes loomed the imposing pre-war apartments of Fifth Avenue. Beautifully kept window boxes splashed brick walls with color, and mature shade trees hung over the curbside, pruned to perfection so they wouldn't scratch the high-end cars lining the streets.

Samuel stopped in front of a stately five-story home. "This is it."

I would have known it before he said it. Its peach walls, white window frames, and balcony had been dragged here straight from the Antebellum South. He jogged up the stairs and rang the bell.

The door creaked open. I wasn't sure how I expected Caroline to appear, but my imagination fluctuated between power suit and devil horns. What I hadn't expected was a woman who was, for all intents and purposes, a mess. Posh exterior abandoned, she slumped to the door in worn jeans and an oversized sweater, though it was early September. Her hair was haphazardly twisted up, a pencil holding it in place. Instead of makeup, glasses framed tired eyes.

"Hello, Caroline," Samuel said softly.

"Samuel." She wavered in the doorway, not knowing how to greet him. Finally, she stepped aside and gestured us into her home.

"Kaye — good to see you again. I'm sorry for the clutter," she said over her shoulder, though the spacious home was immaculate. "I've been inundated by work."

You and me both.

I peered around the open foyer, searching for a humungous portrait of Caro with a poodle or some other yippy animal in her lap. Instead, a large sketch of a sailboat hung at the top of the magnificent curved staircase.

"Not only are we trying to get a new business off the ground, we also have our current authors' needs to attend to," she explained.

"I'm sure you've also been quite busy with Togsy's book," I added with a bitter edge.

Caro paused to appraise me with cool eyes, then nodded. "That, too. I've barely had time to sleep, but it's coming together."

"That's what we want to talk to you about — *BrownStoners*. What's with the melodrama?"

Samuel shot me a warning glance. "We simply want to hear your side of the story, Caro. Kaye didn't mean — "

"Don't scold her, Samuel Cabral. Let her do her job; she's good at it." Her Carolina accent thickened. "She's also right — it *is* a bunch of drama. Coffee?"

I nodded, picking up my jaw from the polished floor. Samuel, however, didn't seem surprised. Instead, he brushed my hand with his and murmured an earnest apology.

"Anyway, the book," her voice carried from the kitchen. "I can understand where you're coming from, Kaye. If I was still Samuel's publicist, I'd be pretty damned wary of me, too."

She emerged with three mugs and a coffee carafe on a tray. Ever the gentleman, Samuel instantly stepped forward and took it from her hands. She led us up the staircase and into a brightly lit hallway. More artwork hung on both walls—a series of dreamy nautical paintings in sea blues and sand. She saw me studying one.

"They're a series I did of the Carolina coast. I have a small studio in the attic where I paint and sketch, though I haven't had much time for it in recent years, what with career demands."

And Samuel's celebrity, I added, seeing him grimace.

We followed her into a room at the end of the hall—her office. A desk and bookshelves took up most of the space, along with a Queen Anne longue and two armchairs that were too classy to be ostentatious. Caroline pushed a pile of papers to the side and indicated for Samuel to set down the tray.

Taking a mug of piping coffee, he stirred it, his brow creased. Finally, he plunked it down and leaned forward.

"Why didn't you fill me in on your plan to leave Buitre, Caro? We may have not treated each other well in recent months, but we've always been honest."

"I couldn't risk you or Kaye accidentally tipping off Buitre. They would have squashed my new company before I could walk with the agents and writers. I assume you want Ace conferenced in?"

"Yes," I answered.

"By the way, Samuel," she continued as she punched in Ace's number, "how did your meeting with the demigods go?"

His face darkened. "Don't play games, Caro. You know. The entire room was subjected to a graphic history of my indiscretions, thanks to Togsy's need to spice up his book."

A baby wailing through the phone receiver silenced him, followed by Ace's bushed voice as Caroline put him on speaker. "*Squirt, for the love of...*Caroline? Hi, sorry about that. This one's got a temp of one-oh-one, but...*oh nasty!*...she won't go to sleep. I can't stay on the phone long."

"We'll jump right in, then." She gave Samuel a tight smile. "I gather you've read *BrownStoners*. What'd you think?"

"I think the book can stand alone without filling it with tripe."

"That's where you're wrong. As literature, it can. But in the marketplace? No way. Togsy's a no-name without his dirt on you. No matter how good the book is, publishers won't put their dollars into it unless it's a guaranteed sell."

"So you're selling out," Samuel said flatly.

"I prefer to call it being realistic."

"You used to have more integrity."

"Youthful idealism alone doesn't get companies off the ground. You think I didn't have to pull strings and insinuate some fierce house competition to get you published, Samuel? When I championed *Water Sirens*, I had Berkshire so worked up over another publisher swooping in, they gave you the 'big name' treatment and offered you an outlandish royalty percentage. Now that's youthful idealism! And it paid off, for everyone." She took a sip of coffee and cringed. "Sometimes you can be so naïve."

That was harsh. I brushed the inside of Samuel's wrist with my thumb, reminding him to stay calm.

Ace blew a stream of air into the receiver. "Ms. Ortega, what would it take to keep this book from being published? Think big...be *idealistic*." I wondered if this was Ace's prelude to the bribe Jerome had suggested.

"Nothing. It's going to be published, Mr. Caulfield."

"Would Lyle consider marketing it as fiction?"

"Not a chance."

"Then we're looking at some major revisions." A child's watery sniffling built in the background. "My client would like his name changed and the inflammatory information removed."

"So, you're basically asking for the same deal I gave Jerome."

Silence flattened the room like a nuke bomb.

"Wait, what deal?" Ace asked.

Caroline grew smug. "I'm not surprised they didn't inform you of my offer. I told Buitre if they left my fledgling agency alone, we'd clean up the unsavory details. We can change his name, too, but readers will still figure out who the character is."

"You blackmailed them," I breathed. "That's borderline criminal." And pretty genius.

"That's the game, Kaye Trilby. My point is, you didn't hear a word of it, did you? Know why? Because Buitre would rather crush any bit of competition than protect its clients. Even you, Million-Dollar Man. I drew up a contract, but they refused to sign it."

"I'd like to see that," Ace said.

"I'll email it to you." She swiveled her chair and fiddled with a laptop, rubbing tired eyes behind her glasses. "I really do give a damn about you, Samuel. But here's the thing—Jerome Buitre is scum. The people who followed me out the door did so because they want a champion and weren't getting it." She shut the laptop. "So it's not like they'll be missed. But Jerome rejected my offer because he's a greedy, power-hungry bastard. The prick said he could manage Mr. Cabral, Hollywood, *and* sink my new company with a twitch of his pinkie. I *made* their company."

"You and Samuel," I mumbled. Samuel said nothing.

"So Jerome refused to sign this," Ace verified.

"Yes." She passed a piece of paper to Samuel and me. Sure enough, it was an unsigned contract detailing a swap—hands off her company: Samuel painted in a better light. Obviously, there was no way to verify Caro's story.

"I don't know if I can believe you anymore, Caroline," Samuel said quietly, voicing my very thoughts.

"You trust them over me?" Caroline tossed the file on her desk. "If I were you, I'd ditch The Buitre Group and find other representation."

I snorted. "Who? You?"

"Please. I wouldn't represent Samuel Cabral now, even if you threatened to drown me in Sofia's vegetable soup. I'm telling you this for your own good. Because, despite the way things ended, I find I still care what happens to you."

I wasn't moved. "That's great. You still give a damn about Samuel. So are you going to remove the controversial details about him from the book? Because *I* find I don't give a damn whether Buitre takes you out or not."

"You're a tough little backwoods cookie, aren't you?" Caro's unpainted lips twisted. "Fine. I'm open to negotiations."

I heard a whoop from Ace's end, followed by an indignant baby shriek. "Now we're getting somewhere. I'm willing to haggle it out line-by-line."

Caro jotted something in a planner. "I'll have my lawyer schedule several conference calls with you. I'm sure he'll fold on half of it—he's young and he's cheap." Translation: a spitfire.

The entire time the wheeling and dealing whipped back and forth, Samuel was silent. He sipped his coffee and bit his lower lip. I knew that look—the Cabral pout—because I'd seen it on his face since he was a fifty-pound runt and I'd pushed him into creeks. He was hurt. Betrayed. My heart broke a little for him.

Finally, he spoke. "Ace, do you mind if I have a word alone with Caroline?"

"Ah…yeah, sure, Sam," Ace stuttered. "My kid just puked on my lap, anyway. No promises, no contracts, okay?"

"Fine."

I rose and smoothed my creased pants. "I'll just go peek at the paintings again, if that's all right."

Samuel squeezed my fingers. But Caroline…she held up a hand. "You two are still together, right?" We nodded. "Then Kaye should stay."

"But it's not business-related," I said.

"All the more reason to hear what we have to say. If my daddy ever sent my mama out of the room so he could speak to another woman in private, he'd be sleeping on the couch for a week."

Samuel gave her a small smile—the first bit of warmth since we walked through her door. Then he turned that gorgeous, repentant smile on me and pulled me back to the longue, entwining his fingers with mine. "I apologize to both of you for my disrespect. Now tell me the *real* reason you didn't fill me in on your plans to break from Buitre. You know I would have supported you."

Hard eyes gentled. "Because I couldn't face you. I didn't know how to tell you…"

"That you were planning to use my life as a bargaining chip to boost Togsy's career?"

She pushed a black strand behind her ear. "It's fair play. You shut me out to get back in Kaye's good graces. I *have* to help Togsy publish his story. He called me. Said he missed me. He begged for my help—he's kicked the drugs, goes to meetings, and is writing again. I was skeptical when I visited him earlier this summer—the week of your sister's wedding? But then I read his book, and oh…I was so glad for him. You would be, too, Samuel."

"I just don't want him to use you," he said kindly.

"Samuel," she sighed, "you and I have been using each other for years. You've been my only friend in a backbiting industry where real friendship just doesn't exist. I don't know how we stuck it out so long. Maybe because you felt guilty over my split with Lyle."

"I never meant to drive a wedge between the two of you. I'm so very sorry."

She shook her head. "Despite his claims, it wasn't your fault he jilted me. You gave him an easy out from a relationship he stayed in because of obligation instead of love."

She rose from her chair and perched on the edge of her desk, across from Samuel. "We've pushed each other to succeed because that was all we had. I always knew, deep down, that I'd be sidelined if Kaye came back. I'm not going to lie—it hurt like hell. But you knew I'd do the same thing to you if I had a second shot with Lyle. So Togsy's book? That's me sidelining you."

Samuel's voice grew tellingly hoarse. "Fair enough. Next question: Why didn't you tip off Togsy about my bipolar disorder?"

She shrugged. "We don't have much left to give to each other; we've punched each other out. Consider my silence on the subject a parting gift."

I jumped in. "But, Caroline, if you publish only half the story—the drugs and cheating but not the bipolar disorder—it will make Samuel look like a tool."

"So, publish your own story."

"*Hydraulic Level Five?*" Samuel was appalled, as if she'd suggested he release a homemade sex tape.

"What else? It's one of your best. It's not fantasy—it's the real you." Her eyes gleamed. "Your readers will adore you even more for it. I don't think you realize how deeply your words reach into them, Samuel. This book will be your *coup de grace*."

"I can't publish it, Caro. I'll be *that* author."

"For a time. And then you'll be that author who has record-breaking movies. Or that author who was on *Ellen* the other afternoon. The masses have a short memory. They'll gossip about it, wait for you to go manic and rip Indigo's Oscar out of her hands during her *Water Sirens* acceptance speech. When you don't, they'll commend you and move on."

"I don't know…" But he was caving. "I've told you before, it's too personal. I'm writing it for myself and for Kaye, not millions of people."

Caroline's eyes burned. Not with anger or triumph in besting him, but something else. It dawned on me: she was proud of him.

It was then I saw what Samuel had always seen in Caroline Ortega, beauty queen from North Carolina. She cared about him. Yes, she was manipulative. She didn't play fair. She was a hard-nosed bitch who went after what she wanted. But she tried to be a friend the only way she knew how—she pushed when others would not. Sometimes she pushed Samuel too hard, because she would rather have him hate her than watch his slow self-destruction. And he *got* that about her.

She got him, too, so she knew which trump to throw on the table.

"If you won't do it for yourself, do it for Kaye. She'll be bone-weary after a month of media cover-up, trust me." Her eyes drifted to mine and locked. Understanding passed between us.

He held my hand, absently scuffing the area rug with his shoes. "I'll think about it."

Chapter 12
HYPOXIA

Divers who spend too much time in thin air and high altitudes will exhibit symptoms of intoxication, such as a lack of judgment and clumsiness.

Our next meeting with the "demigods," as Caroline pegged them, played out like a choreographed Broadway number. Jerome performed a little shuffle when he asked if I'd prepped my client for Monday's press interviews. "Naturally," Samuel smoothly covered for me, though we hadn't glanced at the talking points. A cadre of dancers figuratively swooped on-stage when we grimaced over Caroline's stack of affidavits, including the indie singer, several of his grad school colleagues, and the cocaine-coated brunette who haunted my dreams. Thankfully, Indigo Kingsley's people told Caroline to piss off.

But Jerome stole the spotlight in a thundering finale when he unveiled a fresh copy of Togsy's book.

"I understand you were forced to obtain the book yourself, Ms. Trilby." Reptilian fingers slithered over the binding. "I sincerely apologize for the delay."

I flipped through the pages. It was identical to the copy I'd swindled from Berkshire House. Dang it, I'd hoped to catch him in the act. I was absolutely certain they'd been planning to tweak the hell out of the thing and cast Caroline as Hitler, but now there was no way to prove it. Lexi's eyes were carefully lowered, and I realized she'd tipped off Jerome.

As we packed away laptops and files, Justin sauntered up. "So, what's your boy planning to wear the ninth?"

After a grueling day of press interviews (to make up for Samuel's canceled LA events), Buitre was hosting a swanky reception at the Boom Boom Room. It was a charity event for a New York arts foundation, given under the auspices of Buitre and its need to schmooze. According to Justin, Boom Boom was the jet set's new Studio 54, had the toughest door in the city, and the PR giant was shelling out a fortune. Indigo Kingsley would also be there with her famous flowing hair and pouty lips, and you could bet the press would be more interested in whether Samuel fell to his knees and begged her to take him back than in his bestsellers. Incidentally, the big shindig also fell on my birthday. Yay.

"He's wearing a suit, some number Caroline picked up for him in LA. Why, are you going to coordinate?" I teased.

"Nah. What are you gonna wear?"

"A suit."

"To the Boom Boom Room? For the first time Samuel and Indigo are seen together in public since their split? Oh no. You need to wear a dress, beautiful."

"It's a stylish suit," I said defensively. "In any case, it's work, not a date."

"If you don't wear a dress, you'll stick out like a chubby in Chelsea. I'd take you shopping, but I have incredibly bad taste for a gay man—I'd have you wrapped in some hideous tribal T-shirt. I'm an enigma like that."

It was official. I hated the fashion aspect of my career.

That evening, I rifled through my garment bags hanging in Samuel's closet, pulling out anything that might be acceptable for the Boom Boom Room. Cotton, cotton, more cotton. It was all too casual. A frantic call to Molly, then Danita, produced nothing.

"There's a shop in Queens I've always wanted to visit after I watched a special on the Travel Channel," said Molly. "They make lovely sarongs, beaded skirts, incense; you should check there!"

"A pant suit, are you kidding?" shrieked Danita. "You're in New York! Go to Fifth Avenue!"

But I'd never shopped designer before (other than the occasional mall trip in Denver), and had terrifying visions of some sales clerk going

Pretty Woman on my tush. That was how Samuel found me—cross-legged in his closet, dresses and shoes strewn across my lap, a pout the size of Pike's Peak on my lips.

"What are you doing?" He chuckled, pulling a soft leather belt from around my neck.

"Justin says I need to celebutante it up for Boom Boom so guests don't call me 'Senator' all night. I'm afraid I'll have to buy something."

"And you're worried because you don't know your way around New York?"

I nodded.

Samuel sank onto the ground next to me. "Would the Gentlewoman from Colorado like me to accompany her on a shopping excursion?"

Wow, this man could be sweet. A flash of me twirling in front of a dressing room mirror in a floppy hat a la Julia Roberts while Samuel nodded his approval flittered through my mind, but I shot it down. Best to lay off the hooker fantasies. "Thanks, but you hate shopping as much as I do. If you can tell me how to get to Fifth Avenue, I can go myself."

"You're talking about twenty-five city blocks round trip, Firecracker." I stared at him blankly. "That's more than two miles of shops."

I groaned and dropped my head on his shoulder. He laughed, his lips brushing my ear.

"Why don't I call a friend? Indigo's manager lives here in New York."

Did Samuel have any friends who weren't women? No wonder his exes thought he was gay. But at the moment, I didn't care. Pushing the pile of clothing onto the floor, I crawled into his lap and softly kissed him. "Thank you. That would be perfect."

The following evening, I bounced down the stairs in my eco sneakers, purse slung over my arm and hair in a messy bun—my shopping uniform. The pavement was slick and grimy from the afternoon thunderstorm, and I skidded. But the rain had beaten away the muggy remnants of summer, leaving the air fresh and cool.

A gray SUV with a driver waited for me. Its occupants opened the rear door.

"Are you Kaye?" asked a willowy blonde. She had an Aussie accent and the biggest gray eyes I'd ever seen, and I felt flutterings of recognition.

Oh flippin' sea turtles. My gut clenched when I realized who she was.

"Yes. Hello, Ms. Kingsley." I took the hand she offered and warily slid into the car.

"Call me Indigo. I'm also hitting Boom Boom and need to do a spot of shopping. Do you mind if I crash your trip?"

"Not at all." She was not as soft-looking as I'd expected—sharp collarbone, laugh lines around the eyes—but then, I was used to seeing her in airbrushed photos. Still, she was beautiful and I was really, really glad Samuel never slept with her, or I'd have curled into an insecure bundle right there on the car mat.

To my utter, stiff-backed shock, Indigo pulled me into a tight hug. "Between Neelie Nixie and Samuel's nonstop reminiscing, I feel as though I know you already. I'm glad to finally meet you."

"Ah—you too," I stuttered.

"This is my agent and your blind date, Nat O'Malley." I leaned across Indigo and shook hands with the curvy woman.

O'Malley…why was that name familiar? I chalked it up to celebrity circles. "Thanks for doing this. I'm not a big shopper."

"Samuel mentioned as much," said Nat. "No worries, that's what I'm here for." She appraised me, eyes skittering up and down my person. "You're a Thakoon woman. You like color and comfort," she finally pronounced. "What do you think, Indigo?"

"Definitely. Or Proenza Schouler. She could carry this season's surfer look well."

Surfer? Heck no! "There's no way you're getting me into anything tie-dyed."

Nat and Indigo laughed. "Fair enough. How do you feel about bypassing Fifth Avenue?"

"Yes, please."

Nat suggested shopping in SoHo which was…an experience. I'd been to Barney's in Denver with Danita and, after five hours' shopping with her, nearly threw myself onto the ground in a temper tantrum worthy of the posh toddlers plowing through clothing racks. But Indigo knew her stuff. To my joy, the boutique's selections were small—the fewer options I had, the better. The price tags, however, made me shudder.

Indigo anxiously cracked her knuckles. "Do you see anything you like?"

I gazed over several flouncy dresses displayed on headless mannequins along the back wall. "Those are nice."

"I knew it! Proenza Schouler!" she shouted, startling the sales associate and rattled the dozens of silver chains dangling from the counter. Nat rolled her eyes as she browsed a wall of colorful purses. "Jill, can we try their smocked floral in a six, and that pretty cocoon dress if you still have it in stock? Let's also bring out Thakoon's hook-and-eye silk in black. No, blue—yes?" I nodded, utterly clueless, but I liked blue. "And their tie-dyed mini. That should start us off!"

"No tie-dye."

"It's not what you think. Just give it a shot."

"No. Tie. Dye." I stood firm. "My father wears tie-dye. A *lot* of it."

"Oh." Sympathy filled Indigo's face. "I get it. No tie-dye. Thanks, Jill," she said as the sales associate tackled the dresses. "I assume this is on Samuel's tab."

"In a roundabout way." If I counted my alimony stockpile. "Don't worry, I've got it covered."

Indigo bit her lip. "Please don't take offense, but I should warn you. This might get pricey."

"Ex-wife, remember?" I tapped my nose.

"I forgot." Indigo flashed a row of white teeth. "Yeah, I have one of those, too—a divorce settlement. My ex is a designer. Everyone thinks he's from Italy, but he grew up with Sicilian parents in the Bronx. I met him at New York's Fashion Week. We got married, I started dressing in his designs, and his career took off. Then *he* took off with a Danish twig he was bonkin' on the sly. She had a man jaw, the slag. Fortunately, I got to keep our place in Gramercy and the best part of him—our twin boys. I thought about moving back to Oz, but I couldn't bear to leave New York."

While I tried on dresses and paraded them out for my tiny audience, Indigo talked away, her drawling vowels pleasant to listen to. She thrust a wallet of pictures over the door as I zipped into a dress that was so short, I'd moon the guests if I tilted my chin.

"Those are the twins. They're four, and the nuttiest kids you'll ever meet—just ask Samuel. Whenever he's in town, he swings by to do guy stuff with them like baseball in Central Park, even after we broke up—not that there was much to break between us. Earlier this summer, he took the ankle biters to see the Yankees play, but they kept dragging him to the concession stand and toilet, so they missed most of the game. They left after the…what do you call it? When everyone stands up and sings horridly?"

"The Seventh-Inning Stretch."

I slipped out of the dressing room and leaned against the wall lest a faint draft lift my skirt a half-inch. Lips twitching, I flipped through the pictures of her curly-haired children. They were cute, but probably a handful. And if they were chatty like their mother, I could guess why Samuel kept them mouth-high in junk food. But I was glad he knew a couple of kids to dote on. At the same time, I felt sad. He deserved children of his own.

Indigo returned the pictures to her wallet. "Anyway, my point is this. Samuel's a really, really nice bloke. You've known him a lot longer than I have and you have a history together, but I still want to make sure, you're…you know. Good to him. Please don't be offended," she said in a rush.

"Are you giving me the 'if you hurt him I'll kill you' speech?"

"Yeah, in so many words."

I studied Indigo earnestly—her bright eyes, guileless air—and decided I liked her. It would've been easy to burn with jealousy if I didn't know where his heart was. "I understand where you're coming from," I admitted. "The industry you move in must be filled with greedy people looking to latch onto someone like Samuel. People who would use him for his money and influence. But I'm not one of them."

Indigo released a whoosh of air. "Exactly. I didn't mean to corner you, sorry. The two of us—Nat and me—we're a bit clucky over him. We've talked about how great it is that you and Samuel are so loyal to each other, even though you're divorced. You really could have profited off the *Water Sirens* books, but you never did."

Well, aside from the alimony.

"Kaye, how's the dress?" Nat kindly interrupted.

"Short."

She smiled. "Try the black one with the little ivory blossoms."

I shot her a thankful smile and ducked back into the dressing room.

"And Samuel," Indigo persisted through the vents, "well, I'd be blind not to see how crazy he is about you. Poor me. For the longest time, I couldn't figure out why he went out of his way to avoid some good ol' fashioned pashing. I thought he might…um…'value his privacy,' if you know what I mean."

I smacked my head against the wall. *Not another one.*

Indigo must have heard the thumping. "Oh, but I don't think that anymore. He was helping me find the emotional inspiration behind one of my Neelie scenes on set one day, and the truth finally clicked—he was still pining after you! We all agree it's the most swoon-worthy thing we've ever heard, kind of like an Austen gentleman. Now I have Marco Caldo and we're on fire…Oh, but you didn't hear that from me."

After a while, Indigo informed us she was popping next door to look at shoes. Her absence left a roaring void of sound in the boutique.

"Are you still over there?" Nat laughed quietly from the room next to mine.

"Yes. It got quiet, didn't it?"

"Indigo's a chatterbox, but I love her for it. Any luck with the dresses?"

"I'm just finishing up this black one with the lopsided shoulder. I think I like it the best."

"With the little flowers? Let's see." We stepped out of our dressing rooms and I tugged my smocked waist into place. "Oh, Kaye, it's perfect on you."

"So's yours." We exchanged shy smiles and did a few mirror turns.

"My husband said you were a nice person. Do you remember meeting him?" I shook my head. "You sat next to him on a flight from Denver to LA. He's Indigo's image consultant."

I gasped. "You're Patrick O'Malley's wife? I knew I'd heard your name before! I didn't know he worked for Indigo." I scanned my fuzzy memories of our conversation, praying I didn't say anything embarrassing about his client.

"That's why we're in town."

"W-Wow," I stammered. "Congratulations."

Nat laughed. "I've been fortunate. The biggest bonus was meeting Patrick because of it. When Indigo's career began to take off, she hired both of us. We occasionally crossed paths in Hollywood, but I'd never gotten to know him until we joined the Kingsley family. The rest is history."

"Let me get this straight. Indigo doesn't use a full-service agency like Samuel does with Buitre. You're her manager and Patrick is her image consultant? And she has a separate publicist, stylist, agent, all that?"

"Correct."

Crazy and thrilling ideas took shape in my brain. If Indigo Kingsley—one of the most successful actors in the world—didn't need a Buitre-type agency to manage her career, surely Samuel didn't, either. "Your clients don't mind that you're not with a high-profile agency?"

"Not at all," she said proudly. "We're very selective in our clientele because we can afford to be. The few celebs we take on prefer the personal attention. If there's something we can't handle, we outsource. So you see, you and I have a lot in common."

I bit my thumbnail, growing excited. This might be the solution to our Buitre problem, if I could pull it off. "What about mixing business with family? How does that work?"

"Oh, we disagree, usually when something is made public that affects our private lives. But Indigo's priority is her kids, and she'll always make decisions with them in mind. And Patrick's and my relationship comes first, and our careers, second. I will *always* choose Patrick, and he'll do the same for me. If it hurts my career, so be it. But so far, I've had no regrets."

"That's…that's wonderful," I sighed, feeling some relief.

Indigo returned and by the time we paid for our things (more than two thousand dollars for a dress, shoes, and clutch; I felt sick), it was close to eight.

"I've got to relieve my sitter by ten," Indigo said, "but we have time for a quick drink. Any takers?"

I declined. All I wanted to do was go home to Samuel and put my arms around his neck. Hugging my purchases, I exchanged numbers with the women and waved good night, promising to see them at the Boom Boom Room.

When I tripped up the stairs to the Fort Tryon apartment, Samuel wasn't there. I fumbled with the spare key he'd given me and collapsed through the door, dropping my garment bag, purse, and boxes on the floor. I flipped on the living room lamp, wondering if he'd fallen asleep.

"Samuel?"

I peered into the bedroom. Also empty.

I told myself I wouldn't worry. Even after I called him, then heard his phone ring on the kitchen counter, I decided there was no reason to stress. Still, when I heard a key jiggle in the lock two hours later, followed by Samuel's quiet footsteps, my body sank into the bed with relief. His long shadow fell across the bedroom slats.

"Where have you been?"

"Out writing." His voice was gritty.

"You forgot your phone. I tried to call you."

"I'm sorry I worried you. I'm not used to having someone at home."

I turned in the bed, my eyes taking in his shabby form after a long day of writing. "You didn't have your laptop with you, either."

He simply held up his Moleskine notebook in answer.

I tugged a hand through my own unkempt hair. I hoped — really hoped — it wasn't an eggshells night. Folding back the quilt, I smoothed my palm over the bed in unvoiced invitation. I honestly didn't know whether he'd accept and come to bed with me, or fade into the hallway again. He chose to join me.

Troubled eyes remained on mine as he shucked his jeans, then pulled his shirt over his head and dropped it on the floor. He shivered when his skin hit the cold sheets, and he pressed his long body against my back for warmth. One arm wrapped around my waist, but it was stiff and formal, as if he felt it his duty to hold me.

My hand flexed and relaxed on the pillow, a steady rhythm as I waited for him to speak, or fall asleep, or even leave for the sofa.

He spoke.

"Tell me what to do about our book, Kaye. I don't know."

I lightly dragged my nails over his forearm. "That's your decision. If you want to keep your illness a secret, then I'll stand behind you."

"Yes, and you'll be burdened by it, like my family, like Caroline. But if I go public with the story, there will be no more secrets."

"There are always secrets, Samuel."

He rose from the bed again and opened the window, letting in a rush of cool air and distant car horns, and I immediately felt the loss of him. He leaned against the frame, watching the quiet street below.

"All I've ever wanted to do was write. Before, I wanted people to read my words. The more I shared them, the more real those words became. But now?" He ran a hand through his tangled hair. "I don't want to share them. Maybe it's selfish."

"It's not selfish to want to keep some things private. It makes it sacred, somehow."

"Sacred. Just like friendship." His voice grew stronger, angrier. "From the very beginning, Caro's pushed me to publish this thing.

Now she's backed me into a corner where my only other choice is to build another web of lies. Damned if I do, damned if I don't."

"Her method sucks, but she has a point."

He squinted at me, head cocked curiously. "And what would that point be?"

Tread lightly, Kaye. "Maybe publishing *Hydraulic Level Five* would be a good thing."

Samuel sat on the edge of the bed. "A few months ago, you had rather forceful opinions *against* publishing my memoir," he said coolly. I tried to grasp his hands, but he planted them behind him on the mattress.

"That was before I knew the whole truth. Our story could help people, Samuel. People like Molly's sister. And maybe…maybe it could help you, too."

"Would it?" He gave a short, sardonic laugh. "I suppose it would help TrilbyJones. Imagine the clout your little firm will get, trotting out my personal life for your fund-raiser."

Ooh, he knew how to hit me where it hurt, didn't he? "Hey, cliff-hucker, I didn't ask for any favors. You offered." I angrily whipped the quilt around my camisole-clad body. There was no way I was sharing a bed with him after a jerk statement like that. Yanking my pillow from the bed, I stalked out of the room, half-tripping over the blanket.

"Don't pretend you'll support me if I remain silent, Kaye," he called after me. His feet hit the floor and pounded across the room. "I could see it in your face the moment Caro suggested I go public. You want me to be a poster-child for mental health disorders, because it's easier than cleaning up when my brain goes haywire. I mouth off to the media in a manic frenzy, you arrange for me to do a PSA that'll run nationwide, problem solved. I'll not be turned into a tool."

Eyes blazing, I whirled and found him directly behind me. "Then quit acting like one. I have put *everything* on the line for you. You could at least do the same for me!"

"To what gain? That I'll break from Buitre and go with your firm?" He crossed his arms over his chest.

"You said yourself it was time for a change."

But his accusation hit a little too close to home. Fighting him when he was like this—paranoid and stressed—was putting a match to a stack of kindling. I took a step back, trying to calm myself. What did I expect to happen if he went public with his illness? It wouldn't magically go away. Cautious glances from fans, hugs of pity from talk show hosts. Friends and family asking about his health, when they were really asking if his head was put together. Then the backlash would hit, hard. Every time the tabs caught wind of a display of emotion, they'd blow it into a headline reading "Sirens Author Goes Manic in Public." He would hate that.

This wasn't a decision to rush. But I did know this: Samuel carried too much dead weight and he was collapsing under it. Some burdens needed to be cast by the wayside.

"TrilbyJones doesn't have the capacity to handle you," I replied. "But if what Caroline said is true, breaking from Buitre is a necessity. We could find new people to represent you…"

I tentatively traced his jawline with the tips of my fingers, back and forth…back and forth…soothing him. His eyes closed and he wrapped his hands around mine, burying his face in my palm.

"I don't know who to trust anymore," he whispered.

"Trust yourself. You will do the right thing."

He said nothing. I couldn't tell if he was mulling over what I'd said, or listening to laughing voices outside the door as his neighbors returned home. So I continued.

"Do you trust me when I say I love you?"

Ah, there was a reaction. He raised his head from my hand. "Yes."

"Then believe that I'm telling you this in love. I know about crutches. Secrecy has been your crutch, and everyone's indulged you in it. Secrecy about your illness. Your family. Your addictions. You live in the past, Samuel, in our childhood, your mother, the *Water Sirens* books, heck, even our old furniture—" I gestured around the room "—because it's easier to cling to those things than to give up your secrets. So when I said publishing your book might be a good thing, I really meant for you to let go of it all."

"Kaye, don't."

I took a deep breath and rushed on. "I admit it's my fault, too, with all the careless reminiscing and 'remember whens.' But it's time to make a new start together. Let's just finish the book, published or not, then move on with our lives. Because as much as I cherish your Caulfield, I'd rather have the grown-up version."

A siren blared past the building, then faded down the street. I waited for Samuel's answer. All that met me was a heated look and unfathomable eyes. He was too far inside his head for my words to reach him.

He kissed my palm. "Come to bed with me. I'm sorry I'm in such a fuck-awful mood."

"I'm sorry, too."

The fire was growing. I could see the subtle changes in his demeanor much sooner than I had the last time. He clutched at my hand, thumbs kneading my skin almost frantically. "Samuel, forgive me, but I need to ask—have you been taking your meds?" He turned his face away. I tugged on his hand, bringing his eyes back to mine. "Answer me."

"Yes."

But how would I know if he hadn't?

"Maybe you should see a doctor."

"I just saw one a few weeks ago." He shook off my hand.

I was getting nowhere. Defeated and exhausted, I decided to turn in for the night.

"Where are you going?" he blurted, his panic reaching across the room and grabbing me by the throat.

"To the couch. I thought you might like some space. That you might be cross—"

"There's no need," he pleaded. "I won't touch you tonight, I promise."

"That's not what I meant. I mean, it's okay if you do," I stuttered. "I just didn't want to intrude, that's all." So I followed him back to the bedroom, pillow clutched to my chest. We rolled to our respective sides, whispered our good nights, and slept.

And yet, at four a.m., I woke to find Samuel's side of the bed cold. The faint *clack-clack-clack* of a keyboard ambled around the apartment, and I couldn't deny the truth...

It was happening again.

***

As New York coffee shops go, this one was not noteworthy. From what I could tell, there was one on every block. But we hadn't chosen Starbucks because of its appeal factor. We'd chosen it because it was easy to find.

"All you have to do is hop on the train," Caroline had explained, "hop off, leave the subway and there it is. You can't miss it."

I'd lied to Samuel. This morning, like a shy teenage boy approaching a girl about a dance, he'd asked me if I wanted to attend the neighborhood church with him. "I find peace there, talk to some nice people." He shrugged, flushing at my dubious expression. "I usually go when I'm in town. You don't have to if you don't want to."

"It's not that," I hurriedly explained. "I'm sure it's really beneficial. It's just...I'm meeting someone for coffee this morning."

Now, I sat at a corner table across from Caroline. An already volatile Samuel would have flipped if I'd told him the truth, so I told him my coffee friend was a critic for a magazine here in the city. (I'd never actually followed up with Mr. Avant Garde, and he hadn't called, so I assumed I was in the clear on the cuppa offer.) Here I was, only hours after passionately rebuffing him for his secrets, doing the same thing—keeping secrets.

Caroline rubbed her temples. "Have you called his father? He might be able to convince Samuel to see his doctor."

"No." I couldn't meet her eyes. It was wrong not to inform Alonso and Sofia, but I couldn't bring myself to do it. Not yet, not until I'd tried to help him on my own. "How did you manage it, Caroline? Get Samuel to go?"

"It didn't happen often. Samuel's very diligent in monitoring his moods before they become out of control. The few times it did, I scheduled the appointment myself and then informed him he was going. If he fought me on it, I usually pushed him like a stubborn mule until he relented just to shut me up. I wouldn't recommend it for you, though."

"Why not?"

"Because Samuel appreciates that you don't treat him like a disobedient toddler. Let someone else do that for you."

Like Alonso.

My elbows hit the table with a *thunk* that shot pain through my funny bone. "He has a day packed with interviews tomorrow, followed by a charity event that will be in all the New York social diaries."

"You'll just have to play it by ear."

I drummed my fingers on the table, knowing it was time to bite the bullet. "Look, Caro, I want to apologize for the way things went down between us. Honestly, when I heard you and Samuel were dating, I was crazy jealous. I'd already decided to dislike you before you set foot in Lyons, and that wasn't fair."

She shrugged. "I admit I have an abrasive personality. You wouldn't be the first to dislike me."

"True, but I probably didn't make the best impression when I crashed Samuel's book signing in Boulder."

Caroline studied me with those glittering eyes. "Tell you what," she relented. "I'm really not supposed to release the names of Samuel's doctors without his permission. But you need to take a look at the calendar I kept for him, starting two years ago in February. You might find some old appointments still useful."

Clever. I hadn't thought of that. "Thank you so much."

"Next time, Kaye? Don't be afraid to snoop through his medicine cabinets for names. Invading his privacy is the lesser of two evils, in this case."

"I understand. Thanks."

She caught my forearm, just as I was lifting my coffee mug to my lips. "Do you *really* understand?"

I bristled. "Of course I do. I was there with you in LA. I saw it, firsthand. I lived it."

"No. Seven years is living it. What you saw? Just a taste." She glanced around the nearly empty coffee shop, as if she expected someone to swoop from behind the counter and cuff her.

"I have something for you," she ventured. "Something I was supposed to give you that night in the East Village, when you slept in my room. I never did because, at the time, I didn't know what to make of it." She took a tattered, browning tablet from her briefcase. As she slid it across the table, I recognized it at once — it was one of Samuel's Moleskine notebooks, its pages dog-eared with age.

"I have a box full of old papers, drafts, files of Samuel's writing we backed up from his old laptop. He knows I have it, but he hasn't asked for it back yet."

"I'll send someone over for it later this week."

She shook her head. "No, it's probably wise to pick it up yourself. But this — " she tapped a chipped nail on the notebook " — he hasn't seen it, doesn't even remember this. Open it."

I did. What I saw took my breath away.

It was the note—his good-bye letter—written over and over and over again. Pages and pages of pen scribbles, a notebook full of notes, as if he'd been copying detention lines:

Go home to Colorado. I don't want to see you again. The roots between us are dead, we are dead...

Go home to Colorado. I don't want to see you again. The roots between us are dead, we are dead...

The roots between us are dead, we are dead...

The roots between us are dead, we are dead...

The roots between us are dead, we are dead...

Red, blue, black, even faded pencil, put down and picked up again at a later time, perhaps over days. Some of the lines were illegible, some widely spaced and others over top of each other. Some, near perfect. There were slight variations in the wording, but always, "the roots between us are dead," as if he was trying to convince himself more than me. I drew in a shuddery, terrified breath.

"Samuel's laptop was full of frenetic writing, too, though nothing like this. I told you his work from that time period was harsher? That was an under-exaggeration. It was frightening. Abstract ideas and stories with no cohesion, and all incredibly dark—like stumbling through a nightmare world, then randomly waking only to fall into another nightmare. Samuel would let me use his laptop because my desktop computer was on the fritz. It was wrong to snoop through his personal files, but his other writing—the things he'd shown me—was so amazing, I couldn't help myself. But what I found shocked me. That's how I began to get a clue something was wrong. Somehow I *knew* it was more than the drugs. I should have called someone when I first saw the files, but I had no experience with those sorts of things."

"So a doctor or Alonso has never seen this?"

"Not this. They read through Samuel's other episode writing, thought it was drug-induced. After the incident in Raleigh, they decided it was more."

"Did you copy or distribute any of it? Has Togsy seen it?"

"I didn't. And no."

I could only take her at her word.

"That night, after I put you in my bedroom." She pressed her forehead between shaky hands. "It was horrible. All I could do was watch Samuel torture himself running sprints up and down the street, while that imbecile East Village crew stood outside and laughed, ribbing each other about how high Cabral was. Then Alonso arrived and took his son inside, heartbreak all over his face. Samuel picked up this notebook and began the frantic writing. Alonso just *stood there*. His own father stood there in agony, watching him, soaked through from hours of running."

"Poor Alonso," I murmured.

"Then he stepped out to call Sofia. When Alonso left, Samuel quit writing and slapped the notebook shut. I'll never forget the pleading look on his face. 'Take this to Kaye and put it in her backpack. Make sure you put it in her backpack,' he kept repeating."

By now, tears streamed down my cheeks. "But you didn't give it to me."

"Only a piece of it." Caroline tugged the notebook from my grasping hands and flipped through it, until she found a page with a missing rectangular chunk. I recognized the lines of writing on that page, more than the others. Precise, swooping letters, more carefully written than most of the notebook:

Go home to Colorado. I don't want to see you again. The roots between us are dead, we are dead...

"Rather than give you the entire thing, I cut out one line, folded it into your sweatshirt pocket so you wouldn't find it until later, and placed it in your pack. Deep down, I knew what I did was wrong, but I felt like I was protecting him from more hurt, you see."

"Why?"

"I told you. I thought you were too timid to face the problems of the real world. That you're too focused on yourself. So I didn't give you the book. Even if I had, it's such a small thing, it probably wouldn't have changed much."

I slammed my hands down so hard, our mugs rattled in their saucers and coffee sloshed out. The barista shot me a wary eye. "It would have changed *everything*. Maybe our split was inevitable because of our youth and insecurities. But I would have *known*. I would have *seen*."

"Maybe."

"Without a doubt." I picked up the notebook and hugged it to my chest. "This was meant for me instead of you, Caroline. I should have been the one to call a doctor, to stand by him in rehab, and mental health clinics, and meds adjustments. I should have been the one to hold him and tell him it would get better." Rage and regret churned in my belly like a sickness. "You should have given me the notebook like he asked, but you stole it. Why?"

"Because I thought you were poisonous," she whispered. She couldn't meet my eyes. "Look—I didn't have to tell you about this at all, so don't give me grief."

I swiped runny mascara across my cheek. "I'd hoped…maybe…we might have become friends someday. Probably the stupidest idea I've ever had, huh?"

She shook her head. "It's not possible. I have associates, Kaye, not friends. I don't want them."

"Then I am very sad for you."

I didn't miss that in all of her explanations, not once had Caroline apologized. Never in a million years would she admit to being sorry. She was too proud. Brushing the last of my tears away, I rose from the table and purposefully placed my half-empty coffee mug in the dish bin, then made for the door.

"Kaye," she called after me. I paused. "You and Samuel should publish your book. It's a beautiful love story."

I stared at her, struggling to rise above this flood of emotion. I searched for the flicker of amity I'd felt pass between us the other afternoon. One last chance. But she'd buried it, and it was gone for good. Somehow, that only made me sadder.

"I'll be by for Samuel's papers tonight," I said flatly. "And talk to Lexi at Berkshire House, explain the offer you made to Buitre. She might be willing to champion Lyle's book if he's serious about making those revisions. *Only* if the revisions are made."

Her eyes widened. "I can't crawl back to Berkshire House for help. It would be degrading."

Not even to help Togsy. Interesting. And with those few words, Caroline Ortega told me enough.

"Good-bye, Caroline. I hope you find your happiness."

When I was eleven, I bought a diary. It had a pink plastic cover and a little silver padlock and key, threaded on a ribbon. My father gave me ten dollars for my birthday and there wasn't much for shopping in Lyons. But I carried the ten-dollar bill in my purse on the off-chance I'd find something to blow it on. That chance came when my mother filled a prescription at the pharmacy. I spotted the diary on a magazine rack next to gift wrap and party balloons, and knew it was meant for me.

"But you never write," Mom said when I held up the diary.

"I want this." I was firm.

The thing was, Samuel Cabral wrote in a diary.

He kept it hidden in a box stuffed with baseball cards. But Danita had sibling radar, an instinct that started beeping when there were embarrassing things to be discovered in her brother's room.

"My brother is such a dork!" she shrieked when she triumphantly pulled the stolen diary from her backpack. It was a plain blue journal with a Red Sox sticker on the front and a rubber band around the middle. At the time, I was so caught up in the thrill of reading the clandestine thoughts of my long-time crush, wanted into his world so much, I didn't consider I was doing something wrong. I was barely eleven, and eleven-year-olds are notoriously self-centered.

Much to Danita's dismay, there were no juicy revelations in the book's pages, mainly recaps of baseball practice and the funny things Angel said in geography class. There were also brief, horny snippets about Jennifer — AKA, Cherry ChapStick Girl — which made Danita giggle and me fake vomit.

Before she could return the diary, Samuel busted us.

"I can't believe you read it, Kaye!" he shouted, red streaking up his neck and coloring his cheeks and ears. "I would never, ever read your diary!"

"I don't have one," I mumbled, "but if I did, I'd let you read it."

I think he understood my offer wasn't meant to be petulant. I simply wanted to undo the damage I'd done by offering a piece of myself in return — a child's flawed "I'm sorry for kicking you, would you like to kick me back?" sense of justice. His shoulders slumped, the fight leaving him. "Just don't tell anyone, okay?"

I didn't. But I did buy a diary. I even wrote in it every night for two months, filling it with little details which, in the back of my mind, I thought Samuel might like to read. Whenever Danita came to visit, I left the pink diary in plain view, the key secure in the padlock. She never took it. I played in the Cabrals' basement and blatantly laid the book on top of my pom-pom hat. When I returned, it was always untouched. After a while, it became clear that Samuel meant it when he said he would never read my diary.

But still, I'd wanted him to. Badly.

I gave up on the thing halfway through December. It remained hidden in the bottom of my underwear drawer until I left for college. Now, seventeen years later, I wished I'd filled it to the brim.

That night, I heard the rapid clacking of fingers flying over a keyboard before I even unlocked the apartment. The box of Samuel's papers was heavy and awkward in my arms. I hoisted it onto my hip and pushed through the door, ready to chew him a bit for not hearing my huffing knocks. He didn't even turn his head when I loudly dropped the box next to the coffee table.

"Samuel, what are you doing?"

"I've got to write it all down," he muttered. "All of it..."

Fear shot through my heart. "Write what?"

"The words. The memories. I have to get them on paper before I lose them, because I can feel them slipping away again, every day, further and further, slipping away again and I can't let them leave."

His glasses were pushed up into his hair, which made me realize he was typing blind. Muscles beneath his T-shirt bunched and clenched with frenzied energy, his body not fast enough to release what was in his head. Peering over his shoulder, I squinted at the glowing laptop screen:

> Catch them in your hands, those bitter drops of rain or blood
> like death seeping through brittle bones split over age or
> paving stones. Or maybe she's stone through and through,
> always was and always will be, like the stone angel woman
> towering over us, *la llorona* with her drowned babes and sad
> sad lips gaped in a horror scream, a space of black
> if only she'd crack that cement seal.

> I lift my love, so light so warm, by her waist. I lift you high high high so you can see her dead eyes and hope for some life, but she's dead, you see, staring down at me from her place above, or below, but always staring in her tomb and crying from cold eyes
>
> But oh my, there you are all grown up in brown earth and roots, thriving, hot and wriggling in the sun, and I want to kiss you.
>
> I want to fuck you.
>
> I want to be buried with you in warm flesh so pink and alive when she watches me...

I swept an unruly lock from his forehead.

"It's okay, Samuel," I said, trembling. "You need to sleep, and then we'll go see a doctor in the morning."

"No. I need to write it all down before she's gone."

She? I cast a wary glance at the urn above the fireplace. "Before who's gone? The Weeping Lady?"

Sad eyes met mine. "Aspen. I can't lose her again, Kaye." He returned to his keyboard.

Oh no. Please, no. Was he writing his thoughts before he lost them, or was he confusing fantasy with reality? That wasn't supposed to happen with hypomania, was it? I had absolutely no idea what to do. But I had to do *something*, had to ground him.

"She's right here. *I'm* right here." I knelt beside him and pried his fingers away from the keys then forced them onto my face. "Can't you see her in me? Tell me you can."

Fevered blue eyes locked on mine. His fingers dug into my cheeks, the back of my skull, as he searched for his Aspen. Finally, he nodded. "I see you."

Ground him. I watched his face, mesmerized by the raw craving I saw there. He probably saw the same thing in me. I was terrified and I wanted to feel him, to hold him close and tie him to me in the only way I had left.

I pushed his laptop aside and placed my hands on his chest.

That was all the invitation he required. His lips took mine with a frantic passion. He clung to me, fingers pushing under my shirt, only breaking his kiss to drag it over my head. I heard the metallic clatter of his glasses as they skittered across floor. We tumbled down and my tailbone screamed in protest at the sudden jarring, but I swallowed the pain beneath his heated skin and wrapped my legs around him.

"I love you," he rasped as he dragged his fingers through my hair. "I'm not ready to let you go. I love you. Let me love you. You are so warm."

A gut feeling told me those words were not meant for me. They were for an idea of me and, strangely, I felt guilty for deceiving him, for making him believe he was with a different person…but not enough to stop.

We shed our clothing and pressed our bodies together, driving out the air until there were only rib cages, sharp pelvises, and soft flesh. Still, like his elusive memories, he was slipping away. I fought to find that symbiotic circuit crossing between us so I could overpower his manic mind, to draw out the madness like a fever and replace it with cool sanity. I pushed his back to the ground and straddled his lap, but I couldn't ground him. Keeping Samuel with me was like forcing sunlight to stay on my skin. It could burn and burn and burn until my arm was a charred, aching mess. Even so, its brilliance would vanish when the sun sank.

We made love on the floor. My hands clutched his beautifully shaped shoulders, feeling the lithe, potent muscles shift. I begged him to stay with me. "Please come back, Samuel." His eyes were hooded with pleasure. He flipped me to the ground, his torso weighed me down and his legs twined with mine, pinning me, heavy as a humid night. A clammy palm cupped my face. "I love you…I love you…I love you."

I hugged him to me. Every muscle in his thighs, back, and arms clenched, and he shuddered, groaning into my neck a single word.

"Aspen."

The dream returned. I was cast as the brunette, trapped beneath Samuel's steel arms as he gazed at the broken girl in the doorway. I shoved at his chest, trying to get his attention. I shouted. I must have said or done something in my sleep, because I awoke to Samuel whispering in my ear, trying to calm me with gentle words.

"I'm going to take you to Boston, to Fenway Park. Would you like that? Please don't cry. Don't cry. Don't cry. I haven't forgotten the promise I made to you that morning by St. Vrain Creek. Do you remember?"

"I remember," I choked out, even though I didn't remember.

"It was a sunny day and you skipped your government class to hike with me. Your shoulders were sunburned. I kissed them like this—" he smoothed dry lips over my skin "—and you told me it made them feel better. After lunch we waded in the creek. We dug rocks from the bed and laid them out in the sun. When they were dry, we drew faces on them with markers and then threw them back in the water for other people to find."

I buried my face in my pillow as he spoke, stifling my breaking heart. I'd begun to hate *Hydraulic Level Five* and my youthful doppelganger.

Chapter 13
STUPID HURTS

An idiotic decision that results in injury to the diver or another person.

S—They found your laptop and returned it to me. I hope you don't mind, I read what you wrote those days in New York. I'm no expert, but it doesn't really gel with the rest of our story. So I'll write it for you, even though I'm crap at it. I can't exactly screw it up because I'm Aspen...right? I think I am, but sometimes I'm afraid I'm not. I love you anyway. ~Kaye

Hydraulic Level Five {working title}
Draft 5.34
© Samuel Caulfield Cabral & Aspen Kaye Trilby
34. *Using Up Stamps*

Aspen squints at her young husband in his smelly undershirt and jeans, hunched over his guitar, and wonders whether he'd look hot with Cobain hair. No, definitely not. She smooths smoke-heavy locks from his forehead. It's been months since he's had it cut, and the shagginess ventures beyond Sexytown and into Grungeville. He turns his face into her palm and gently nips the base of her thumb.

"I'm heading back to campus," she says. "Can you buy stamps and mail my internship applications before two?"

Caulfield nods, red-rimmed, glassy eyes not leaving the guitar strings as he plunks out "Pale Blue Eyes" for the fiftieth time – a far cry from the grinning, golden boy baseball star of their high school days. "Linger on..." And on, and on, and on.

She tugs his T-shirt sleeve. "Why don't you toss that in the hamper and I'll do laundry tonight."

He pauses in his playing to jerk the ratty thing over his head, then chucks it in the vicinity of the hamper. She catches a whiff of sex and stale beer and oddly, it's a turn on.

"You don't always have to take care of me," he says.

She shrugs. "I'm used to taking care of stuff. Besides, you take care of me, too."

"Not very well." He closes his eyes and his Adam's apple bobs as he swallows.

They had a late night covering an area band. She doesn't know how he could stumble home with her half-drunk tush, have mind-blowing sex, and still be coherent enough to turn around a review for the paper by deadline. It's typical for him to write his reviews the same night, when his mind is still fresh with details. Somehow, he always pulls it off.

She vaguely remembers him crawling into bed sometime around five and wrapping his arms around her waist. But the fruity drinks he bought her at the bar and sound-system overkill made her head throb, so she pressed her face into her pillow and went back to sleep. Earlier this morning, her mouth was so mucky she questioned whether she'd been throwing back sours or sewer water. Even now, her hangover lingers like a barfly who can't take a hint. As she gargles mouthwash, she hears quiet chords and his even softer baritone drift from the couch.

"Caulfield?" He doesn't answer. Aspen glances at her watch – eleven forty. She has to hurry or she'll be late for her internship. *Strum... strum...strum...*Nothing short of kneeing him in the balls will get his attention, so she just leaves.

She grabs a can of instant soup from the cupboard and scribbles a quick "don't forget mail & stamps" for Caulfield on a Post-it note. Then she drags her bike downstairs and pedals into the Boulder sunshine.

Her tires skid around a smashed and rotting jack-o'-lantern, splattering orange gunk on her sneakers. It is miserable October

days like this that make her restless to run away from home. Fortunately, this is all limbo until the grown-up phase of their lives begins. By this time next year they'll do some apartment hunting in New York over fall break, if nothing screws up her five-year plan:
Year one: campus internship (scored one in the Alumni Office).
Year two: graduate, land paid New York internship while Caulfield attends NYU.
Year three: find entry-level job and get two years' experience.
Year four: save money.
Year five: move back to Colorado and start business with Molly.

Most college students didn't think of their futures past graduation, but Aspen is not one of them. She has goals. No one can accuse her of being rash and naïve, not anymore. She is twenty now. She is an *adult*.

She hopes Caulfield remembers to buy stamps.

Later that afternoon, her phone rings as she rummages through stacks of old alumni pictures.

"Hey, Caulfield."

"Hey, I'm at the post office. Do you want a book of stamps or just a sheet?"

She frowns and glances at the clock – four fifty. "You're just now mailing those? That means they won't get to New York before Friday."

"Well next time, mail them yourself," he grumbles.

"I barely had time to get home between classes and work, let alone go to the post office. The *only* thing you had to do was mail that stuff for me." She doesn't know how the frick he is going to manage grad school.

"It won't kill anyone to wait a day. I just didn't feel well. Sorry." He exhales and the raspy, tired sound loosens the anger knotted in her chest.

"Listen. I know everything feels really temporary right now. When we find our footing, it will get better."

"Firecracker." She hears the frown in his voice. "Yeah, it's temporary, but it's still life, here and now. Case in point – look at the attacks last month in New York and DC. The Towers, the Pentagon, all those people with the photographs, hunting for the people they love. If you're always looking ahead, saying it will be better if this happens, or if that happens, you'll never actually *live* your life."

"Hangovers and playing your guitar until noon isn't living."

She wants fire from him, but he doesn't take the bait. There is a long pause, then a resigned, "I'll see you tonight. I love you."

"Caulfield?" She shoves a file of old photos into the cabinet and presses her aching head against the cool metal. "We only need a sheet of stamps. It will take too long to use a book and who knows when postage will go up again."

After Aspen hangs up, she realizes she forgot to say "I love you" back.

•••••••••••••••••••••

> Sam—I've often wondered what kind of person I'd have become if our (and when I say "our," I mean "my") New York plans had come to fruition. I don't think I would have liked her very much. Just one of those "looking on the bright side" moments, I guess. ~Kaye

"Happy Birthday, Kaye."

"Thanks, Mom."

My mother's voice was a welcome sound early Monday morning as I dropped two slices of bread into the toaster. I'd already been up for an hour, having called Samuel's psychiatrist before the sun rose. By some miracle, Samuel was still asleep.

I remembered it was five in the morning in Colorado. "Why on earth are you awake so early?"

"Putting a batch of tomatoes in the pressure cooker for canning. Wish you were here, but it's a relief not to worry about a party this year."

"Mom, we go to the Cabrals every year for my birthday. Sofia always takes care of the cake." My heart twinged at the thought of Sofia's spicy chocolate cake.

"Well then, I don't have to buy a birthday hat."

We chatted for a while. My arms ached to hug her neck when we said our good-byes, even though we rarely embraced.

"You take care of yourself, Aspen Kaye. Only carry a little cash when you go out."

"I will, Mom."

I hung up the phone then jumped when Samuel's arms snaked around my waist. Still warm with sleep, his scruff tickled my cheek as he nuzzled it.

"Happy Birthday." He yawned. "Any news from Gail?"

I peered up at him with wary eyes. "Other than Hector getting busted for doing fifty down Main Street? No."

"Sounds like business as usual."

"Yeah, the big lug asked the sheriff if he'd hold his six-pack while he pulled his license from his wallet."

His eyes crinkled in laughter. Well. Now he seemed completely normal. Still, Samuel had behaved normally yesterday morning, too, and look how he'd deteriorated by evening. "Hey," I said gently, "how are you feeling?"

"Fine. Rested. Hungry. I was going to make you breakfast, Birthday Girl, but you beat me to it."

I pecked him on the cheek. "You can play me 'Happy Birthday' on your guitar. I'm sure you were exhausted after last night."

"Last night?"

"Yes. It was…" I froze when I saw bewilderment, then blatant fear seep into his eyes. His arms tightened. A single shudder raced through his body and slackened. He kissed my neck with trembling lips and released me.

"Last night was great," he lied. "Do you want coffee?"

"No, thanks."

Crap crap crap. He didn't remember. I could see it in his face, even though he tried to hide it. How could he possibly not remember something so important? A dreadful weight settled in every joint of my body, threatening to press me into the floor with pain and guilt as I grasped the far-reaching hurt my rash choice last night brought down on both our heads. Tears pricked my eyes. I had to get him to a doctor.

"Toast's up." I sniffled. "Jelly?"

"Just butter's good." He grabbed a slice and took a big bite, then fled down the hallway. Moments later, I heard the shower run. My thoughts strayed to the old Moleskine notebook in my messenger bag—the one he didn't know existed. I'd have to show it to him, and it would suck worse than scraping my knuckles on concrete. This would complete Caroline's betrayal and he'd feel it keenly.

Licking the jam from my fingers, I pattered down the hall and knocked on the bathroom door. "Samuel?"

"Come in," he called. "Did you need something?" he asked when I still hadn't spoken.

"I collected a box of hard copies from Caroline. It's your earlier writing."

"Oh?"

"Yes. It might send you into a tailspin when you read it. And I, um, scheduled a doctor's appointment for you this morning."

A pause. The shampoo bottle snapped open. "I can't. I have press interviews."

"We can reschedule them."

"No, we can't—not after the LA debacle. Kaye, I'm fine, truly." Nothing but the quiet plopping of suds. Then he stuck out a wet head from behind the shower curtain. "Will it really make you feel better if I go?"

"Yes."

"I propose a compromise: I'll go tomorrow, first thing. Just one more day."

"I don't know…"

He used that disarming crooked smile, darn it. I hungrily watched water drip from his hair and trickle down his neck. "I'm much better than yesterday, and I know I can make it through today without any issues. We'll get the interviews out of the way, Jerome's disgusting display of opulence tonight, then the doctor tomorrow. Okay?"

"Okay," I relented, because I very well couldn't hog-tie him and drag him to his psychiatrist. "First thing tomorrow."

He began to whistle—he was actually whistling in the shower—and that boded well for the rest of the day. But I knew better. I'd read the notebook. I heard him confuse my names. I'd seen too much to turn off the lights on last night.

I hadn't needed a babysitter since I was ten. (Save for an unfortunate introduction to Gospodin Vodka and his jiggly mistress, Jell-O, at a freshmen mixer. Molly had to peel me off the floor.) I got why Jerome wanted to micromanage Samuel's interviews: the behind-the-curtain world of celeb PR was abuzz over Caroline Ortega's departure. But after the third interview in which the smarmy man shut me down when fielding questions, I itched to pummel his shiny bald head.

I decided not to fight him on this. Soon, with luck and a little tap-dancing, I'd make sure he and the rest of his self-important crew no longer represented Samuel.

The silver lining was that Jerome's micromanagement left me with time to ponder. The last instance when Samuel had large chunks of time wiped from his memory was his cocaine spree in Raleigh. Cocaine had also exacerbated his illness that night in New York, causing a memory lapse. The only conclusion I reached was that he was using again. I hoped to God he wasn't. But then, what if there was something dreadfully wrong — something out of his control, like a brain tumor — that caused the black out?

I wound my arms around my torso. Tomorrow morning's doctor visit couldn't come soon enough.

I stared out a window of the Standard Hotel at the mini-circus below, just beyond the railroad tracks. Paparazzi paced like a pride of lions and waited for Indigo Kingsley's arrival. The camera-happy photogs had hoped for a money shot of Samuel handing Indigo out of car. I could feel waves of disappointment when I'd climbed out of the car instead of Indigo.

Just beyond the hotel was the Meatpacking District, an area once known for its slaughterhouses, drugs, and prostitutes. Rotting packing plants gave way to dens of hipsters and trendy hotels like the Standard, which catered to celebs seeking low-key visits. The hotel was so futuristically retro, I half expected George Jetson to fly in and say "get out of my chair, you big strata-jerk." Justin called it *Le Corbusier*. I called it awesome.

Samuel sat on an uncomfortable-looking sofa, absently twisting a cocktail napkin.

"Lastly, Mr. Cabral, do you prefer boxers or briefs?"

"Seriously?" Justin whispered. "What an unimaginative question. The poor girl works for *You Magazine*, though, so I shouldn't expect any less."

"Your claws are showing, kitty."

At least Samuel could respond to this stuff in his sleep. "Unless you catch me at the Laundromat, I'm afraid you'll never know the answer." He winked robotically.

My eyes drifted across the skyline to the cloudless sky. If I was in Boulder, we'd take advantage of a Monday like this and blow off work to canoe. Heck, our clients would grab their life vests, and bongs, and join us. I covered my mouth to stifle a yawn. I'd seen practically nothing of the city, though I understood it would be this way. Once the movie promotion was over, I'd come back for a real visit.

"Don't forget about the press junket and *Water Sirens* screening in November," Jerome said.

The girl thanked Samuel for his time, just as another interviewer strode in, such-and-such from *The New Yorker*. I didn't need Jerome to tell me this one was important. *The New Yorker* was the first big publication to run Samuel's short stories years ago.

The man sat, all business with a leather binder and a goatee that hid a weak chin. "Sam, good to see you again. Since we only have fifteen minutes, I'm just gonna get to the good stuff."

"Okay." A napkin shred fluttered to his lap.

"What's this I hear about Caroline Ortega beating feet?"

"I can answer that," said Jerome. "Ms. Ortega has left The Buitre Group to pursue a new business venture and Mr. Cabral has chosen to remain with us."

"You're not going to give me anything, are you, Jerome? Okay, Sam, is there any truth to the rumors she's got a book in her pocket written by an old friend of yours?"

Samuel started from his bored stupor. He crumpled the napkin and tossed it on the floor. "What the fuck kind of question is that?"

I stifled a groan.

New Yorker lifted his story-sniffing nose. "I haven't seen it, but word is Togsender has some pretty strong opinions about you. Judging from your reaction, I'd say it's true."

"I can respond to that, too," Jerome simpered. "The book does nothing but regurgitate tabloid trash, which obviously upsets Mr. Cabral. It will probably never see book stands. Do you have any questions related to *Mr. Cabral's* books?"

"Yeah, if you're gonna let him answer."

A commotion in the hallway stole our attention, followed by a flurry of action on the street below. Photogs surged toward Indigo Kingsley's gray SUV in a mad rush to snap pictures and were instantly pushed back by a wall of bodyguards.

"Finally, just in time. "She's here," I said to the room.

Relief flashed in Jerome's face. "I believe I can arrange a special feature for *The New Yorker*, if you can give us another twenty minutes of your time. Justin, please confer with Nat and see if Ms. Kingsley is willing to sit down with Mr. Cabral for a joint interview." Why did it sound as though he was setting up a play-date?

Mr. New Yorker's eyes widened. "Hell yeah, I can give you twenty."

I had to hand it to Jerome—he was shrewd beneath that oily exterior.

I watched as the top of her blond head emerged from the car. She paused for a few photos, waved to fans, then disappeared into the hotel. It was over in half-a-minute, but it was enough to make my stomach flip again.

Soon, *the* Indigo Kingsley sashayed into the room, all legs and slit skirt. Maybe it was that Aussie confidence, or simply fame, but she commanded a room's attention with a lift of her chin.

"Samuel, stellar to see you again." She clasped his hands and kissed his cheeks. Gray eyes scrutinized the room. "Will you look at this place? I feel as though Scotty's beamed me up."

Nat followed behind her and gave me a small wave. She could easily fade into Indigo's long shadow, if not for the bright mind beneath her sober face.

"Indigo, Nat. You know Jerome and Justin. But I'd like to introduce you to Kaye Trilby," Samuel said softly.

Confusion flashed over Nat and Indigo's faces, but they tapped it down. "Kaye, glad to see you again. Samuel, thank you for arranging our shopping trip," Nat hinted.

Indigo smiled at me. But it faltered as she watched Samuel sink into the sofa like a deflating balloon. Her gaze swept over his weary slouch and resigned expression. Then she watched as Justin snatched up the napkin shreds at Samuel's feet. Indigo was sharp. I think she understood something was wrong, and she'd have to carry the interview. I found I was grateful for her steady presence. She sat next to him on the spaceship couch and crossed her long legs, gazing politely at Mr. New Yorker. He'd taken copious notes throughout the exchange.

"Speaking of Neelie Nixie," the man began, "in what ways were you able to identify with your character?"

"The love she has for her friends and family. It wasn't hard to channel—Samuel wrote her beautifully. I also like to think I have a bit of her adventurous spirit..." Indigo Kingsley was a pro at giving just enough to sate the media's appetite.

Nat took her place next to me, and together we watched the interview unfold.

"I didn't have a chance to say thank you for arranging the subterfuge last month," I said quietly. "I was afraid the tabs were gearing up to crucify me for coming between Indigo and Samuel, Brangelina-style."

"They probably were," she whispered. "It was no trouble, and Indigo's thrilled to show off her hunky Latin lover. It was win-win."

I liked Nat. Both she and Indigo were flower-beautiful, but as different as lilies and wattles. We chatted in hushed voices, one ear on the sitting area. As we spoke, the skin on the back of my neck prickled, and I felt the blistering gaze of two beady eyes. Jerome watched me. A dark look passed over his face, then diffused into his ruddy skin.

"Time's up, I'm afraid." He gestured to the clock on the wall.

Hours passed and interviewers trickled in and out. Catering wheeled in a cart loaded with lunch items. Samuel ate nothing.

It was more confounding than an abstract algorithm. Last night had been, frankly, terrifying. I was sure I'd wake to find him a manic mess, fingers worn to the bone from a night of typing. This morning, he was all smiles. Now, it was as if he'd set his body on autopilot while his brain retreated to Shangri-La. Was I witnessing one episode or several? I'd read about rapid cycling, but I thought there were long stretches of "normal" sandwiched between highs and lows, stretches that could last weeks.

I stole away into the side bedroom and rifled through Samuel's messenger bag. I found his two prescription bottles and counted: twenty-two Depakote tablets, twenty-two antidepressants. One less than yesterday, each. Relieved, I stuffed them back in his bag.

Damn it, I needed a sunblock with the highest fricking SPF available for Samuel's rays.

By three p.m., birthday wishes were rolling in. Molly and Cassady…Dani from the welding shop…Angel from the hangar…Sofia even phoned, her voice faltering. I hadn't heard from her since Rocky Mountain Folks. She and Alonso seemed to be giving us our space after I'd reamed them.

Another call came in, and I gleefully stepped out of the room.

"¡Hola, mamacita!"

"Hey, Hector."

"How's life in New York? Seen lots of tall buildings?"

"I've lived in the clouds since I arrived." Mostly thunderclouds, but clouds, nevertheless.

"I've got a birthday present for you. Ready?"

"You didn't need to—"

"What do you call Hippie Tom's wife?"

"I'm guessing not Gail or Audrey."

"*Ay*, that was an insensitive joke, sorry."

"Well, give me the rest." I bit back a grin.

"Mississippi!"

My gut twisted, longing for home. "Man, I've missed those. Hey, big player, what's this I hear about a love triangle?"

"Oh. That." He proceeded to fill me in on the infamous Tricia/Jaime scandal, his head growing to the size of a Goodyear Blimp. "And then Jaime hung up on me."

"Let me get this straight. Jaime asked you to go biking with her in the National Park and you said yes. Then Tricia asked you to skydive with her, and you said yes. How is this not two-timing?"

"Because the thing with Jaime isn't a date. Her words were, and I quote, 'I need someone to bike with so I don't get attacked by pervert frat boys camping in the forest.'"

"It's a date, trust me. And if you want to escape with your manhood intact, I'd break one of those dates. I don't know Tricia, but Jaime expects exclusivity."

"*Lo que sea*. So, you ready to give Longs Peak a good spankin'?"

I groaned. "Work has been so insane, I've barely had time to do a single sit-up, let alone wall-climbing."

"You better get on that or we'll make you carry the food."

I gasped. "You wouldn't! We always give that to the rookies."

"Well, get your butt harnessed so you don't disappoint the Guzman kid. Seriously, you know the rules. The minute fatigue sets in, you make crap judgment calls and end up tumbling down an ice crevasse."

"Geez, bossy. Okay."

There was a long, awkward pause when neither of us said a word. Finally, we exchanged our good-byes.

"I miss you, Kaye."

"I miss you, too." But as the words rolled off my tongue, it hit me that I didn't miss him as much as I thought I would, I'd been so busy. Actually, I didn't miss any of the Lyons crowd as much as I thought I would, and feeling that way about my friends made me uneasy. "See you in November," I mumbled, and hung up.

Sometimes I forgot that Samuel had marvelous hearing, especially when he was borderline catatonic like today. I emerged from the bedroom after my call and found a nearly empty room. Samuel waited for me.

"What did Hector say?" he demanded.

"Nothing important. Birthday wishes, wanted to make sure I was getting ready for the climb."

"Did you tell him you aren't going?"

I scowled. "No I didn't, because I'm still doing the climb."

Anger flared in his blue eyes. Fury, even. I thought he was going to unleash hell and all its minions on me. But he said nothing, and the fire fizzled to a defiant flicker. "I'm going to take a fifteen-minute break. Can you see if the next interviewer is willing to wait?"

"I think that's a good idea," I said delicately. "You have to watch your health. Maybe we shouldn't do the event tonight, yeah?" He stalked past me into the bedroom, not even bothering with his usual head kiss.

I sighed and pressed my forehead against the grain of the closed door. Swallowing, I forced down fear before it besieged me. If I took in everything on my plate, I'd crack. *Like steel, Kaye.*

When I turned around, I saw Jerome, hands clasped behind his back, staring again.

"Is there something I should know about my client, Ms. Trilby?"

"Nothing I can't handle, Mr. Buitre."

He pursed his thin lips, calculating. "I'll remind you that Samuel Cabral committed to this charity event months ago. Many prominent people will expect him to be there, and if he doesn't show—especially after his illness in Los Angeles—people will speculate. Rumors will crop up about nervous breakdowns, rehab, the whole gambit."

Now I was faced with a dilemma: Samuel's health or Samuel's reputation? Like a machine, I mentally checked off our friendship vows…no matter how I chose, I'd violate at least one of them. Son-of-a-monkey.

"I'll give you one hour at the charity event." Put in a quick appearance, then duck out.

"Three."

"*One* hour, non-negotiable, then he's calling it a night."

His eyes glinted with a hardness that conveyed how cruel he could be. And then, that silver tongue. "Certainly. Mr. Cabral's well-being is our first priority, as ever."

He knew I didn't believe him.

It had come to this. I, Kaye Trilby, small-business owner that catered to B&Bs and ski shops, would have to find that single ruthless bone in my body and exploit, exploit, exploit. I hated the idea. Hated the manipulation, the games, the back-stabbing. But I could tell, without a doubt, Jerome was gearing up to strike.

The minute the interviews were over and I was ensconced in the privacy of my own hotel room, I called Jaime.

"Guzman."

"Jaime, I need you." I jerked away my slacks and blouse, and unzipped the garment bag containing the cocktail dress I'd bought with Indigo and Nat.

"It's about time. Do you want to wear the strap—?"

"Ha-ha," I interrupted, lest she take us to a place from which we could never return. "I need you to do some digging into Jerome Buitre's background. That weasel's gonna take me out, I can feel it. I need dirt on him, something to hold over his head ASAP."

She whistled. "Tall order. First Caroline, now her boss. Are you sure you want to go down this road? I'm telling you right now, if there was anything to be found, the guy's probably swept his tracks clean."

I squeezed the phone between my shoulder and ear as I shimmied into the filmy black material. "Try. I'll make it worth your while."

"I want double what you paid last time, plus a date with Hector Valdez."

Crap, he would kill me. I jabbed a bobby pin into my scalp. "You're asking me to use Hector as a bargaining chip?"

"It's your way or my way."

Jaime's way probably involved dog collars and leashes. Well, Hector was always on the hunt for new thrills. Jaime Guzman wouldn't disappoint.

"It's as good as done. Happy digging."

My smugness vanished when I looked in the vanity mirror and saw Samuel leaning against the door frame, astute eyes boring into mine, more alert than he'd been in days. He was already dressed in a sharp black suit, elegant down to his cuff links and pocket square. The way he looked at me…his disapproval pelted me like dime-sized hail. Well, what did he expect when he brought me on board?

"Trading in extreme sports for other adrenaline rushes?"

I glared at him. After Samuel and Jerome overheard my previous conversations, I should have learned my phone voice carried like a klaxon.

"Don't play their games, Trilby. Not you. Especially with people you care about."

I bent to buckle the straps on my heels, giving him a generous view of what little cleavage I had. "You yanked me off the bench and put me in your starting lineup, Cabral."

"Hector is your friend." He held my gaze for a long while. "You're sidelining me, you know. Cutting me out of whatever you've got brewing. Why?"

"That's ridiculous."

His gaze grew flinty. "I may have bipolar disorder, but my brain still works—very well, actually. I have to wonder if this is a delayed attempt at retribution for cutting you out all those years ago." I opened my mouth to protest, but he held up a hand. "Please. Just think it over." He gave me a small nod and left.

"I'm doing this for *you,* Samuel," I called after him.

Because I *was* doing this for him. I wasn't trying to prove a thing, or shut him out, oh no. If he'd only consider publishing his book, I wouldn't have to play these games.

But you are *cutting him out, Kaye. Are you doing it to protect him, or pay him back?*

I jerked open my makeup bag so hard, I tore off the zipper. Fan-flippin'-tastic. Eye shadow…liner…mascara, like Danita taught me my first day of high school. I uncapped a tube of lipstick and dabbed it over my lips, painting them a killer red. I never wore dark red lipstick. I gazed at the woman before me, all smoky eyes and sleek hair in the glow of vanity lights. Powerful and classy, legs pale and long against a dramatic black. This woman could rival the biggest PR players in New York City. She was heart-attack beautiful. She was scarlet and steel. She was arrogant.

She wasn't me.

Just as Caroline painted sailboats, my heart painted hiking boots, and rivers, and snow-capped mountains.

A funky *boom-shaka-laka-laka* pounding down the hallway warned of what awaited in the Boom Boom Room, moments before we stepped past an anorexic-looking doorwoman and into its seventies decadence.

Oh sweet superfly.

White leather sofas. Wood paneling and starburst chandeliers. Floor-to-ceiling glass windows, the city glittering below. In the adjoining room was a span of glossy black tiling, broken by a sunken triangle-shaped hot tub, of all things. I'd have to watch my footing so I wouldn't take a classic Kaye tumble into its bubbly depths. Celebs and authors, designers and debutantes mingled with martini glasses in one hand and shooters in the other. Tall models circulated with hors d'oeuvres and wine trays. Along one of the glass walls was an elaborate table highlighting local artists' work for silent auction. And at the center of the space? A two-story, cone-shaped bar, golden and glowing.

It was Mick Jagger's living room.

I gripped Samuel's elbow and wandered through the A-list hideaway. It was like some trippy dream sequence, where everything's a blur of dim lights and swirling people, and occasionally, you recognize a face, but you aren't sure if you've actually met that face or saw it on a magazine rack in a check-out line.

"Cabral, good to see you." A man in a leather jacket fired a finger gun at us. "Loved the new book. Cute girl."

"Hey, Samuel, welcome home," crooned a pretty little thing who couldn't have been more than nineteen.

"Sam, can I buy you a drink? Ha!" Another man with freaky sunglasses and a trophy wife on his arm slapped Samuel's shoulder. I felt him stiffen.

"I was just on my way to the bar, excuse me," he mumbled, sidestepping the pair with a hand pressed to the small of my back. Sunglasses man stared after us, mouth gaping.

"I think you offended that guy."

He snorted. "He's a rat. Still bitter I've knocked three of his books off the number one slot on *The New York Times'* bestseller list." He snatched two wine glasses from a tray and handed one to me. "Drink half of this, please. If I want to be 'socially acceptable,' I'll need a glass in my hand."

I did as he asked, coughed, then swapped drinks. "Clever. Where did you pick up that trick?"

"Endless parties like this. Buitre likes to be up to their elbows in *Lafite Rothschild*. If you ever need to get on Jerome's good side, ask his opinion of their cellars. It won't matter if you don't know what the hell he's talking about; he'll appreciate the chance to brag."

I took a sip of wine and wrinkled my nose—too dry for my taste. I wiped red lipstick off the rim with my thumb. Oh, forget it. I snatched a cocktail napkin and rubbed the gunk from my lips, too. A man laughed heartily just behind us.

"What do you think of Buitre's snazzy Grand-Cru, Ms. Trilby?" Patrick O'Malley greeted us, and I could have kissed his friendly face. His blinding white teeth glowed beneath the mood lighting.

"I think if they served the cheap stuff, no one would know the difference."

"Agreed. You'd be surprised how many focus groups—wine experts included—prefer the cheaper bottle when labels are stripped away. Wine expertise is the biggest swindle in our society, along with academia and golf. It's too easy to become snobbish about the labels."

"Or snobbish about non-conformity," Samuel came back.

Patrick raised his glass. "Very true."

"Kaye's accused me of being the snobbiest anti-snob in Manhattan." He gave my hip a tender squeeze.

I rolled my eyes. "It's our Colorado upbringing. They fed us granola instead of Cheerios. You don't ascribe to labels, Patrick?"

"I do not."

"Odd philosophy, coming from someone who creates images for a living."

"Ah, Ms. Trilby. I don't *create* them, per se. I simply highlight qualities which already exist in my clients. Fewer fraud perpetuations that way." He clapped Samuel on the back. "You've got an enchanting one here, Cabral. Don't let her slip away again."

"I don't intend to." The warmth of his words burned through my limbs like the wine I drank. Then he nodded to someone behind me. Indigo Kingsley waved us over to her entourage. Among them were Nat and a gorgeous, tan hunk who could only be Marco Caldo.

"Excuse me for a moment," Samuel said quietly, then turned in the opposite direction.

I tightened my grip on his elbow. "Where are you going?"

"To the little boys' room. You'll have to release my arm, Kaye."

"Oh. You won't like the restrooms. Rumor has it the floors are clear glass." My fingers relinquished him for the first time tonight. He kissed my head and sauntered through the room, drawing every eye to his graceful frame.

Patrick shook his head. "He doesn't even realize how much they watch him, does he? Amazing."

My eyes stayed on Samuel until he disappeared. "He does. He's just not comfortable being watched." I took another sip of wine to bolster my courage. "Patrick, do you remember, on our flight to LA, you said I could call you if my client ever needed a consult? Well, I'd like to call you."

He lifted a dark eyebrow. "Negotiating a change of guard in the old guards' barracks? Now I truly adore you. Let's talk in private." He glanced around the room, then hustled me away from the crowds to a quiet table. I slid onto the stool and was about to swipe my napkin across the sugar-covered table when Patrick grabbed my wrist. He held it still, shaking his head.

"Best not to touch that."

"The sugar?"

He chuckled. "I don't think it's sugar."

My face reddened. "Crud, I'm so naïve sometimes."

"It's refreshing. Now, Ms. Trilby, won't you tell me about Mr. Cabral's career plans?"

Between my chat with Patrick and Indigo's dragging me around like a show dog, the night went faster than I expected. Relatively uneventful, save for a disheartening confrontation with a very bitter Robin.

"Are you Kaye Trilby?" he sneered. I immediately recognized the effete voice from our ambiguous phone conversations. "You nearly cost me my job." His knuckles tightened around the stem of his wine glass, and I was sure he'd snap it in two. An untamable cowlick made him appear even more boyish, poor kid, like someone's little brother. He probably was. Mother cliff-hucker, I was a harpy.

I jumped into an apology before he had a chance to chew my lying behind. "Robin, I'm so sorry—"

"Save it," he clipped, and stomped across the room to a circle of young New Yorkers burning holes in my back. It left me feeling like I was back in high school and a box of tampons fell out of my locker, or something equally embarrassing. I slammed back the rest of my drink, willing away humiliation as sangria thrummed through my veins.

Samuel came up behind me just as the kid stormed off. He rubbed my neck. I closed my eyes and leaned into his hand.

"I take it Lexi let him have it over *BrownStoners*?"

I grimaced. "At least he's still employed."

He gave my neck an affectionate squeeze. "Don't dwell on it. Come with me—I want to show you off."

I kept one eye on my wristwatch and the other on Samuel as we circulated. Eleven forty. We'd been at Boom Boom much longer than the promised hour, to Jerome's delight. But now it was time to turn in. Samuel wasn't well, though he wasn't poor. He just...was. He hovered politely in conversations, offered terse replies when needed, coasted on autopilot. He kept the same half-full glass of wine in his hand the entire night, fooling them all.

I sidled up to the flamboyant bar for a watered-down night cap, ogling Samuel from across the room as he shook hands and said good nights.

"Samuel Cabral is as beautiful as ever, isn't he?"

I turned at the dulcet voice by my side. My eyes widened. My mouth went dry. Spank me and call me a slut. *Her.* Fluffed brunette hair, lethal dress, curling lips, it was as if she'd hopped from my nightmare and landed in the waking world. I'd know her anywhere. I'd never felt such a fanatical urge to gouge out someone's eyes. It was the brunette of my brownstone nightmares.

"You," I spat.

She blinked. "You remember me. I thought you wouldn't."

"How could I forget? Your little affidavit for Lyle Togsender sure hasn't helped to block you from my brain."

Her critical, eyelash-feathered gaze swept over me. "I don't know if I would've recognized you, if not for Page Six. Your lack of hoodie and backpack threw me off. That, and a noticeable absence of drama."

My stomach roiled in disgust, and I had to clutch my glass between both hands to keep from tossing red wine in her face. I wanted to yank that mane of hair from her scalp and hang it above my mantle. Like a *Maury Povich* episode, I wanted to scream that she was a skanky crack-whore and to keep her powder-covered claws away from my husband. But I managed to restrain myself. I'd learned my lesson with Caroline at Danita's wedding, and I wasn't going to embarrass Samuel in that fashion. I studied her again, the brittle face and bony shoulders, and decided she truly was human and not the insuperable vixen my nightmares made her out to be.

But my oh my, she was trying. "Damn, he was sexy when he was high." Her eyes followed Samuel, drifting down his body. "He certainly was an intense, confused young man, like he was tied to the bumpers of two cars driving in opposite directions. I thought maybe he…you know. Had a wide stance."

Jesus, Mary, and Joseph. "He's not—"

"Kaye!"

And Saint Patrick. You've got to be KIDDING me. I watched with disbelieving eyes as Mr. Avant Garde himself purposefully strode my way, arms spread for a hug. He was gaunter, and he'd grown out his hair. It was slicked back into a stubby tail and honestly, it made him look skeevy. A striped silk scarf was flung around his neck and he sported an intentionally rumpled blazer over an equally rumpled T-shirt with a print of Toulouse-Lautrec. I had a hard time recalling why I'd found him attractive. Could this night possibly resemble a French film more?

"I see you've met my date."

The brunette. *Oui.*

When I didn't accept his hug, he shrugged and wrapped an overly friendly arm around her shoulder. "Our magazine is publishing a selection of her coffee house poetry next month."

"Congratulations," I said acidly.

Brunette actually winked at me. "Kaye and I go way back. I knew her husband seven years ago."

Mr. Avant Garde froze, hand raised mid hair-slick. "Husband!"

Yeah, probably should have left an hour ago, before Fate had a chance to kick me in the teeth. "*Ex*-husband, thanks in part to your frisky friend here," I muttered.

The brunette pointed to Samuel. "That guy over there."

Avant Garde followed her finger, and his eyes bulged like a bullfrog's. "Samuel Caulfield *Cabral?* Oh shit, you're *that* Kaye?"

To my horror, Samuel swung around at the sound of his name. His eyes caught mine, silently questioning the panic in my face. He was at my side in a moment.

"Kaye, are you ready to…" And then he saw her. "You."

She flashed neat Chiclet teeth. "Hey, Samuel."

His arm crept around my waist, as if he would throw me behind him like a caveman if the woman so much as puckered her lips.

Mr. Avant Garde sputtered something terrible. His hands seemed to have unfrozen and dug paths through his gel-encrusted locks. "You're her husband! Oh crap, I slept with Samuel Cabral's wife. Please tell me you don't have kids."

I felt Samuel's shock before I even dared to look at his face. He released me as if I'd burned him. We downright should have left an hour ago.

"For the love of all that's holy," I hissed desperately, "lower your voice! You're not a home wrecker."

"You fucked him?" Samuel's voice was low and treacherous.

"Samuel," I begged.

His face grew wild. He growled. Then, it was as if all the energy quit the vicinity and concentrated in his clenched fist. It surged forward and before I knew what happened, Samuel threw himself into Mr. Avant Garde, pummeling him into the ground.

"You fucking stay away from her," he bellowed. "Don't you ever touch her with your filthy fucking hands again, or I'll hunt you down and break every bone in your body!"

Blood splattered across the black tiles and Samuel's shirt as he landed a second blow to the writhing man's face. People screamed, and

I think one of them was me. I was vaguely aware of Justin and Patrick leaping forward and grasping Samuel's biceps, pulling him away from his victim. Then Mr. Avant Garde, blood smeared over his nose and cheek, grasped the opportunity to attack and dived, shoulder-first into Samuel's gut. He was a lot feistier than his Toulouse-Lautrec shirt implied. The sheer force sent all four men skidding across the polished black tiles and, as fate would have it, into that bubbly, ill-placed hot tub.

Cameras flashed. Party-goers gasped and chattered excitedly as bouncers shoved them to the side, yanking the sopping wet men from the tub. Somewhere behind me, above the roaring crowd, Jerome demanded to know what had happened.

"Get him out of here!" Patrick shouted at me. The minute Samuel crawled out of the water, I latched onto his hand.

"Good night Brunette, Avant Garde — sorry about the nose," I called, scurrying past the hot tub mess.

"You can forget about coffee, Kaye!" he howled after me as I dragged Samuel through the crowds before Jerome could find us.

The moment we stepped into the elevator, I pounced. "What the —? You can't just go around punching people out, Samuel! What if he wants to press charges?"

He gripped my arms like a vice. "You slept with that man!"

"Yes, a long time ago." Never mind his brunette also put in an appearance. His eyes, inches from mine, burned with hurt and rage as water streamed around them. "He was Number One — friend of a friend. I told you about him in the cave, remember?"

"You were going to meet him for coffee," he accused.

"No, I wasn't. He helped me get a copy of *BrownStoners*. I was being polite, and I am so sorry you found out about it this way. Samuel, listen to me," I said calmly, "you need to get a hold of your temper. Look at you, you're dripping a lake in the elevator." For someone who hated to be the center of attention, he certainly was, tonight.

His grip on my arms slackened, and the blood rushed back to my fingers. I clenched and unclenched them as they tingled.

He closed his eyes and breathed deeply. "You could have told me."

"I'm truly sorry for lying to you about contacting that guy. You have a tremendous jealous streak, Cabral. I didn't want to risk it."

"So who were you having coffee with Sunday morning?"

"Caroline. I wanted her advice on how to convince you to see a doctor." I grabbed his shirttails and began to wring water from them.

"Don't hide things from me, Kaye," he snarled.

"Don't be hypocritical, Samuel. Do you truly remember last night?"

He froze. "No. I don't remember."

"There was coke at the party. Have you been using again?"

"No! Quit with the fucking interrogation!"

The elevator doors opened and an older couple was poised to walk in. But one glimpse of Samuel, drenched and bloody, a towering psychopath in the corner, and they decided to catch the next one. When the doors slid shut, I watched with horror as his face crumpled. His hand shot up to shield his eyes from me.

I brushed sodden brown strands from his forehead. "Hey. Talk to me."

"I'm...not in control. I terrified those people."

"Well, babe, you're soaking wet." And a tad gory, but I somehow thought that wouldn't help. "I'll call your doctor right away and we'll sort this out."

I let Samuel into the hotel room where we'd stashed our things. Digging out his dry clothes, I placed them on the bed. He looked utterly lost as he wandered through the room.

"Goodness knows what was in that hot tub; I'd venture a mixture of piss and booze. You might want to take a shower. Just leave your wet things in there and I'll have someone launder them." I gestured to the spacious bathroom and he padded in, shoes squeaking, and shut the door.

I crashed onto the sofa. Kicking off my heels, I rubbed life into my sore feet. Not the worst night of my life, but close. With a sigh, I grabbed my phone and punched in the number for Samuel's New York psychiatrist.

"Dr. Vanderbilt speaking. Ms. Trilby?" said a sleepy voice. Yes, a Vanderbilt. There was a reason he got the big bucks.

"I'll pay you a small fortune to make a house call tonight."

"I'll be there in an hour."

I gave him the address of the Standard Hotel, along with the room number. Then I sat. And waited. And freaked out.

Stupid pride. Stupid, stupid need to prove myself. We should have left the party earlier. I should have told Jerome no to begin with.

Heck, I should have called Dr. Vanderbilt the minute I arrived in New York. But I didn't. So tomorrow morning, Samuel's angry fists would be splashed across Internet sites, magazines, and TV stations worldwide. Togsy would get a boon for his book. Ace would warn about potential lawsuits and assault charges. Alonso would be on the first flight to New York. Any moment, the calls would start.

I heard the shower turn on. *Samuel.* That's what hurt the most… The negative media blitz would utterly whip him.

My phone buzzed in my hand. *So it begins.* I answered, ready to woman up and do my job.

"Kaye Trilby speaking."

"Flower?"

"Dad?" My voice cracked.

"Hi, baby girl!"

"Whose number is this?"

"Audrey's brother's. I was worried I wouldn't get to wish you a happy birthday before midnight."

"Actually, it's two minutes after midnight here."

"Man, that's right. Audrey's entire family is visiting from Montreal and it's just crazy here. Why are you still up?" Somewhere in the background, Audrey tittered that "the Cabral boy" was giving me a nice birthday present. My father groaned.

"Oh, Dad, it's a long story."

"You can tell me."

"No…I really can't. It's business-related. But you know, I don't want to think about it right now. Care to distract me?"

"Gladly." For the next half hour, I listened, arm flung over my eyes and wretchedly homesick, as my father and Audrey soothed me with stories of his organic nuts on display at the Garden Market (I had to laugh), her pink highlights, and Lyons High's seven homeruns at the Friday night football game (touchdowns, Audrey, touchdowns).

I didn't notice when Samuel turned off the shower. At some point I was aware it wasn't running. I said good night to my mother and peered into the bedroom. The bathroom door was open, remnant steam billowing from the shower and fogging the mirror. Samuel's wet clothes lay in a heap on the dressing bench, water trickling from the cuffs.

But the bathroom was empty.

So was the bedroom.

The entire suite was empty, save for a small white box tied with a red ribbon. An envelope with my name rested under the bow. It was creased, as if he'd carried it for a while. I slid a fingernail under the flap and ripped it open.

> *Happy Birthday, Firecracker.*
>
> *This isn't a conventional gift, I suppose. But then, you've never been one for gifts unless there's meaning attached. Kaye, you are more precious to me than my own life. I've known as much since I was a scraggly, six-year-old boy. It's always been you. It always will be. You are so strong. I trust you. I love you, Samuel.*

I untied the ribbon with trembling fingers. It looked like a jewelry box. More specifically, a ring box. A thought rose, unbidden. *Please don't let it be an engagement ring. I'm too overwhelmed, I'm not ready, he promised me a trial period then he'd move to Boulder...*

And then, *Oh my, I want this. I've waited so long for him...*

No jewelry. My heart sank a bit. I frowned at the tightly folded piece of paper wedged in the box.

It was a legal document.

> Medical Power of Attorney
>
> Effective Upon Execution
>
> I, SAMUEL CAULFIELD CABRAL, a resident of 16 Margaret Corbin Drive, New York County, NY; designate ASPEN KAYE TRILBY, presently residing at 902 Fifth Street, Boulder, CO, as my agent to make any and all health care decisions for me, except to the extent I state otherwise in this document. For the purposes of this document, "health care decision" means consent, refusal of consent, or withdrawal of consent to any care, treatment, service, or procedure to maintain, diagnose, or treat an individual's physical or mental condition. This medical power of attorney takes effect if I become unable to make my own health care decisions and this fact is certified in writing by my physician...

I scanned the document...the additional powers, the indefinite duration unless Samuel chose to revoke said power of attorney. His signature was at the bottom, followed by two witnesses: Justin and his business manager. The document had been notarized by Ace the very day we arrived in New York City. A sticky note from him explained the original was already on file.

My eyes burned. Like so much about Samuel, I didn't know whether this was sweet or morbid. He was giving me the power to make the calls for him, should he ever become incapacitated again. He didn't want me steamrolled like seven years ago. He thought I was strong enough: not Caroline, Alonso, Neelie, or Aspen. Me.

He trusted me with his life.

And then I turned around and lied to him about Mr. Avant Garde. It wasn't a stretch to figure out why he hadn't given this to me in person.

The late hour and the remnants of alcohol made my temples throb. I squeezed them, praying that when I opened my eyes, the pain would be gone. But the light only made them ache again. I called his cell phone. A ringing sounded in the other room, coming from the depths of his overnight bag. I tried not to panic. Well, that meant he *had* to be coming back, if he'd left his phone behind.

But my gut...or symbiosis, or love, or simply understanding of Samuel Cabral...told me otherwise. Truth hit me like a loaded-down semi.

He was running again.

Chapter 14
CUT AWAY

*In the event of a parachute malfunction,
a skydiver must make a quick, life-saving decision
to jettison the main canopy
to allow the reserve canopy to deploy.*

Hydraulic Level Five {working title}
Draft 3.35
© Samuel Caulfield Cabral & Aspen Kaye Trilby
35. *Hiding Easter Eggs*

"I'm thinking after graduation, I'm going to travel the world. Australia, China, Thailand – as far away as I can get," Lacy says as she nestles an Easter egg beneath a hedge.

Aspen hands her another from the basket. "You know, you can still travel when you work."

"Psh, you sound like a career counselor. I'm not hitting the work force right away, but maybe in a couple of years. Don't look at me like that, all disapproving. You get this funny crease between your eyebrows. Anyway, apparently the continental US is still too close for my stepmom." She reaches for a branch, then decides if it's too high for her, it's too high for the children in her Bible class.

She hides the colorful egg in a tree knot. "Who knows, maybe I'll venture out to New York with you and Caulfield next year and look into grad schools, unless you don't want a third wheel hanging around you newlyweds. Hey, isn't your first anniversary just around the corner?"

"Next month." Aspen tucks an egg in a cluster of yellow daffodils. "Caulfield's planning to whisk me away to a B&B in Vail as soon as my classes are over. I heard him talking to his dad about it through that air vent in their basement." The convenient air vent Maria showed her years ago.

Lacy sighs. "So romantic. That guy has always been too perfect for his own good. Where'd he go, anyway? The minute worship ended, he bolted out of that church pew like the minister was going to ask him to stay for another sermon."

"I think his mom sent him to the grocery store to get crushed pineapple for the ham glaze. I bet he got dragged into baseball talk with my dad." But now that Lacy mentions it, Aspen realizes he has been gone nearly an hour. She scans the churchyard, searching among Easter service stragglers and antsy kids with empty baskets. No Caulfield.

Lacy reads her mind. "If you want to go find him, I can hide the last of these eggs."

"Thanks. Save one for us to split." Aspen hands her friend the basket and walks around the side of the church to call Caulfield. But before she dials, she glimpses her rosy-faced husband across the lawn near the forest edge, the only spot of real color against a drab sky.

The ground is soft and muddy from an early morning rain shower, so she ditches her heels and wades barefoot through the squishy grass. She calls out to him.

"Hey, Hubby, the point of an Easter egg hunt is to hide the eggs, not yourself."

He hurriedly tucks something in his back pocket and turns to her with devastated eyes.

"Caulfield?" Her grin fades.

"Is the egg hunt over already? That was fast." He's jumpy. She cautiously places her hand on his crossed arms then jerks it back when he recoils.

"What's wrong?"

He leans against a tree, heedless of the bark sap staining his pale green oxford.

"Talk to me," she tries again.

Caulfield takes a deep, shuddery breath. "I'm troubled – no, disgusted – by what I'm doing."

Aspen freezes. "What have you done?"

"I was sitting in that damned pew I've sat in since I was six, listening to the minister talk about love, forgiveness, faith, and all these things I'm supposed to care about. And you know what's going through my head?" His voice breaks. "How long before I can escape through those doors and forget everything I'm hearing?"

She hums. "To be honest, half the congregation was probably thinking the same thing. I know for a fact that the guy who kept nodding off in front of us wasn't paying attention."

Frustrated hands tear through his hair. "I'm not talking about wanting to make a beeline for Easter dinner. I've bastardized everything I've ever held sacred, Firecracker. My faith, my writing, my love for you." He ticks each on his fingers. "Especially my love for you."

The thing about Aspen, though, is that she hasn't experienced enough to truly understand the depth of her young husband's pain. What is there in life that can't be fixed by having someone at your side, loving you? Aspen bites her lip in confusion. "Is this some sort of God-guilt thing?" she asks. "If you want to go to church more often, I won't fight you on it anymore. We can get involved at that Boulder one you like."

Caulfield offers her a small, sad smile. "Just let me hold you for a while."

He pulls her into the fold of his arms and rests his chin on the top of her head. Together, they watch as children in flouncy dresses and Easter suits trample down the steps of the church, swinging baskets and falling over each other to uncover the most eggs. They remember a time not all that distant...yet an eternity ago...when they'd been those children, fingers still tinted pastel from eggshell dye. Even now, Aspen's fingertips are pale purples and pinks from the eggs she and Lacy hid.

"You are so warm," he murmurs.

Sam—Since you left a week ago, my days have been a whirlwind of people, with their maddening curiosity and condolences. But when night comes, it's too silent. Which is a conundrum, because I've had seven years of nights alone. We only shared them a short while and yet, I need your steady breath on my neck to fall asleep. So I've had some time late at night to study your writing more closely—the way you phrase things, words you would use—and I think I'm getting better at it.

I'm finding as I learn more about what you went through in the months we were married, a lot of things that didn't make sense are suddenly clearer. Writing this out is cathartic—I see why you enjoy it so much. Put all that guilt and regret on paper, exorcise it, and send it back to the past, where it belongs.

I love you.

P.S.—Has it really only been a week since you ran from the Standard Hotel? It feels as though it was another lifetime...~Kaye

Samuel was running again.

It was apparent he was not returning to the hotel, so I hoped he might be at his apartment.

I dropped a wad of cash in the cabbie's hand, hefted both my garment bag and Samuel's duffel bag over my shoulders, and barreled up the stairs of the Inwood apartment building. I prayed he was upstairs. But when I flung open the door—darkness. A quick search of the place told me he'd already come and gone. The jeans and T-shirt he'd carelessly tossed over the bedpost were missing, as was his old Red Sox hat. He'd taken nothing else...no luggage, toothbrush, razor. So perhaps he'd just stepped out for a while.

At two a.m. In Washington Heights. Crud.

Jerking on sweats and sneakers, I tried not to think about how big and scary New York City was at night. I didn't care that I was in an unfamiliar city, alone. Still, I grabbed Samuel's familiar Lyons High ball cap and plopped it on my head, a talisman.

The elevator was too slow. I tapped my foot; why was it so flipping slow? The doors opened and I skidded into the lobby, nearly tripping over the soles of my shoes.

"Excuse me," I said to the wide-eyed night man, "did you see Samuel Cabral leave?"

"About half an hour ago, ma'am."

"Did he have anything with him? Bag, luggage, anything?"

The man squinted, thinking. "A backpack. Oh, and a laptop bag."

I took a calming breath. *Breathe…breathe…* Maybe he just went somewhere to write, like a twenty-four-hour diner. Eccentric, but Samuel. I asked the doorman if there were any such places in the neighborhood. He jotted down three and handed me the paper, with a stern warning to be careful and maybe even consider waiting until dawn to go exploring. I took the paper and thanked him for his help.

Fortunately, I wasn't robbed. Unfortunately, none of the greasy spoons produced my AWOL lover. I hunted for him in the park. He wasn't on any of the lighted paths and it was impossible to search the wooded areas in the dark. I wandered out of Fort Tryon and along Broadway, clutching a pepper spray key chain, my shirt clinging to my sweaty back. I shivered in the cool air. I hadn't realized how cold the weather had grown the past few weeks and its chill bit my cheeks. The street was relatively quiet, save for club music pounding behind neon signs and well-worn residents wandering in and out of Dominican convenience stores with flickering fluorescents. I gave a cursory glance in each of the stores, used my Spanish. Each store clerk shook his head — *no sé.*

My skin began to prickle, and I slowly became aware of all the eyes following me. They probably only wanted to know why a white girl was tearing through the Heights after midnight — I think they believed I was jacked up on something — but it scared the crap out of me. What on earth was I doing? New York City, alone? My behavior was completely reckless. Samuel would give me an earful when he returned. I choked back the fear clawing up my throat.

He will return. He's coming back.

Fear for my safety sent me jogging, then running, up Broadway. I didn't know if anyone followed me, but I felt like a hundred people were on my heels. My lungs wheezed and my legs ached as I plowed into the apartment once again and collapsed on the couch.

It was dark, just as I'd left it. No Samuel.

At four thirty a.m., I started calling our New York acquaintances, fingertips still numb from the outside air. Justin. Lexi. Jerome. Even

Caroline. Voice mail, every one, except for Justin. He hadn't seen Samuel since the Boom Boom blowup.

I called Dr. Vanderbilt. "I'm sorry, Kaye," he said. "He wasn't at the hotel. There's nothing I can do for Samuel until he's found. In twenty-four hours, if he hasn't returned, you can call the police…"

I dialed Samuel's number again, on the off-chance he'd returned to the apartment for his cell when I was out. Once more, I heard it ring in the bedroom where I'd left it. No one was picking up. For the love of everything holy, why wouldn't someone *answer* me? Snot dripped from my thawing nose. I grabbed a wad of tissue paper and fisted it, then angrily hurled it across the living room where it plopped unsatisfyingly on the area rug. Who else was left to call?

There was someone else…

I stared at Alonso's name in my contact list, my finger hovering over the send button. Not again. Never again.

Desperate, I scrolled further down. Molly? No, as much as I loved my friend, her solutions didn't always pan out. Dani? Angel? Hector? No.

My finger paused over my father's number, and the little girl inside of me ached for her daddy. I dialed the one person I knew would always answer the phone, no matter the hour.

"Hello?" answered a sleep-heavy voice. "Flower?"

"Dad!" I cried.

"Kaye?" I heard him scramble out of bed. "Kaye, what's wrong?"

"Dad, I n-need you. Samuel's m-missing."

"Criminy," he mumbled. "Baby girl, I need you to take a deep breath…good girl…try to stop crying. Now explain what's going on."

A stream of words poured from my mouth. I tried to slow them, but they rushed through the receiver and into my father's patient ears. I told him about the fight at the Boom Boom Room, how he had punched out Avant Garde. How Samuel was fit-to-be-tied, and scared, and all muddled. I explained how he'd been back to the apartment to change clothes and was last seen leaving with his backpack and laptop.

"You should know that Samuel…he's got bipolar disorder, Dad." I heard him curse softly. "But something's not right. He's been switching back and forth, and I'm afraid he's gone manic or something."

"Huh. Well, that explains a lot. I've heard about that illness before, especially when people go missing."

"I'm really scared for him. He gave me power of attorney for my birthday…"

There was a pause, then a sigh. "Flower, I'm going be real honest with you. I love you, but I'm not the person for this. You want someone who can stay level-headed and do what needs to be done. Baby girl, that's your mom."

I tried not to feel the sting of his rejection, and instead thought this through. Then I did as my father suggested. I called my mother.

My mother could be as cold and hard as the ground before sunrise. But at a time like this, emotions couldn't trump common sense, could it? When I finished telling her what I told Dad, I heard a car door slam over the phone.

"Kaye, honey, I'm leaving Lyons for Denver right now and I'm gonna fly out there. Look around the apartment again. Is anything else missing, something that might give you a clue to where he's gone? Passport, keys, weapons."

I rifled through his desk then his overnight bag. "Passport's here… keys are gone, along with his wallet…crap, he forgot his meds. I don't think he has a weapon. Kitchen knives, maybe? No, those are still there."

I gazed around the living room. It felt off. Slightly different. Then my eyes fixed upon the empty mantle above the fireplace and I knew why.

"Mom," I whispered, "he took the urn."

"What?"

"His mother's urn is gone. And…" I flipped open the cardboard box next to the coffee table, "some of his writing's gone, too. I know where he's going. Listen, when you get to Denver, catch the first flight to Boston, okay?"

"Boston!?"

I dashed through the apartment, gathering up my purse and messenger bag, still packed from yesterday at the Standard Hotel. I stuffed Samuel's medications and a change of clothes for both of us in my things. Then I turned off the lights, slammed the door, and locked it. Subway or cab? Call a cab.

"Phone me when your flight gets in and we'll find each other. Mom…I'm so sorry." Because I just needed to tell someone I was sorry.

"You have nothing to be sorry about." She cleared her throat. "Be safe."

"I love you."

"Love you too, Aspen Kaye."

There were ghosts in Boston and Samuel chased them. I didn't understand why they still had such a hold on him after all these years, though it was all tangled in the fear he'd end up like his mother. I was petrified his flight was some sort of self-fulfilling prophecy.

In a way, aren't we all afraid we'll become our parents? Our parents could be saints or the scum of the earth; most fall somewhere in between. But because they are our parents, we see the flaws. Sometimes we remember the faults more than the good and we swear, up and down, we'll never do that to our children, spouse, friends. Yet, no matter how much we fight the tide, we see a little more of them in ourselves with the passing of each day…

"Just to be clear," I said to the woman at the gate check-in for my shuttle flight to Boston, "a person can fly with human ashes, as long as the urn is a carry-on and goes through X-ray? You don't need some sort of prior dispensation from the airline?"

The woman sighed. "I told you three times, ma'am. We understand how painful losing a loved one is, and we respect anyone traveling with crematory remains. Typically our security screeners will allow an opaque urn through if they can see what's inside."

"And you can't tell me whether my friend was on the previous flight?"

"No, ma'am. If you ask again, I'll have to call security."

Damn it, she'd tell me if this was a chick flick, then sob about the rarity of true love.

I dropped into my seat and crossed my arms, glaring at travelers as they wheeled through the concourse. Two whole hours on standby until the next available flight! I should have taken the train, but Justin swore up on down this was the quickest way to get to Boston. Mom'd beat me to Boston, at this rate. Nine o'clock…seven in Colorado. Alonso and Sofia would just be waking up. She'd play her up-an'-at-'em music in the kitchen and he'd read the paper. They'd smile at each other over coffee, both unaware their son had now been missing for eight hours.

I should call them.

My fingers shook as I scrolled to their number. I'd call them. They'd tell me not to panic, that Alonso would meet me in Boston and take care of everything, and wouldn't it be best if I just went back to Boulder and saw to my lagging TrilbyJones accounts?

I couldn't do it.

But Samuel is their son. They need to know.

Not yet. Not until I find Samuel.

He gave you power of attorney. They won't shut you out.

I can't.

The gate attendant's voice crackled through the speakers, announcing the first boarding call for my flight. I didn't have time now, anyway. I chucked my cell phone in my messenger bag and fell into line with other bleary-eyed passengers.

I tried to sleep on the brief flight to Boston. I'd been awake for twenty-eight hours straight. Not just any twenty-eight hours. Press interviews. Celebrities. PR coups. Fisticuffs. Legal documents for birthday presents and missing boyfriends. And a brisk jog through Washington Heights. Mr. Sandman would have knocked any normal person flat on their face. But sleep was as elusive as ever. The waiting was killing me. I willed the plane to go faster, to cut through the next cloud bank and poof!—there's Boston.

Just as Samuel chased his ghosts, I chased him. I'd always chased Samuel…in age, achievement, friendships, family, secrets. He was my best friend. My lover. My world. And still, he was forever an arm ahead of me. He told me he belonged to me, but I'd never really truly caught him, had I? Was I doomed to repeat this chase over and over until the day I died?

If something happened to Samuel, if he…

A horrible pain in my heart ripped through me, and I bit my clenched fist. I thought…maybe…I might die, too.

"Take me to Fenway Park," I said to the grizzled cabbie as I slid into the backseat, outside Logan International.

"In town for the game? It's going to be a zoo, ma'am, just a head's up. I'll get you as close as I can." I noticed he had a tiny plastic Red Sox helmet dangling from his mirror.

"That's fine," I sighed. Of course there was a home game this afternoon. "Who're they playing?" I needed noise or I'd go crazy.

"Second game in the Orioles series. Pedroia's lookin' to surpass one hundred RBIs, so it'll be a good 'un if the Sox can keep their heads out of their asses."

I nodded, my eyes widening at the foreignness of the choppy Boston Harbor as we sped along the turnpike and into the city. I squinted against the midday sun, glinting against the downtown skyline. Traffic was heavy. All inbound lanes crawled to a stop, crept along, then stopped again. "Some sort of delay," said the cabbie. "Typical weekday. We're heading into the Back Bay Fens." A semi pulled up alongside us, blocking my view of the river. I slid to the other window and watched as the road narrowed and passed into a neighborhood dense with brown brick, trees, and a towering Citgo Oil sign in the distance. I remembered the sign from televised Red Sox games, and I thought we must be close to the ballpark.

I tried to imagine Samuel seeing all of this as a child, from the backseat of his mother's car. Were we anywhere near the place he used to live? Beacon Hill, he'd told me.

"Where's Beacon Hill from here?"

"Back east a half mile or so. You got friends in one of those big ol' mansions?"

"My husband used to live there," I murmured.

The cabbie whistled. "Some husband."

"He is."

I checked my phone. Four missed calls from Jerome. Two from Samuel's doctor. One each from Lexi, Justin, Indigo, Caroline, Patrick. Nothing from my mother. And nothing from Samuel, obviously. I had his phone in my purse.

I listened to Caroline's message:

"*I haven't heard from him since the day you both visited my home. Let me know when you find him…*"

Every single voice message from the others was the same, except for Jerome's.

"Ms. Trilby, you must *call me*. I need to confer with Mr. Cabral if we're to manage last night's unfortunate event effectively and to our advantage…"

Fat chance, Mr. Buitre. Spin was on the back burner and last night seemed so far away.

"Only a few blocks," said the cabbie. "I don't think I can get you any closer."

"Son-of-a-monkey." I took in the thousands of people buzzing around Fenway Park like red and white bees, a massive swarm of Sox caps, jerseys, and foam fingers. And this was an hour before the game. Fans poured in and out of a dozen sports bars surrounding the compact ballpark, and the entire neighborhood unleashed a strangling claustrophobia. Prospects of finding Samuel in this mess? Bleak.

"Is it always like this?"

"Most game days, unless it's raining. Even then, there's always the diehards. I think they're handing out bobble-heads today, so it's a good thing you got here early. That'll be twenty-two dollars."

I handed him my card. Well, there went my plan. I couldn't exactly go up to a security guard and ask him if he'd seen a thirty-year-old man in a Red Sox hat and jeans wandering around the ballpark. Hefting my bag onto my shoulder, I set out blind, hunting for some sign that Samuel was here.

I pushed my way through the crowds, standing on tiptoes to see over thunderous people raising their beer cups like toasts and shouting to their buddies. I was jostled by sticky kids on leashes dragging parents laden with strollers and diaper bags, street vendors selling Red Sox gear. The entire place was rife with festive excitement. If Samuel was with me, he'd be blinking up at Fenway's shabby brick entrance like it was the Gate of Heaven. He would have laid down a fortune on pennants and gear within the first five minutes.

That's where I started — the street vendors.

I sidled up to a bearded vendor not far from Ted Williams' bronze immortalization, hocking plastic beer hats.

"I'm looking for a man." A slow grin spread over his face. I flushed as red as the B on his hat. "No no, a particular man. Red cap, backpack, laptop case. He's tall and extremely handsome — he may have been wandering around for a while, kind of twitchy? Oh! And he's carrying a cremation urn."

The vendor gave me a helpless shrug and said something. I cursed my bad ear in the midst of the ballpark cacophony and asked him to repeat it. "Lady, that could be half of Beantown," he shouted.

"But an *urn?*"

"Like I said."

Four more vendors and two security guards—no luck. "Is he here for the game?" one of them asked, handing me a hot dog.

"Um, maybe. He didn't have a ticket."

"Unless he's paying big bucks on the street, he won't get in. Wait around an hour until the crowd thins out. You might spot him."

Hope blossomed in my chest. "Right. Absolutely right, thank you." I took a bite from the dog, cringing as repulsive green relish oozed over my fingers.

My phone vibrated. I wiped my hands then whipped it out. My mother.

"Mom?"

"Kaye, I'm at Logan Airport. Now what?"

I wandered north, looking for a landmark. Citgo sign, perfect. "Look for the big Citgo sign in Kenmore Square, and there's a coffee shop where we can meet. Take a cab and I'll wait for you there."

Forty minutes later, my mother strode into the coffee and donut shop, outright exhausted in a faded flannel shirt, her eyes baggy. Even her curls drooped. I flew at her.

"Mom." She scooped me into a hug as if I were five. I cried into her shoulder, sucking in air and that earthy, Lyons scent that was all Gail. She stroked my hair.

"It's all right, Aspen Kaye, we'll find him. Right after I get a coffee."

We settled into a booth. She blew across a cup of steaming black coffee and I told her what I knew.

"No one's seen him, huh?"

I shook my head. "I'm beginning to think I was wrong, that maybe he didn't come here."

"What made you so sure it was Fenway Park?"

"He dwells on this place. His mother—his birth mother—promised to take him here a long time ago. Right before she killed herself, she was obsessed with spreading her husband's ashes at Fenway. It was a manic fixation of hers and I thought, well…with the way he's been eyeing her urn as of late…" Geez, it sounded crazy, even to my ears.

"Are you afraid he's going to…?" She grimaced and dragged a thumb across her neck.

"I don't know," I whispered. "Yesterday, I would have said no way. But now? I'm realizing I don't know how deep this fear of his runs—or anything about this illness, except nothing about it is logical."

"Fear?"

"Fear of hurting me like his mother hurt him. That's why he left, the first time."

"Kid never did do things half-assed, did he?" She studied her chipped nails with sober, pain-heavy eyes. She took another sip then tossed the rest of the contents in the garbage. "Well, I guess it's useless to sit around and try to make sense of an illness that doesn't make sense." She tightened the bandana over her hair. "We should start looking."

"How hard can it be to find a manic man trying to dump his cremated mom beneath the Green Monster?" I grumbled.

Someone tapped me on the shoulder, causing me to jump. "Excuse me. I'm sorry to eavesdrop. Did you say you're looking for a man with a cremation urn?"

My breath caught in my throat. I looked up at the portly man and then beyond him, saw a tableful of off-duty security guards in bright red polos, walkie-talkies at their hips.

Mom winked at me and tugged me toward the table. "Yeah. Seen one of those around, lately?"

One of the guards chuckled. "You'd be surprised how many fans try to dump ashes on the field. Just heard some buzz over the radio, though. Security's bringing out a guy right now who jumped the barrier. Crowd went nuts over it."

"Young guy, dark brown hair, lots of hum about being famous. Didn't you say that, Wayne?"

"Yup. Was lugging around a backpack and an urn. Security tackled him because he smuggled in that bag—bomb scare and all, but it was just filled with papers. They've called for police backup to arrest him for trespassing and disorderly conduct."

"Samuel," I breathed. He was okay. On his way to jail, most likely, but okay. Oh, thank God, thank God. I pressed my hands over my heart and felt it race. My mother squeezed my shoulder.

"That was his name, yeah." Wayne gave me a curious once-over. "Last I heard, security was trying to get in touch with someone who knew the guy. They called the phone number on record and didn't get a response." I dug into my purse and pulled out his phone. Sure enough, there were missed calls from an unknown number. "Then they tried his emergency contact—Caroline something—but the number was disconnected."

"Caroline Ortega." She'd still be on record, wouldn't she?

"I assume they'll take him to lockup?" my mother asked. I widened my eyes; she watched too many *Law & Order* marathons.

"Yeah, D-4. That's next to the Cathedral of the Holy Cross, can't miss it," the first man said, jabbing a thumb behind him.

"Thanks so much for your help." I actually hugged the security guard. He politely patted me on the back as my mother rolled her eyes.

I grabbed my purse and Mom slung her bag over her shoulder. We pushed through the crowds around Fenway Park, much lighter now that the game had started. Organ music pumped over the brick walls and along Yawkey Street, gearing the fans up for what sounded like a Sox up-to-bat.

We'll go to a game sometime, Samuel, I silently promised.

I heard his impassioned shouts mingling with the crowd noise, though I couldn't see him. My mother grabbed my elbow and we sprinted toward a cluster of security guards leaving Fenway Park. A small gathering had begun to form around the scene, several taking pictures with camera phones. Crap, this mess would be on the Internet in two minutes flat—Samuel Caulfield Cabral, arrested in Boston.

"Fucking fat-asses, let go of me," he bellowed. "Don't you know who I am?"

"Samuel!" I pushed through the crowd.

"Kaye? Kaye!" he screamed. His head strained above the security guards, his unmistakable mess of hair matted from a hat that was now long gone. There was no sign of his laptop, either, but one of the guards carried his backpack and the urn. Every inch of him pulsed with manic energy, from his feral eyes to his wrenching limbs. I insinuated myself in the huddle and placed a hand on Samuel's chest. A guard shouldered me out of the way.

"Ma'am, step back, please."

"Kaye!" Frenzied ice eyes swept over me. "Oh fuck, I can't believe you're here. Tell them to stop taking my goddamned picture. Tell them who I am, Kaye, tell them I'm fucking famous. You know who I am. *Tell* them."

A guard snorted. "Sure you are. We'll just let you go then, Mr. Pitt."

"Don't antagonize him," I sobbed. "Please, please let me touch him."

"She's family," my mother explained.

The guards silently conferred, then nodded, keeping Samuel's hands firmly trapped behind his back.

I stepped up to him and pressed a cautious palm to his face, feeling its flush.

"Hey, Sky Eyes," Samuel slurred, gazing down at me. "That's what she called me, you know? Sky Eyes. She said I was a fucking disgrace. She didn't want to see my goddamned sky eyes staring at her. Fuck her. I don't know why I even bothered, but here I am, at Fenway, and she can smack her own ugly face and keep her foam fingers and Wade Boggs posters. I can buy my own shit."

My fingers trailed his jawbone. "I know. I'm so sorry."

"They're going to let me go, right? So I can go back in there? I have to take care of this, Kaye; that's what she wanted me to do. She'll never leave me alone until I do it."

"Try to calm him down," my mom hissed. "If he assaults a cop when they get here, that's a felony."

I nodded. "I love you, Samuel, so much. But you need to calm down, okay? Go with the officers when they get here. Don't fight them." I reached up on tip-toes and placed a soft kiss on his chin.

"I love you," he mumbled. "I'll try to be a better person. I swear I'll be so good for you."

"You *are* good for me."

Samuel began to settle down, just as sirens grew louder and two police cars arrived.

"They'll take me into Fenway, Kaye? Tell them, tell them, *tell* them they need to take me back in there."

"We'll go back in some day," I soothed. God help me, I would not lie to him, not again.

My mother pulled me from the scene, but I couldn't look away. Two cops forced him to the ground and cuffed him. Another read him his rights. Jerking him to his feet, they guided him toward the squad cars. His eyes went wild as realization painted him red, and he tried to twist out of their grip.

"You fucking tricked me! You're *helping* her, Kaye! You lied to me! Kaye!" The police shoved him into the back of the car and closed the door, but I could still hear his fury.

He doesn't mean it. He's not well. Tears dripped from my chin and coated my neck. Mom handed me a tissue. I took it and scrubbed my face, then returned it, vaguely aware of her stuffing it into her pocket.

We stood there, somberly watching Samuel struggle and flail, hitting the reinforced car window with his shoulder. At last, the squad car flipped its lights and sirens, and pulled away.

"I don't think I'm strong enough for him, Mom," I whispered.

"Whoever ends up with that man will need the patience of a saint, that's for sure." My mother sighed. "Your father's going to tell you to race the other way and don't look back."

"What do you think?"

She pressed her lips together. "Are you willing to fight this thing he has?"

"I'd like to try. You probably think I'm being foolish, don't you?"

Capable arms turned me around. She tilted up my chin and solemn hazel eyes fixed on mine. "You are one of the strongest people I know, Kaye Trilby. You'll get through this, one way or the other."

I placed my hand over hers and squeezed her rough fingers. "If I'm strong, it's because I take after my mother."

Mom winced, and I could see her own ghosts stir in her head. "Here's what I think—you better get him back to Lyons. That way, if this happens again, you can call in a favor to the sheriff and he'll put him in lockup till he's sorted out."

I never understood my mother's love for cop shows. Dramas, docudramas, those Friday-night spotlights on killer wives and man-of-God con artists that made you question everyone within a one-mile radius. Winter was the worst, when Mom was out of the field and freak snowstorms made travel treacherous.

But now, I'd never been more grateful than this moment for my mother's vice. Mom spoke cop.

"Trying to locate Samuel Cabral—white male, DOB six, twenty-three, seventy-nine. Picked up on DOC and CTTP, detained half an hour ago." She leaned into the counter at the police station's receiving area, cool and commanding as she stared down the rookie officer and ignored his glance down her camisole. "We'll post bond when it's set."

"Oh yeah, the D&D. Looks like the guy's already got a rap sheet, huh?"

"He's not a D&D," she said firmly, "he's sick. Didn't they catch that in booking?"

We claimed a couple of straight-back chairs in the lobby and waited. Samuel's nonsensical, rage-filled shouts ricocheted down the corridors. I flinched at each, a physical wound. Finally, after an hour, it was obvious to everybody at the D-4 police station—officers and inmates alike—that Samuel Cabral was *not* drunk or high, and needed immediate psychiatric attention.

It didn't take long for Ace Caulfield to arrive (I hadn't even needed to call him, which wasn't a good sign), chat with a magistrate, and arrange to have him transferred to Massachusetts General—just north of Beacon Hill and the Caulfield ancestral home. Once a medical team arrived, they administered some sort of injection and he calmed considerably.

"Security found his laptop outside Fenway Park," said an officer, breaking me from my stupor. Two sturdy-looking boots stepped into my line of vision. I blinked up at his badge, wondering if I'd actually slept with my eyes open. "He probably ditched it to get through the gate." He handed me the laptop and I hugged it to me, along with his backpack.

"Thanks."

Honestly, the cops were glad to wash their hands of the whole thing. Public intox arrests filtered in as the baseball game finished and drunken fans hit the streets to numb the loss. When we left, the police station resembled a rowdy sports bar.

Later that afternoon, Mom and I twiddled our thumbs in yet another waiting room—the hospital's. Ace paced the floor, quietly arguing with someone over the phone.

"I was hoping WBZ wouldn't run it. We gotta get those charges dropped." He pocketed his phone and turned to me. "I'm going to head out, pay a visit to a judge friend. You'll be okay here?"

I nodded.

He paused, gaze scouring my hunched body and haunted demeanor. Scratching the back of his neck, he sighed.

"Kaye, I don't know what to say. With his parents' tragedies, I always kind of wondered. Look. He's a good guy. Our family should be damned proud of him, you know? They're idiots."

"I suppose none of them will be dropping in for a visit, huh?"

"Just me and my wife."

"If they don't want anything to do with Samuel, why does Caulfield Law Firm represent him?" I fired back. Lord, I was on edge.

He searched my face. "You don't trust me, do you?"

"No."

"That's understandable. The truth is, we originally sought him out as a client to make sure the family remained unsullied. Once he began to make a name for himself, they sent me to feel him out, befriend him. But I could see right away he'd never blab their family secrets—he's not the type, even if he has every right to retaliate against us. I have a lot of respect for my cousin." Ace loosed a humorless laugh. "The first time I met him, he told me to go to hell. But I was persistent and he finally agreed to let me work for him. I think, deep down, he wanted some sort of family connection."

"Well, I'm glad he was raised by the Cabrals instead of the Caulfields. No offense to you, but I can't imagine being part of such a horrible, cold family. They only fight for him if his interests are Caulfield interests."

"I can't argue with that. I wish things had been different…"

"And so I have to ask you, Ace. If Samuel's personal life, his past, his illness blows up in the media like it very well might—something I know your family won't be happy about—whose interest will you be championing? His or theirs?"

"If he's doing the right thing, I'll be behind him one hundred percent," he said firmly.

"That's all we can ask, I guess."

Ace awkwardly patted my shoulder and retreated.

During the entire exchange, my mother flipped through local television channels without a word. The TV quietly aired an afternoon talk show—Samuel was supposed to appear on that very program next week.

The area was blessedly empty. Windows overlooked the tar-patched roof of a hospital wing, and beyond that, the skyscraper forest of downtown Boston. More steel. More clouds. A fake plant in the corner was the only spot of green. Some previous waiting room occupant had left a pile of snack bags on the table, and I realized how hungry I was…but not hungry enough to eat mysterious food in a psych ward.

I juggled my phone between my hands, counting the missed calls piling up. The longer I waited to do damage control, the worse the situation would get. When my voice mails hit double digits, I decided it was time to quit being a pussy and re-enter the PR world.

The first thing I did was touch base with Justin and ask him to postpone all of Samuel's appearances until further notice.

"What's going on, Kaye? You wouldn't believe the speculation running rampant in all corners of the media. Samuel's lucky that guy in the Toulouse-Lautrec shirt at Boom Boom didn't call the cops." Heh, if he only knew. "Now there are photos surfacing online of a crazy person who looks an awful lot like Cabral being carted out of a Red Sox game. I need to know what to tell these people."

"On the record, we're not confirming anything, other than Samuel is under the weather."

"Off the record?"

"It was him, Justin. Samuel's…not well. He's at Mass General."

"I figured as much. I had a hunch in LA, but after yesterday, I was sure."

"That obvious, huh?"

"Yeah. This is gonna come out, beautiful. No stopping it now."

Mother of Tom.

Next, I spoke with Molly to give her a heads up in case they too started getting calls.

"What are you going to do about Jerome?" Molly asked.

I groaned. "I don't have the slightest clue. Put him off as long as possible. He was willing to risk Samuel's reputation to take down Caroline, so I don't want him handling something this personal."

"Let me deal with Jerome," she said gently. "You have enough on your hands."

Thank goodness for friends.

Lastly, I made that promised call to Patrick.

"Saw the Internet," he said right off the bat. "Would you like me to bring Nat? It sounds like you could use a female shoulder."

I smiled a bit for the first time today. "That would be really nice. I want you to meet with Ace Caulfield to sign an NDA first, then we'll talk damage control."

My mother kept to herself, shuffling the pages of a *Reader's Digest*. I slipped my phone into my purse and sank into my chair, but I couldn't let exhaustion claim me—not yet. The television program was in commercial break. I cringed when the evening news ran a promo. The highlight?

"*A man was arrested for disrupting a Red Sox game today, after jumping onto Fenway Park…with a cremation urn. More at ten.*"

The police had the urn, but Samuel's backpack rested in my lap. Every time I shifted, his old college papers inside rustled and sang. I glanced at my mother; she still read her magazine. I stuck my hand through the zipper and yanked out the first paper I grasped.

The lack of punctuation and paragraph breaks were difficult to read past, but I soon found Samuel's patterns. I read on…lots of pain…more crackling bones…bloody handprints on the pavement, walls…a woman shrieking. No, it was a little boy shrieking. It was so dark; I felt I was intruding on a very personal nightmare. My face reddened. I shoved the paper into the pack and zipped it away again.

My knee-jerk reaction was to be scared by his words. I could see why Alonso had been worried for my safety that night in the brownstone. But even in the height of his mania, Samuel had never physically hurt me—not once. Through his madness, I'd seen moments of lucidity…love, security. I *knew*, deep down, these hellish thoughts would never leave this page. That's all they were. Thoughts. Bad dreams, remnants of a scary childhood, and I could no more fault him for having them than I could blame myself for my own nightmares.

"Kaye, have you called the Cabrals yet?" Mom asked, not looking up from her magazine.

"No."

"Don't you think you should?"

I stared at my hands.

"You can't do to them what they did to you."

I was saved when Dr. Tran entered the waiting room, clipboard in hand. *Finally.* She was a slight, middle-aged woman with salt-and-pepper hair and shockingly, a grip that could win arm-wrestling trophies. She stared at Mom, who tossed down the magazine and pushed up from her chair.

"I'll head downstairs and pick up dinner from the cafeteria."

The doctor waited until my mother was gone before peering at me over square glasses. "Ms. Trilby, I understand you have power of attorney for Mr. Cabral."

"Yes."

"I'd like to discuss his medication with you. His current prescription regimen is Depakote and Zoloft, treating a Bipolar II diagnosis. Do you know if he's been taking them?"

"Every day, as far as I can tell."

She jotted something on her chart. "It's the antidepressant we're concerned about. Blood tested negative for illegal substances that might exacerbate an episode, so that leaves us with his prescribed meds."

"No drugs?" I asked, just to be sure.

"No drugs," she said, and I exhaled in relief. "Not illegal ones, anyway. His physician in New York indicated Mr. Cabral's last medication adjustment was in April, when the low dose Zoloft was added to combat the depressive end of his disorder. Can you give me a picture of what his demeanor was like before and after the medication change?"

"I'm afraid I can't. I've only been familiar with Samuel's moods since May. The past few months, he's been…mercurial. Mainly normal. But when he has moods, they're more hypomanic than depressive. I suppose you'd call him edgy? Nothing has been as bad as today, though."

"We'll need to observe him for a time, consider a new diagnosis."

"New diagnosis?"

"After a full-blown manic episode like today's, we'll look at Bipolar I, as well as a medication adjustment. My early suspicion is the antidepressant aggravated the mania and caused the mixed state he seems to be experiencing. Dr. Vanderbilt and I are in agreement here."

"When you say 'mixed state,' you mean…"

"When mania and depression occur simultaneously. It's very distressing for the patient and a dangerous combination—impulsiveness combined with despondency."

The implication sank into my tired mind. "I see. I think you'll want to speak with Samuel's father. He's better acquainted with Samuel's history than I am."

"Just so we're clear, Ms. Trilby, his treatment decisions ultimately lie with *you*, for the time being. He'll need inpatient care for at least a week, which we can provide here at Mass General, followed by a strict regimen of outpatient psychotherapy. You can look at psychiatric hospitals here in Boston, New York—"

"Wherever's the best."

"There's New York Presbyterian, John Hopkins in Baltimore, UCLA..."

East coast or west coast. Frick. Home grew fainter and fainter. Well, like Nat said, it was all about priorities. Samuel was my priority.

And he needed his parents.

I stared at the contact screen for a full five minutes. *This isn't seven years ago. He won't cut you out again. He can't cut you out.* I touched the folded piece of paper in my pocket for comfort—my odd little birthday present—and dialed.

"Cabral residence," answered a warm, familiar voice.

"Sofia," I sighed, "I'm calling about Samuel."

Chapter 15
BOOGIE

Skydivers will often gather to cut through the air, hackey sack, and simply jump together.

Hydraulic Level Five { working title}
Draft 2.36
© Samuel Caulfield Cabral & Aspen Kaye Trilby
36. Mountaineering

"Do you know how fast you were going around that curve, miss?"

Aspen peers up at the Bear Creek sheriff through the Jeep's open window, his aviator glasses hiding his eyes. His wife was Aspen's favorite grade school teacher and they have watched her grow in their small town aquarium, but that doesn't seem to matter when one has broken speed laws.

"Just answer the question, Aspen."

"Yes," she groans, her head dropping to the steering wheel. "But in my defense, you know I never speed."

"Let's keep it that way." He passes her a slip of paper through the window, lips quirking. "I'm going to let you off with a warning this time. Have a safe drive, and tell Caulfield to behave."

"Thanks, sir." She stuffs the flimsy carbon paper in the glove box, waves to the sheriff, and creeps onto US 36 toward Estes Park.

As she drives around pine-lined curves, she glances at the patrol car in her rearview mirror until he finally U-turns at the edge of the National Park, well out of his jurisdiction. Her mother must have put him up to it.

Aspen's mother has lingered on the periphery her past few weekend visits to Bear Creek – an odd thing for her normally non-invasive parent – watching her and Caulfield as if she expected some sort of massive screw-up from the pair. It unnerves Aspen, and though she appreciates her, she is glad to be returning to Caulfield.

But if she's honest, she also feels a nameless unease simmering in her marriage, and as much as she explains it away, it bubbles higher and higher as summer temperatures climb. It nearly boiled over two days ago, the night before she left for her weekend trip to Bear Creek. Caulfield stayed behind in Boulder to cover a downtown gig. He's been moody...everything about him is flat, from his voice to his eyes to his demeanor, and she isn't certain she can write it off as stress.

They had sex before she left, and Caulfield buried his face in the pillow beneath her head. Then he raised himself to kiss her forehead. She tried to see his eyes, but he kept them closed until she was nearly frantic for the intimacy of a locked gaze. So she nudged his shoulder, again and again, gasping and pleading until his lids fluttered open. Instead of a fervent blue peeking between long brown lashes, it was dull. Flat. Distant.

At last, Aspen admitted there was a problem, and she was terrified it was too big for her to fix. After sex, she choked and cried in the shower, hoping the pounding water would obscure her tears. But still, she saw Caulfield through fogged glass, hovering in the bathroom doorway. He gripped the knob, then turned and calmly closed the door.

They took their cues from each other. This time, the cue was to keep their eyes closed...

Rocky Mountain National Park is upon her before she even realizes she's flown past the old Stanley Hotel. She pulls into the entrance, where she meets Maria and Lacy for one final jaunt up into the tundra before classes start.

"Hey, old married lady." Maria grins as they pile into the car. Lacy smacks Maria's arm and turns to Aspen.

"Her day is coming too, and then you can give her twice as much grief."

Aspen flashes her season pass at the Park entrance and begins the meandering climb up Trail Ridge Road. "Do you have somebody in mind?" Aspen hopes her friend will finally see what's right in front of her, especially since Esteban will soon be deployed.

"I just can't fathom being married yet. No offense." Maria catches herself. "The idea scares the crap out of me."

Aspen shrugs, feigning nonchalance. "I wouldn't recommend getting married young, especially if you're not ready for it. It'll save you a lot of uncertainty. Just don't break anyone's heart, okay?"

"Totally, especially since people change so much in their twenties. That's what my stepsister says all the time, and she's been married twice already." Lacy misses the implication, but Maria does not. She narrows her eyes at Aspen.

"Are you and my brother having problems?"

"Do you really want me to tell you about your brother's sex life?"

Her deflect works and Maria makes a face. "*Ave Maria Purisima*, I don't want to picture that twerp pounding into my best friend. Ugh! And there it is in my mind, anyway."

Aspen sniggers, and the tension eases as the air grows thinner and the breeze chills. When they reach their favorite overlook, she zips her fleece up to her throat and tromps toward the rail.

The whole sweep of the Rockies lay before them in feathered greens and blacks, light and shadow, each mountain peak climbing into the clouds. The sky is a fanciful blue, so like Caulfield's eyes. The encroaching range is still all crackled ice. Just beyond it is the crown jewel – Longs Peak. Even now, at the end of summer, patches of snow furiously cling to its rocky zenith.

Aspen breathes in air touched by pine and ice. "I've circled Longs my entire life, and I've never set foot on it. Not once. How is that possible?"

"Maybe you should just commit to climbing it," Maria says, her words revealing an understanding Aspen's never given her credit for. "If you start training now, you could be ready next summer."

"Maybe." Her eyes water as wind blasts and dries them, but she can't turn away. More than anything, she wants to own the mountain that has watched her wander around its feet like an ant, skirting and side-stepping, but never climbing. In the years to come, she'll hike to its summit three times, calves aching and lungs wheezing. She'll chuck snowballs at her climb team. She'll pitch tents in its enclaves, dodge its marmots and break fingernails against its deep-rooted trees. But there, at that moment on Trail Ridge Road, she can't fathom having the courage to do any of this.

With a last, wistful look, she gestures to the Jeep.

"Girls, I need to hit the road. It'll already be a late night, and I have to get up early tomorrow to buy my books for class..."

Here we are, Sam. I've taken us to the morning you left for New York, and I can't take our story any further without you. ~Kaye

Day Three of the Great Boston Boogie: that's what Justin dubbed it, capitals and all.

It was fortunate I called Alonso and Sofia when I did. Not two minutes after that tough talk, my phone rang. It was Molly, telling me she and Danita both received social media links to a video of the Green Monster debacle, and they were flying to Boston.

My hotel room across the street from the hospital became a makeshift command center for the small group doing round-the-clock damage control. Justin and Nat fielded media calls. Patrick bit the end of a pen as he proofed press releases I'd whipped up. In the sitting area, Ace Caulfield quietly discussed Samuel's misdemeanor charges with Alonso. Danita was on her cell phone in the bedroom, talking to Angel, who had drills this weekend. Molly sorted the flood of cards, flowers, and balloons that made their way up to the suite every half-hour. She'd catalogued them as Family, Celebrities, and Politicians.

"Hey, Kaye, is Terry Francona one of Samuel's work colleagues? Oh wait, she's his great-aunt in Baja, California, right?"

"Er, no. *He's* the Red Sox manager. Why? What did he send?"

"Oh! That would explain the baseball." She turned the ball in her fingers, puzzling over it as if it were a moon rock.

"Lemme see that." I took the card and ball from Molly's hand; the surface was covered in signatures. "Nice. Samuel'll love this. I'll make sure one of the nurses takes it to him."

Molly crouched over a box from my father and Audrey (a peace offering), ripped away packing tape and uncovered bags upon bags of organic snack foods. Dad wanted to ship a box-load of home remedies for Samuel's "condition"—ginseng, St. John's Wort, and crystals—but between me and Audrey, we convinced him that the hospital staff knew what they were doing. I promised to see him the minute I was back in Lyons, and that appeased him.

I'd heard his displeasure through the receiver when we spoke two days ago. "I just hope you realize whatever's going on with him will tie you down, and not in a good way."

"Dad, please. I can't do this with you now."

"This is too big of a commitment, baby girl."

I tugged at my ponytail in frustration. "Question—why did you stay in Lyons after you and Mom split? Why didn't you leave, have your great adventure?"

"Oh flower, I wanted to. I just couldn't leave you behind like that. I know I'm not the steadiest of people, but you needed a dad in your life. Still do, I hope."

"Do you regret not moving to San Francisco, or Seattle, or someplace more exciting?"

He sounded surprised. "Sometimes. I wanted to study Vedic science at the Maharishi University in Iowa. But I think about your childhood, and how you had a fairly stable home, friends, parents. Then I met Audrey. It was worth the sacrifice. You were worth it."

"Thank you." I swallowed, my voice hoarse. "So maybe you can understand that I love Samuel, and if he'll let me, I want to make a home for him—a real home, not a bunch of old furniture and photos he salvaged from our place in Boulder. He's worth it, too."

"Aspen," my dad sighed, "just try to practice some semblance of self-preservation."

I hadn't yet seen or spoken to Samuel since he was admitted to Mass General. With each hour that passed, and each time he turned away visitors, a bit of me wondered if, perhaps, my dad was right. How could I be there for him when he wouldn't let me set a single toe in his hospital room?

But this morning, I hadn't left the hospital empty-handed. Just as I signed out on the visitor's log—exactly two minutes after I'd signed in—a nurse caught my elbow. She handed me an envelope.

"From Mr. Cabral."

I'd ripped it open with quaking fingers and slid out a single sheet of hospital stationary. Another note. The handwriting wasn't even his, but the words were, and I'd clutched it with hope:

Kaye,
You're lovely. I want you. Please wait a few days.

Simple, ambiguous. Still, I got it. He'd asked for a little faith, reminded me not to give up on him or to doubt myself, as he had asked the night he'd uttered those very words at the Valdez bonfire. Like me, he was in uncharted territory and it was scary. If space was what he needed right now, I would bide my time.

A beam of autumn sunlight shifted across the box from Dad when my mother opened the hotel room curtains. She shuffled from foot to foot at the window, her worn overnight bag hanging over her shoulder. She didn't belong in big cities. Her flight home wasn't until this afternoon, and I could tell she was anxious to return to her mountain shelter.

I wrapped my arms around her waist. "I don't know what I would have done without you, Mom. Thank you for helping me."

She patted my hands. "I can't help with all this media stuff, but if you need anyone buried under an old farm shed…I can see to that."

Tempting, but I declined.

We were fighting a fire burning faster than it could be contained. Speculation over Samuel's disorderly conduct arrest spread swiftly and covered every angle, from drug abuse to nervous combustion. Buitre released a statement—a vague thing about his being treated for exhaustion, blah blah blah. The tabs had bloodhound noses. They saw right through it.

A new rumor surfaced, implicating me in a massive blowup with Samuel at the Boom Boom Room, which led to our alleged breakup and his breakdown. Before long, fans would call for my head and burn my effigy in the streets. The source of the rumor, *HollywoodDays*' gossip blog, was also responsible for the "Friend Behind the Forehead" drivel back in June. Back then, an "unnamed source" had revealed that Caroline had taken a Sharpie marker to Samuel's forehead before a national talk show appearance. Similarly, this new article, "Hard-Partying Cabral Slugs Ex-Wife's Beau," also cited "an unnamed source close to the duo."

Was the unnamed source Caroline, gearing up for Togsy's book release? Or did the mag throw a wild dart that happened to land close to the truth? I had no clue.

But when the blog followed with another headline, "Bad Boy Cabral Tortured by Breakup," and mentioned Samuel's admittance to Mass General's psych unit — information that *wasn't public* — I suspected an inside job.

Just before lunch, I called Jaime.

"I've got nothing on your Buitre bastard," she snapped. "Like I said, he's covered his tracks. However, I thought you could do a little Nancy Drew sleuthing. Use the oldest trick in the book."

"And what's the oldest trick in the book?"

"Stick a recorder in your pocket and goad the hell out of the slimeball next time you chat. See what you come up with."

I snorted. "I'll give it a shot. I'd like you to look into something else for me. *HollywoodDays Magazine* has run several articles about Samuel, citing an 'unnamed source close to the duo.' I'm fairly certain I know who it is, but I need ammo. Can you find out the name behind the source?"

"I can try." There was a low murmur on the other end, followed by Jaime's snerk. "Um, Hector says hi, and don't let the nurses catch you ass up beneath Samuel's peek-a-boo gown," she muttered, and hung up.

I rolled my eyes. Well, well, well, Mr. Valdez. It seemed as though he'd finally cut one of his women loose.

By noon, my mother had left for the airport. Alonso and I were bent over room service salads, silently munching. Each bite landed with a heavy plop in my stomach. His calm, appraising gaze was on me. He was struggling to find a way to broach what needed to be broached — why I'd waited so long to call them. But with the media assault weighing on my shoulders, I think he didn't want to push.

The hotel door opened and Sofia slipped in. She dropped her purse on the kitchenette counter—the only surface not covered by flowers from well-wishers—and pulled up a chair next to Alonso, burying her face in her hands.

"How is he?" Alonso asked, rubbing her back.

"The same. Still refusing visitors. And since he doesn't want to see us, the nurses can't force him."

"Maybe if Kaye tried again."

"*Hágalo,* Kaye. Try." She grabbed my hand, oozing regret and panic as she had since they first arrived in Boston. *Save my son,* her clenching fingers said, *bring him home.*

If only I could.

I pressed them in apology. "I went this morning. He won't see me until he's in better shape, and I don't want to upset him further."

It stung. It wasn't logical—we'd all seen him at his worst. Heck, anyone who tuned into WBZ Boston saw him at his worst, clutching that horrid urn, security dragging him away. But I understood why he did what he did. Samuel Cabral didn't want pity. He wanted his dignity, because he was hard-wired to fix and protect. And to him, protecting meant staying away so he wouldn't burden us. I think he knew, somewhere in his heavily sedated mind, that we were outside the door, waiting, supporting.

I finished my salad, wadded up my napkin, and chucked it in the trash can. Alonso did the same.

"Walk with me? I could use some air, and it's been years since I've been in Boston. I'm feeling nostalgic."

That's right. I'd forgotten Alonso once lived here.

Instead of heading into town, we turned west, toward the Charles River and Cambridge. As we walked, buildings tapered off until all that was left was a wide sky and curling gray water. Bright sailboats flecked the horizon. Gulls swept down, much closer than I preferred, and I imagined they were used to dinner deliveries courtesy of tourists and their half-eaten hot dog buns. Alonso led me over a bridge that crossed the river and opened onto a path. We walked along the waterfront, taking in the breeze and slapping waves, not speaking for a long time.

"Let's sit," he said, pointing to a bench. A Harvard row crew skimmed along the river, and my eyes followed their strokes until they rounded the river curve. "My brother—Samuel's father—used to drag me to the river for a breather when my professors frustrated me."

"I can see why."

He smiled down at me with sad eyes, and I vaguely saw Samuel in their beauty. "I am so very sorry for what our secrecy has done to you, Kaye."

I shrugged. How does one explain to the man once epitomized as the perfect father that he let you down? That it's tearing you up and flipping your childhood ideals end-over-end?

Somehow, he saw it anyway. "You've handled everything admirably."

"It doesn't seem like it. I feel as if I've failed him."

"How so?"

I fidgeted with my charm bracelet. "I was too caught up in work, so I didn't see how serious the situation had become until it was too late, even after his episode in LA. Once is understandable, but twice? I should have called his doctor sooner."

"This is all very new for you, and you've done as best as you could, *hijita*. Deciding how to handle someone with an mental disorder is like going on a road trip with no map and one of those cardboard accordion shades still covering the windshield."

Ain't that the truth.

"But I know how you feel. That night in New York, when you asked me to come to the brownstone…" He closed his eyes, overcome. "I was watching my brother and Rachel all over again. Rachel entrusted Samuel to my care before she took her own life. Did you know this?"

"Her letter in Samuel's backpack?"

Alonso nodded. "It was messy and wild, and at the same time, oddly straightforward. She asked me to 'put up' with Samuel, as if he were a burden. She begged me to forgive her for killing my brother, for driving us apart. But there was no letter for her own son, asking *his* forgiveness. He was all skin and bones when he came to us in Lyons. Do you remember?"

"It's hazy." I could only recall the unsociable little boy in a ghost costume.

"Traumatized, frightened…Before I even became his father, I'd failed him. I should have tried harder to visit him, to make sure he was all right. It is a guilt I will carry for a lifetime. But now, I find I've failed my son again. And you."

"Alonso—"

"No, Kaye, I did. You know it, my children know it, Sofia and I know it. We took a broken little boy and tried to give him that American dream—Sunday school, dinner around the table, Little League games, music lessons, family vacations. We raised him to believe he could accomplish anything with hard work. But we also raised Samuel to believe it was acceptable to keep secrets for the sake of appearances. Sure enough, that's what he did. It cost him seven years without the person he loves most in this world." He ran an agitated hand through his hair, and I remembered where Samuel had picked up that habit. "Still, we kept his secrets."

"Danita says you enabled his shame."

He grimaced. "That sounds like an accurate assessment. But I believe it's not too late for us to change. And I'm positive it's not too late for Samuel."

"I don't understand *why* you did it."

"Why does anyone behave a certain way? I suppose we often do what our parents did. You've read the pot roast story?"

"No."

He smiled a bit, and it barely touched his weary eyes. He looked so old. "A reader submitted it to our magazine years ago, and we still run it now and then. A child watches her mother prepare a pot roast for dinner: dice the carrots, slice the potatoes, cut off the tip of the roast before baking. She says to her mother, 'Why do you cut off the end of the pot roast?' and her mother tells her, 'That's what Mama always did. It makes the roast better.' So the child goes to her grandmother and asks, 'Why are we supposed to cut off the end of a pot roast?' Her grandmother answers, 'Because my mother did it that way. It cooks better.' Then the child asks her great-grandmother, 'Why do you cut off the end of the pot roast?' The great-grandmother laughs and says, 'The only reason I cut off the end was because it wouldn't fit in my eight-inch baking pan.'"

I hid a tiny smile behind my hand.

Alonso sighed. "My own *abuela* suffered from what I now believe was depression, and it became a skeleton in the closet. In those days, no one mentioned mental illness on pain of shunning. It was shameful to have a relative in an asylum, worse than tuberculosis. They treated manic episodes with lobotomies, for God's sake. Today…I understand there is no shame in Samuel's disorder. Yet a part of me—that protective part—is still compelled to secrecy. I'm afraid he will be regarded unfairly if others know. And he probably will be, but not like thirty years ago.

"We are taught that certain things, like mental illness, are taboo. So we stay silent and keep family secrets because our parents did, and their parents, and their parents, and so on. If medicine operated in this fashion, we'd still be bleeding with leeches. Why don't we ask 'why' in other facets of our lives? We should. Sometimes there are good, sound reasons for doing what we do. Other times, not so much."

I nodded. "I've wondered the same thing, lately, especially about my parents' craptastic relationship. I was so *eager* to marry Samuel. But it had less to do with love, or even Samuel, and more to do with wanting to be the exact opposite of my parents. But then I divorced him just as quickly. Now, I can see how my need to protect myself made me act really rashly—a knee-jerk reaction, like holding up your hands to ward off a blow. I *knew* what was and wasn't out of character for him—I've made a study of him almost as long as I can remember. I should have fought harder for Samuel, exhausted all options. But I was so certain I'd fail, I didn't even try."

"We are products of our parents, Kaye. But we are not them."

"*Gracias*, Alonso." I reached across the bench and touched his brown hand. The past few years, it had become more wrinkled than I was comfortable with. "Don't be offended, but I'm going to speak plainly. A big part of me wants to tell you and Sofia to back off and let Samuel and me live our lives. Practically, I know we'll need your help. So we're going to have to find a balance between supporting and interfering. I love you guys, never doubt that. But it'll take time to repair things between us."

"We can do that. Just remember, if it gets too rough to handle alone, we'll always be here for you. Choosing to stay with him is the more difficult of two paths."

"I love him. How could I choose any differently?"

Day Five of the Great Boston Boogie: dyswhatsit mania?

That was the official cause of Samuel's flight. Dr. Tran told me that dysphoric mania was a manic episode mixed with symptoms of depression. It would explain Samuel's rage, confusion, and fear, delusions of persecution, even memory loss. Most likely, it was brought on by his regimen of antidepressants.

"In retrospect, he could have suffered from such an episode seven years ago. I can't say for certain, but the presence of cocaine in the system can also cause dysphoric mania. It's likely, given he can't recall those nights."

"So you're telling me his meds caused it? I thought they were supposed to help him." If we couldn't trust the meds, what could we trust?

"The correct combo of meds works wonders. But finding that balance is often difficult, as the disease is prone to shift and change. Mr. Cabral has done everything he's supposed to. In this case, the treatment failed."

"How do we make sure it doesn't happen again?"

"Right now, we have him on antipsychotics to rapidly stabilize his mood. Long term? We'll rediagnose him with Bipolar I, ditch the antidepressant, and put him on a higher dose of Depakote. In any other case I'd consider something less archaic, but unfortunately, antidepressants have messed up the system. The good news is, we're on the right road. I also recommend a round of couples therapy for the two of you."

I pressed my fingertips to my forehead. "When will you release him?"

"When his mood stabilizes. I'd give it another few days, just to be certain."

"Does he want to see me yet?"

"I'll ask." I don't know why she bothered. His answer would be no. She returned, eyes full of pity. "Maybe tomorrow."

That evening, I had drinks with Molly and Danita at the hotel bar. It was either the pungent martinis or Molly's crocheted shawl that made me think of my grandmother, deceased nearly a decade. I recalled the best advice she'd given me that I'd never taken: a man can be your best friend, but don't expect him to be your best girlfriend.

I'd spent many summers at her home in Durango, sustained by Samuel's infrequent letters and even more infrequent phone calls. The letters were wonderful, detailed, revealing…when he sent them. Half the time, he'd take so long rewriting and perfecting, they never saw a stamp and only made it into my hands after I'd returned to Lyons and he dug them out of his desk drawer.

The calls? Paaainful. They went something like this:

"Hey, Kaye, it's Samuel."

"Hey, Samuel, it's so awesome to hear from you! How's Lyons?"

"Okay."

"How's the parents?"

"Okay."

"Danita?"

"Good."

"Erm…how's the baseball season?"

"Oh man, you should have been at the game the other day. We were playing Princeville, right? And of course it's gonna rain half the afternoon, but the ump's never going to cancel unless there's lightning, which never happens. So Pedro's rounding the bases, but Princeville sucks at field maintenance so third base is this giant mud hole…"

And thus, the conversation dissolved into baseball for fifteen minutes. Then he made the mistake of asking "How's Durango?" and I spent the next fifteen minutes gushing my little thirteen-year-old heart out about how I didn't have any friends in the neighborhood and my grandmother made me go to bed at nine. His reply?

"Oh. That sucks."

"Yeah."

"Listen, I have to go 'cause dinner's ready."

"I really miss you, Samuel."

Silence. Then…

"You too. Bye."

Later that night, my grandmother laughed away my teenaged angst and told me the reason Samuel talked about baseball all the time was because it was a topic he could discuss with confidence.

"Men hate to use the F-word." I blinked up at her in faux innocence, and she smirked. "*Feelings.* Men don't like to let us know they aren't sure of themselves. They feel like frauds most of the time, but it's preferable to us believing they're failures. You, dear granddaughter, seem to think Samuel hung the moon, and he's not going to let on otherwise."

Psh, Samuel didn't hang the moon? Nonsense!

Fortunately, I managed to glean a couple of lessons from Gran during those summers. I could just feel her smacking me upside the head right now as I sipped martinis with my girlfriends and silently bemoaned Samuel's self-imposed quarantine. She'd tell me, "Kaye, it's not the end of the world if you have to wait a couple days until that boy has a modicum of composure. In the meantime, quit moping. He'll appreciate that you're taking care of yourself." Then she'd wink and I'd cringe, because grandmothers should never, *ever* hint about sex to their grandkids.

Day Six of The Great Boston Boogie: Samuel Cabral, here I come.

I got the call from Dr. Tran in the middle of a hotel bagel and cream cheese—Samuel wanted to see me.

I dug through the suitcase Danita and Molly had packed for me. Everything was so wrinkled, I might as well have ripped down the drapes and fashioned a dress a la Scarlett O'Hara.

"I hung your blue knit dress in the closet," Danita said behind me. She tugged the dress from the hanger and tossed it at my head. "Samuel loves it when you wear blue."

"I'm not dressing for him," I grumbled. "He hasn't wanted to see me, so why should I?"

"It's okay to admit you want to look pretty for him. He'd jump your bones, even if you wore one of Tom's old Dead T-shirts. But make him suffer a bit for the past week. He'll appreciate it." Apparently Danita had been communing with Gran.

"He's probably too doped up on meds to jump onto the toilet, let alone me."

Her velvety brow furrowed. "What is this, Kaye? Are you seriously going to stand here—a woman who's thrown herself off mountains with two small strips of plywood attached to her feet, nearly drowned herself year after year in the Colorado River, and dived headfirst from planes thousands of feet in the air—and tell me you're intimidated by one manic episode? This is right up your alley. Wear. The. Dress."

I couldn't argue with both Danita and Gran. Wordlessly, I slipped on the dark blue dress, fastened a pretty turquoise necklace, and grabbed a jacket on the way out. The temps had cooled as Boston slid firmly into a golden autumn. Just as I shoved on a pair of sunglasses and walked out of the Wyndham, a flurry of camera flashes blinded me.

"Kaye, are you on your way to see Samuel?"

Crud. Tweedledee and Tweedledum had camped outside the hotel since stupid *HollywoodDays* leaked Samuel's location. I tried not to scratch my nose, or sniff, or trip, or kick them in the balls.

"Hey, Neelie Nixie, do you straddle him in that hospital bed?"

"Morning, guys. Hope you get hit by a car."

I couldn't believe I once gave those jerks blueberry muffins.

Tweedledee and Tweedledum trailed me until I reached Mass General. They didn't follow me in, because several days ago, one of their cronies got brave and ended up behind bars when the front desk receptionist called security. "We frequently have celebs here," she explained, "so the paps tag along. Once, someone even pulled a fire alarm when a celeb's wife was having a baby, trying to force the poor guy onto the street. It was crazy."

A gaggle of diehard Neelie fans also camped outside the hospital, clasping bunches of helium balloons and Red Sox gear (clearly his readers now knew he was a baseball fan). For security purposes, the hospital wouldn't let them loiter in the lobby. Each morning, they pressed gifts on me and begged me to carry them up to Samuel, making me feel like the pope on his way to say intercessions. Security told me to leave the stuff at the front desk.

But this morning was different. I could only attribute the dark glares and hisses to the garbage the tabs churned out. I wove through the small crowd, absently accepting their presents, skirting their questions and dodging spiteful elbows until I zipped through the rotating door. The receptionist waved me over. I dropped an armload of teddy bears and collapsed, breathless, over the desk. She held up a bear wearing a tiny *Deep in the Heart of Nixie* T-shirt and pursed her lips.

"Keep it, if you want," I told her.

All chubby cheeks and giddiness, she tucked it next to her computer monitor. "Lean over here, honey."

Confused, I did as she asked. She pulled a tissue from a box and dug something from my hair, then held it out for me to see. A chewed pink blob of bubble gum. I grimaced. "Disgusting."

"They're turning on you. Best call someone to escort you home when you're ready." I nodded my thanks as she pitched the tissue in the garbage. "I'm not supposed to do this," she whispered, "but I have a huge favor to ask. Can you ask Mr. Cabral to sign my copy of *The Last Other*?"

I started to protest, but remembered this gal all but broke a photog over her knee for me. I took the book.

My palms were a clammy mess when I reached the psych unit. I wiped them on my dress and followed the nurse. A Red Sox game on a mounted television in the lobby quietly buzzed. Could Samuel hear it? The only other occupant in the room was an old woman, tangled white hair all askew and her lipstick even more so. She wrung her leathery hands as she watched the game, but I didn't think she actually followed it.

The nurse knocked on the third door down.

"Mr. Cabral?"

She pushed the door open. There he was, and my heart pounded.

His skin was chalky. That was the very first thing I noticed—how stark his brown eyebrows and eyelashes were against his pale face. His lips were cracked and as bloodless as the rest of him. Books were stacked on a table next to his bed, all of them new and untouched. His eyes were closed, head resting on a pile of pillows. Six days' worth of stubble covered his jaw and chin, and it hit me that I'd never seen him wear a beard before, even in our Boulder days.

"No razors?" I whispered to the nurse. She gave a shake of her head. "What if I brought an electric one?"

"Not even that. No cords allowed, not unless an orderly watches him and Mr. Cabral has been adamantly against that."

I could only imagine.

"I'll leave you to your visit." She patted my shoulder and left.

He looked so, so tired. Lifeless, like one of those tagged corpses in thriller movies. I reminded myself he was heavily medicated and probably battling off a post-manic crash, but seeing his death-like pallor scared the crap out of me, and I focused on the gentle rise and fall of his chest.

Then those beautiful blue eyes met mine. They were dull and foggy, but damn it, he was still alive and I was grateful for it.

"How do you feel?" I hung back, near the door.

"Like I just woke up, all the time." His voice was coarse, slurred. "I can't shake the fuzziness."

"It's the antipsychotic. They'll put you back on Depakote, but even then, you'll feel sluggish for a while. And you'll have to exercise like an Olympian to keep that pretty form."

"I know. I've had to before." He gave me a lazy smile. "Would you still love me if I was fat?"

The corners of my mouth curled in spite of myself. "I suppose it would give me leeway to pack on a few pounds. We could be one of those happy, pudgy couples that hold hands in the park."

"We'll laugh about this someday."

"Definitely a funny story to tell the grandkids." But I wasn't laughing. Still, Samuel ran with it.

"Oh no, Kaye. The grandkids will never hear a word of it."

"Sure they will. The minute little Samuel the Third does a school report on Grandpa, the whole sordid Fenway affair will spill out."

We let the fantasy linger in the air, reluctant to admit that's what it was—a fantasy. Right now, children seemed as unlikely as a hurricane hitting Lyons.

"You look so beautiful." He motioned me closer. "What do you have there?"

I pushed the book into his hands. "The paparazzi slayer in the lobby would like you to sign this as payment for my safe passage."

"You'll have to ask the nurse for a pen. They won't let me have one."

"It's just a precaution, Samuel."

He rolled his eyes. I jogged out to the nurses' station, asked for a pen, then handed it to him while an orderly hovered behind me. Samuel scowled as he signed the inside flap. "Offing myself was never my intention, you know."

"I *didn't* know. Thanks, though I would have preferred that clarification a week earlier." He may have been doped up, but he still heard the bitterness in my tone, and he paused mid-signature. I continued, "The city's going to let you off with community service, which can be served in any state. Ace is a miracle worker."

"I'm running out of chances, aren't I?" He snapped the book shut.

"If something happens again, you might have to do time."

His dry lips pressed into a thin line as the thought of prison hung between us. He capped the pen and returned it to the orderly, glaring at the man's back until he was gone. Then he held out a hand, trembling from the meds. I took it, and he pulled me onto his bed, burying his face in the folds of my jacket.

"I didn't want this life for you."

"It was never your choice."

His hands tenderly clasped my hips. "Do you know what my biggest regret is, about that night? Not telling you how lovely you looked on your birthday."

My fingers combed through his soft, thick hair until his body sagged against me. Kissing the top of his head, I left him so he could grasp at much-needed sleep.

When I returned to Central Command, Justin thrust another printout from the *HollywoodDays* blog in my face.

"'Ex-Wife Singing for *Sirens* Author's Fortune,'" I read aloud. Peachy. I grabbed the article from Justin and skimmed.

"I liked the bit about your enlistment of a top Boston Law Firm to fight for conservatorship. Oh, and the speculation about Ace and me entering and exiting your hotel room. That was particularly seedy. Other gossip mags are starting to parrot *HollywoodDays*, too."

I crumpled the paper. "This has got to stop, Justin. They have someone on the inside, and I think you know as well as I do who it is."

"Who has the most to gain by painting you as the bad guy?"

Who had the most to gain by painting me as a bad guy? I silently repeated. My status as Samuel's publicist didn't affect Caroline anymore, but it mattered to The Buitre Group.

"You're makin' enemies, Kaye. That means you've reached the big time. You want me to release a statement?"

"What would be the point? They'll just twist it into a lie." Would Jerome stoop that low? Dish dirt on Samuel's illness — his own client — to gossip mags? You bet he would. I punched in Jaime's number.

"Have you found anything new on the *HollywoodDays* source?" I asked.

"Give me some time, Trilby," she grumbled. "You can't rush weasel-fucking."

I cringed. That was a resounding no.

I visited Samuel every morning for the next three days. Each visit, he seemed a little less tired, a little more together. He was able to jog on a treadmill. He read. Went to therapy. Soon, he permitted his family to visit.

Switching from the role of devoted lover to that of publicist soon gave me a Jekyll-and-Hyde complex. I wanted to wear each hat as well as I could, but I balanced a stack of hats on my head all at once, and that stack soon began to teeter. Each time I returned to the hotel Command Center from Mass General, I strained to detach my heart from the business calls I made.

When I arrived at the hospital one morning, the chaplain was in the room with Samuel, immersed in soft conversation.

"He's visited several times since Mr. Cabral was admitted," the nurse next to me whispered.

In fact, he'd been the *first* visitor allowed access by their celebrated patient. I tried not to feel hurt by this new information. Samuel's grapple with God was nothing new. With a sigh, I let it go. If I couldn't keep Samuel grounded, the Almighty was the only one for the job.

The chaplain shook Samuel's hand and rose, greeting me as he exited the sterile room. When Samuel saw me, his entire face glowed brighter than a Colorado sunset, and it burned away my petty jealousy.

"How are things?" he asked.

I awkwardly swung our arms, not sure if he was asking his lover or his publicist. "Busy. We've canceled your appointments and released a statement—"

"Kaye."

"—and Nat, Justin, and Patrick are running interference, at least until you can decide what you want to do—"

"Kaye." He tugged my hand. "That's not what I meant. I guess…I want to talk about us. Not work."

"Oh."

"First of all, is there still an 'us?'"

I nervously twisted the aluminum rails of his bed as if they were jail bars. "I'm up for it if you are."

He frowned, not liking my flippancy. "Please be—"

"—serious, I know. Sorry. Yes, there is still an 'us.' I refuse to believe our window is gone for good."

"I want to fight for us, too," he said, his voice brightening. "I will always fight for you. I know the selfless thing to do would be to encourage you to get the hell away from me, but I'm not willing to do that. Do you understand why I couldn't see you right away?"

"I think so. You were angry and needed time. Samuel, I'm very sorry for not telling you I was in contact with Mr. Avant Garde." He raised an eyebrow and I waved my hand. "The scarf you punched. If I had known it would drive you away..."

He sighed and beckoned me onto the bed with him. "Firecracker, this isn't your fault. It wasn't rational anger. But it was still anger, and some part of me, through the haze of mania and meds, recognized I loved you too much to expose you to that sort of abuse."

I relaxed against him, weariness seeping from my muscles. I liked this new honesty between us. He brushed a long finger over my knuckles, white from clutching the bed railing.

"I'll find a way to make this easier for you," he said. "What questions do you have?"

"How much do you remember?"

"I remember everything, except the night before your birthday."

"Um, we..."

"Had sex? Yes, I was able to piece that together."

I rested my head on his shoulder, biting back tears as the guilt of that night bowled over me. Even on heavy meds, Samuel still saw. He wrapped strong arms around my shoulders and sighed into my hair. "We'll have our chance again, Kaye. A time when it's significant for both of us.

"The flight, the cab ride to Fenway Park, everything was odd," he continued, "like that sense of exigency people sometimes have just after waking. A persistent dream tells them there's something important they have to do, something irrational like buy a pair of socks, but they can't remember why it's important. Then they snap out of the dream and the feeling vanishes. It was like this for me—I *had* to take my mother's ashes to Fenway Park. I believed I was somehow exorcising her from my past, my head, my life. If I could get rid of her, I'd get rid of the illness and I wouldn't hurt you anymore."

"You said she'd leave you alone if you did it."

"But it's not that simple, is it?" His whole body was fatigued, as if he were a lot older than thirty. "'God, if there is a God, save my soul, if I have a soul.' I have cried those words many times, so much so, that gradually, my plea simply became 'God, save my soul.' Because when the moods take me, I can't save myself. You are not responsible for saving me, either, Kaye. But you should know, I live for you. I've always lived for you." Heavy eyes searched my face.

"Samuel—"

"Please, I need to say this." His voice broke. "Forgive me for everything I've put you through. The horrible things I said, the way I left you behind in New York. I am ashamed."

"You've always had my forgiveness," I breathed into his soft T-shirt. "Forgive me, too, for avoiding our issues, all those years ago?"

He nodded sharply, and relaxed beneath me. "I hope you understand I wasn't running away from you."

"I know you weren't running from me. You just want closure."

"I want liberation."

My fingertips flitted over his overwrought eyebrows, smoothing them. "Well, Boston's a good place to start. We can stay here if you want."

"Is that what you want?"

"I want to go wherever's best for your health. New York, Baltimore, Boston—"

"Boulder?" he interrupted.

My mouth dropped open. I wasn't expecting home.

"That's what we agreed to, correct? I'll move there after Thanksgiving, if you still want me."

"But what about your therapy and doctors?"

"It's nothing the local mental health clinic can't handle. I'll have Dr. Vanderbilt on call, and Denver's not far. Most importantly, we'll have friends and family who can help us should something like this happen again."

"Will it happen again?"

"Most likely." I already knew as much. "Kaye, I'm not going to take you away from Colorado unless you want to leave. You love it too much. The Front Range is home."

"You're home, too," I whispered. He pried my hand from the bed rail and tangled our fingers together.

That night, just as the team packed up laptops, Jaime Guzman called.

"Hold on to your phone, sugar-bottom. I know a dude who's now a copy editor at *HollywoodDays'* parent company."

"Really? That's great!"

"Yeah. His mom got picked up for hooking a few years back and I took the case pro bono because he was a poor college student."

"Prostitution in Lyons?"

"Just go with it, the real story's boring. Anyway, it was easy to get the gossip bloggers umm…gossiping about the Cabral situation. Your man meat's the talk around the water cooler. Some snitty little Indian girl—the ones that don't wear eagle feathers—writes those stories—"

"Jaime," I gasped, "you just can't *say* stuff like that. How are you not held in contempt every time you open your mouth in court?"

"*Anyway*," she ground out, "this girl was bragging about how an important insider approached her with information a couple of years ago. He's fed her tidbits ever since."

"Does the insider have a name?"

"All my source could get from the chick was a 'Larry Rothschild.' Sounds like a pseudonym. That, or the House of Rothschild's redneck cousin—the guy they don't invite to weddings."

I clenched my teeth. "It's Jerome."

"How do you know?"

"He has a crush on *Lafite Rothschild* wines."

Yes! I punched the air, did a shuffle-skip through the suite, amazingly, not landing on my tail, and then bounced onto the couch. I had Jerome. Had him by the *cojones*. Now Ace and I just needed to have a heart-to-heart with one "Larry Rothschild" about a little document he signed, called a non-disclosure agreement.

As I arrived at the hospital Wednesday morning, Sofia was just leaving. She dabbed her eyes with a handkerchief, but she seemed peaceful, now that her son wasn't barring us from the psych unit. For all the scraped knees she'd cleaned and baseball uniforms she'd bleached, it had taken Samuel years to accept her as his mother. For Sofia, Samuel's rejection touched veins of fear I couldn't comprehend.

I rapped the frame. His head snapped up and the clouds cleared his troubled face. His eyes were sharper today. Dr. Tran was weaning him off the antipsychotic medication before his hospital release tomorrow.

"You're lovely," he sighed. "You've been working hard, haven't you?"

"Yes." I self-consciously touched the bags under my eyes. "Do I look tired?"

He held out his hand for me. "*Mamá* said you've been fronting a publicity team nonstop since last Monday."

"There's a lot to clean up. But don't worry about that right now."

"What are they saying out there?"

"Lots of things. Drugs. Breakdown. Lovers' spat. But my favorite is that I'm holding you hostage until you give me control of your estate."

He chuckled. "How very gothic of you. In short, the longer I remain mum on my illness, the crazier the speculation will get. I suppose the only thing to do is go public."

My hand froze on his chest. Was he saying what I thought he was saying? "Not necessarily. We could pass it off as exhaustion."

"No, we can't. Not any longer. I spoke with the hospital chaplain about this—he reminded me if I want liberation, the best way to get it is to be truthful." He scrubbed his bearded jaw and stretched. "Funny, it's the same thing you and Danita have been trying to hammer into my head."

"Sometimes it takes an impartial person to say it, I guess. You'll have plenty of options when the time comes. Several news programs are battling it out like gladiators for an exclusive first interview. And you'd have your pick of publications if you prefer to write about it. But it would be in your best interest to decide before Togsy's book hits the stands."

His lips softly kissed the skin beneath my ear, his scruff making me squirm. "What's the latest?"

"Togsy toned it down, but it's still pretty harsh. Ace has done all he can do."

"When will it hit the shelves?"

I scoffed. "The week before *Water Sirens* premieres, of course. Caroline found a publisher who'd do a rush job."

My eyes held his and I wavered. Would it be too much too soon to show him the old Moleskine notebook Caroline gave me in the coffee shop? But Samuel had thrown open the doors today, clearing the stale air between us. I dug through my messenger bag.

"Speaking of reading materials, I have something for you," I said carefully. "I'm not sure how you'll feel about it." I placed the notebook in his lap.

His eyes widened as he flipped page after page. "This is mine... but...I don't remember writing *any* of this." He paused when he came to the page with the missing piece, realizing what had been clipped from the page. "Where did you get it?"

"Caroline. I think a part of you wanted me to know what was going on in your mind, even then."

"It's as if I was desperate to separate myself from you, and at the same time, desperate to keep you with me." His fingers skimmed over the elastic band that was holding in his secret.

I told him how he'd asked her to give it to me that night in New York, but instead, she'd only delivered a small portion of the big picture. "In the end, Caroline will get everything she wanted," I finished sourly.

"And she'll never be content with it, because what she wants won't bring happiness." He set the notebook aside and took my hands, kissing each. "Give me a year, Kaye."

"For what?"

"This life I've built for myself—the wealth, the acclaim, the fame—it's all meaningless. They've become my shackles. Give me a year to free myself and become a man who can stand beside you with both feet firmly planted. Then I will give myself to you, in whatever way you'll have me. All yours. *Only* yours."

Only mine...in a year. A year of relationship limbo.

So very typical of him—time to hash out, think through, and deliberate. You'd think, after what we'd just been through, I would have danced the cha-cha at Samuel's promise to be mine with no vows and no wedding ring branding my hand. Instead, his offer left me with a pit in my stomach. I wanted him to want me beside him now, shackles and all.

Disillusionment shadowed the ray of surety I'd basked in, and once again I shivered in the cold knowledge that I was still chasing Samuel, and might always chase Samuel.

Chapter 16
SUNSET LOAD

*The last skydiving run of the day
is typically veteran divers with an affinity
for the beautiful evening sky, a laidback dive,
and nudity (or not).*

Day Twelve of the Great Boston Boogie: Jerome trumped me.

And boy, did it hurt my pride. Almost as much as the time in seventh grade, when Jennifer Ballister invited me to her slumber party. She made fun of my braces and my tomboy braid, which couldn't really be helped at age twelve. At last, I'd had enough. My mother was AWOL. My father was in Denver visiting some bearded hippie who operated an Old West portrait studio at an amusement park. So I called Samuel to walk me home. By then, he'd grown into his big blue eyes and cemented his heart-throb reputation. So, when he showed up at Jennifer's, collected my sleeping bag, and tucked me beneath a protective arm, it was a pretty big deal. The other girls flushed under his cold stare, and Jennifer never made fun of me (to my face) again.

But what Jerome had brewing was going to sting a lot worse than Jennifer's mockery of my lacking décolletage if I didn't bring his PR machine to a grinding halt. I wasn't sure Samuel could "walk me home" from this party, this time.

I was having trouble tracking down the elusive Buitre weasel, and Jerome's assistant was roughly as helpful as a tapeworm. He must have possessed a sixth sense that warned him a smackdown waited, because his clueless assistant returned each of my calls with a "Mr. Buitre is in meetings all day."

The Wyndham Command Center was empty save for Samuel and me. He huffed over newspaper clippings, magazine articles, and blog print-outs that were spread across the coffee table. I'd warned him not to read that garbage, especially since he was freshly released from the hospital. Maneuvering him from the revolving door and into a cab had been like shoving through thick forest brush, only the scraping branches had flashing bulbs and a stockpile of prying questions. The minute he set foot in my executive suite, he asked me to put him to work, too.

I drummed my desk in time to the tinkling on-hold music. My brain paged through an enlightening conversation I'd had with Groovy Adventures Kevin yesterday morning. When he asked if I'd heard of Buitre PR and Media Group, Jerome's stonewalling clicked into place.

"Please tell me he hasn't contacted you."

"Yeeeaaah, I wanted to send a big heads up your way. Dude's totally high-strung. I asked him why a little caving club in Colorado would need a PR agency in New York. He told me Buitre could do the same work for half the price as TrilbyJones."

"Holy fish buckets! How'd you respond?"

"I told him the Babes were my caving buddies, and asked him what he had against you. He just got all huffy at me so I bid him adieu. Something was off about the whole thing, ya know? I got that vibe, but I can't speak for your other clients. If this dude's using those smooth moves on them, too, you might be in for an über-rough ride."

Mother cliff-hucker, Jerome was swiping my clients. Needless to say, the entire TrilbyJones team contacted our B&Bs and ski clubs all of yesterday.

"Molly," I'd pleaded over the phone, "I am so very sorry for bringing this down on TrilbyJones. I'll make this right, I promise you."

"Kaye, calm down, this isn't the apocalypse we're dealing with. You've always been resourceful in a pinch. Killer instincts, remember?"

There was silence on my end.

"Should I continue with the validation?" she asked.

"Please."

Molly chuckled. "The good news is the profit you brought in with Samuel as a client equals five of our local accounts. Yes, we've earned every single penny of it and we're all taking vacations the minute you return to Boulder. But in the long run, it's been great for business. The downside is, the interns might have a mild case of mercury poisoning from all the sushi they've ingested. Back-to-back business dinners isn't a good business practice. Now go get 'em, killer, before the lackeys eat their weight in raw fish…"

"Ms. Trilby?" Jerome's assistant yanked me back to the present. "Mr. Buitre is at an important client luncheon and can't be bothered."

"Aren't you going to ask if I'd like him to return my call as soon as he's able?"

"Ah…um…I suppose."

"Better yet, maybe I'll just phone the restaurant and have a word with him at his client luncheon. Where are they dining again?"

Samuel's eyes darted up, took in my rigid back and fisted hands, and quickly returned to the article he was scanning.

"I'm sorry, Ms. Trilby, I can't…"

There was a time in my life when the idea of flying to New York City to confront a conference room full of PR executives about their lack of professionalism would have reduced me to one of those squishy invertebrates chilling in their reception room aquariums. But now, I was one spine away from booking a flight. Stupid Buitre.

"Forget it. Tell Mr. Buitre if I don't hear from him by tomorrow, I'll have to return to New York to meet with him in person. And Mr. Cabral *will not* be happy about it."

"I'll do that."

I collapsed into the desk chair and swiveled, watching Samuel. Grinding jaw, squinting eyes…I waited for his outburst as he twitched over some tabloid clipping. Finally, he wadded it up and furiously chucked it across the room near the wastebasket.

"Kaye, hear me out before you say no."

This didn't sound good. He shoved two hands through his hair.

"I want you to resign as my publicist."

I bolted up from the desk. "What? Why?"

"Firecracker, you have been amazing," he said hurriedly. "You've worked so hard for me, and I love you for it. I couldn't have a better publicist. But it wasn't fair to ask you to take on this burden."

"You've got to be kidding me! After all the sweat I've...um... sweat." I narrowed my eyes. "Is this because you don't want me to go back to New York?"

"In part." He crossed the room and pulled out the chair next to mine. "This industry warps people, makes them do things they normally wouldn't do. I will never hear from Caroline Ortega again, and I'll live with that. But I'd be a wreck if that happened with us."

"Hate to break it to you, but Caroline was warped before you became famous."

"Nevertheless, I hate how it sucks you in."

"It won't, if you plan to cut down on your public appearances like you said you would."

"Well, I don't want to put you in the tough position of having to be my publicist instead of my significant other. I'd rather you were by my side as the woman I completely and openly adore. Let me take this off your shoulders." He dragged his fingers along my jaw, his eyes softening. "This is, naturally, your decision."

Yeah right, it was my decision.

The man was silky smooth, I'd give him that. Even so, I couldn't help but feel sacked, and like the PR brew would go to muck if my hand wasn't stirring it. "Who'll take my place?"

"I think you can answer that yourself, little conspirator."

"Nat and Patrick," I conceded. "You'll need a new agent, too."

"Yes. Buitre has proven themselves to be untrustworthy." That was an understatement.

"And if I want to remain your publicist?"

"Then we'll find a way to make it work."

He would, too. He wanted to make me happy. But I think he was beginning to understand what made me happiest. It was him. Not success, or adventures, or even a life free of burden. I remembered that having Samuel, even on his worst days, was better than not having him at all.

I knew when to bow out gracefully. Well, maybe not *grace*fully—two could play the smooth game. With a sultry smile, I found my way to Samuel's lap and breathed slow air across his neck. His meds were wreaking havoc on his sex drive, but dang if I didn't feel a stirring there.

"Fine. Mr. Cabral, I quit this lousy, stinking job. What do you think? Dramatic enough?"

His mouth dragged over my temple. "Very dramatic. I hope this isn't how you quit your job at Paddlers after high school."

I smiled against his lips. "Señor Valdez would have dropped a paddle. Samuel?" I trailed a finger over his bobbing Adam's apple. "There's one thing I want to do before I hand over the reins. Let me be the one to fire Jerome."

"No."

I rushed on before he could protest further. "Ever since I was a little girl, you've tried to keep me safe. Let me do the same for you."

"Do you ever stop plotting and planning?"

"Nope."

I could see the things he wanted to say: *That's too risky. What about TrilbyJones? He'll come after you. Let me do it for you.* But he simply shook his head, a corner of his mouth turning up. "How can I possibly stop you?"

~

Frickin' Nancy Drew.

I checked the small recording device pinned inside the cuff of my jacket. Still there, still on. Jerome was ten minutes late. Either he was delayed by the thunderstorm dumping reservoirs of rain on Boston streets and rattling the windows of the low-lit sports bar… or he was making me squirm. I tried to eat a slice of pepperoni, but the only thing I could handle was the cold brewski condensing all over the Red Sox coaster until it was ruined. Friggin' water stains, I'd been planning to snag that coaster for Samuel. I removed the mug and tried to salvage the cardboard souvenir.

After Groovy Adventures Kevin's tip-off, I wasn't shocked when Jerome's assistant called to inform me Mr. Buitre was traveling to Boston for an in-person chat. "I've booked a small meeting room at The Mandarin Oriental for your convenience." Luxury hotel. Crap, I'd still be on his turf.

"I can do you one better. Please inform Mr. Buitre I will meet him for lunch at Papa Baffi's Pizza and Sports Bar." I rattled off the address Ace gave me.

Now, I rubbed bleary eyes and studied the patron in the booth next to mine. His head was lowered over his plate, and he had on a backward ball cap. I tried to read the logo—a baseball, and something Bluefish? The waitress came and I sent away my barely eaten pizza slice. Beacon Hill Bluefish, maybe? Sounded like a little league team. I spun the coaster and pondered how Ace's phone call to Jerome went this morning. Explosive, I hoped. We needed him spitting nails for this confrontation.

Minutes later, a sour-faced Jerome Buitre slid into the booth on the bench across from me, blocking my view of the ball cap. His hair and gray suit were rain-speckled, his tie knotted around his neck, tight even for Jerome's standards. He was utterly out-of-place in this dive, and I realized Ace just might be a strategic genius.

"If your contract was with me instead of Samuel Cabral, I'd have fired you," he hissed.

"Hello, Mr. Buitre." Hoo boy, he was mad. Polished and polite were out the window.

"Where do you get off having Caulfield Law Firm threaten to terminate my contract if I *interfere* with Mr. Cabral's current media crisis? The man was in the psych ward, for Christ's sake! How is he supposed to confirm his publicity wishes via writing?" Nice one, Ace. Contract loophole. "We're his agent, his PR machine. We control his career! You are ruining everything we've worked for, Ms. Trilby."

"*Controlled* his career. Past tense. That's why I've been trying to call you, Jerome. I'm sorry to inform you that Mr. Cabral considers his contract with The Buitre Group null and void and has chosen to cancel your services, effective immediately. I have it in writing, right here."

As I set Samuel's written wishes between us, our booth grew deadly silent, invaded only by faint clanking of beer mugs and forks against pizza plates. The silver-tongued ferret was gone, and in his place was a snarling, pissed-off pit bull. The warm, red glow of the suspended lamp above our heads nearly made him look demonic. A demonic, snarling, pissed-off pit bull. Ugh, I was getting nervous. *Don't show fear, Kaye.*

"Pray, tell me, how have we broken faith with Mr. Cabral?"

I pulled a stack of tabbed magazines from my messenger bag. I tossed them on the table next to the other paper. "You've been leaking details of his personal life to *HollywoodDays Magazine* for years without his consent, using the pseudonym Larry Rothschild. You violated your non-disclosure agreement."

"Their reporting certainly lends Mr. Cabral that tortured artist sheen, doesn't it?" He narrowed his eyes. "Don't waste my time, Ms. Trilby. You can't prove it was me."

"Ace is working on it." That was a bluff, because Jerome was right. We couldn't prove it was him — only the mysterious "Larry Rothschild." But he didn't know that.

He leaned forward, his breath stinking of stale coffee. "You don't comprehend this business at all, do you? You sit in your high seat of judgment, snide and ignorant because in your miniscule backwoods sphere, you've never had to dirty your hands. But even *you* should know that all publicity is good publicity. Mr. Cabral's books will only carry him so far. If he wants to keep his high profile career, he's got to be what the small people talk about around the water cooler."

I shook my head. "He's never wanted the spotlight. He just wants to publish his books. But you never understood that. Caroline didn't, either."

"Until her imbecile move with Togsender, Caroline was a brilliant PR strategist. You know why she was brilliant? Because I mentored her. You'd do well to heed my advice instead of scorning it, Ms. Trilby."

"That doesn't surprise me. I'm glad she wised up and bailed." *Focus the conversation.* "If we're finished here, the only thing left is to sign the termination papers. Ace will meet you at your hotel, later this afternoon — "

Suddenly, Jerome grabbed my forearm, holding me in the booth. Crap, that hurt. My eyes flew to his.

"You think I'm going to let your pathetic little agency steal my biggest client, just like that? I've been busy, too, these past few weeks." He released my arm, then took a file from his briefcase — a list — and shoved it on top of my magazine stack.

I scanned the paper: Rocky Mountain National Park…Colorado Caving Club…Boulder Fine Arts Center…Longmont B&B…It was TrilbyJones's client list. No bombshell there. Yet, as I stared at those names, I couldn't help but feel Jerome had me between locked jaws.

"I believe you recognize these businesses. I can assure you, if you think you can persuade Samuel Cabral away from Buitre, I can do the same to each and every one of your clients."

Play it cool, Kaye. Don't freak out. Easier said than done, considering that, beneath the table, nerves had my knees clapping like castanets. "You really believe these mom-and-pop businesses would rather have a big New York agency handling their PR than someone local?"

"Of course. We have the connections you lack and, if the price is right, the choice is obvious."

I snorted. "Then you know nothing about rural America, Mr. Buitre. My clients wouldn't touch The Buitre Group with a ten-foot pole. Heck, half of them ski with my father." A corner of my mouth slithered up. "And the other half ski with me. That's all the connection I need."

But Jerome, with his thick skin and even thicker skull, wouldn't back down. "They would hire us if they thought TrilbyJones was no longer competent. Financially, professionally—use your imagination."

Ah, here it comes—Ace told me to watch for this. Competitive pricing was not illegal. But bad-mouthing was.

I subtly shifted my jacket sleeve, hoping the tiny recorder picked this up. "That sounds a lot like trade libel, Jerome. Are you saying you'd actually go to my clients and intentionally damage TrilbyJones's reputation if Mr. Cabral fires Buitre?"

"Take it as you will. Don't think we haven't done it before and gotten away with it. Most companies fold because they can't afford the legal fees. Bottom line: If Cabral walks, TrilbyJones is done."

Got it. I smiled sweetly, now completely in charge.

"Wow, extortion, too. I think we could afford the legal fees, Jerome. The same man who pays for your PR services also signs my alimony checks."

Jerome loosened his tie, and I could tell he was losing his tight control. Time to throw down the ace. I steeled my trembling hand, then leisurely slid the tiny digital recorder from my sleeve and placed it on the table between us, red record light still blinking.

His pasty complexion became angry and mottled. He slammed two fists onto the Formica in an indulgent fit, knocking the Red Sox coaster off the table. *Nice try, but you don't scare me, neutered pit bull.*

"You go after TrilbyJones—" I coolly picked up the coaster and placed it in my purse "—and I'll screw you over with this little bit of damning evidence."

And then Jerome snatched the recorder from the tabletop before I could pocket it. He dropped the device on the ground, beneath the table. There was a metallic crunch, and I guessed he'd ground it under his heel.

"Your case just got a lot harder to prove, Ms. Trilby."

I raised an eyebrow. "Mr. Buitre, you've forgotten the golden rule of crisis management: always have a Plan B." I cleared my throat, and Beacon Hill Bluefish man turned. "Did you get everything, Ace?"

"Sure did. I'll upload a copy after I finish my beer."

Jerome whipped around, just as Ace Caulfield rested his arms on the booth divider and twisted his little league ball cap, revealing a microphone taped on the underside of the brim. "You're just racking up the charges, there, Jerome. Slander, breach of NDA, trade libel, extortion. And now destruction of property." He tapped his mic. "You can smash this puppy, too. The entire recording is already saved to six separate servers in secret sites."

"Nice alliteration, Mr. Caulfield."

"Thank you, Ms. Trilby." I may have disliked the Caulfield family on principle, but I sure loved Caulfield Law Firm right now. Corrupt as Boston politics, but a boon when they worked for you.

Jerome sneered. "Illegally recorded conversations don't hold up in court."

"No, but it won't be pretty if it's broadcast by the national media. The Firm's done it before and gotten away with it." Ace tapped the side of his nose. "I can see the headlines now."

I snapped my fingers. "'*Water Sirens* Author Hosed by PR Tycoon.'"

"'*Water Sirens* Author Hosed by *Former* PR Tycoon,'" Ace countered.

"Nice. Oh! Even better, '*Water Sirens* Author Hosed by Former PR Tycoon, *Seeking Damages*.'"

"I like it." Then Ace stared down Jerome, all business. "Plain and simple — if you follow through on your threats to Mr. Cabral, TrilbyJones, or anyone connected to Mr. Cabral or TrilbyJones, those actions *will* hold up in court. Extortion's a criminal offense."

"And I bet you don't want to spend the next few years behind bars. I doubt they serve *Lafite Rothschild*, even in white-collar prison."

Jerome's eyes widened with rage. His fists wrapped around the stack of magazines, and it was then I noticed how tellingly sweaty his palms were. You and me both, buddy. I stood and flipped up the hood of my rain slicker, scattering drops across the table and Jerome.

"Gentlemen, I'll leave you to your business. Don't forget to sign those termination papers." I'd decided I probably shouldn't be around for the discussion that would go down between the two. Better to have fewer witnesses.

"We can do that now, if it's convenient." Ace grinned, sliding into my vacated seat and taking command of the helm.

I practically skipped from the restaurant despite the thunderstorm. Frickin' Nancy Drew, now *that* was a rush. Despite its crazy fans and BS-slinging seagulls (and politicians), I really loved Boston.

Day Sixteen of the Great Boston Boogie: Check-out.

Danita was the first to leave, because Angel was living on Cheez Whiz and Chicken-in-a-Biskits. Justin left for New York not long after, followed by the O'Malleys' return. Alonso, Sofia, and Molly flew out that morning, and now, only Samuel and I remained.

We spent our last few days in Boston, Samuel tracing his past from Beacon Hill to Fenway Park, my hand in his as we trekked across harbor city blocks and hailed cabs. When we gazed up at his old family seat—a discreet yet imposing row home on the south slope—I asked him if he wanted to knock. He shook his head. "I think I've effectively closed that door," was all he said on the matter.

We had a direct flight to Denver in three hours. But before we left Beantown, there was one final stop on Samuel's early childhood tour: the hotel where his mother died.

"Are you sure about this?" I asked as our taxi drew closer to the grim behemoth that haunted the dark side of his writing.

"Yes. I've given this too much power for too many years. I think, once I see it again, it won't grip me so tightly."

We sat on a bench outside the momentous place, long since converted to luxury apartments. It was towering and white and classy, encased by a wrought-iron fence and shrubs shaped to perfect cones that cast long shadows against an otherwise sunny day. We'd tried to enter the lobby, but the chandeliers, marble, and sky-mural ceilings were the same as they were twenty-four years ago. It freaked Samuel out, so we stayed outside. Silent. Staring at the sidewalk. With an urn between us.

"I'm going to take her remains to Zermatt." His long, slender finger traced the porcelain lid.

"Why Zermatt?"

"Somehow, I don't think she cares anymore whether she makes it to Fenway Park. I know it seems strange, but our ski vacation to Zermatt is a good memory. I want to remember us in that ski lodge with wind-burned cheeks, eating room service hamburgers and watching cable TV. I love that version of her. I like to think if someone had been there to help her, to understand her mind..."

"You were just a little boy. It's not your fault she died."

I squeezed his hand. He smiled at me, but his eyes were fogged in sadness.

"And what happened at Fenway Park wasn't your fault, either," I added. "It was nobody's fault."

He said nothing for a long while. Then he simply stood, tugged my arm, and we left.

As our plane soared over the earth, quilted farmland gave way to jagged mountains peeking through banks of clouds. Soon, the ice of the fourteeners sprawled in the distance. I longed for their summits—that rush of strength, even as my body wearily hauled itself into the snow-filled bowl at the top of the world. I pressed my fingers to the glass, sure I could ease them through the window and skim them along the mountaintops.

Samuel stiffened beside me. He ground his jaw, refusing to look at me or the mountains. He was irritated. But I could see fear behind the irritation. I didn't know what to do, so I took his hand in mine, playing with the blunt ridges of his fingernails until we landed.

We hadn't asked anyone to meet us at Denver, because there was no real itinerary we followed—leave when we're ready to leave, stay if we need to stay. It was dark when we lumbered out of a cab and into our hotel near the downtown. The Broncos were home, so everything was booked, save for this shabby bit of history in Capitol Hill. Its radiator heat hissed half the night and its old-fashioned door chains conjured up bad horror films from the fifties. But a soak in my room's claw-foot tub made up for the creep factor.

Samuel knocked on my door an hour later, and we ducked into a claustrophobia-inducing elevator that had no business boasting a capacity of six.

The hipster manning the front desk recommended a hole-in-the-wall Vietnamese restaurant across the street. I was so hungry, I would have eaten one of my father's nasty blender concoctions. But the restaurant was far from blueberry sludge.

I hummed over my noodle bowl. "This is quite possibly the best fish sauce I've ever tasted. How'd we not find this place when we came here for concerts?"

Samuel wasn't listening to me gush over the food. He only picked at his salmon, lost in his head. Finally, he raised heavy eyes.

"Help me understand."

I quirked a questioning eyebrow.

"Longs Peak." He waved his hand. "Actually, this entire fixation. This summer, you told me you used extreme sports to fill a hole left by the dissolution of our marriage. But we're together again. So why do you still need to do this winter climb?"

I took a minute, trying to answer him honestly. "I have this…this *drive* within me to conquer. I guess it's no different than an artist's need to paint or a writer's need to write."

"Why not do something safe? You love your guitar."

I shook my head. "Music's always been *our* thing. But this is all mine."

"And Hector's," he muttered.

"No, it's mine." I thoughtfully gnawed the end of my chopstick. "I think it's because I feel strong when I'm tackling wild places like mountains and rivers. Less of a feeble little girl, unable to stand up against life's hard hits. It reminds me that I'm not…well, not Aspen."

A shadow passed over my thoughts as I remembered how much I'd hated her for coming between Samuel and me when we'd had sex the night he was manic. If the same thing ever happened again, I'd be devastated. But wasn't it bound to recur, or something like it? Pain wrenched through my gut and I wrapped my arms around my middle to hold it at bay.

"What is it?" he asked, apprehensive.

My words were hoarse as I talked to the tabletop. "The night before the party at Boom Boom, the night we…you thought I was the Aspen in your book. I know you don't remember it, but I do. Samuel, I felt so helpless when everything I tried couldn't keep you with me, like I failed some test…"

He saw where my mind was going and ran two frustrated hands through his hair. Then he breathed deeply, closed his eyes, and released

325

the air with a whoosh. "Kaye, I don't know what more I can do to make you believe that when I say 'I love you,' I'm speaking to the woman in front of me, right now. You are not some remnant scrap of a seven-year-old's security blanket. I *love* you. And you have not *failed* me. If anything..." He shoved his water glass out of the way and grasped my hands, beautiful eyes seeking mine.

"You are extraordinarily strong. But the only time you're one-hundred-percent confident in your strength is when you're taking risks. Tell me what I can do to make you feel that way about me, too," he begged.

I watched how hard he struggled to keep his composure—twisted clammy fingers around mine, squinted his eyes then blinked owlishly—and I realized he was still quite edgy. It was thoughtless to put him through unnecessary anxiety over my mountain climb. Mother of Tom, the independently functioning woman in me wanted to thrash my behind for letting this thing, this illness, rule me. But the loving woman in me understood I shouldn't climb Longs Peak, not right now, not if it did this to him.

I gently traced a thumbnail over his knuckles. His eyes flew to mine, and I let him see my concession there. *I will give this to you*, I silently told him, drawing in his arm, *if it will make you happy.*

He held my gaze a long moment, and then let his head fall back, groaning.

"Truth, Kaye. Can you be ready for the climb by November?"

"I...yes, if I put time and energy into some day-hikes. But what—"

"I want you to climb that damned mountain."

"*What?*" I gripped his forearm. "Samuel, no, not after what happened to you. You need me right now, and I can't just—"

He rolled his head forward, the blue startling me in its fierceness. "Yes, you can. I see how badly you want to climb the thing. I can't lock you away in a closet, so I'm going to have to trust you to take care of yourself up there. It'll be worse for both of us if I hold you back from the things you love."

"But I love you, too."

I searched his face for a trace of resentment, but found only earnestness. Still, his hand trembled in mine.

"Samuel."

"I'm not going anywhere. Maybe you can use the climb time to think about what you want for us."

He was serious. I began to feel lighter, freer as his words sank in. Seven years ago, he never would have uttered them. I grinned like a danged idiot. "Are you telling me to look for the robed old man on the top of the mountain for a bit of wisdom?"

"*Kaye.*"

"*Samuel.* I don't think Longs Peak has an old man. Just overzealous thrill-seekers making snow angels and gasping for air."

Samuel sighed and released my hand for his chopsticks, and I saw they didn't quake as he stabbed at his food.

I teased on. "Climb mountain, you must. Clear, to scale slopes, your mind must be."

He pursed his lips, holding in laughter. At last it broke through. Delighted, he reached under the table and dragged my chair closer to his, then wrapped an arm around my shoulder. "What was *that?*"

"Yoda, obviously. What wisdom would you share?"

He kissed my forehead. "Just be safe and be smart, because I won't lie — I'll be a mess until you return in one piece."

"Well then, I fully expect you to be huffing and puffing next to me while I log some practice time in the Front Range."

"That's exactly where I should be."

We hadn't shared a room since New York. I was left in limbo by Samuel's desire to date me, court me, whatever he called it. I called it ridiculously cautious. But after dinner, as we walked through our hotel's creeptastic corridor, he halted me.

"Stay with me tonight?" he ground out. I hesitated, and he lifted my chin. "No sex. Just your company. Please."

I could have cattily reminded him that his year hadn't passed. I could have thrown his request to "date" me back in his face. But I didn't, because now wasn't the time to rehash our fears and failings. I'd brought him home, just as Sofia had requested. So I nodded and took his hand.

That night, as the radiator hissed and steamed into the blackness... as my fingertips smoothed over the soft hair on his chest, lean muscles, ribs...I realized what the main difference was between fictional Aspen and me. Aspen needed her man for her happiness. Me? I *chose* to be happy with mine. I was grateful it wasn't too late to tell him so.

"Wednesday at nine. Belinda Walker sits down with Water Sirens *author Samuel Caulfield Cabral to discuss his startling arrest and a long-kept secret…"*

The radio cut through the quiet of the Campervan as we whooshed through the blackness of the pre-dawn mountains. Our climb team and significant others were scattered about the interior in various stages of sleep, but Jaime fixed that.

"If I have to hear that twisted publicity hound's name one more time, I'm going to rip Betty's stereo system right out of her pretty dashboard," she growled over the crackling AM station.

"Hey! I'm sitting right here." Samuel yanked out his earbuds and scowled at the couple opposite us.

"I'm talking about Belinda Walker, not you, mental case."

"Frickin'-A, Jaime! Quit being such a harpy."

She ignored me, like always. "I question any television journalist's integrity by rule."

I turned to Hector, who was all too ingenuously fiddling with a compass beneath the circle of an interior light. "You need to control your woman."

"Nuh-uh." He squinted at the tiny needle. "She'll put a hex on my balls. Luca, she's your sister."

"Yeah, man, but she's beaten the crap out of me since I started walking."

Molly turned in the front passenger seat and glared at the five of us. She was wearing the pinkest fleece cap I'd ever seen, pom-poms and all, and it took the scary out of her glare. "Will all of you shut up? It's like I'm chaperoning the *Children of the Corn*'s field trip bus."

"Don't make me call down He Who Walks Behind the Rows," Cassady chimed in, all paternal-like. It was an idle threat, considering we were three cars deep in a slow-moving caravan winding into the Rockies.

Moonlight peeked through the towering canopy of evergreen, casting dappled shadows across the roadside. Growing up in the mountains, I'd never really noticed how tall our trees were, knobby and bare in their "highwater pants" branches. The fat midget trees of

New York and Boston left me feeling exposed beneath an open sky. Right now, the sky was clear. Later today, sun would be a welcome addition to our climb and would dry out the sole-sucking mud pits of the trail. Jaime was especially averse to the great outdoors, and I felt bad for leaving Samuel while we climbed the fourteener. Though I'd never tell Samuel, I almost longed for the days of Caroline, the cliff-hucking floozy.

Almost.

"*Mierda,* Jaime, can it!" Luca hissed. Samuel was either a masochist or madly in love with me to willingly stay behind with her at base camp. I hoped for the latter, but it might have been both.

"So, Cabral, did David Ortiz pay you a visit in the nuthouse?"

Samuel leveled cool eyes on Jaime. "Nope. But Ted Williams did."

Her mouth fell open and she blinked. Then a wide, well-pleased smirk found her dry lips. "*Ay.* You do have a sense of humor after all."

That's my man.

We clamored out of Betty and into the biting wind at the base of Longs Peak. My pack was lighter than it was at Paddler's, when we'd split and stashed our food store. I glanced at Hector's pack, mysteriously bulkier. He caught me staring, and offered me a sheepish smile. I returned it, then circled the van to find Samuel.

"Do you have your—"

"Meds? Yes."

I slid my arms around his waist. "I was going to say Taser."

"I think I can manage Jaime for a day." Samuel wrapped his arms around me, and I could feel his warmth even through layers of fleece.

"I should tell you something about Caulfield," he whispered in my ear. "Sometimes he's afraid the woman he loves doesn't need him, not the way he needs her." I started to protest, but he shushed me. "He's afraid he'll lose her again, but he doesn't want to seem clingy."

"You won't lose me," I whispered back.

He nodded against my cheek. "I'm telling you, so you know. I need you, Kaye."

"Samuel…" I pulled back so I could see his face. He was so beautiful, and so worried. "I don't have to go."

"Yes, you do. I want this for you." He brushed two thumbs along the apples of my cheeks, and I closed my eyes at his gentleness. I could tell he meant every word.

"I'll be careful, I promise. And for the record, I need you, too. Symbiosis, remember?" I pecked his cold lips, then leaned in for another, deeper kiss. The heat soon warmed our lips and neither of us wanted to pull away. With a final kiss to the corner of my mouth, Samuel leaned back and smiled, tucking a few loose strands of hair beneath my cap.

"I trust you." He lifted a sly eyebrow. "But, just to make sure." He pulled a thin, red Sharpie marker from his coat pocket, uncapped it, and then brought it to my forehead. "For Hector's benefit," he explained as he scrawled something across my skin.

Scowling, I ducked to Betty's side mirror and tried to make out what he'd written. Then my scowl faded, and I was grinning, too:

I LOVE SAMUEL CABRAL

I held out my hand for the Sharpie. "May I borrow that, please?"

Playful eyes met mine as he placed the marker in my open palm. I uncapped it and motioned for Samuel to bend over a bit. Standing on tip-toes, I scrawled my own words across his brown forehead:

I'M STILL NAUGHTY

"It says 'I Love Kaye Trilby,'" I fibbed, hoping I'd be on the trail before he bothered with a mirror.

He beamed and helped me hoist my pack onto my shoulders. "I'll wear it proudly. Now go kick that mountain's butt."

As my climbing team hit the pitch black trail and wandered away from base camp, excited thoughts raced through me...

Odd, how only a few weeks ago, I'd fought like an Amazon to climb Longs Peak; Samuel had been just as fierce. Now the opposite was true.

But that's the way real love works, isn't it? It's not calculating or conditional, or self-serving. It doesn't subjugate another to the demands of one's happiness, but it rejoices when happiness is found. *Especially* when it's found hand-in-hand. Real love is placing your unmolded years in the palm of another and, despite circumstance, trusting them to shape it into something exquisite before they return it to you. And then you do the same for them because you love them.

I'd never loved Samuel more than when I gave up the Longs Peak climb for him...and he gave it right back to me. I absolutely, truly believed—for the first time since I saw Samuel again, his mud-colored hair flopping over his forehead as he signed copy after copy of *The Last Other* in a Boulder book shop—we would be okay.

And I didn't need to scale a snowy mountain to discover what I already knew: I would marry Samuel Cabral.

Again.

Continue reading for a short preview of the upcoming sequel: *Fourteeners*

FOURTEENERS

When a mountain crosses the towering threshold of fourteen thousand feet, it is known as a "fourteener." Fourteeners shadow the twisting spine of the Colorado Rockies, and mountaineers, in their desire to be "above it all," will face grueling terrain to place these peaks on their mantles.

Chapter 1
ANCHOR

To offer protection against a potentially fatal fall, mountaineers will bolt their rope to rock, ice, or snow at an anchor point.

Hydraulic Level Five {working title}
Draft 1.100
© Samuel Caulfield Cabral & Aspen Kaye Cabral
100. *Emotivus Drownicus Nixius*

Caulfield sees the half smiles of his wife.

Having her safe in their Bear Creek home, rooted to the ground while he writes and she canoes and hikes, works with her art galleries and cave clubs...she has all of her fingers and all of her toes. But she withers in his hands.

Her mountains have become casual acquaintances – warranting a nod, but never an invite. The top-of-the-line hiking pack he gave her for Christmas collects dust in the closet. Next to it rests his own unused pack, bought in a flash of optimism. Every morning she watches the sun hit their mountains in a blaze of gold. Then, at night, they fall into shadow, and another day has passed in which she refuses to conquer their peaks.

Ever since the avalanche.

Their third wedding anniversary is approaching. Three years ago, they promised themselves to each other again, and when they repeat their vows on this date, every year, they say them with the painful knowledge of what it means to forsake those vows. Their anniversary is a time of celebration. But for Aspen, the days preluding it are a bitter token of ice and panic. She marks them alone, from the safety of her desk chair.

Caulfield subtly asks, "Has H contacted you about another climb?" He dislikes the man on principle, and has long suspected H is in love with his wife, or was, once upon a time. Now H has his own wife, and he no longer watches Aspen with burning eyes.

Aspen shrugs away his inquiry with a counter question. "How's the new book coming?" She knows this will shut him up. He feels his manhood shrivel at the mention of that book – the book with great expectations attached to it. The fledgling fantasy series was supposed to be better than his nixies, and critics couldn't wait to prove those claims wrong. It was lambasted before it hit the shelves. The reviews sit in his brain like his mother's ancient upright piano: dissonant and immovable.

"By the standards of his auspicious career, Sea Rovers is a cliché-strangled shipwreck destined for the foreboding depths of dust bins..."

Still, he's a storyteller. He sifts through his brain, and seeds of ideas tumble through his fingers where they root on paper. Caulfield writes, not about far-away nixies or water horses, or universally panned pirates. He turns to his beloved Colorado. To the drama of its mountains, where life thrives and dies through sun, and snow, and thin air fourteen thousand feet above the earth.

"And so, Aspen, my wife," Caulfield says, "I propose this: I'll write mountains for you, and we'll conquer them. As much as I want you in my hands, I will not watch you wither there."

·············•●•·············

> Kaye—It's been a long while since we've worked on our book. Are you game? ~Sam

> Sam, I'm game for most anything. Not once have I regretted what I did for that Klondike bar. ~Kaye

The first time I ever heard "four-by-four" used as a verb was huddled over the breakfast stove at our Longs Peak high camp, between nibbles of freeze-dried food. It was also the first time I'd met someone with a "gold claim in the bush." Not a euphemism—I asked.

Dusky pinks of the alpenglow swirled over the rocks, though the air was still as cold as the dead of night. There wasn't a cloud in sight, but that could change in a heartbeat. Today would be sunny and warm—relatively speaking—for a tundra zone. We watched as early-morning climbers trickled onto the field and others stretched stiff cold limbs out of tents. A pair of park rangers picked their way over boulders, checking ground and weather conditions. I dug through the "marmot-proof" box and handed out a round of granola bars.

"If you were up in Prince George, you'd just four-by-four those off-roads," crowed one of our new friends, chewing through a bar. "You don't bike the forest during moose-calving season." There was laughter and back-slapping, even though Hector didn't know what the heck they were talking about. My friend was already half in love with his new climbing buddies, and a part of me was relieved he'd made a new adrenaline junkie connection. I had a feeling my cliff-hucking days were over, unless they involved a brown mop of hair with a Latin flair.

A heavy boom echoed across the Boulder Field. We stilled, panicked stares flying to the great Diamond slab, then the Keyhole, searching for the beginnings of an avalanche. The loud crackling which followed was too far away to be our snowfield, but the warning was clear. Cassady had been right—warm sunlight after days of snow meant avalanches, and somewhere, a bank of snow had cracked and tumbled down the mountainside.

Minutes later, one of the rangers—I mentally called him Ranger Rick—barreled over to our campsite, a two-way radio clutched in his hand. "Avalanche at Glacier Gorge, just off the west ridge. Don't make plans to take the Keyhole approach today."

Cassady raised an *I told you so* eyebrow. Dang it, that was our return route.

"Was anyone hurt?" I asked.

He smoothed down his grizzled beard. "Not sure yet. Once the sun's high, we'll be seeing lots of slides. Any of you planning to summit today?"

We all tentatively raised our hands. The ranger grimaced.

"It'll be dangerous. Personally, I'd hold off for the next climb."

There was a collective groan.

"Think we could still make the technical on the North Face before the day heats up?" asked Hector. The technical was the most difficult portion of the climb, where all the vertical rock wall training came in handy.

Ranger Rick squinted at the massive face, still a midnight blue hulk in the early morning hours. "It's your risk to take. You're looking at a good five to six hours *minimum*, if you decide to do it. That'd put you up there 'round noon. Then there's the descent."

"We're gonna slide down the Keyhole route for the descent," said one of the Canadians.

"Right on." Hector fist-bumped him. A rabble of butterflies tumbled excitedly in my stomach at the thought of descending after the summit. Sweet Tom, it would be an unbelievable rush. I gazed up the vast snow slope. That summit beckoned me, all craggy ice, thin air, and audacity—a siren song to a woman who battled giants. A bushy-tailed fox picked its way over the snowfield and disappeared into what was left of the night. I stared after its path, mind-boggled. This was the sort of thing I loved about mountaineering—something unexpected defying textbooks, nature. Finding life in the middle of nowhere. A Kit Kat bar tucked away like buried treasure. Huffing over rope and ax, higher and higher until there's nothing higher than me—physically and emotionally—in a white, windy place in which humans have no business inhabiting.

I wanted it. Badly.

Could we summit Longs? We'd have to hoof it, push our bodies hard before the sun turned solid snow to fallible slush. No time for pictures or Kit Kat detours; heck, we'd barely have time to slick on sunscreen and melt snow before we absolutely had to leave.

Hector's bright eyes met mine, making the same calculations. He gave me a nod. "Let's climb it."

Acknowledgments

To my husband and beautiful children: You will always have first claim on my hours and my love. Thank you for your ceaseless support and encouragement.

To Mom and Dad: You raised me to believe I could achieve most anything with hard work and creativity. Thank you for your guidance.

To the Kutoskys, Spanglers, Sheeks, Swartzes, Widners, and Joel Nettles: You have helped me to take ownership of my writing and be mindful of for Whom I write. May God bless you.

To the English teachers of Benton-Van Horne and Iowa State University's MFA program of Creative Writing and Environment: Thank you for tossing fuel on the creative fire.

To my editor Sean Riley: You fought for Kaye and made me truly understand her, along with Samuel. I appreciate your insight.

To Elizabeth Harper and the Omnific Publishing staff: Thank you for your respect, time and care in making this book "shine." You've taken something significant to me and made it significant to you, too.

To Nina Bocci: I'm glad to have your talents for this book. You are fabulous.

To Amy Plummer: Thank you for having my back.

To Jenny, the poet: You were the first to tackle these pages with the "red pen of honesty." Thank you for helping to shape this tale. The world needs to see your moving words and stories.

To Team WTFISGOINGON and the online community: Thank you for your enthusiasm and endless patience these past years. You made me want to keep writing.

Lastly, and most importantly, thank you to the brave and beautiful souls who allowed me to interview them, shared their victories and pains, and helped me to glimpse what it is like to live and love with mental illness. Kaye and Samuel belong to you.

About the Author

Sarah Latchaw was raised in eastern Iowa and appreciates beauty in mud-splattered gravel roads and fields. She also loves to explore faraway places, thanks to countless family minivan trips across the States. This passion for finding stories led to college adventures in many different countries, and each place's story rests in the back of her mind and in her photo albums.

Sarah received her BA in public relations and media from Wartburg College and entered the workforce ready to climb the ladder. However, when researching MBA applications evoked feelings of dread, with the loving support of her husband, she pursued a career in creative writing and was awarded her MA from Iowa State University.

These days, Sarah wakes every morning thrilled to cuddle her small children, show them the world, then capture that world and shape it into stories on paper. She is not thrilled when she wakes to her cats smothering her face. She and her family reside in Des Moines, Iowa—one of the best places to live and work.

check out these titles from
OMNIFIC PUBLISHING

←→ Contemporary Romance ←→

Keeping the Peace by Linda Cunningham
Stitches and Scars by Elizabeth A. Vincent
Pieces of Us by Hannah Downing
The Way That You Play It by BJ Thornton
The Poughkeepsie Brotherhood series: *Poughkeepsie* & *Return to Poughkeepsie* by Debra Anastasia
Recaptured Dreams and *All-American Girl* and *Until Next Time* by Justine Dell
Once Upon a Second Chance by Marian Vere
The Englishman by Nina Lewis
16 Marsden Place by Rachel Brimble
Sleepers, Awake by Eden Barber
The Runaway Year by Shani Struthers
The Hydraulic series: *Hydraulic Level Five* & *Skygods* by Sarah Latchaw
Fix You by Beck Anderson
Just Once by Julianna Keyes
The WORDS series: *The Weight of Words* & *Better Deeds Than Words* by Georgina Guthrie
The Brit Out of Water series: *Theatricks* by Eleanor Gwyn-Jones
The Sacrificial Lamb by Elle Fiore
The Plan by Qwen Salsbury
The Kiss Me series: *Kiss Me Goodnight* & *Kiss Me by Moonlight* by Michele Zurlo
Saint Kate of the Cupcake: The Dangers of Lust and Baking by LC Fenton
Exposure by Morgan & Jennifer Locklear
Playing All the Angles by Nicole Lane

←→ New Adult Romance ←→

Three Daves by Nicki Elson
Streamline by Jennifer Lane
The Shades series: *Shades of Atlantis* & *Shades of Avalon* by Carol Oates
The Heart series: *Beside Your Heart*, *Disclosure of the Heart* & *Forever Your Heart* by Mary Whitney
Romancing the Bookworm by Kate Evangelista
Flirting with Chaos by Kenya Wright
The Vice, Virtue & Video series: *Revealed*, *Captured* & *Desired* by Bianca Giovanni

←→ Historical Romance ←→

Cat O' Nine Tails by Patricia Leever
Burning Embers by Hannah Fielding
Seven for a Secret by Rumer Haven

Young Adult Romance

The Ember series: *Ember* & *Iridescent* by Carol Oates
Breaking Point by Jess Bowen
Life, Liberty, and Pursuit by Susan Kaye Quinn
The Embrace series: *Embrace* & *Hold Tight* by Cherie Colyer
Destiny's Fire by Trisha Wolfe
The Reaper series: *Reaping Me Softly* & *UnReap My Heart* by Kate Evangelista
The Legendary Saga: *Legendary* by LH Nicole
Fatal by T.A. Brock
The Prometheus Order series: *Byronic* by Sandi Beth Jones
One Smart Cookie by Kym Brunner

Paranormal Romance

The Light series: *Seers of Light*, *Whisper of Light* & *Circle of Light* by Jennifer DeLucy
The Hanaford Park series: *Eve of Samhain* & *Pleasures Untold* by Lisa Sanchez
Immortal Awakening by KC Randall
The Seraphim series: *Crushed Seraphim* & *Bittersweet Seraphim* by Debra Anastasia
The Guardian's Wild Child by Feather Stone
Grave Refrain by Sarah M. Glover
The Divinity series: *Divinity* by Patricia Leever
The Blood Vine series: *Blood Vine*, *Blood Entangled* & *Blood Reunited*
by Amber Belldene
Divine Temptation by Nicki Elson
The Dead Rapture series: *Love in the Time of the Dead* by Tera Shanley

Romantic Suspense

Whirlwind by Robin DeJarnett
The CONduct series: *With Good Behavior*, *Bad Behavior* & *On Best Behavior*
by Jennifer Lane
Indivisible by Jessica McQuinn
Between the Lies by Alison Oburia
Blind Man's Bargain by Tracy Winegar

Erotic Romance

The Keyhole series: *Becoming sage* (book 1) by Kasi Alexander
The Keyhole series: *Saving sunni* (book 2) by Kasi & Reggie Alexander
The Winemaker's Dinner: *Appetizers* & *Entrée* by Dr. Ivan Rusilko & Everly Drummond
The Winemaker's Dinner: *Dessert* by Dr. Ivan Rusilko
Client N°5 by Joy Fulcher

Anthologies and Sets

A Valentine Anthology including short stories by
Alice Clayton ("With a Double Oven"),
Jennifer DeLucy ("Magnus of Pfelt, Conquering Viking Lord"),
Nicki Elson ("I Don't Do Valentine's Day"),
Jessica McQuinn ("Better Than One Dead Rose and a Monkey Card"),
Victoria Michaels ("Home to Jackson"), and
Alison Oburia ("The Bridge")

Taking Liberties including an introduction by Tiffany Reisz and short stories by
Mina Vaughn ("John Hancock-Blocked"),
Linda Cunningham ("A Boston Marriage"),
Joy Fulcher ("Tea for Two"),
KC Holly ("The British Are Coming!"),
Kimberly Jensen & Scott Stark ("E. Pluribus Threesome"), and
Vivian Rider ("M'Lady's Secret Service")

The Heart Series Box Set (*Beside Your Heart, Disclosure of the Heart* & *Forever Your Heart*) by Mary Whitney

The CONduct Series Box Set (*With Good Behavior, Bad Behavior* & *On Best Behavior*) by Jennifer DeLucy

Singles and Novellas

It's Only Kinky the First Time (A Keyhole series single) by Kasi Alexander
Learning the Ropes (A Keyhole series single) by Kasi & Reggie Alexander
The Winemaker's Dinner: RSVP by Dr. Ivan Rusilko
The Winemaker's Dinner: No Reservations by Everly Drummond
Big Guns by Jessica McQuinn
Concessions by Robin DeJarnett
Starstruck by Lisa Sanchez
New Flame by BJ Thornton
Shackled by Debra Anastasia
Swim Recruit by Jennifer Lane
Sway by Nicki Elson
Full Speed Ahead by Susan Kaye Quinn
The Second Sunrise by Hannah Downing
The Summer Prince by Carol Oates
Whatever it Takes by Sarah M. Glover
Clarity (A *Divinity* prequel single) by Patricia Leever
A Christmas Wish (A *Cocktails & Dreams* single) by Autumn Markus
Late Night with Andres by Debra Anastasia
Poughkeepsie (enhanced iPad app collector's edition) by Debra Anastasia

coming soon from
OMNIFIC PUBLISHING

Loving Lies by Linda Kage
Variables of Love by MK Schiller
Redemption by Kathryn Barrett
The Brit Out of Water series: *Jazz Hands* (book 2) by Eleanor Gwyn-Jones
The Dead Rapture series: *Love at the End of Days* (book 2) by Tera Shanley
The Playboy's Princess by Joy Fulcher
The Jeweler by Beck Anderson
The Vice, Virtue & Video series: *Tied* (book 4) by Bianca Giovanni
The Divinity series: *Entity* (book 2) by Patricia Leever
The WORDS series: *The Truest of Words* (book 3) by Georgina Guthrie

CPSIA information can be obtained
at www.ICGtesting.com
Printed in the USA
LVOW12s0614280917
550387LV00001B/22/P